GRIFFIN'S DAUGHTER

GRIFFIN'S DAUGHTER

BOOK ONE OF THE
GRIFFIN'S DAUGHTER TRILOGY

LESLIE ANN MOORE

Avari Press

Lancaster, Pennsylvania

Published by Avari Press
Lancaster, Pennsylvania
http://www.avaripress.com

Cover Art Copyright © 2006 Matt Hughes
Map and Photo by Ted Meyer
Interior designed by Anthony N. Verrecchia

First edition: January 2007

Library of Congress Cataloging-in-Publication Data
Moore, Leslie Ann.
   Griffin's daughter / Leslie Ann Moore. - 1st ed.
     p. cm. - (The griffin's daughter trilogy ; bk. 1)
   ISBN-13: 978-1-933770-01-7 (pbk.)
   I. Title.
  PS3613.O5643G75 2007
  813'.6-dc22

                                            2006024335

0 9 8 7 6 5 4 3 2 1

Printed and bound in the United States of America
ACB 001

To my family - Doris, Sylvia, and Ted - for their unwavering love and support, to Ed for his invaluable advice and comments, and to Mr. Terry Brooks, whose kind words of encouragement set me on the road to becoming a professional writer.

Table of Contents

Part I

Part II

Part III

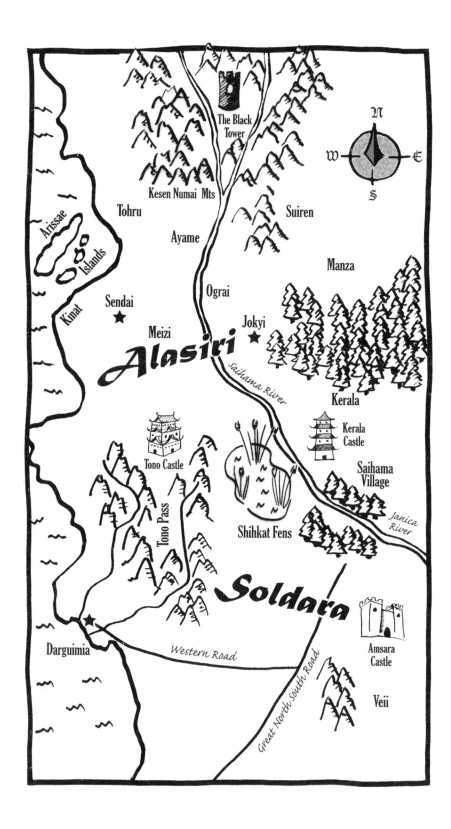

PART I

PROLOGUE

A Spell is Cast, A Child is Born

Part I

On the crest of a small hill, a woman stood alone, gazing off into the distance. She was dressed for battle, her once bright armor now grimed with mud and gore. A broadsword hung at her left hip. The woman and the blade were old comrades, having seen many a battle in their time together, but never had they witnessed such a slaughter as this. The unmoving results littered the plain below; grotesque shapes lay twisted in the churned earth, the corpses of creatures too horrible and unnatural to be of this world.

The woman's hair, unfettered by helmet or ties, streamed out from her head like black banners snapping in the wind. A pall of weariness hung about her, stooping her shoulders slightly under its gray weight. Her pale, still face contrasted sharply with her green eyes, which burned with a fierce intensity, mirroring her thoughts.

How has it come to this? How?

We must succeed, or Goddess help us all.

A soft *ahem* from behind broke her melancholy reverie. The sounds of an army settling in for the night now brushed against her awareness, like a great beast at her back. She turned.

"Highness," the man said, ducking his head in a quick salute. He was slightly out of breath and clearly agitated.

"What is it, soldier?" she replied. She took a step forward to see the messenger more clearly in the rapidly diminishing light.

"Lady Junko has returned. The Kirians await you at your tent."

She ran.

Her heart slammed against her breastbone as if it would tear itself free and fly from her chest. Terror bayed at her heels.

What if Junko has failed?

Well, then, we are all dead.

Men and women threw themselves from her path, upending plates of food and spilling mugs of hot tea, but yelps of outrage were quickly stifled when they realized who had torn through their midst. She saw none of it. Her vision tunneled down to a single point as all thoughts crystallized into one.

The ring.

She skidded to a halt in front of a tent that was larger, though no less plain, than its neighbors, and set apart by an open space. Two soldiers stood guard on either side of the doorway. They saluted briskly as she paused for a moment to catch her breath and gather her composure. She closed her eyes and offered a silent prayer to the Goddess.

A soft buzz of voices fell silent as she entered.

A group of people stood in a loose huddle around a camp stool, upon which sat a young woman. The woman rose to her feet, and the entire group bowed their heads in obeisance. A white-haired man stepped forward, his age and great air of authority clearly marking him as their leader.

"Princess Syukoe, Lady Junko has returned, successful. We have the ring."

Syukoe breathed out a long sigh and closed her eyes. She felt as if she would fly apart at any moment, her entire body drawn up tight as a bowstring. She didn't realize she was swaying on her feet until she felt the steadying hand of Master Iku under her elbow. She put a trembling hand to her forehead. *When did I last eat?* she wondered.

"I must sit for a moment," she murmured.

Master Iku steered her to the just vacated camp stool. She sat, and someone immediately handed her an ornate silver goblet. The clean, sweet smell of her favorite wine tickled her nostrils. She took a long pull and wiped her lips with the back of her hand in a very un-princess like manner, frowning at the grime she saw caked there. She was a soldier as well as a princess, and right now, she felt bone-weary, filthy, and she reeked of the battlefield. She desired nothing more than a hot bath and deep, dreamless sleep, but she knew she would have neither this night.

"Master Iku," Syukoe began.

"Highness, we have very little time. Your father…"

"Knows, Master. He already knows. Of that you can be sure."

Despite his advanced age, the Master of the Kirian Society stood straight and tall. The ruby Eye of Lajdala upon his breast, symbol of his high office, gleamed softly in the mellow light of the oil lamps. His long white hair hung in a single, neat plait down his back. Stern-faced and somber in his black robes, nevertheless, he inspired feelings of comfort and safety in Syukoe. She trusted him completely.

"My fellows and I must begin the spell immediately if we hope to succeed. There is no time to prepare you. I fear that your strength is depleted after this day's terrible work."

"I am strong enough. I have to be," Syukoe replied. "The ring. Let me have it." Master Iku placed it into her upturned palm. It felt cold, so cold, and yet it burned her skin, searing the flesh without leaving any mark. She could barely stand to hold it, but she could not release it either.

This is my father's ring.

There is blood on it.

Syukoe looked first to Master Iku, then to Lady Junko. "How did you get this from my father?" she questioned, her voice sharp.

Junko came forward and knelt before Syukoe. She was very young, but her eyes were already hard and sad. "I cut off his finger, Highness," she replied, matter-of-factly. "I drugged his wine. I'm the only one he trusts these days…or trusted. When he fell asleep, I tried pulling it off, but it wouldn't come, so…" She fell silent.

Syukoe closed her eyes and struggled to keep from retching. The bitter taste of bile stung her mouth, and her skin prickled as if a thousand spiders had worked their way under her armor, trapping themselves beneath her clothing. Junko, because of her position as the king's favorite concubine, was the only one who could get close enough to him to steal the ring, and even so, she could not have succeeded without the help of the Kirians. Junko did what she had to do, but, Goddess, did she have to cut off his finger?

A dark anger settled over Syukoe, dense and cold. Junko must have seen it in her face, for she backed away quickly, putting

Master Iku between herself and the princess. Syukoe stood up abruptly, overturning the stool. She glared down at the cowering concubine. Shiura Onjara, practitioner of the vilest form of magic, brutal and despotic though he had become, was still her father. He had once been a loving and attentive parent, adored by his only daughter, until the lust for power twisted him into the beast that she now stood against. Still…

He is my father, the hurt child within her cried. *This girl cut off my father's finger!*

Get a hold of yourself, Syukoe! She did what had to be done, by whatever means necessary. She assumed a terrible risk, and she succeeded. Now you have the White Griffin Ring in your possession, the only thing that may keep you alive and free your people.

If the spell could be completed in time.

"He is coming," Master Iku breathed.

The eldest Kirian stood with his head cocked slightly to one side, like an old hound that has caught the scent of danger. The others stood very still, bodies taut, eyes unfocused, as if they, too, could feel the approach of the king, like a great, onrushing storm. Syukoe cried out in pain as the ring, enclosed within her fist, burned with such sudden intensity that she had to drop it to the floor, where it lay shining with a white light like a star fallen from the heavens.

Quick as a striking serpent, Master Iku snatched up the ring. Its cold fire did not seem to affect the old sorcerer.

"Highness! We must act now, or all is lost. For the elven people, you must be strong through what is to come. They will need a queen when this is finished."

For a brief moment, Syukoe hesitated. What choice had she, really? She must either go along with the Kirians or face another day in which she watched while brave men and women fought and died, torn apart by an army of loathsome and unnatural creatures called up from the depths of the Void by her father's vile magic. No, she hadn't any choice at all.

She nodded once, decisively. "Let's to it, then, and be done."

"Hold onto my sleeve, Princess," the Master instructed. "If you've never teleported before, it can be very disorienting, and you may be quite dizzy when we arrive."

"Where are we going?" Syukoe asked.

"To the only place where he will not hold the advantage," replied the Master. "The stronghold of the Kirians."

The Black Tower. Syukoe swallowed hard and tried to stop shaking. Her mouth tasted of ashes. She took hold of Master Iku's elbow, as instructed. Beneath the heavy black fabric, the muscles of his arm felt hard, more like those of a warrior's than a magician's. Still holding fast to the ring in his left hand, he raised his right hand and traced a glyph in the air before him. He spoke a single word, and the glyph became visible, a softly glowing silver tangle of lines, meaningless to Syukoe's untrained eye. The other Kirians obviously knew their part, for they all gathered close, surrounding Master Iku, Syukoe, and now Junko, who had wormed her way into the center of the group and stood with her back pressed against the princess's.

The mages began to chant softly, rapidly. The air within the tent started to crackle and pop with energy. Syukoe felt the bare skin of her face and hands begin to prickle unpleasantly as if she were being stung by nettles. Just as the prickling intensified into true pain, Master Iku spoke three words loudly, in rapid succession, closed his fist and pulled downwards.

The room folded in on itself.

PART II

Syukoe's mind couldn't quite interpret what her body had just experienced. One moment, she had stood with the Kirians, surrounded by the canvas walls of her tent. The next, she hurtled through freezing darkness to land upon hard stone, dizzy and sick. Her knees buckled, and she would have fallen, but a pair of strong arms encircled her waist, holding her firmly until she could stand again.

"My thanks, Master Iku," she murmured, pushing herself gently out of the embrace of the old mage. She glanced around her. The group had alighted in a small room, barely large enough to contain them all. The walls were constructed of wood, the floor of stone. The corners still crackled with the blue fire of dissipating magical energy. A single doorway opened onto a dimly lit corridor.

"Come, everyone," the Master called. "We must go to the Spell

Chamber and activate the wards. Quickly!" He turned and rushed out of the room into the corridor. The other Kirians followed en masse, their black robes flapping like the wings of crows, sweeping both Syukoe and Junko along in their midst.

"Hurry! He comes!" Master Iku shouted over his shoulder, and for the first time, Syukoe thought she heard a note of fear in the mage's voice.

They ran now, fleeing ever downwards through a series of corridors and down staircases illuminated by softly glowing globes set into the walls at regular intervals. Master Iku still held fast to the ring. Syukoe could see his left hand ablaze with the cold starfire of the ring's terrible energy, and she marveled at the Master's strength that he could withstand its dreadful power.

At last, Master Iku skidded to a halt in front of a set of massive double doors fashioned of highly polished black stone. Syukoe gasped in wonder at the sight of them. Glyphs and sigils covered their mirrored surfaces, and to her eyes, they seemed to move, swimming like a school of fantastic fish that alternately surfaced, then retreated into the inky depths of a dark, still pond.

The Master spoke a word of Command and the doors swung inwards with a great inrush of air, as if no atmosphere had existed within the chamber until the instant the doors opened. Despite their previous haste, the Kirians entered the room slowly, reverently.

This place, their inner sanctum, lay at the very heart of the fortress known as the Black Tower. Here, the Kirian Society performed its most powerful Workings. Here, they would work the Spell of Sundering, which would separate the Key that unlocked the power of the Griffin Ring from the ring itself. They would then attempt something that could only be described as an act of desperation.

It would take every particle, every last bit of the collective energy of all of the Kirians to perform this Working, with no guarantee of success. No one in living memory had ever tried such a feat, and the elves had very long memories.

If they succeeded, a hole would open up in the very fabric of Time itself. Through this portal, the Key would be cast into the living body of a person not yet born, a person of the blood royal, a descendant of the House of Onjara. The divinations had already

LESLIE ANN MOORE   7

been performed. The House of Onjara would endure, and there would be living members a thousand years hence. Theoretically, the spell should work.

If it failed, they would all die. The Kirians, having drained themselves dry, would have nothing left with which to battle the vengeful fury of a sorcerer king betrayed by his onetime allies. Syukoe could expect to suffer an especially bitter fate as the treacherous child who dared to turn against her own father and aim to set herself in his place.

Worse than anything Syukoe's father could do to her would be the suffering of the elven people. Their pain would be everlasting.

The spell had to work.

The doors swung shut with a soft *whoosh*, sealing the room.

The octagonal chamber had been cut from the living rock upon which the fortress stood. Its walls were made of the same polished black stone as the doors. Here too were the drifting symbols, giving Syukoe the impression of being in a glass-walled room submerged in black water. No symbols marred the dark perfection of the floor. In the exact center of the room, affixed to a square base, rested a slab, also fashioned of black stone. It stood at a height to make it comfortable as an altar or work table, measuring as long as the height of an average elven man, and about three times as wide as that same man's body. Upon it rested many objects that Syukoe took to be the tools of the sorcerer's craft.

Master Iku stepped over to the table and dropped the ring into a bronze bowl, then fell back and folded his left hand into his right, hissing with pain.

"Master!" Syukoe cried out in alarm. Two of his fellows supported him as he doubled over, chest heaving. Syukoe knelt beside the stricken mage, her throat clogged with fear.

"The magic of the ring is very potent, especially with the king so near. It is a wonder that I was able to hold onto it for so long," the old mage said through gritted teeth. He stood straight once more, having mastered the pain, and unfurled his clenched fingers.

Where the ring had contacted his palm, a blackened hole gaped, seared into the Master's flesh by the ring's power. No blood seeped from the wound; the tissues had been cauterized by the intense energy.

"Master, you must let us tend to your hand," one of the Kirians, a woman of middle years whose name escaped Syukoe, said.

"No! There is no time," Master Iku replied, his voice full of urgency. "This wound is nothing compared to what I and the rest of us will suffer if we do not accomplish what we must this night. I will bind up my hand if I can find a bit of cloth, and make do."

"Master, please take this." Junko stepped forward and proffered a red silk ribbon that, moments before, had bound back her waist-length golden hair. Master Iku took the ribbon with a word of thanks and began wrapping it tightly about his injured hand. Junko, eyes lowered deferentially, backed away and retreated into a corner of the room where she then sat, back pressed against the unyielding stone.

Syukoe knew little about her father's favorite concubine, other than she was very young and came from the north. The princess wondered just what the Kirians had offered her to betray her master and king. Perhaps sharing the king's bed and receiving his favor had not been enough for this ambitious girl. Perhaps she had desired much, much more, and when she could not get what she craved, her mind had turned to treachery.

Syukoe shook her head in frustrated anger. None of this was Junko's fault.

She is a victim of Father's evil, just as we all are. Your problem is that you still love him. You would run to him and fall into his arms without a second thought. All he would have to do is speak a kind word, and all of the horrors of the last three years would be forgotten— that is, until he slit your throat for betraying him.

She had to stay focused. Her survival, and that of the elven nation, depended on it.

Master Iku had finished wrapping his hand and now stood at the stone table, the bronze cauldron containing the Griffin Ring before him. The light from the ring still blazed, throwing the upper half of the elder Kirian's face into eerie shadow, making of it a bizarre, featureless mask. The others stood to either side of their leader, arms raised, palms turned outward. Master Iku spoke a single word, and the aimlessly drifting symbols in walls and doors began to swirl and dart, forming themselves into linear patterns, which then froze into place. Syukoe could now see that they had formed what looked to be the sentences of a massive text, written in a language unknown to her.

The Kirians began to chant.

A sudden wave of concussive force hit the chamber like an enormous hammer blow, throwing everyone off-balance. The chanting faltered for an instant, then resumed with even greater speed. Another shockwave rocked the chamber a heartbeat later, sending a fine powder of rock dust pattering to the floor.

Blue-white fireballs of energy sprang into being in all eight corners of the room. Syukoe heard Junko scream as the concubine flung herself out of the way. The energy balls raced along the floor toward the center of the room, leaving burning trails in their wakes, which shone in the semi-darkness like the spokes of a giant wheel. They met and coalesced under the base of the stone table. The entire structure lit up, becoming as transparent as rock crystal.

Upon the glowing coals of the lit brazier, Master Iku cast a handful of powder. Tendrils of spicy smoke curled up into the supercharged air, tickling Syukoe's nostrils. Abruptly, the chanting ceased.

The energy in the room thrummed with such intensity, Syukoe could barely remain standing. Out of the corner of her eye she saw Junko, collapsed upon the floor like a discarded doll wrapped in a pile of silken rags.

Master Iku, a fine sheen of sweat upon his brow, clapped his hands together three times and spoke a single word. To the uninitiated, a Word of Power was felt, rather than heard. Syukoe squeezed her head in her hands, fighting to remain conscious, as the Word blasted her mind and body like the sonorous voice of a great bell.

A sphere of energy manifested inside the bronze cauldron. Master Iku slowly raised his hands and the sphere followed until it hovered at eye level. The ring floated within.

Still off-balance from the residual effects of the Word of Power, Syukoe fell to the floor as a third massive shockwave hit the chamber. She stared in stunned disbelief as the seemingly solid stone of the doors bulged inwards, as if their substance had been somehow fundamentally altered, making them more like clay than rock.

Somehow, the Kirians remained standing, all thirteen pairs of eyes fixed upon the ring. A steady shower of rock dust sifted down from the ceiling. Syukoe coughed as the fine grit worked its way into her throat and lungs. She scrambled to her feet and whirled to face the deforming doors, drawing her sword because her warrior's instinct compelled her to fight, even against impossible odds.

The room shook steadily now. The Kirians began a new chant, this one slow and deliberate, each word a Word of Power. Syukoe moaned in pain, struggling to keep a grasp on both sword and consciousness. The Words kept a steady beat, in rhythm to the synchronized pulses of the mentally joined sorcerers.

Syukoe heard a loud pop and turned in time to see the ring fall through the sphere back into the cauldron, its light extinguished. That light now burned within the sphere itself, with such intensity that Syukoe could not look directly at it. In a moment of clarity, she realized that the magic of the Key had been separated from the ring and placed within the sphere.

"Princess!" Master Iku called out. "We require you now!"

Syukoe moved as quickly as she dared, fighting to keep her balance. She slipped into the circle of magicians beside Master Iku, who indicated that she should hold out her hand. She braced herself for what she knew would come next.

The Master had briefed her only this morning on how the Kirians would form the link to the future Onjara. The magical principle was based on the blood tie between the generations that stretched unbroken down through the years, connecting Syukoe with her descendent. Her living blood would catalyze the spell that would open a hole in the fabric of Time, allowing contact with the target. The Kirians would then cast the Key through the hole and into the body of its new host, thus effectively sealing it off from the king's control.

Without the power of the Griffin Ring at his disposal, Shiura Onjara could no longer command his armies. The foul creatures he had conjured up from the Void were compelled to serve him by the magic of the ring; freed from that compulsion, they would be thrown into disarray and made far more vulnerable. Syukoe's forces would then have a chance to defeat them, and perhaps some semblance of victory could be won from the disaster of the rebellion.

Bereft of his deadliest weapon, the king himself would also be weakened, giving the beleaguered Kirians a chance to neutralize his magic. Syukoe had made Master Iku swear to her that if they ultimately succeeded in bringing her father down, the Kirians would find a way to imprison, rather than kill, him. She still loved him, despite everything.

The floor heaved sharply. Syukoe gasped in dismay as the solid stone of the walls began to ripple in glistening black waves.

"He is unraveling the magic that holds the very substance of the Tower together," Master Iku stated grimly. "Soon, the rock will be like putty, unable to hold its shape. We must hurry." He grasped Syukoe's wrist in his left hand and held it over the lighted charcoals of the brazier. In his right hand, he held a small ritual blade, poised over Syukoe's waiting flesh. He closed his eyes and began to intone the opening verse of the spell.

Master Iku spoke rapidly, the words running together in a continuous buzz of sound. The other Kirians stood silently, eyes closed, brows furrowed. Some perspired heavily, others betrayed the intensity of their effort with barely a twitch of an eyelid or lip. Oddly, despite the chaos of the dissolving room, the group seemed locked in a bubble of stillness, shielded from the worst of the punishing energy blasts directed at them by their enemy. Syukoe spared a quick moment of concern for Junko, still sprawled unmoving in a corner. She hoped the girl could survive the coming storm.

The chant reached a crescendo as Master Iku shouted out the last Word. Syukoe's head exploded in noise and white light. Simultaneously, she felt a searing pain lance across her left palm. She cried out and felt herself slumping to the floor, where darkness enveloped her like a velvet cocoon.

PART III

How long she lay in a swoon, she did not know, but when Syukoe regained her senses, she found herself still on the floor, eyes level with the hem of Master Iku's robe. The sour taste of vomit filled her mouth. She gagged and spat, then levered herself up on one elbow and attempted to focus her eyes. Her head throbbed with pain. Looking up, she cried out in astonishment and climbed shakily to her feet in order to get a better view of the extraordinary phenomenon.

Hovering at eye level within the circle of the sorcerers, a window-like opening appeared through which Syukoe could look out and see a forest clearing. Water drizzled from the dreary sky. Syukoe smelled the pungent odors of wet earth and rain, and felt the moisture-laden wind gusting coldly against her sweating face.

"What…what is happening?" she whispered, but Master Iku seemed not to hear. All of his attention remained focused on the scene before him. Ominously, the chamber had stopped shaking, but the walls continued to ripple and flow. Syukoe, even without any trained Talent to speak of, could sense that her father now gathered his power for a final, cataclysmic assault. *Whatever the Kirians are going to do, they had better do it now*, she thought.

The sound of footsteps, squelching through mud and leaf litter, drifted through the open portal. Master Iku drew in a sharp breath. "The target is here," he said softly. He raised his right hand, and the drifting sphere containing the Key settled gently into his palm. All eyes were riveted onto a path that snaked out of the forest and across the clearing towards the portal. A figure, swathed in a dark cloak, approached through the trees.

A hood obscured most of the face; even so, Syukoe still recognized the distinctive gait of a non-combat trained female. She walked with the deliberate step of one who knows the path well and is eager to arrive at its end. Abruptly, the woman stopped dead in her tracks and pushed back the hood of her cloak. She stared directly at the portal, her mouth forming an "O" of surprise. She seemed more puzzled than afraid.

The Kirians all gasped in dismay.

The woman was human!

"Master, there must be some mistake!" cried Ankai Noemi, the most senior member of the Kirian Society after Master Iku. The murmured agreements from the rest of the group echoed the consternation in her voice.

"The calculations were carefully checked and rechecked. They were completely accurate. There is no mistake. This… no, she… *is* the target. But how…" Master Iku's voice trailed off in mid-sentence.

"Master, look!" Syukoe pointed at the woman's midsection. The pronounced swell of her shift told the tale of her condition.

"Ahhh, I see now!" Master Iku exclaimed. "She is with child. Of course! It is not this human who is our target, but the child she carries. It must be so!"

"But, you said the target was my direct descendent. How can a human child be the target, unless…" Suddenly, Syukoe understood. The child must be only half-human, sired on this woman by an elven man, a son of the House of Onjara.

The woman—a girl really—sidled closer to the portal. Her eyes held no fear, but rather an intense curiosity, coupled with a natural wariness. She was comely, for a human; a wild shock of black curls framed her smooth, heart-shaped face. She paused, close enough now for Master Iku to reach through and touch her, and peered into the portal as if she were looking through the window of a house. She spoke aloud in her own tongue—meaningless to Syukoe's ears—but the upward inflection of her voice seemed to indicate a question. All within the chamber of the Black Tower held themselves in complete stillness.

At the same moment, Junko regained consciousness and let out a blood-curdling shriek. Simultaneously, the great stone doors of the chamber exploded inwards, sending rock shards hurtling through the air with deadly force. The lethal fusillade ricocheted off the energy shield surrounding the Kirians and the Time Portal. Junko, still outside the shield's protection, was pulped in the space of an eye blink, reduced to tattered shreds of flesh and bone.

Within the doorway stood Shiura Onjara, King of Alasiri.

The Kirians were out of time.

"Master Iku, I believe you and your fellows have something that belongs to me," the king said, his voice satin-smooth and full of the dark promise of torture and death. Even so, in this direst of moments, Syukoe still felt a pang of guilt, for was she not part of the betrayal that had brought them all to this terrible place?

The king glided into the room on silent feet, carefully avoiding the gobbets of meat that had once been his favorite concubine. Syukoe thought him magnificent, garbed as he was in full court dress—an elaborate layering of richly decorated robes, belted at the waist with a jeweled girdle. His long black hair—so like her own—was bound back with a gold clip. Upon his brow sat the Crown of Alasiri, a simple circlet of gold set about with blood-red rubies. He approached the energy shield that protected his enemies and raised his right hand. A single tear leaked from Syukoe's eye at the sight of her father's mutilated hand, the stump of his ring finger bound with a strip of bloodstained linen.

A startled yelp tore Syukoe's attention away from the advancing menace of her father. She looked up in time to see Master Iku lunge through the portal, and with his free hand, seize the human girl by the wrist.

"Someone help me!" he cried, as the terrified human struggled wildly to escape, clawing and slapping at the old sorcerer's face and hand, all the while screaming out a steady barrage of gibberish. Syukoe dove in and grabbed the girl's flailing free arm and together, princess and sorcerer hauled the heavily pregnant human up off her feet and part way through the portal, where she dangled, her body straddling the boundary between the two worlds.

The energy sphere of the Key, still balanced on Master Iku's right palm, began to pulsate in time to a heartbeat; whether to the king's or the unborn Onjara's, Syukoe did not know. Using her warrior's strength, Syukoe had successfully pinned the human girl's arms behind her and now held her steady. The girl had gone quiescent, her face slack, eyes half closed.

"Hurry, Master! Do whatever it is you're going to do, while this girl is still in a swoon!" Syukoe urged.

What happened next took only a few heartbeats, but to Syukoe, time seemed strangely expanded, each moment drawn out and rolling before her eyes in excruciatingly slow motion.

A sunburst erupted overhead, sending a sheet of flame roaring downwards to engulf the group of fiercely concentrating mages. Several of them cried aloud as they strained to maintain the integrity of the energy shield—the only thing that stood between them and the devastating power of the king's magical attack. Despite their combined strengths, Syukoe could feel the shield failing as the air around them began to heat up.

Master Iku appeared oblivious to the king's presence, so focused was he on his task. Muttering rapidly in a singsong chant, he traced a sigil upon the human girl's belly, then to Syukoe's amazement, he plunged his hand containing the Key deep into her body. The girl convulsed and let out a strangled cry, then collapsed back into a stupor. The Master withdrew his hand and Syukoe saw that no trace of blood stained it. The Key had disappeared.

Needing no prompting, Syukoe shoved the unconscious human back through the portal where she lay sprawled in the wet grass, her unruly mane of dark curls spread about her head like a tangled bush. She moaned softly as the rain pattered down upon her upturned face.

"Ai, get back, Princess!" she heard Master Iku shout. Syukoe barely got her arms out of the way in time as the portal slammed shut with a blast of air and a noise like a thunderclap. The air within the chamber shimmered, superheated now to the point of combustion. The Kirians had clearly reached their limits of endurance. Hair and clothing began to smoke, just moments away from igniting.

"Get down behind me, Princess," Master Iku gasped. He raised his hands towards the ceiling. Syukoe did as the Master bade, curling herself into a tight ball and covering her head. She began to pray to The One for deliverance and an end to all of their suffering. She prayed for her father's soul, that it be washed clean of the foulness and corruption that had warped it into something so unspeakably evil.

The Key lay safely in the future now, locked away from Shiura Onjara, hidden in the body of a half-elven child. Syukoe prayed for the Goddess's protection for that child, for as a half-blood, its life would surely be a difficult one, filled with hardship and uncertainty. What was to become of the Key, no one, not even the great and powerful Kirian Society, had been able to divine.

"Kirians! To me!" shouted Master Iku. Twin bolts of blue-white energy exploded from his fingertips. The resulting blast hammered Syukoe's senses into tatters. She tumbled down into darkness and knew no more.

PART IV

In a dusty chamber high atop a semi-abandoned tower, a midwife delivered a baby from its dying mother's body. She cut the cord and wrapped the newborn girl—wrinkled, red, and capped with a thin shock of dark curls—in an old wool blanket. The old woman who had struggled to save both mother and child held the baby close, tears running in rivulets down her lined cheeks. She had failed.

"My poor, Dru…my poor little Dru!" the woman sobbed quietly.

The dying woman—barely out of girlhood, really—stirred and cried out weakly. "My baby… Where is my baby?"

"Here's yer sweet little babe, my lamb… a beautiful little girl," the old woman crooned, laying the whimpering infant next to her mother. Weakened from blood loss, the new mother could do little but gaze at her child. It would have been clear to anyone witnessing the sad tableau that her love burned fierce and hot for the daughter she would never know beyond these last few moments of her life.

"Claudia," the young woman whispered.

"Yes, my lamb," the old woman answered.

"I want to name her Jelena…I've always loved that name."

"Jelena…Weren't that a name of an ancient queen? From one o' those old stories you an' yer brother loved so much?"

The dying girl nodded weakly. "Promise you'll look after her, Claudia, because no one else will. Promise you'll not let them hurt her because…because of what she is."

"I promise," Claudia sobbed.

"Promise…you…you'll keep the ring…safe until…" The girl's voice trailed off and her eyes fluttered closed.

"Dru?...Drucilla?" Claudia leaned close and peered into the girl's waxen face. She could already feel the cold presence of Lady Death, come to gather her precious Drucilla up into her cloak of blackest velvet and carry her away on silent wings to Heaven.

Drucilla stirred and opened her eyes, but they focused now on something beyond the living world.

"I swear I'll keep th' ring what belonged to yer baby's dad, and give it to her when she's ready fer it." Claudia kissed Drucilla's cold forehead. "Rest now, my lamb. Go to sleep," she murmured. Gathering the baby up into her arms, she sat in the room's only chair to wait.

She did not have to wait long, and when it was over, she placed the baby in an old laundry basket and set about the task of preparing the young mother for her grave.

When she had finished, she gathered up all of the soiled linen and picked up the newborn in her basket. She took one last look at the shrouded form upon the bed, then exited the room, pulling the heavy oak door closed behind her. She negotiated the narrow tower stairs with caution, fearful that one misstep could send her and the baby tumbling to serious injury or worse.

At the bottom, Claudia breathed a sigh of relief. *So many things to take care of now,* she thought. The duke must be told, and a wet nurse found for the child. She recalled a kitchen maid who had just lost a baby not more than three days ago. *P'rhaps she can be persuaded.* She set the laundry basket down and rubbed the small of her back in an attempt to ease the pain that plagued her. The baby began to wail.

"Oh, poor little lamb! Yer hungry, o'course, and with no mam t'feed ye," she said. "Well, let's get a move on, then. C'mon Claudia, old girl. You've got work t'do!" She hoisted up her burdens and headed for the castle kitchens.

~~~

Later that evening, Claudia lay in bed, the sleeping baby tucked in a makeshift cradle alongside. The duke, not surprisingly, had expressed no desire to have anything to do with the child, commanding Claudia to take it away and keep it with her, in the servants' hall. Claudia was only too happy to obey. The kitchen maid who had lost her own baby balked at first but eventually allowed herself to be persuaded by the ten copper a week fee—double the usual charge—that Claudia agreed to pay her. Claudia could have used that extra money for other things, but she had no alternative.

She gazed down at the baby, sleeping peacefully on a full stomach. On impulse, she got up and went to open the wooden chest at the foot of her bed. She reached in and removed Drucilla's ring from its hiding place at the very bottom. She held the ring up to catch the light of the room's single oil lamp and examined it thoughtfully for a while before returning it to the bottom of the chest.

The baby awoke and began to fuss. Claudia scooped the infant up and cradled her against her large, soft breasts. Instinctively, the child began to suck.

"You'll get nothin' from these old tits, little one," she said, rocking the baby gently back and forth. She traced the shape of one tiny, pointed ear with a fingertip. A sudden, fierce determination swept through her. "I promised yer mam I'd protect you from folks' abusin' you 'cause of what you are, and by the gods, I'm going t' do my best. And when yer old enough, I'll give you yer dad's ring and maybe, just maybe, you can find him."

Claudia kissed the baby's forehead and rocked her until she drifted off to sleep again.

CHAPTER 1

AN UNEXPECTED INVITATION

The day started much like every other for Jelena. Emerging reluctantly from her cozy nest of rough woolen blankets, the young woman shivered as her bare feet touched the old rag rug lying on the flagstone floor beside her cot. Spring was in the air, but apparently, the stones of Amsara Castle hadn't gotten the news yet. Dawn's first flush had just begun to lighten the indigo sky. The day would be warm and dry, perfect for a festival.

A few live coals left over from last night still smoldered in the grate. With a handful of kindling and a chunk of fresh wood, Jelena soon had a small fire cheerfully burning. She hunkered down in front of the grate and held her hands to the flames, sighing with pleasure. The brutal cold of winter had begun to ease during the last few weeks, but nights and mornings remained chilly. From behind her, Jelena could hear old Claudia snoring softly. From experience, she knew Claudia's uncannily accurate internal time sense always roused her foster mother at the same hour each morning.

A loud cough and a grunt heralded the old woman's return to the waking world. "Big day today, my lamb. Lot of extra work t' be done. Best get to it, I reckon," Claudia said. She threw aside the rumpled bedclothes and rose ponderously to her feet, then ran a gnarled hand through her thinning, steel-gray hair.

"Umm," Jelena answered, still huddled before the fire and loath to move. How wonderful it would be to be able to sit here all morning with a mug of hot tea and a sweet roll!

"C'mon , girl! Get yourself movin' now! Them fires in the kitchen won't make themselves. Cook'll want 'em nice and hot before she comes down."

Jelena groaned out loud as she reluctantly left the bubble of warmth created by the flames and made a show of stomping to her chest to pull out her day clothes.

Claudia chuckled affectionately as she pulled on her robe and slippers. "Off to the necess'ry," she announced, and slipped out of the room, closing the door softly behind her.

Jelena preferred to use the chamber pot early in the morning; she found it infinitely better than sitting over a malodorous hole while a freezing draft chilled her backside. After relieving herself, she washed her face and hands in an old ceramic wash basin, then donned a coarse cotton smock with a rust brown overdress of linen. Very fine embroidery decorated the dress at the neck and hem, but it was old and worn from hard use. It was not something an average servant girl would wear, but then, Jelena was not an average servant. She had acquired the dress as a castoff from her cousin, the Lady Thessalina.

Lastly, she pulled on gray cotton stockings and slipped a pair of sturdy leather sandals onto her feet, then turned her attention to her hair.

She gazed at herself in the small square mirror nailed to the wall next to the door and sighed. With a boar bristle brush in one hand and a wooden comb in the other, she attacked the tightly coiled, re-calcitrant mass of mahogany curls that sprang from her head with a vengeance born of years of frustration. All her life, she had envied girls like Thessalina who had been blessed with shining waves of luxuriant hair that fell gracefully down their backs. Hers, by con-trast, stood out from her head in a great bushy shock, refusing to be tamed by comb, pin, or hair grease.

During Jelena's babyhood, Claudia had often tried in vain to cajole some semblance of order from her foster daughter's chaotic tresses. "A gift from your mam," Claudia would ruefully say as she tugged and twisted and smoothed. In the end, both child and nurse had grown weary of the struggle, and so Jelena's hair had finally been allowed to do what it would with little interference, save an occasional trim.

On her eighteenth birthday, just two months past, Jelena had taken shears to her locks, and now had only a shoulder-length tangle to deal with. She would have cut it man-short, except then she would no longer have been able to hide her ears.

With a final tug, she finished the daily battle, securing the sides with a pair of ivory combs. These combs were her most cherished possessions, for they had belonged to her mother.

Jelena might have her mother's hair, but the rest of her features bore the unmistakable stamp of her father's elven blood, from the slightly upturned eyebrows and gently pointed ear tips, to the slender build of her body.

Because of the undeniable fact of her mixed human-elven parentage, she had lived her entire life on the margins of castle society, the barely tolerated bastard offspring of the duke's late sister, Drucilla. The duke could not accept her as a full member of his family, but neither could he turn his back completely on his sister's child, so the infant Jelena had been given at birth to Claudia so that she could be raised in the servants' quarters.

Claudia's face had been the loving visage floating above Jelena's cradle; her voice crooned lullabies when sleep would not come. Claudia's ample bosom had given shelter and comfort to her little girl, so hurt and tormented mercilessly by both castle children and adults alike. Claudia was Jelena's heart-mother, the dearest person in her universe.

The older woman returned just as Jelena finished tying her work apron on over her dress. "What? Still here? You better get goin' or Cook'll be yellin' for sure," she said as she pulled her voluminous nightdress up over her head. She shook out the garment and carefully folded it before tucking it away in her chest.

"I'm going, I'm going," Jelena replied. She gave Claudia's seamed cheek a quick peck, then dashed from the room and down the stairs to the door leading out into the yard. A blast of fresh cool air hit her as she pulled open the heavy oak door. A ray of golden, new morning sunlight dazzled her eyes. Somewhere, a cock crowed.

Gods, I'm late. Cook will be furious!

She hurried across the yard, still shrouded in cool shadows, heading toward the kitchen. She reached the door and paused just long enough to chirp a greeting to the small pride of castle felines that had congregated on the threshold. They responded by raising a raucous chorus of hungry meows, patting at her skirt hem with insistent paws and twining around her legs in an attempt to cajole from her their morning feeding. Jelena laughed at their antics, and bid them be patient. Just as she pushed through the half opened kitchen door, a great shout rang out.

"Girrrl! Why aren't them fires made yet?! I've got a feast to get on! I need m' fires now!"

Cook, a great she-bear of a woman, had the disposition to match her formidable bulk. She stood now, hands on hips, glaring at Jelena from beside the main hearth.

"I'm sorry, Cook. I was a little slow this morning. I'll get right to it," Jelena apologized in her most deferential tone of voice. Her hands shook a little as she got busy. When Cook's temper flared, she was fierce indeed. Jelena had often heard rumors that she had once been a soldier in the Imperial Army. Jelena had never doubted those stories.

Cook harrumphed and stalked away. Jelena soon had the main hearth fire going and had just finished the lighting of the big oven when the rest of the kitchen staff began to straggle in. Save for a cursory acknowledgment of her presence, most of them didn't speak to her; in fact, she had worked beside some of these people for years, and had barely exchanged a handful of civil words with any of them. Now that she was older and strong enough to defend herself, the more persistent bullies limited themselves to verbal abuse, or they simply ignored her. Jelena didn't mind; she had grown used to the solitude imposed on her by the pervasive bigotry of the castle's residents, and it no longer bothered her.

The kitchen soon bustled with activity. The breakfast needed making for the family and the staff, and the enormous task of preparing the festival feast had to be started. After Jelena had finished lighting the fires, Cook put her to work chopping vegetables.

The Festival of Sansa was one of the most important holidays on the Soldaran solar calendar, celebrated during the month of Dul when winter's harsh grip on the land began to ease. The people offered prayers to San, Goddess of Spring, and asked for her blessing on the new growing season. It was also a traditional time for matchmaking; an important part of every Sansa celebration was the marriage market, to be hosted this year by the Duchy, thus insuring a much larger crowd than usual for the castle's public feast.

In addition to the public meal, the duke would be holding a private feast for his neighbors. Several nobles from afar were also expected to attend. The most senior members of the kitchen staff were to prepare this very special meal, including a spectacular Sansa cake made entirely by Cook herself—her night's masterpiece.

Jelena had no expectations that she would be allowed to celebrate the holiday with the family this year. She had never been invited before, despite the protestations of her cousin Magnes, so this year should be no different. This also no longer bothered her much. She was content to spend the holiday with Claudia, as she always had. The two of them would celebrate by eating their own little Sansa cake together.

Magnes was Duke Teodorus's eldest child, future Duke of Amsara, and the only member of the Preseren clan who treated her like family. Magnes had been her only friend and playmate during their childhood. Three years her senior and by virtue of his station, he suffered no adverse consequences by befriending her. When they were together, his mantle of protection shielded her, and the worst of the bullying ceased.

Magnes had taught her to read and write, to ride a horse, and to shoot a bow, which she now did with great skill. Jelena loved him dearly, as much as she loved Claudia.

Break time arrived, and Jelena stopped work to get her breakfast along with the rest of the kitchen staff—oatmeal with dried apples, mild yellow cheese, and fresh bread, hot from the oven. Jelena collected her food, and with a mug of honey-sweetened tea to wash it all down, settled into a corner to eat and wait for Claudia.

The older woman soon appeared, and after getting her food and having a few words with some of the other staff, she waved to Jelena and sat at the kitchen's long trestle table, which ran along the back wall. Jelena almost never sat at the table with the others unless Claudia sat with her. She rose from her corner and went to join her foster mother.

Since both of the duke's children were now adults, Claudia's services as a nurse were no longer needed by the family. She had therefore been put in charge of the castle's laundry. She still acted as the castle midwife and informal healer for the staff, dispensing advice and herbal remedies. She also served as liaison between the staff and the duke if a serious health problem requiring the services of the district physician arose.

Claudia patted the bench beside her, indicating that Jelena should sit. Her clothes were still damp from the moist air of the laundry, and a few stray wisps of wet, gray hair straggled from beneath her linen cap. She had a slightly quizzical expression on her face as if she were trying to make sense of something puzzling. "Saw yer uncle the duke just now, afore I came t'get my breakfast. He told me to tell you to come to his study straightaway. I told 'im you'd still be eating, so he says oh well, then, have her come when she be finished. Now, what d'you suppose he wants with you this mornin'?"

"I have no idea," Jelena replied. Her uncle rarely paid any attention to her at all, much less summoned her into his presence. He seemed to prefer that she stay away from him. A vague sense of unease sent tiny prickles down her spine, like spiders skittering over her skin. What on earth could he possibly want with her on this particular morning? She found that her appetite had deserted her, and the food that she had already consumed had turned to rocks in her stomach.

"I'd better go now," she murmured, pushing her dishes aside.

She stood up and removed her apron. Claudia took the garment from her and draped it across her shoulder. She reached out and squeezed Jelena's hand in reassurance. "Nought to worry 'bout, my girl. He prob'ly just wants to invite you to eat with the family this year, is all."

"After all this time?" Jelena shook her head in disbelief. "I think it must be something else." She gulped down the remainder of her tea and left the kitchen by a side door. In order to reach the castle keep where the duke had his private quarters, Jelena had to first negotiate a maze of tables that had been set up in the yard for the public feast.

Jelena rarely entered the keep. Since she had no official place in the ducal family, and her duties did not involve chambermaid's work, she had almost no reason to cross over its massive stone threshold. The few occasions when she had been inside, it had almost always been at the invitation of Magnes. Despite their long and close friendship, she had only ever been to his private quarters once, and that had been several years ago when they were still children. Both she and her cousin recognized the impropriety of her coming to his chambers now that they were grown.

Jelena remembered the way to her uncle's study from the last time she had been there, a little over three years ago. The day of her fifteenth birthday, the duke had summoned her to tell her she had officially come of age now, and could choose to stay at Amsara Castle to live and work, or she could leave. If she chose to stay, she would remain his ward until he could arrange some sort of match for her, if possible. At the time, she felt as if she'd had no other choice. She had chosen to stay, for where else could she go? As difficult as her life was at Amsara, she knew no other home.

The keep's massive, iron-banded oak door stood open. Jelena stepped through and stood a moment, blinking owlishly while her eyes adjusted to the dimness.

Dust motes swirled and danced in the shafts of sunlight spilling down from slit windows set high up in the walls. Ancient banners hung from wooden poles set at regular intervals into the stone. The grunts of horses and the good-natured shouts of men-at-arms at their morning exercises drifted through the open door. An elderly wolf-hound lay in a patch of sun near the great hearth, soaking up the double warmth of fire and solar heat. His tail thumping rhythmically upon the stone floor, the dog's liquid amber eyes tracked Jelena as she moved farther into the room.

"Come here, Ghost," Jelena called softly to the dog, and the old beast climbed laboriously to his feet and ambled over to her. He pushed his massive, grizzled head into her hands and stared up adoringly into her eyes.

In his prime, Ghost had been Magnes's favorite hunting dog and his constant companion. Despite his ferocity in the field, he had always been patient and gentle with people. Now, stiff and slow with age, he spent most of his days either lying before a fire or sleeping in the sun.

Jelena bent to press her cheek against the wiry fur atop Ghost's head, breathing in his musky aroma. She had always loved this dog for his sweet nature and because he belonged to Magnes.

With a final scratch behind the ears, she left Ghost at the foot of the stairs leading up to the second floor of the keep. Climbing took too much out of him now, so after uttering a soft *whuff* of farewell, the big dog went back to his patch of sunshine.

Jelena made her way up the stairs and down a short corridor to the polished oak door of her uncle's study. Before knocking, she smoothed her skirts and made sure that the tips of her ears were hidden beneath her hair; concealment of the most elven of her features had become automatic. This simple act of protective camouflage somehow always made her feel a little safer and stronger. She drew in a deep, shaky breath, and rapped firmly.

"Come!" a deep voice called out from within.

Jelena pushed the door open just wide enough to slide her slim body through, closing it carefully behind her. She paused, her quick, hazel eyes taking in the scene before her. Dark, heavy wood and shadowy corners made up her uncle's study. A small fire burned in the stone hearth to her left. Tapestries hung against the walls, depicting various scenes from the Stories of the Gods. Numerous cases and tables were scattered about the room, all serving as display areas for an extraordinary collection of scale models. There were models of ships, siege engines—even a complete replica of Amsara Castle itself. All had been lovingly constructed out of wood and metal by the duke's own hands. The smells of dust and wood smoke infused the air, and a telltale tickle in Jelena's nose heralded a sneeze, which she quickly stifled.

"Come here, girl. I can't speak to you when you're across the room," her uncle commanded.

"Yes, Uncle," Jelena answered, and quickly crossed the expanse of Sermatian carpeting to stand before the duke, who sat at a small writing table. The *scritch-scratch* of quill pen upon parchment was the only sound in the room for several heartbeats as the duke worked, ignoring his niece completely. Just as Jelena began to fidget, he put down his pen and fixed his steely blue eyes upon her.

Duke Teodorus Preseren looked much like his castle's keep—squarely built, imposing, and strong. He had a broad, plain face, with a heavy jaw and beetling brows, which at first glance could give the false impression of brutish stupidity. However, one would only have to look into his eyes, which gleamed with a shrewd intelligence, to realize that underestimating the Duke of Amsara would be a serious mistake. He was a man completely devoid of any sentimentality, an able administrator, hard and extremely demanding with his people, yet well respected for his fairness and judgment. Jelena knew that he took very good care of the folk of Amsara, and because of this, she had never borne her uncle any ill will.

"I'll get straight to the point, so you can get on with your work," the duke said, never one to waste time on trivial things like greetings and pleasantries. "Tonight, you'll be allowed to feast in the great hall with the family and our guests."

Jelena gasped, uncertain that she should believe what she had just heard. "Uncle! I…" she began, but the duke cut her off.

"You can thank me later, after the feast. Go see Fania." Fania was the castle's seamstress. "She has some old gowns of Thessalina's that my daughter doesn't wear anymore. You can choose one. You'll know where she is, I trust."

"I know where Fania works, Uncle," Jelena answered, trying hard to keep the excitement from her voice.

Her uncle scowled, as if irritated by Jelena's interruption. "Have Claudia help you with your hair. Here, take this. It may help to keep that thatch of yours in its place." He held out a circlet.

Jelena's embarrassment turned to wonder as she took the circlet from her uncle's large, callused hand. Finely crafted of pure silver and beautiful in its simplicity, the circlet gleamed softly in the natural light streaming in from the window behind the duke's desk. Jelena turned it over in her hands, admiring the tracery of leaves and flowers engraved on its surface.

"I can't believe you're allowing me to wear this, Uncle. It…it's much too fine…" Jelena's voice trailed off. At the back of her mind, a little bell of alarm began to chime. She shivered.

"That circlet belonged to my sister, Drucilla… your mother. I reckon you're entitled to wear it, at least tonight, anyway. It should fit. Your head is about the same size as hers… same hair, too."

"Thank you, Uncle. I'll wear it proudly," Jelena replied.

"You can go now," the duke said by way of dismissal. He picked up his pen and resumed writing, as if Jelena had suddenly vanished from the room.

Just then, the door swung open and Thessalina entered. "Father!" she cried. "You can't be serious!" She stomped across the room, radiating fury like the blast from a forge.

The duke's only daughter had a face too hard to be pretty, but the force of her personality nonetheless drew men to her like a magnet and allowed her to bend them to her will. The full strength of her power emanated from her like the heat of the sun as she stood facing her father. Even the duke seemed to shrink a little in the face of her towering anger.

"I will not marry that…that *toad!*" Thessalina shouted. She hammered her gloved fist down onto the duke's writing desk, sending the ink pot tumbling to the floor, where it disgorged its contents in a black spray upon the carpet. This proved to be too much. The duke catapulted himself up out of his chair and thrust his face to within a nose-length of his daughter's. Neither of them acknowledged Jelena's presence.

"I, uh…" Jelena stuttered as she backed away a few steps. Thessalina had nearly knocked her over.

As if seeing her cousin for the first time, Thessalina turned to face Jelena, blue eyes blazing. "Get out!" she growled.

Jelena fled.

Down the stairs and past the loudly snoring Ghost she ran, her mother's precious circlet clutched tightly in her sweaty hands. She didn't stop running until her feet passed over the threshold of the keep and she found herself back out in the yard. Her heart fluttered in her chest like a panicky rabbit, and her mouth seemed to have lost all of its moisture.

What a scene! she thought. Jelena had witnessed Thessalina's rages before, but never up close. She shuddered to imagine the scorching heat of her cousin's wrath turned upon her. She would be reduced to ash!

As the rush faded from her limbs, leaving her drained and shaky, Jelena made her way back to the room she shared with Claudia in the servants' hall. Once there, she sat on the edge of her cot to examine the silver circlet. Holding this object that had once graced the head of her mother mined a deep vein of emotion within Jelena's soul. It brought forth grief and loss, and tears for the young woman who had died to give her child life, a young mother whom her daughter would never know. Yet, the daughter did know something of her mother, in a way.

Surely there's a lot of my mother in my own looks and personality, she thought. *Claudia is forever telling me so.*

Jelena dried her eyes and blew her nose upon her sleeve. She then placed the circlet lovingly in her chest, on top of the one other dress she owned. She would go now to see Fania and pick out something to wear from among Thessalina's castoffs, but even a castoff from her cousin would be a far finer garment than Jelena could ever hope to acquire on her own. Then, she would return to work.

As she walked back down to the yard, she had a sudden change of heart. After she chose a dress, she would not return to the hot, noisy kitchen. Instead, she would go up to the battlements to think. The windy solitude on those man-made heights always seemed to help clear her head. She needed to try to make sense of things.

Why, after all these years, has Uncle suddenly seen fit to allow me to attend a family feast? There has to be a specific reason behind his decision.

Jelena suspected it had nothing to do with any newly discovered affection for her. So, that could only mean her uncle needed her there for a particular purpose, one that would ultimately be to his benefit, and not necessarily to hers.

Of that, I'm certain.

CHAPTER 2

UNWELCOME NEWS

"Good mornin', an' happy Sansa to ye, Lord Magnes," the groom said as he took the reins of the bay gelding and held them for his young master. The son and Heir of Duke Teodorus had just returned from his morning rounds, satisfied and cheerful.

"An excellent morning it is, Dari! The sun is shining, the orchards are in full bloom, and we shall all have a very happy Sansa, indeed!" Magnes threw his booted leg up and over the bay's withers and slid to the ground. He ruffled Dari's ginger hair, and the boy favored him with a gap-toothed grin.

"Heard tell Cook's outdone herself on the vittles, milord. My old mam says never in her life has she seen such a Sansa cake as this 'un. It be huge, says she!"

Magnes laughed. It delighted him to see the boy so excited. "Well, if you give Storm here a good, thorough rubdown, I'll see to it that you get an especially big piece of that cake." He slapped the gelding's shoulder affectionately, and the horse whickered in reply.

"Aye, Lord Magnes, I will!" Dari tugged on the horse's bridle, clicking his tongue to encourage the animal to follow him to the stables. Magnes smiled as he watched the boy walk away with the horse ambling along in tow. He had always liked Dari, a good boy and a hard worker. He seemed to have a special way with horses, an instinct almost. It allowed him to get beneath the skin of his charges, to inhabit their minds, to *think* like they did. Magnes had no doubt that someday Dari would be Amsara's Horsemaster.

Magnes Preseren was not an overly ambitious man. By accident of birth, he was the Heir to one of the richest duchies in the Empire, but he cared nothing about his position. Magnes's true passions were twofold. He loved the very land itself, with a deep, emotional connection few others understood.

He also loved Livie, the raven-haired daughter of Amsara's chief game warden—a respectable girl from a respectable family. She and Magnes had loved each other since they had first met as children. Whenever the warden came up to the castle, Livie would accompany him, and she and Magnes would quickly steal away and lose themselves in adventure. Eventually, she started coming to the castle on her own, to work in the kitchens until she reached the age where she could apprentice at her mother's trade. As a young boy not yet burdened with the social restrictions of his station, Magnes could befriend a common girl, and no one would disapprove.

As the years passed, their innocent affections gradually transformed into adult passion with the maturing of their bodies and emotions. But with maturity had come the painful realization that their love could never be openly acknowledged, at least not without devastating consequences. Livie's family might be respectable, but as the daughter of a commoner and servant, she would never be a suitable marriage prospect for Duke Teodorus's Heir.

Unable to be together openly, they had carried on their love affair in secret, but the fear of a pregnancy had put a stop to any physical intimacy. Now, with Livie's eighteenth birthday rapidly approaching, her father would be looking to find her a husband. Magnes felt unsure how he would cope with seeing her wed to another man, but what choice did he have? The grief of their predicament had been keeping him awake at night, tossing and turning with worry.

Magnes shivered with the memory of their most recent time together. They had been unable to control themselves and had made love, filled with all of the desperate passion of doomed lovers. He sighed, and with great effort, pushed the memory aside. Any decisions about his situation with Livie would have to wait for now. He had duchy business to attend to, and his father was expecting him.

Magnes left the stables and made his way across the yard towards the keep. All around him, the hustle and bustle of festival preparations proceeded at a frenetic pace. He had to weave his way through rows of trestle tables and dodge scurrying servants, their arms laden with baskets of linens, crockery, and tableware. His spirits, brought low by the impossibility of his situation with Livie, were soon lifted as the cheerful hubbub of the yard re-instilled within him the happiness of the season.

Anyone who didn't know him by sight might easily mistake Magnes for a farmer. He usually dressed simply in a linen or cotton tunic, leather jerkin, breeches, and sturdy leather boots. This morning was no exception, for he had spent it, like he spent most mornings, riding over his father's vast estate, overseeing the duke's agricultural interests. He had been competently performing these duties since coming of age at fifteen. Gifted with an instinctive understanding of how the land, weather, and the turning of the seasons worked to produce the bounty upon which all of Amsara depended, Magnes desired very little else out of life.

Unfortunately, Fate and the gods had decreed that he be born a duke's eldest child, and with that station came a birthright that he could not escape, no matter how much he might wish otherwise. So, in exchange for allowing him to run Amsara's agricultural operations, the duke had insisted that Magnes train at arms and study the classic subjects usually included in a young nobleman's education so that he would be prepared to take over as duke upon his father's death.

Each time Magnes scooped up a hand-full of rich, black Amsaran soil and inhaled its heady aroma, redolent of the promise of growth, he imagined life as just a common-born man, free to marry the girl he loved.

The keep felt like an oasis of calm after the controlled chaos of the yard. A fire burned in the large hearth, for despite the growing warmth of the day, the stones of the keep's thick walls still retained their nighttime chill. Old Ghost lay sprawled on the stones before the fire, snoring loudly. Magnes took the stairs two at a time up to the second floor where his father's study was located. As he approached, he could see that the door stood partially open. The sound of voices, raised in anger, drifted through. Cautiously, he entered.

Magnes's sister Thessalina was as unlike in physical appearance to their father as Magnes himself was akin. Whereas he shared their father's same stocky build, square face, and curling brown hair,

Thessalina was their deceased mother reborn. She stood a good two inches taller than both her kinsmen, with mahogany hair that hung in thick, lustrous waves to her waist, and a slender body honed to the peak of fitness by years of arms training.

Right now, she and Duke Teodorus were squared off in a shouting match, nose to nose. Thessalina appeared to be winning, for the duke threw up his hands in exasperation and turned away.

"Uh…Is it safe to come in?" Magnes asked, a tentative smile playing across his lips. Both combatants turned as one to face him.

The duke irritably waved his arm. "Yes, yes, come in, son. Your sister and I were just having a small disagreement, that's all." Duke Teodorus turned hard eyes upon his daughter.

"A *small* disagreement? Father! I would hardly call…"

"Thessalina, please! We will discuss this later!"

"I could come back in a little while, Father," Magnes offered.

"No, of course not. You have my morning report, and I want to hear it now." The duke glared pointedly at the seething Thessalina, who narrowed her eyes and set her mouth in a hard line but kept it shut. The duke returned to his desk chair and sat. "Look at this mess," he muttered, peering down at the ink splattered carpet. "I paid a lot of money for that carpet. Hmmm. Well. Talk to me, son."

"The orchards are in full flower, including all of the new apple trees we planted. We should have a record harvest this year, if all goes well."

"That was a smart move, increasing the number of trees and when the new ones mature, we'll probably have to expand the mill to keep up."

"We should easily double our production over last year with just the old trees alone," Magnes added, a touch of pride in his voice.

"We'll be able to increase our profit without raising our price. Well done, Son," the duke said, nodding his head in approval. It had been Magnes's idea to expand the very profitable cider business. Amsara was famed throughout the empire for the exceptional quality of its cider.

"There'll be no profits for anyone, 'cept the arms makers if there's a war on," Thessalina interjected. "We should be discussing improvements to the fortifications and how soon we can raise and train our levies. We are a border duchy after all, Father, or have you forgotten?"

The duke shot his daughter a pained look. "There'll be no war. The elf king has shown no interest in anything outside his borders. It's been over a hundred years since the Empire and The Western Lands had any hostilities between 'em, and that was Silverlock's father started that business. So far, Silverlock himself has been nothing but peaceful, as was his brother before him."

"I agree with Father," Magnes said. "The elves have been good neighbors. They've left us alone, pretty much. Why should things change now?"

"You've heard the rumors, Father. You can't just ignore them," Thessalina countered.

"I've heard them, yes. The empress wants to take back territory her great-great grandfather lost to the elves during the last war. The elves have had the Portanus Valley for a long time now. They are not about to give it up without a very nasty fight. It's too important to them. I don't think the empress'll be foolish enough to spend the enormous amount of money it would take to wage that fight, just to satisfy some musty old debt of honor."

"How do we know that they won't try any more land grabs? Perhaps use Portanus as a base to invade further south?"

The duke shook his head. "They may be lacking souls, but they are not lacking intelligence, Thessalina. They don't have nearly the troop strength to mount any kind of invasion. They may not even have enough to mount an effective defense."

"Yes, there are a lot more of us than there are of them," Magnes pointed out. "I think they just want us to leave them alone. And I don't believe that myth about them having no souls."

"Well, you wouldn't," Thessalina commented sarcastically, the unspoken meaning behind her words clear.

"You and Father really should treat Jelena better. She is our family, despite both of your efforts to deny the fact," Magnes said angrily.

"Oh, not that old song again. It is sooo tiresome!" Thessalina rolled her eyes and heaved an exaggerated sigh.

Magnes could feel the pressure of fury building within him. "You are such a bitch sometimes, Thessalina!" he lashed out.

"That's enough!" the duke barked. "Magnes, you will not speak to your sister in that way. She is a lady, and you will treat her with respect!"

"Sorry," Magnes muttered grudgingly, but the hard look in his eyes warned of his enduring anger.

"Now, then. I have some news for you, Magnes," the duke began. "As you know, we'll be hosting several of our neighbors at this year's feast. Duke Leonus of Orveta will be attending. He'll be bringing his daughter, uh…" the duke massaged his temples in an attempt to coax the girl's name from his memory.

"Lowena," Thessalina supplied.

"Lowena, yes. The girl just turned sixteen a month ago, and Leonus has made me an offer. He has agreed to a match between you two, as long as agreeable terms can be reached. I have graciously accepted on your behalf. You will be meeting your future bride tonight."

"What?" Magnes cried.

"Oh, no, Father, not Magnes, too! You can't be serious! I've seen that girl. She's a simpering little twit! You can't make Magnes marry her, any more than you can force me to marry that toad Artos!"

"I beg you, Father," Magnes pleaded. "I'm not ready to marry yet. Let me…"

"*Enough!*" the duke bellowed, slamming both hands down hard onto the desk top. "You are both my children, and *you will obey!* You will marry *when* I say, and *whom* I choose! Your wishes have no bearing on the matter. This is business, by the gods!" Both Magnes and his sister stood silent, he with his arms hanging by his sides, she with hers folded tightly across her breasts.

"Magnes, the deal is as good as done. Our family stands to gain handsomely by joining with Orveta, so you'd better get used to it. As for *you*, Daughter, Lord Artos hasn't given me an answer yet. He may not accept my offer. I am sure he has heard the stories of your legendary temper, and he may not wish to take on such a willful wife as you'd be."

"I pray that's so, for his sake," Thessalina muttered under her breath. The duke acted as if he didn't hear his daughter's last comment. He began to gather up the papers he had been working on, stacking them into two neat piles. The room grew very still. A log collapsed in the hearth with a loud pop. The faint sounds of laughter and shouting drifted up from the yard through the high, narrow windows, open now to let in the fresh air.

"Is there anything else to report?" the duke asked Magnes, not bothering to look up at his son.

"No, Father. May I go now?"

Teodorus waved his hand in dismissal.

"I'll come with you," Thessalina said.

The joyful mood engendered by his morning's work had completely dissipated, to be replaced by one of almost unbearable sadness. All of Magnes's hopes and dreams for a simple life were being consumed, destroyed on the pyre of his father's ambition. Thessalina followed him out of the study and closed the door behind them.

As Magnes turned towards the staircase, Thessalina reached out and placed her hand on his shoulder. "Magnes, wait," she said. He turned back to face her. "I'm sorry for what happened just now," she began. "Despite our different beliefs, you are still my brother, and I love you. Father is thinking only of his purse, not of your happiness, or of mine."

Magnes sighed. "What are we to do, Thess? Is there no escape?"

"Well, I'm going to go change out of these clothes. I'm sure I must reek of horse. I was out breaking that new Raks'sh'Am stallion Father bought me last week, when Horsemaster Nolus came up to congratulate me on my upcoming marriage to Lord Artos! Imagine my surprise, since it was the first I'd ever heard of it."

Magnes laughed. "How do the servants always seem to know things even before we do?" he said.

"Huh!" Thessalina shrugged her shoulders by way of an answer.

"I think I'll go up to the top of the wall awhile, to clear my head," Magnes said. He had a lot to think about.

"I'll see you later, at the feast." Thessalina turned and headed off toward the staircase leading up to the third level where both she and Magnes had their private quarters. Magnes went down and out of the keep, back across the yard, and up the narrow stairs to the battlements atop Amsara Castle's curtain wall.

Up here, so high above the earth, peace and quiet reigned. Magnes could look out and see the whole of Amsara, or so it seemed. At the base of the hill upon which the castle stood, the small cluster of houses and workshops that made up Amsara village nestled. Below the village, the fields and orchards began, spread out like a green and brown patchwork quilt. He placed his palms down flat against the rough stone of the wall, and took in great breaths of the sweet spring air, and slowly, slowly, the anger and sorrow roiling his heart began to settle down to a dull ache.

"Happy Sansa, Cousin," a familiar voice said, breaking into his reverie. "We always seem to end up in the same place when we need to think."

Magnes smiled. "It does seem that way. Happy Sansa, Jelena."

CHAPTER 3

THE FIRE WITHIN

By the look on your face, Cousin, I know you need a drink," Jelena said.

Magnes laughed. "Is it that obvious? What are you doing up here?"

"The same thing as you. We both of us need a place to hide once in a while."

"That we do. Life is so difficult sometimes."

"Just sometimes?" Jelena's voice was sly and teasing.

"Yes, yes, I know. I, of all people, really have no cause to complain."

The cousins rested their elbows on the parapet and gazed out over the outer wall, watching the horizon in companionable silence. A hawk screamed overhead, held aloft on rust-brown wings. The spring sunshine bathed the backs of their necks and shoulders with gentle warmth.

Jelena, with her keener vision, spotted the approaching party first. "Look there! Coming up the road," she cried, pointing to the group of moving specks that soon resolved into a sizable party of both mounted and un-mounted people. The group appeared headed straight for the open gates of the castle.

"Must be the first of our guests," Magnes said. He strained to make out the device on the fluttering pennants. "Looks like an azure field, a silver ibex *passant* with two six-pointed silver stars. That's Duke Sebastianus Lucien of Veii."

Veii was Amsara's immediate neighbor to the south, famed for the quality of the horses bred there, second only to the fabled Raks'sh'Am of the southern deserts.

Magnes nibbled thoughtfully on a fingernail. "You know, Duke Sebastianus was widowed recently," he said. He turned his head and spat out a nail fragment. "He's been putting it about that he's in the market for a replacement wife. The last one failed to give him an heir, even after seven years of marriage."

Jelena sighed. "Poor woman. He probably had her poisoned to get her out of the way."

Magnes turned to his cousin with a look of feigned shock. "My dear cousin! Such cynicism, and in one so young!"

Jelena rolled her eyes.

"For your information," Magnes continued, "Duchess Trina died of a fever, or at least that's the official story. Anyway, he'll not have much of a selection. Most of the girls of noble families in this area are either already spoken for, or they're too young."

"Maybe he's come to ask your father for Thessalina," Jelena suggested.

"Ha! Not bloody likely. Veii isn't nearly rich enough for my father to even consider the idea of an alliance between our families. Besides, he already has a husband picked out for my sister, but I'd lay a sizable wager against Thessalina marrying any man not of her own choosing. She'd sooner throw herself off the battlements. Maybe that's what I should do. My situation's not much different..." Magnes's voice trailed off into silence, his face pensive.

"What do you mean, Magnes?" Jelena asked. She already had a pretty good idea, though, of what he was referring to. She and Magnes had been confidants since childhood, and Jelena knew of his intense love for the chief game warden's daughter.

Magnes let out a soft, bitter chuckle. "My father has been very busy matchmaking lately. Seems I am to be betrothed this very night. The lady in question is from an old, very rich family, and this alliance is going to be extremely profitable for both houses. For you see, cousin..." Magnes fixed Jelena with such a look of hopeless sorrow that it pierced her heart and caused tears to start in her eyes, "I and my sister are but pawns to my father, to be used at will, for the maximum benefit of both himself and Amsara."

Jelena leaned close and placed her small, slender-boned hand over Magnes' larger one. She felt powerless to help him, for she had even less status and influence with her uncle than Magnes had. "Magnes, I…" she stammered, but he shook his head and smiled at her.

"It's all right, Jelena. I know." He gathered her into his arms and held her close. He smelled of old leather, musty wool, and horse. "I just wish things could be different."

Jelena wished, with all her heart that things could be different as well, for both herself and her cousin. They were each trapped by the circumstances of their births, the courses of their lives dictated, not by free will, but by the mandates of others more powerful than they were.

After a few moments, Jelena squeezed Magnes hard then slipped out of his embrace. She gave him a quick peck on the cheek and straightened her dress. "I've got to get back to the kitchen. I'm going to catch hell from Cook for sure." She turned and headed for the stairwell that led down from the wall.

"It's not fair how my father treats you, Jelena," Magnes said. "You should be living as a noblewoman, not as a servant."

Jelena turned and shrugged. "I am just a stupid little tink bastard, after all. Isn't that what everyone has always thought of me?" she replied, matter-of-factly.

"Stop it, Jelena. Don't talk about yourself that way," Magnes retorted angrily.

Dear Magnes, Jelena thought. *You always defend me.* "I guess Uncle hasn't told you yet. I'm to eat with the family tonight at the private feast. He's even allowing me to choose one of Thessalina's old gowns, so I won't look too embarrassing. The best part is he gave me a silver circlet to wear that belonged to my mother."

Magnes cocked his head to one side. "You don't seem all that excited about this," he commented.

"Oh, I am. It's just…" she bit her lip and tugged nervously at a stray coil of hair. Magnes raised his eyebrow questioningly. "Why would he invite me now, after all these years? What's so different about this Sansa? It just makes me a little scared, is all."

"Jeleeenaaa!!!" a voice cried out from the yard below.

"Oh shit! I've got to go!" With a quick wave, she turned and scrambled back down the steep stairs to the yard.

When she emerged from the stairwell, she saw Ruby, one of the scullery drudges, standing outside the kitchen door, hands cupped to mouth. She was just about to give another shout when she spotted Jelena jogging towards her.

"Hey, where've you been, then? Tryin' to duck out of your fair share of the work, I'll reckon, you lazy good for nothin'..." Ruby stood, hands on hips, a belligerent expression twisting her bovine face.

As aggressive as she was stupid, Ruby had always been one of the worst of the castle bullies. Jelena loathed her with a particular passion.

"Shut up, Ruby," Jelena spat as she tried to brush past the other woman.

"Why, you little tink bitch!" With startling swiftness, the back of Ruby's hand slammed across Jelena's mouth, snapping her head to the side. Jelena gasped in shock, and her own hand flew up to her stinging lip, coming away with a smear of blood. The two of them stood staring at each other in silence for several heartbeats.

Something in Jelena tore loose then; all the pent up rage from years of abuse boiled up from her deepest core and spilled forth in a bitter wave. As it came, it released something else, something completely outside of anything Jelena had yet experienced.

What happened next left her even more stunned and shaken than Ruby's unexpected assault.

A tingling sensation in her right hand caused Jelena to raise it up to eye level. She cried out in fear. Her fingers seemed to be on fire; each digit was haloed with pale blue flames that flowed down her forearm like water, and yet her flesh was unburnt. How could this be?

Ruby let out a strangled cry and rushed forward. Instinctively, Jelena threw up her hands in defense. The two collided, and a shockwave blew through Jelena's body, rocking her backwards. Ruby was lifted off of her feet and flung through the air, arms and legs flailing. She slammed into the dirt of the yard with a heavy thud and lay still.

The blue fire died away.

On trembling legs, Jelena approached the fallen Ruby, who lay sprawled untidily on her stomach, her skirts flung up around her waist to expose her naked backside. Gingerly, Jelena knelt down and peered into the other woman's slack face, and breathed a sigh of relief. Ruby was still alive.

Still reeling from shock, Jelena sat back on her heels and tried to calm her frantic heart.

What the hell just happened? How did I do that?

Ruby groaned and began to stir.

Jelena gently probed her split lip with the tip of her tongue and felt a new wave of anger building within. Quickly, she squelched it. Whatever had happened, whatever this was that she had summoned, she realized that she had no idea how to control it, but Ruby needn't know.

The other woman groaned again, then rolled over and sat up, rubbing at her dirt-streaked face. Jelena remained crouched where she was and allowed her face to settle into what she hoped seemed like an appropriately menacing expression.

"You'd best leave me alone from now on," she warned, her voice low and dangerous. "I'm through taking your shit!" Ruby's eyes widened and Jelena saw uncertainty and yes, a little fear within them. Wordlessly, Ruby scrambled to her feet and fled, disappearing through the kitchen door.

Jelena rose, dusted off her knees, and followed, a wicked sense of satisfaction adding a little swagger to her gait.

"Girrrrl!!!" Cook shouted as she entered. "Get over here an' start on them turnips!"

"Yes, ma'am," Jelena answered, her newfound confidence evaporating like frost on a sunny windowpane. She grabbed a paring knife and, seizing a root, began furiously peeling.

Later that day, when she had a few moments to herself, she sat and turned over in her mind the extraordinary occurrence of the blue flame. What exactly was its nature? What had triggered it? Anger, perhaps? She'd been angry plenty of times before. No, there had to be more to it. Most importantly, could she learn how to summon it at will and control its effects?

Magic!

The word whispered through her mind, conjuring up images both seductive and terrifying. Only a tiny fraction of the human race had any innate magical abilities, and those that practiced openly were more often than not shunned or punished for it. Powerful magic had always been the province of the elves.

All elves were born with magical abilities—an inheritance from their demon progenitors, or so the priests taught, and because their magic came from the demon realm, it was inherently evil. A favorite bogey of all priests was the elf witch, a creature whose beauty ensnared righteous men and whose magic corrupted their souls.

Jelena's stomach clenched with dread. What if Ruby denounced her as a witch to the castle's resident priest, Father Nath? What would happen to her then? The people of Amsara barely tolerated her as it was, and only because of the very thin mantle of protection her blood ties with the Preserens afforded her. If she were accused of witchcraft, she would be driven out and possibly worse, blood ties notwithstanding.

Still, the mere fact that she seemed to have inherited at least a little magic from her unknown sire instilled in her a new sense of courage. She decided not to live in fear of denunciation. Ruby was so stupid that no one would believe her anyway.

Jelena determined to keep the blue fire a secret at least for now, until she could figure out a way to call it forth again. Eventually, she knew that she would confide in Claudia and perhaps Magnes. This was too important a development to keep from them for long. Perhaps, between the three of them, they could figure out what it all meant.

Reluctantly, Jelena rose from her seat outside the kitchen door and returned to her duties.

~~~

"Well! You are a sight, my lamb. As beautiful as yer dear mam, I reckon." Claudia stood with hands clasped beneath her chins, a look of pure delight suffusing her heavy features. She gestured with a forefinger in a circular motion, indicating that Jelena should spin around again for a second viewing. The girl obliged, laughing a little despite her attempts to keep a tight leash on her excitement.

The gown she had chosen consisted of a cornflower blue over-dress with a matching pale blue undertunic. Both garments were of silk, and to Jelena, who was used to the rough feel of coarse wool, cotton gauze, or plain, serviceable linen against her skin, the whisper-soft way the fabric glided over her body seemed almost ob-scenely luxurious. High-waisted, with a tight fitting, scandalously low-cut bodice and a full, slightly flared skirt, the gown had last seen use several seasons ago—out of fashion, but still beautiful, nonethe-less. The oversleeves were slit from shoulder to wrist to reveal the fine embroidery of blue flowers that embellished the sleeves of the undertunic. Embroidery also decorated the neckline and hem of the overdress, carrying through the floral motif. Matching blue slippers completed the ensemble.

"Humph," Claudia rumbled, tapping a stout finger against her jawline thoughtfully. "That neck of yours needs summat to set it off. It be too bare…Ay! O' course! I've got just the thing!" Jelena watched with growing curiosity as her foster mother went over to the large wooden chest at the foot of her bed and began rummaging through its contents. After much digging, she brought forth, with a small crow of triumph, a little box made of cedar.

"I want you to have this, my love. It'll go just perfect with the dress," Claudia said as she pressed the box into Jelena's hands.

Jelena sighed with wonder. The box was exquisitely crafted, with an inlay of different colored woods forming an interlocking pattern of vines upon its lid. Jelena had never seen the box before and had no idea Claudia even owned such a fine object. She lifted the lid.

Nestled within its lining of black velvet rested a strand of blue beads.

Jelena carefully lifted the necklace free and held it in her hands as if it were made of the most precious of sapphires. In truth, the beads were fashioned of blue Kara glass; although not as costly as sapphires, still, a servant like Claudia would never have been able to afford such a piece of jewelry.

Claudia must have seen the question in Jelena's eyes. "This was a gift, given t' me by the late Duchess Julia, may the gods bless an' keep her soul. As good an' kind a mistress as anyone could want, she was. She gave me this necklace as a token of her thanks, after I seen her through the birthing of young Lord Magnes. Ay, what a hard birth that was! The poor duchess suffered the pains of Hell, she did, but it was worth it, for she gave your uncle his Heir. Now, turn 'round an' I'll fasten it on."

With the necklace now encircling her neck, there remained one last task to be completed before Jelena could make her way to the great hall for the feast.

After a great deal of vigorous brushing and the judicious application of almond oil, Jelena's hair was subdued enough to allow Claudia to place the silver circlet upon her foster daughter's head and adjust it so that it sat correctly. She then clapped her hands together and let out a great sigh.

"Well, girl, off you go now."

Jelena threw her arms around her foster mother and laid her head on Claudia's shoulder. She could feel Claudia's love enfold her like a warm, comforting blanket, and her own intense feelings momentarily threatened to overwhelm her.

Claudia held her close, clucking softly like an old contented hen. "You don't want to be late, my lamb. Won't do, keepin' the family waitin'."

"No, it won't," Jelena agreed. She laughed and wiped the unshed tears from her eyes. "I guess I'm just a little nervous. After all, I've never been allowed to eat with the nobles before. I'll have to be especially careful not to let them see that I'm really just a kitchen maid."

Claudia shook her head. "There'll be none in that room who'll mistake you for anythin' but what you are…a true Preseren."

My mother may have been a Preseren, but that doesn't matter to anyone but Magnes, Jelena thought. *All they'll see is the mark of my father's blood on me. That's all they've ever seen.*

"Don't wait up!" Jelena said airily as she swept through the door. She didn't want Claudia to see how scared she really was.

The wooden stairs squeaked like indignant mice as Jelena made her way down, mindful of the full skirt, which she had partially gathered up in her hands. The rustling of the silks seemed preternaturally loud in the close, narrow stairwell. She reached the bottom landing and pushed open the door leading to the yard.

Twilight had fallen, but the yard glowed with the light of lanterns and torches. The public feast was in full swing.

Jelena paused for a moment to take in the scene, a riotous conglomeration of colors, noise, and aromas.

The common folk of the district looked forward all winter to the

Sansa public feast held on the castle grounds, and it seemed to Jelena that the whole lot of them had come here tonight, dressed in their holiday finery. Servants scurried back and forth from the kitchen, bearing great platters of steaming roast beef and pork. There were heaps of meat pies, baskets of bread, boiled turnips, onions, and carrots, wheels of hard, brown cheese, red and yellow apples, and, to slake the crowds' insatiable thirst, endless flagons of beer and famous Amsara hard cider.

Children and dogs were everywhere, rolling underfoot and chasing each other with wild abandon. Jelena recognized the words and melodies to several different and equally lewd drinking songs, all of which added to the general cacophony.

She had no trouble slipping by in the shadows, unnoticed, and she reached the doorway to the great hall without incident. The heavy oak double doors stood open and light from the many lamps within formed a golden pool upon the paving stones without. Jelena paused, just outside of the circle of light, and gazed inward.

No one will mistake you for anything other than what you are!

Claudia's words echoed softly in Jelena's mind. With shaking hands she pulled at the borrowed gown, then checked one last time to make sure that her ears were hidden. Drawing in a lungful of the scent-charged air, she stepped into the doorway.

CHAPTER 4

A VEILED PROPOSITION

At first glance, the scene within the great hall seemed not much different from that of the yard. Jelena saw trestle tables and benches full of eating, drinking people; however, they were fewer in number and much more richly dressed than those outside. Torches burning in sconces affixed to the support posts illuminated the high-ceilinged chamber, and dozens of beeswax tapers in candelabra lit each table. The aroma of the burning candles added a sweet note to the mingled smells of roasted meat, beer, wine, and wood smoke that filled the air. Heraldic banners hung suspended from the heavy ceiling beams, and a series of faded tapestries depicting bucolic hunting scenes decorated the walls.

At the far end of the hall, a proper table and chairs stood upon a raised platform. At the high table sat her uncle. Beside him on his right sat another man whom Jelena had never seen before. She assumed that he must be someone very important to her uncle. Next to this special guest sat Thessalina, looking like she'd just smelled something extremely distasteful. Magnes was seated to his father's left, and next to him sat a young girl with pale blonde hair, dressed in dusky rose.

The man Magnes had identified up on the battlements earlier that day as Duke Sebastianus Lucien occupied a chair one place beyond the blonde girl. There were several other men and women seated at Duke Teodorus's table, all of whom had to be persons of high rank to merit such an honor.

Feeling a little like a rabbit walking into a den of foxes, Jelena stepped through the door, gathered up her skirts, and began walking down the center aisle towards the high table. The rushes strewn over the flagstones beneath her borrowed slippers made a crunching noise as she walked. At first, no one seemed to notice, but as she drew closer, the buzz of conversation trailed off into a charged silence. Her uncle sat coolly, regarding her over the edge of his wine goblet. Thessalina stared, expressionless. Jelena faltered for a moment, then stopped, poised on the knife-edge of panic.

Magnes must have sensed her fear; his instinct to protect her galvanized him into action. "Cousin! You're here at last. Come and join us," he said. His words were spoken at normal volume, yet they seemed to ring out like a trumpet call in the tense stillness of the hall, bolstering Jelena's failing courage.

"Uncle," she murmured, dropping into a deep curtsy.

She heard a sharp little giggle as she rose and saw the blonde girl raise a pale hand to her mouth, her blue eyes fastened on Jelena and twinkling with amusement. Magnes glanced at her and frowned.

"Yes, yes," Duke Teodorus growled, beckoning to her with a curt wave of his hand. "Come on up here and sit down, so we can get back to the food. Magnes, help her."

Magnes was by her side almost before the duke had finished speaking. He placed her hand in the fold of his elbow and led her up onto the dais and to the empty chair next to Duke Sebastianus. He made a great show of pulling it out for her, as if by demonstrating his commitment to her, he could turn the tide of prejudice.

The guests turned their attentions back to their food and conversation. A small musical ensemble, which had fallen silent at Jelena's entrance, once again took up their instruments, and soon the room filled with the sounds of music and feasting.

Jelena was acutely aware of the many pairs of eyes that watched her, some surreptitiously, others openly. She quickly scanned the faces of the crowd, and saw expressions ranging from mild curiosity to frank disgust. There could be no hiding who or what she was, not in this place. She had never in her life felt so naked, so utterly and completely exposed.

How am I ever going to get through this?

"Have some wine, my lady."

Jelena started a little in her seat. She had never before been addressed with any sort of honorific, and it shocked her. Every nerve in her body was stretched taut and jangling, as if at any moment, she would fly apart into a thousand bloody pieces. She turned to look at the man seated to her right.

Duke Sebastianus of Veii was not a handsome man, but neither was he ugly. Rather, he had the kind of face that was like a mask—calm on the surface, but hiding something underneath. He held a ewer in his hand, poised to pour.

Jelena could only nod in mute consent. The duke smoothly filled her goblet to the brim then topped off his own. He lifted the cup to his lips and regarded her with enigmatic eyes.

"My lord, this is my cousin, Jelena," Magnes said, leaning forward to look past the girl seated next to him, who seemed not to notice that Magnes was intentionally ignoring her. Her attention was focused on Jelena, vapid face alight with malicious glee.

"Yes, I know," the duke replied. Something in his tone made Jelena shiver.

"What would you like to eat?" Magnes asked.

"Maybe she'd like a cup of blood, or some raw meat. She won't bite, will she?" the blonde girl purred, fluttering her eyelashes coquettishly.

"Be quiet," Magnes retorted, his voice low and tight with anger. The girl sank back into her chair, her full pink lips set in a pout.

Jelena's stomach roiled with suppressed rage and fear.

"Your uncle sets a very fine table," Duke Sebastianus said. "It all looks quite delicious." He once again turned his peculiarly intense gaze upon Jelena.

There were a great variety of dishes to choose from, all of them familiar to Jelena from her years of working in the kitchen. She saw several of her favorites—rabbit and fruit pie, cold fish in aspic, game stew with turnips and carrots. It all might as well be rocks and wood, for she felt certain that if she tried to eat anything, her stomach would immediately rebel.

Praying that no one would see her hand trembling, Jelena reached for her wine goblet and brought the brimming cup slowly to her lips. She took several deep swallows and immediately regretted it. The dry, woodsy vintage, unhindered by any food that could absorb and slow its intoxicating effects, blew straight into her head. She closed her eyes and leaned back in her chair. From somewhere further down the table, she heard the porcine snort of a man's laughter.

"Ah, let me take that from you, my lady, before you spill it." The pleasant baritone of Duke Sebastianus's voice so close to her ear startled Jelena. Before she realized it, he had the cup and her hand firmly in his grasp and was gazing intently into her face, as if to memorize every detail of its topography. His dark eyes seized upon hers and held them, relentlessly, burning straight through into her innermost core. She felt trapped like a mouse under a cat's paw.

The duke gently pried Jelena's fingers from around the goblet and set it back on the table. "You had better eat something, or I fear the wine will go to your head," he said. "What may I serve you?"

"Some of the cold fish, and a little of the rabbit pie, Your Grace," Jelena replied, finding her voice at last. She watched silently as the duke served her plate with his own hand, acutely aware that many others were watching as well. She thanked him and began eating, taking the smallest of bites, afraid that, if she tried eating any more, she would choke.

"Your uncle described you to me in great detail, Jelena. I must say, though, that his description did not do you justice."

Jelena kept her eyes lowered, studiously avoiding the duke's gaze. "I was not aware that my uncle cared enough about me to describe me to anyone, let alone to a person of your high station, my lord," she replied softly.

"Your uncle has sent me several correspondences concerning you, Jelena. It has been almost a year since my wife died. I've lived the monastic life for long enough and now it's time to move forward."

Jelena felt awash in confusion. Why would Duke Teodorus write to one of his noble peers about her, his half-breed bastard niece whom he barely acknowledged? It just didn't make any sense. "I...I don't understand, Your Grace. I count for little or nothing in my uncle's eyes. Why would he wish to bring me to your attention?"

"You really have no idea why I've come to Amsara, do you?" Duke Sebastianus asked, his voice more thoughtful than puzzled.

Why do I feel like I'm walking through quicksand, and any moment, I'll be swallowed up whole? Jelena wondered.

"The Sansa Feast, of course. Other than that, I know of no other reason you might have to come here, my lord."

The duke leaned back in his chair, silently stroking his close-cropped, gray-shot beard. He opened his mouth as if to speak, but at that exact moment, the Sansa Cake arrived, to a tumultuous response.

Cheers, clapping, and raucous shouts accompanied the magnificent confection as it made its way up the center aisle, borne on a pallet hoisted upon the burly shoulders of four male kitchen drudges. It wasn't so much a cake as an edible sculpture. It was molded to look like a large basket filled up with fruits, nuts and grains—a promise of the harvest to come, if the goddess San bestowed her blessings on the spring plantings. Sheathed in gold leaf, the cake gleamed softly in the lamplight. Common folk jammed the door of the great hall, pushing and shoving each other in an effort to catch a glimpse of the beautiful creation.

Duke Teodorus stood up from his chair as the drudges set the cake down at the center of the high table. The room fell silent in anticipation of the duke's invocation. Even the common folk in the door quieted down to listen.

"Gentle San, goddess of renewal, new life, new beginnings, bestow your blessings upon us, your children. We ask that you quicken our fields, orchards, our livestock, and our women, so that the cycle of life may continue. Amen."

The muted response rippled through the crowd, followed by loud shouts for more beer and wine.

"Happy Sansa, Cousin," Magnes said brightly, but the melancholia Jelena could sense in him belied the cheerful smile on his lips.

Several tables were moved aside to clear an area for dancing. The musicians struck up a high-spirited country tune, and the floor filled with happy revelers, skipping and spinning to the melodic notes of harp, lute, and recorder. The Sansa cake would sit for a while on display before being cut and served. The festivities were only just beginning.

This was the time, in years past, when Claudia brought out a little Sansa cake for Jelena and her to share. They would find a corner somewhere, either in the kitchen or the pantry, and eagerly gobble down the special treat. It was not the cake that mattered to Jelena, although she certainly looked forward to it. It was the special quiet time she'd shared with Claudia, a time when they could just be mother and daughter, sharing a cake together in perfect love and trust.

How I wish I were with you now, Heartmother, Jelena thought. She dared to sneak a look at Duke Sebastianus. He sat watching the dancing with hooded eyes, his face unreadable. Abruptly, she had had enough.

She pushed back her chair and stood up. Magnes, who had been having a rather tense, but muted, conversation with his father, turned in his chair and looked up at her. "You're not leaving already, are you, Jelena?" he asked. His eyes seemed to beg her to stay. "The cake hasn't even been cut yet. You'll miss out on the best part of the feast."

"Yes, Jelena, do stay awhile longer," Duke Sebastianus drawled. The hunger in his eyes now was unmistakable, and it had nothing to do with food.

"Perhaps she's tired of trying to fit in where she doesn't belong," the blonde girl said. "Someone should have told her that dress is all wrong."

"Jelena, don't listen to her. Please stay," Magnes pleaded. The girl shot him a venomous look.

"I'm sorry. I suddenly don't feel well. I must go." She dropped a short curtsy to the duke. As she turned to leave, he reached out and grabbed her hand. She could feel the calluses on his fingertips and palm—put there, no doubt, by many hours of sword practice.

"We will see each other again, my lady," he said, his voice full of unfathomable implications.

Jelena pulled her hand free and bolted.

"Where is she going? Tell her to get back here this instant!"

Her uncle's angry voice carried well over the noise of the reveling, but Jelena had no intention of returning. She had to get as far away as she could from Duke Sebastianus and his dark, hungry eyes. She pushed her way through the dancers, curses and insults following in her wake. The last thing she heard as she fled through the open doorway into the yard was the throaty, arrogant laughter of Thessalina.

Jelena fled into the shadows at the fringes of the yard, running until she reached the wall of the keep, where she stopped to catch her breath. Her heart hammered against her ribs, and the clammy sweat of fear soaked the armpits of Thessalina's castoff gown. She crouched in the darkness, breathing deeply to calm herself. The public feast was still going strong, and watching the revelers had a soothing effect on her panicky brain.

I'll just go back to the room and go to bed, she thought, suddenly very weary. Rising to her feet, she began heading slowly towards the servants' hall. A cool breeze stirred the hair at the nape of her neck. She reached up and wiped her sweaty brow with the back of her hand.

As she approached the door to the servants' quarters, she heard noises coming from behind a nearby tool shed. It sounded like a girl crying. Thinking that someone might be hurt, she started towards the shed to investigate, then hesitated. Why should she care what happened to anyone here at the castle, other than Claudia or Magnes? When she had been hurt or crying, not a one among them had ever reached out to her, other than to further her pain.

Stop it, Jelena. Do you wish to sink to their level? Someone may need help.

She hurried toward the shed, but the two people she found behind the small wooden structure were in no need of her, or anyone else's, help.

The Festival of Sansa had always been about the celebration of fertility. With liquor freely flowing and sexual energy rampant, expectations were that there would be much merry-making of the carnal kind.

The girl sprawled on her back in a pile of straw, her skirt hiked up around her waist, legs in the air. The pale, naked buttocks of her lover pumped vigorously between her plump thighs. It was her cries, not of pain, but of pleasure, that Jelena had heard. The heat of embarrassment warmed Jelena's cheeks as she hastily backed away, certain that the lovers were too far gone in the throes of their passion to have seen her.

Jelena was no innocent. Growing up in the insular world of the servants' hall, where men and women spent most of their time living and working in close proximity, she had seen her fair share of couplings. However, at age eighteen, when most castle girls were already sexually active, Jelena was still a virgin. She had remained so partly because of her status as an outcast, but mostly by choice. No castle man, no matter how lowly his own status, would ever consider her anything more than an object upon which to relieve his sexual needs. Jelena had decided long ago that she would rather remain untouched for life than submit to the use of her body in such a demeaning way. She already endured enough debasement as it was.

Sometimes, while lost in the realm of dreams, Jelena met a faceless man who folded her into a lover's embrace. The touch of his hands upon her body would awaken a fire within her so intense that she would start up from sleep, her entire being aflame with ecstasy. After the sensations had subsided, she sometimes cried, knowing that there was almost no chance of her ever experiencing such bliss in the real world.

Slowly, Jelena made her way back toward the room she shared with Claudia. Her foster mother was most likely still be down in the kitchen lending a hand, and wouldn't be back until very late.

Their room stood empty, as Jelena had expected, but Claudia had left some burning charcoals on the grate to ward off the chill of the spring night. As the door shut behind her, all of the stress of the ordeal she had just endured drained from her body, leaving exhaustion in its wake. She put a splinter into the fire, and with its glowing tip, lit the little oil lamp next to her cot.

With a deep sigh, Jelena began to undress. Even without Claudia to help, she still managed to undo the laces at the back of the overdress and loosen them enough to pull the garment down off her shoulders, allowing it to fall in a heap at her feet. She gathered up the crisply rustling silk and laid the dress out on her cot.

She traced the delicate line of embroidery around the neckline with a fingertip, admiring the artistry of the work. Never again would she wear such a splendid gown, of that she was certain. After her embarrassingly abrupt exit, she imagined that there would be no more invitations forthcoming to any future feasts in the great hall.

It doesn't matter anyway. As beautiful as this dress is, I'm still lower than dirt to them.

She stepped over to the small mirror nailed into the wall by the door and stood staring at the image reflected in its hazy surface. She pulled her mother's circlet from her head and pushed back her mass of dark coils to reveal her ears.

Jelena had never seen a full-blooded elf, but all her life she had been told that they were beautiful, soulless creatures, completely vicious and amoral, incapable of any of the higher emotions like love and compassion. The priests always taught that the elves were the spawn of demons that had escaped from the Abyss to procreate on Earth with human women, many thousands of years ago. All manners of crimes, both high and low, were attributed to them. They soured fresh milk, caused miscarriages, brought the ague and the flux, stole human babies for their dark rites of magic—all because they were jealous of the souls of humanity. They knew that death meant oblivion for them, and that those of their race could never enter into the presence of the gods, and dwell in Paradise for all eternity.

Claudia had always told her that her mother had loved her father.

How could my mother fall in love with such a man, believing everything she'd always been told about elves? She must not have believed any of it at all. I'm living proof that none of it is true.

I'm sick to death of all of this. I'm leaving.

Jelena slipped out of the underdress, and gathering up the gown from her cot, she folded both garments and laid them in a neat pile atop her chest. She pulled the embroidered slippers from her feet and laid them, together with the silver circlet, in the center of the pile. The last thing to come off was Claudia's necklace, which she laid in the center of her foster mother's cot. Tomorrow, she would return the borrowed ensemble to Fania and the circlet to her uncle.

She felt so tired, she barely had the energy to pull on her nightgown and extinguish the lamp. She slipped into bed and pulled the rough blankets over herself with a heartfelt sigh. As she lay waiting for sleep to come, she wondered again just why she had been invited to the nobles' feast, and why she had been seated next to Duke Sebasianus. The mere memory of the way he had looked at her was enough to send a shiver of fear coursing through her.

None of it mattered anymore. She had made up her mind. Amsara was a border duchy. Just north of the Janica River lay elven territory—the southeastern-most province of the Western Lands. Chances were good that her father or his family lived in the area. As soon as the spring rains stopped, she would leave Amsara for good. She would seek out the man who had sired her, and cast her lot with him. And if she could not find him… well, she would think about that when and if she had to. Life couldn't possibly be any worse among the elves than it was among humans.

By the time Claudia returned in the wee hours of the morning, Jelena slept deeply, dreaming of a man she called Father and of pale, blue fire.

CHAPTER 5

HER INTOLERABLE FATE

Jelena! Jelena, wake up, girl. You've gone an' overslept!" Jelena groaned and scrubbed her sleep-heavy eyes with closed fists. Blinking like a hapless mole torn from its burrow, she reluctantly crawled from her warm nest of blankets and groped under the bed for the chamber pot. Claudia stood in the center of the small room, fully clothed, hands on hips.

"Must 'ave been quite a time y'had at the feast. Too much wine, I reckon," she said, a little smile playing about her lips.

Jelena shook her head. "No," she replied, and her stomach knotted up with the pain of remembering. "I left early, actually." She set the chamber pot by the door so she'd remember to empty it later, then went to her chest. She moved aside Thessalina's gown, lifted the lid, and began pulling out her work clothes. *No time for a wash,* she thought ruefully.

"Why, whatever didya leave early for? You looked so pretty in that gown... Surely you wanted t' show off a bit?" Claudia's surprise seemed to come from a genuine belief that, because she saw beauty in her foster daughter, others would as well.

Jelena laughed sharply. "No matter how fancy my gown or how pretty you think I look, I'll never be accepted here, Heartmother. I could hardly wait to get away from all of them. Especially him." Her hands began to shake.

"Who d'you mean?" Claudia probed.

"No one. I...I...uhhhhh!" She fumbled with the strings of her apron, unable to tie them properly. The terrible emotions of last night crowded in close around her, pawing and scratching. She suddenly felt like bony hands had fastened around her throat, cutting off her breath. The barrier she had erected to keep the pain at bay abruptly gave way and she collapsed to the floor, sobbing.

Wordlessly, Claudia gathered her up and held her until the flood of tears subsided. Jelena clung to her, snug against that same soft bosom that had sheltered and comforted her as a child. Now, as then, she felt safe while enveloped in that great haven of motherly flesh, secure in the knowledge that there would be no more torment as long as she stayed within.

As much as she desired to, she couldn't stay. Eventually, she always had to leave.

Claudia mopped at Jelena's tear-streaked cheeks with the hem of her apron. Gently, she lifted her foster daughter to her feet and tied up the recalcitrant apron strings. Jelena felt comforted, knowing that Claudia needed no details, and that her foster mother understood the pain of her ordeal, an extension of the larger ordeal of her life as an outcast.

"Now, you go on," Claudia said. "Don't fret about the dress. I'll take it back to Fania m'self."

"My mother's circlet..." Jelena started, but Claudia interrupted.

"You can give the circlet back to yer uncle later, durin' yer break time. Hurry, now, child. I'll see you at breakfast."

As Jelena hurried off to the kitchen, the image of Duke Sebastianus sprang, unbidden, into her mind and filled her with foreboding.

~~~

"Jelena!" Cook bellowed. Jelena jumped, nicking her thumb with the small blade she had been using to slice carrots for the staff's midday meal. She stuck the wounded digit into her mouth and turned to see Cook beckoning to her from across the room.

Gods, what have I done now, she thought.

Dropping the knife amidst the partially sectioned vegetables, thumb still firmly between her lips, she hurried over to receive her scolding.

"Git yer thumb out of yer mouth, girl," Cook growled.

Jelena obeyed immediately. "I cut myself, ma'am," she explained, wrapping a corner of her apron hem around the oozing wound. She braced herself for the verbal barrage. To her surprise, Cook had a message for her.

"His lordship wants to see you."

"Now?" Jelena asked meekly.

"Yes, now!" Cook replied sharply, her jowls quivering in annoyance. "Gods only know when you'll be back. Who's goin' t' cut all of them carrots, eh?"

Jelena resisted the urge to answer with "Cut them yourself." That would only get her a cuff on the head from one of Cook's ham-sized fists. Instead, she remained silent, eyes lowered.

"Go on, then! Don't keep His Lordship waitin'!" Cook waved her hand in dismissal, and Jelena hastily departed.

The yard lay quiet, bathed in watery, midmorning sunshine. The castle gates stood open and through them, Jelena could see a pair of guards lounging just beyond the raised portcullis, leaning on the butts of their spears. Pigeons fluttered and cooed in the eaves of the outbuildings. A pair of cats snoozed contentedly atop a hay bale.

I'd better go get the circlet. Now's as good a time as any to return it, Jelena thought. She hurried back to her room and retrieved the circlet from her chest. As she descended back down into the yard and made her way toward the keep, she couldn't help but feel that monumental changes were in store for her. Her life had come to a crossroads; she felt certain that her uncle intended to tell her which path he had chosen for her.

She thought about the blue fire and wondered again where it had come from and how she had summoned it. Why had it not appeared last night, during the Sansa feast? Surely, if strong emotions were the trigger, it should have manifested then, yet it had not.

Jelena knew the answers to her questions lay elsewhere. Only by seeking out her father's people could she ever learn the true meaning of the magic that had awakened briefly within her, with such startling results. Only the elves could teach her how to control it.

I've made up my mind. No matter the price, I must walk my own path. I've got to find out who I really am.

"Come!" Jelena heard her uncle's voice command through the

thick wood of his study door. Quickly, she obeyed.

Duke Teodorus was not alone. Brennes, Amsara's steward—a lanky scarecrow of a man—was there as well. He sat on a stool beside the duke's writing table, diligently scribbling in a big, leather-bound book resting on his lap.

"I believe we're finished here, Your Grace," Brennes said, slamming the ledger shut, and briskly rising to his feet. To Jelena, he looked like one of the herons she often saw out in the flooded spring fields, wading about on thin, bony legs in search of crayfish hidden in the black mud.

"I'll coordinate with Lord Magnes on those matters we discussed," the steward said as he tucked his quill behind one ear and started for the door.

"Yes, thank you," the duke replied. Brennes brushed past Jelena, pausing just long enough to rake her with a disdainful glance down his great beak of a nose before exiting and closing the door softly behind him.

"Good morning, Uncle," Jelena said politely. "Here is my mother's circlet. Thank you for allowing me to wear it." She proffered the circlet to the duke, who took it without comment and set it down on his desk. He folded his hands before him and fixed Jelena with a hard-eyed stare.

"Why'd you leave the feast like that? Were you deliberately trying to embarrass me in front of my guests?"

"No, Uncle, of course not. It's just that I…"

"That you what?" Duke Teodorus interrupted, clearly irritated. He shook his head and took a deep breath as if to calm a rising tide of anger. "Anyway, it doesn't matter. No harm done, thank the gods."

"I'm sorry, Uncle," Jelena replied. An ache in her hands drew her eyes downward. She was clutching her apron hem so tightly, her knuckles stood out like white knobs. She forced herself to relax her grip and remain steady.

"I have news for you, girl, and it's good… The best news you're ever likely to hear from me."

Jelena dared to look up at her uncle's face. The hard lines around his mouth had softened a little, as if he were going to take great pleasure in what he was about to say.

"I sent a letter to Duke Sebastianus several months after his wife died, describing you to him and inviting him to come have a look at you at Sansa. Well, he did, as you know, and he has agreed to take you off my hands. Do you understand what I'm telling you, girl?"

Her uncle's words fell on Jelena like freezing rain, rooting her to the stone floor.

"I…I'm not sure," she whispered, barely able to get the words past lips that refused to work properly.

"Veii has made an offer for you, girl, that's what. He's willing to take you on as his legal concubine. It's not marriage, of course, but then, you didn't really expect that, did you? This is an excellent offer, the best you'll ever get. Veii will be legally obligated to care for you for life, and provide for any children that you may bear him, even if he marries again. Furthermore, he has agreed to pay me a decent sum for you, much more than I'd thought I'd get. Everyone profits." The duke leaned back in his chair, smiling broadly now.

Everyone profits?! How do I profit by being sold into slavery?

A white-hot anger rose up in Jelena, melting the ice encasing her stunned brain and unfreezing her limbs. A shout forced its way up from her belly and into her throat. "No!" she screamed. "I won't let you do this to me!"

Duke Teodorus's smile vanished. Slowly he stood up, a storm of rage settling upon his brow. His voice was deadly calm. "You ungrateful little bitch. How *dare* you speak to me that way? Don't you realize that you have no say in this? As your legal guardian, I have the right to decide for you in these matters. The bargain's been struck, and the contract has been signed and witnessed."

"Contract! Don't you mean bill of sale?" Jelena shot back bitterly.

Like a charging bull, the duke rushed her before she could react. His closed fist connected with the side of her head like a hammer blow, knocking her to the floor, where she lay stunned. Blearily, she saw the toes of her uncle's boots appear just beyond the tip of her nose.

Where is it? Where is the magic!

She felt herself being hauled to her feet by the back of her dress. Her uncle shook her hard, like a terrier shakes a rat.

"Stand up, damn you," he growled, holding Jelena under her armpits while she struggled to get her feet underneath her.

I need the magic! her mind screamed, but it refused to come.

"Veii leaves for home in three days' time. You'll be going with him. Now get out." Jelena stumbled as the duke gave her a shove toward the door. Dizzy and sick from the blow to her head, she barely made it out into the hallway before she doubled over and retched.

"Gods! Jelena, what happened?"

Jelena felt Magnes's arms loop around her waist to steady her. She turned and leaned into him, close to losing consciousness.

"Gods!" Magnes exclaimed again. "Who did this to you, Cousin? Who hit you?" He gently probed the blotch of rapidly purpling flesh on her face. She winced and tried to pull away, but he held her firmly.

"Come on. I'm taking you back to my chambers. You can tell me there," he said. Jelena felt too sick and disoriented to protest. Instead, she allowed Magnes to sweep her up and carry her back to his apartments, a suite of rooms that took up half of the keep's third floor.

Once there, he laid her down on a couch in the outer chamber. Jelena closed her eyes while he disappeared momentarily, opening them again when he returned with a damp cloth in his hand. He laid the wet, cool cloth on her injured face, and she sighed gratefully.

"Tell me what happened, Jelena. Who hurt you?" Magnes asked quietly. She studied his face for a moment before answering. Magnes, so much like his father physically, had nothing of Teodorus in his own personality. The two men were a study in contrasts.

"Magnes, remember up on the wall, you told me Duke Sebastianus was looking for a wife?" she whispered. Magnes nodded. "Well, he didn't come to Amsara to get one."

Magnes looked puzzled. "What do you mean?"

Hot tears welled up and spilled down Jelena's cheeks. Magnes gasped in dismay and gathered Jelena close against him, cradling her head on his shoulder.

"Your father has sold me to the Duke of Veii. I am to be the duke's concubine, Magnes...his slave," she sobbed into the soft leather of his jerkin. "I told Uncle that I refused, and that's when he hit me."

Jelena felt the curve of her cousin's shoulder tense in outrage. "He can't do this to you," Magnes whispered. "I won't let him."

"But he can, Magnes. He has every right to do with me whatever he wills." Jelena pushed away from Magnes and wiped her eyes. Her head ached abominably, but her mind had focused more clearly now. "I can still refuse to allow this to happen to me. No matter what, I am not going back to Veii as Duke Sebastianus's concubine."

"What are you going to do, then?" Magnes asked.

"I'm going to go search for my father," Jelena replied.

"You what?" Magnes exclaimed. He took Jelena's hands into his own. "Cousin, you can't. It's too dangerous. You don't know anything about your father's people. They might just kill you outright as soon as they discover you trespassing in their territory. You may not look wholly human, but you look human enough."

"I'm willing to take that chance," Jelena said quietly.

Magnes shook his head. "How do you even know where to look for him? You don't know anything about him, except that he's an elf. Let's suppose you do find him, and he rejects you, what then? Jelena, this is crazy!"

"So what would you have me do, Magnes?" Jelena asked. "Go with Duke Sebastianus? My only other alternative is a dive from the battlements."

Magnes buried his face in his hands. "Gods," he sighed. "Of course you can't go with Veii." He stood and went over to a sideboard where an earthenware jar and two mugs waited. He poured cider into the mugs and brought them over to the couch where he handed one to Jelena.

"The last of last season's batch," he said. "One of our best." He took a long pull and wiped his mouth with the back of his sleeve. Jelena chose to sip hers slowly. "Have you put any thought at all into this plan of yours?" he asked, sitting back down beside Jelena.

"No, but then I just found out a little while ago that your father has sold me." She made no effort to hide her bitterness. "I only have three days."

Magnes rubbed his chin the way he always did when thinking about important things. "We'll need some supplies and weapons. I can get most of that for us. The toughest thing will be a horse for you. We might have to go on foot."

"What do you mean *we*, Magnes?" Jelena set her mug down on

the sanded plank floor and looked her cousin in the eyes.

"I'm going with you, of course. You didn't think I'd let you go alone, did you?" he answered.

Jelena shook her head vigorously. "No, you can't. I won't let you pay the price for helping me," she stated firmly.

Magnes laughed mirthlessly. "You met the odious creature who is to be my wife at the feast last night. Charming, isn't she? That is what I have to look forward to, if I stay—marriage to that shallow, stupid girl. It makes me sick just thinking about it. I could have killed her where she sat, for her cruelty to you."

Jelena sighed. "Magnes, you've been my protector since we were children. If it hadn't been for you, I never would have learned to read and write, or handle a sword, or shoot a bow. You and Claudia have made my life bearable. I love you, and I'll be forever grateful. I can't ask you to make this kind of sacrifice for me. You'd be giving up everything."

"You're not asking. I'm volunteering."

"I can't talk you out of this?"

"No." The stubborn set of her cousin's mouth convinced Jelena that further argument was pointless, but she had to ask one more question.

"Magnes, what about Livie? Are you willing to leave her like this?" Magnes leapt to his feet and began to pace around the room. Jelena could sense the great tension within him as he appeared to struggle with some unresolved problem, a dilemma that weighed heavily on his mind. Finally, he turned to face Jelena, and she could see in his eyes that he had come to a painful decision.

"I've loved Livie for as long as I can remember, Jelena. Truth is, though, the only way we could be together would be terribly unfair to her. She deserves a husband and family, a life that I can't give to her now. If I leave, then she'll be free to find a good man who can give her those things."

Magnes's words tore at Jelena's heart. Why did the world have to be so full of cruelty to those who least deserved it? Jelena rose and embraced her cousin. They stood with their arms around each other for a long while, drawing comfort from the bond and closeness they shared. They had always been allies and would continue to be, well into an uncertain future.

"There's something else I need to tell you about," Jelena said when they at last broke their embrace.

"By the look on your face, I can see that, whatever it is, it's big, and it's got you worried," Magnes responded. He sank back down onto the couch, pulling Jelena with him. "Tell me," he prompted gently.

Jelena paused to gather her thoughts. How could she explain what she herself did not understand? For an instant, she was filled with uncertainty. What if her cousin reacted to her words with horror and rejected her? She didn't think that she could survive that. Then, she looked into his eyes, so like the color of the rich Amsaran soil that he loved, and saw there only love for her. Her fear evaporated. Magnes would never judge her, no matter what.

Magnes remained silent, regarding her expectantly. If he had caught any hint of her momentary confusion, he gave no sign.

"Something very strange happened yesterday," Jelena began. As Magnes listened, Jelena related the incident with Ruby and the mysterious blue fire.

"Gods!" Magnes croaked. He sat as if stunned, staring over the top of her head.

Jelena held her breath.

"Jelena, you've…you've got *magic!*" he whispered, his voice infused with wonder.

Jelena exhaled.

"I'm very confused by it," she said. "I have no idea how I called it up against Ruby and it hasn't surfaced since. I thought for sure it would come when your father attacked me, but it didn't."

Magnes's brow furrowed with the intensity of his thoughts. "Of course you'd have magical abilities. It's in your elven blood." He paused, then abruptly seized her hands, face clouded with worry. "This could mean very big trouble, Jelena. You know what will happen if it's discovered that you have magic, even if you don't know how to use it."

Jelena nodded. Neither one of them needed to say the words. They had both been raised with the Soldaran state religion.

"Do you think Ruby understood what happened?" Magnes asked.

Jelena shook her head. "Ruby is a stupid cow. Besides, if she did have any idea, I'd already be locked up in the castle jail by now."

"Hmm. I think you're right, but I'd still better have a word with Ruby, just to make sure," Magnes said.

"No, Magnes, don't do that!" Jelena pleaded. "If you start questioning Ruby, she might remember that she saw something odd. Best to let her be."

Magnes looked unconvinced, but he finally nodded in agreement. "All right. I won't question Ruby." He paused. "Of course, it's even more urgent that we leave Amsara as soon as possible. Since you have no idea when this ability of yours will choose to manifest again, we can't take any chances that it will flare up in front of witnesses."

"How am I going to tell Claudia?" Jelena murmured sadly. "How can I tell her that I have to leave her?"

"Just tell her the truth, Jelena," Magnes responded. He reached out to tenderly stroke her hair. "She'll be terribly sad, but she'll understand."

"I know, but it's still so hard. I don't know if I have the strength."

"You are the strongest person I know, Jelena Preseren," Magnes said. He leaned in and lightly brushed her forehead with his lips. "You'll get through this, and I'll be with you every step of the way."

"I know you will," Jelena said. *You always are.*

CHAPTER 6

A STORY, A GIFT, AND A CLUE

Jelena did not feel steady enough to return to the kitchen until well past mid-day. Unable to conceal the ugly bruise that discolored the left side of her face, she endured the stares and whispers of the other drudges in cold silence. Her thoughts were consumed with escape—she would need to plan carefully if she were to succeed—and how best to break the news to Claudia.

Ruby steered clear of her most of the time, and when she did have to pass near, she pointedly refused to even so much as glance at Jelena. Jelena couldn't tell if the other woman felt motivated by a newfound respect for her former victim or by fear of Jelena's newly revealed abilities. If Ruby was aware of Jelena's magic, she gave no direct sign.

The mellow gold light of late afternoon had faded to the purple shadows of evening by the time Claudia came to the kitchen in search of her foster daughter. "Gods preserve us!" she exclaimed in dismay upon seeing the bruise staining Jelena's face. "What happened, child?"

"Nothing, Heartmother. I fell, that's all," Jelena lied, unable to meet Claudia's discerning stare.

"Don't lie t'me, child. Tell me what truly happened," Claudia demanded, taking Jelena's chin in her hand and turning her face first one way and then the other, as if hunting for clues.

"Please, Heartmother, not here," Jelena whispered imploringly. "After the evening meal…I've something very important to tell you." Claudia frowned, clearly upset, but she did not press. Jelena gave her a quick hug and hurried off to fetch plates and cups for their supper.

When the last dish had been put away and the kitchen fires were banked for the night, only then could Jelena return to the small room she shared with Claudia. Her foster mother waited for her, nervous anticipation evident in the way she held her large body, much like a she-bear poised to leap against any danger that might threaten her cub.

Jelena sat down beside Claudia on the edge of her bed and in a soft voice told her all that had happened in the duke's study that morning. "I can live as a kitchen drudge or a maid… even a stablehand if need be, but I'll not live as any man's slave, Heartmother."

"You'd have a far better life bein' the concubine of a duke, child, than you'd ever have otherwise," Claudia responded gently.

"I'd still be a slave!" Jelena cried. "Duke Sebastianus would own me like he owns his horses or his cattle, and he would be free to use or abuse me however he wishes. No. I won't let my uncle dispose of me like a spare piece of livestock!" Jelena paused, took a deep breath, and forged ahead. "I've decided to leave Amsara Castle."

Claudia's lower lip began to tremble. The fire hissed and crackled in the grate. The room suddenly felt overheated and stuffy. Jelena edged closer to her foster mother, and waited for the storm to break.

Claudia let out a wail and began to bawl uncontrollably.

"Please, Heartmother, don't cry!" Jelena begged as she fell into her foster mother's arms. She tried to hold back her own tears, but she couldn't—the pain of the moment overwhelmed her. She laid her head on the soft mound of Claudia's bosom and allowed her foster mother's grief to wash over her like a rain-swollen river, turbulent and strong at first, but gradually subsiding to a gentle flow, then to stillness.

Only when the storm had passed and Claudia calmed down enough to listen did Jelena tell her of what had happened during her run-in with Ruby.

Claudia seemed unsurprised at Jelena's revelation. "If Ruby dares t' try an' denounce you, I'll strangle 'er with me bare hands," she said. She sniffled and wiped her eyes on her apron.

"Now do you see why I've got to leave here and go north, into the country of the elves?" Jelena brushed a strand of Claudia's gray hair away from her watering eyes. "I won't be going alone, though. Magnes has offered to come with me. He's promised to help me find my father."

Claudia nodded, as if coming to a decision. Her expression settled into one of quiet resignation as she rose and went to her chest. Lifting the lid, she shoved aside its contents and reached deep within, drawing forth a leather pouch. Wordlessly, she dropped the pouch into Jelena's cupped hands.

"What is this, Heartmother?" Jelena asked.

"Open it, child. There be somethin' inside that belongs to you, somethin' you'll need on yer search." Jelena loosened the thongs holding the pouch shut and upended it onto her palm. A small metal object fell out.

It was a man's signet ring, crafted of heavy white gold with an inlay of black stone. The figure of a griffin, also wrought in white gold, had been intricately worked into the center of the stone. Jelena held the ring up so that it could catch the light from the lamps. The craftsmanship of the ring was exquisite, and she knew that it could have only graced the hand of a nobleman.

Jelena looked into Claudia's eyes and saw the truth. "This ring belonged to my father," she whispered.

"Aye, that it did, my lamb. Yer mother gave it into my keeping on the day you were born. Told me I wasn't to give it t'you 'til you were ready. Ay, gods, I knew this day would come!" Claudia lowered her bulk onto a sturdy wooden stool, clutching at her lower back and wincing in pain.

"I've a story t'tell ye, child. Yer mother told it t'me whilst I cared for her durin' her confinement. It seems that, one day yer mother was out walkin' in th' woods when she came upon a young man who needed her help."

As Claudia spoke, Jelena rolled the ring between her fingers, feeling its weight, trying to imagine the man who had worn it. Claudia told the story of how Drucilla, Jelena's mother, had found a man half out of his mind from pain and thirst, lying at the bottom of a ravine. When she drew closer and saw what he was, she almost fled. All of the stories she had been told, every supposed truth the priests preached about elvenkind warred in her brain with her instinct to aid a fellow living being in dire need.

In the end, she did not flee. She brought the man water instead, holding his head steady so he could drink. It calmed him and brought him back to his senses.

"Yer mam could hardly believe her ears when th'elf spoke to her in Soldaran! He told her that his leg was broke, an' that he needed her help. Seems he'd been tryin' t' get away from a patrol when his horse spooked and throwed him into the dry stream. He'd banged his head on a rock and knocked hisself senseless. Been there for days, in the summer heat, with no water and a busted leg."

Drucilla knew of a small hut in the woods close by, occasionally used by the gamekeepers when they needed to stay out overnight. She would take the man there—if she could get him to his feet and moving—but in order to do that, his leg would need a splint.

"She had no way at hand t' make such a thing, but she knew she could get some boards an' cloth back at th' castle, so she left him with her waterskin an' a promise t' return." Here, Claudia paused in her narrative.

"Go on, Heartmother," Jelena urged.

"Patience, my girl. I'm an old woman, an' all this happened a long time ago. I want t' get it all straight in the tellin'" Claudia replied. "Now, where was I?"

It took some doing, but Drucilla managed to gather up the things she needed for the splint, as well as some food. She was, after all, the duke's sister, and no one would dare to question her. Afternoon had turned to dusk by the time she returned, and the man seemed to be either asleep or unconscious.

"Yer mam said she just sat for a bit, starin' at him. She'd never seen a man so fair… As beautiful as the gods must be. After a while, he woke up and caught her lookin' at him. He said not a word, just smiled, and my Dru fell in love."

"Did my mother describe him to you? Did she tell you exactly what he looked like?" Jelena eagerly asked.

"She said he had eyes the color of the sky in winter… her exact words!" Claudia chuckled. "And dark hair shot through with silver, like an aging man's, 'cept that his face was that of a young man.

That's all she could say of his looks, other than he was beautiful in a way no human man could be."

Claudia continued her narrative.

"Well, Drucilla told me she was able t'make a splint from the things she'd taken from the castle." She found a fallen branch for him to lean on, and with that, and her help, the man could stand, then walk. Many times during the long, slow, journey to the gamekeeper's hut, the man had to stop and rest. Pain, hunger, and thirst had sapped his strength.

" By th' time they reached the hut, the poor man was just about done in, and yer mother could barely hold him up." Claudia raised her hand to her mouth and coughed. Grimacing, she waved towards a little shelf upon which sat a plain, ceramic jar and two cups. "Bring me some o' that water, child. My throat is parched of a sudden." Jelena quickly complied, and after Claudia had taken a drink, she continued her story.

"Well, she got him settled and took a closer look at his leg. There weren't no bones sticking out through the skin, lucky for him, tho' it were a bad break just the same."

The man had fallen unconscious, and Drucilla took the chance to re-do the splint, cutting his boot off with his own knife beforehand.

"The hut was bare, not much but a cot, a table, and a stool. No fuel for a fire, no blankets, no food. She'd have to bring everything the man would need from the castle without anyone, 'specially her brother, findin' out. And, she'd have to pray that none of the gamekeepers came along and discovered her elf."

"Yer mam was very clever and careful," Claudia continued. "It took her several trips, but she managed to bring everything she'd need to care for the man proper like. He was helpless as a little babe, an' he didn't say much those first few days, mainly please and thank you, but as time passed and he grew stronger, she got him to talk to her."

"He said he was a traveler, out t' see the world before he had to take up his official duties. What those duties were, he never told. He'd wandered by mistake into our country. As soon as he got his strength back, he said, he would have to leave and get back 'cross the border into his own land. He seemed very worried 'bout what might happen to them both should he be found. Dru told him not to fret, that she'd take care of him."

"Did my mother tell you his name?" Jelena asked.

"She said his name was Zin," Claudia answered. "Not much to it, but that's what he told her. Anyways, th' two of them had a lot of time to talk together. He spoke very good Soldaran, and told Dru many, many interestin' things about his homeland. There's just somethin' about bein' that close to another person, taking care of 'em and all. It brings up things... feelings that might not otherwise be brought up, if you catch my meaning."

Jelena tried to imagine her mother's thoughts and feelings. The danger and excitement of knowingly breaking one of society's most important taboos, combined with the powerful physical urges of young womanhood—such a heady potion had obviously proved impossible to resist.

"She must have confessed her feelings to him at some point, otherwise..." Jelena began, barely able to keep her own excitement in check. For the first time in her life, she felt a genuine connection to both of the people who had come together to create her.

"Aye, she did. How could she not? She was so young and trusting. She believed him when he said he loved her, too."

"Are you saying that you think Zin lied to my mother just to have her?" Jelena asked, a little miffed that Claudia might make such a suggestion. "Why would he do such a thing after all she'd done for him?"

"No, no, child! I'm not sayin' that at all. We can never know what was in Zin's heart, not truly. He had a beautiful young girl in love with him. He was a man, after all, even tho' he weren't human. I hope he meant what he said. Anyway, the two of them just did what came natural 'tween a man an' woman."

"Not according to the priests and just about everybody else! Haven't you heard? Elves are supposed to be soulless and unclean," Jelena retorted sarcastically. "My mother committed an act of abomination when she lay with my father!" Her anger tasted of bitter gall on her tongue.

"I never believed that nonsense, child, an' the gods know I tried to raise you to not believe it. Yer cousin Magnes, good man that he is, doesn't believe it, either." Claudia took another drink from her cup and wiped her mouth on the back of her hand.

"So, what finally became of Zin?" Jelena asked.

"He left, like he said he would. Yer mother knew he couldn't stay, nor could she go with him, no matter how strong their feelings for one another. He gave her the ring as a keepsake. What he couldn't know is that he also left her with a child… You."

Claudia fell silent, lost in the country of remembrance where a young girl she had once loved still lived, laughing and happy. Jelena felt so tightly wound up that she could barely breathe. She knew so much more now than she did this morning. The mere possession of her father's name, and an object that belonged to him, gave her hope that finding him would not be such an impossible task after all.

"Mother, why didn't you tell me any of this before now?" Jelena asked. She continued to play with the ring, slipping it on and off her thumb.

"I could tell ye that it was because yer mother didn't want you to know until you were ready, but that would be a lie. The truth is, I was afraid that if I told you, you'd want to go off and try t' find him…yer dad, I mean." Claudia shook her head sadly. A single tear leaked from the corner of her eye and trickled down her lined cheek. "I am a selfish old woman. I didn't want to lose my baby."

"You'll never lose me, Heartmother, not really," Jelena said. She reached out and placed her hand over Claudia's. Conflicting emotions stirred her soul. She felt a little angry that Claudia had not told her about her mother and father, but at the same time, she ached for the loss that Claudia would suffer when she left.

"I have to find Zin, Mother. He's the only one who can tell me what the blue fire means."

"Ay, gods…I know you do," Claudia murmured sadly.

Jelena raised the ring up to eye level and stared intently at the white griffin inlaid into its surface.

I will find you, Father… Or I'll die trying.

CHAPTER 7

REGRETS, RISKS, AND RESOLUTIONS

Zin has to be a son of a noble house. He wouldn't wear a ring like this otherwise," Magnes commented as he inspected the heavy white gold signet. "It should make him, or at least his kin, much easier to find. I'll get you a chain so you can hang it around your neck." He dropped the ring onto Jelena's palm.

The late afternoon sun hung low in the sky, and atop the battlements the wind was picking up. The official banner of Amsara—three black lions *rampant* on an azure field—snapped crisply overhead. After recounting the story of her parents to Magnes, Jelena now listened as her cousin outlined his plan for their escape.

"I've got us some packs, a couple of old blankets, a knife, bow and arrows for you. It's all safely hidden in my rooms. You'll have to see about getting us some food. You'll arouse far less suspicion if you're seen in the kitchen than I would. I don't see how we'll get away with taking horses, though. We'll just have to walk very fast." Magnes grinned ruefully. "I'm really going to hate leaving Storm. He's the best horse I've ever had."

"I won't be able to take too much food," Jelena sighed. "Cook always seems to know exactly how much of everything she has, and if too much goes missing, she'll not rest 'til she finds out why."

"We'll have to forage, then. Shouldn't be too hard at this time of year."

"With your knowledge of herbs and your trapping skills, at least we won't starve." Jelena was far more concerned with pursuit and capture once her uncle discovered that she had run away. Without horses, it would be nearly impossible to outrun a mounted posse.

"We're running out of time. Duke Sebastianus leaves for Veii in two days. I think we should get out of here tonight," Jelena said.

"I agree," Magnes replied. "My father intends to officially announce my betrothal to the fair Lowena tonight at a small supper gathering. Of course, I'm supposed to behave in a manner befitting the Heir of Amsara. I just hope I can get through the meal without puking." He raked his hands through his thick dark curls, a familiar gesture. His distress was palpable.

"You're thinking of Livie, aren't you?" Jelena asked softly. She always seemed able to guess his mood.

Magnes laughed, but there was no humor in it, only sadness. "You know me so well, cousin. I wanted to tell her about all of this myself. Now, she'll hear of it secondhand, and the pain will be that much worse for her. She will think that I didn't love her enough to tell her about my leaving."

"Why can't you go and see her now?"

"She's off visiting her married sister in Greenwood Town. That's a full day's ride from Amsara. I'd never get there and back in time." He stared out into the distance, his eyes clouded with bitterness. Far below, cowbells clanged softly, providing a mellow counterpoint to the rhythmic cooing of the doves settling in for the night beneath the eaves of the great hall. Soon, the village girls would come to drive the cattle in for the evening milking. How peaceful the land looked, Jelena thought, then she suddenly realized that she stood on the edge of a deep, black chasm into which she was about to jump, with no clue about what lay at the bottom; yet, she felt no fear, only elation. She was finally taking charge of her own destiny, and there could be no turning back.

"I'm sorry Magnes," she said, laying her hand on his forearm. "I know how much you are giving up to help me. Someday, I hope I can repay you."

"Nonsense." He looked at her and smiled. "You don't owe me any repayment. Don't you know I've always wanted to go off on a big adventure, especially if it involved keeping my annoying little cousin out of trouble? " Jelena punched him playfully in the shoulder, and Magnes let out a mock cry of pain. His naturally cheerful temperament never let him stay depressed or angry for long.

"There's no moon tonight, but we'll still have to be very careful," Magnes continued. "The best time to leave will be during the changing of the watch at midnight. The guards won't be paying as much attention then. Meet me in the kitchen garden. Remember that old gate we found in the wall when we were kids?"

Jelena nodded excitedly. "The one covered over with the wild grapevines. I remember we used to pretend it was a doorway that opened up into a faraway land full of strange creatures and fierce savages."

"Well, I just happen to have the key. After old Jano died, just before Brennes took over, my father gave me the master key ring to keep until he could find a new steward. Well, you know me, ever the curious one. I had to see if any of the keys would open that lock, and sure enough, one did, though it wasn't marked. I don't believe Jano knew about the gate, or he would have marked the key. When I turned the rest of the keys over to Brennes, I kept that one. I didn't really have a specific reason at the time...just a feeling that, someday, I might have a need for it. I guess that day is here."

"Lucky for us," Jelena said. "After the evening meal is done, I'm supposed to put away all of the staff crockery. I'll just move very slowly tonight. I should be able to draw it out long enough to be the last one to leave. The kitchen boys may present a problem, though. They sleep by the main fireplace. I'll have to hide in the pantry until they're asleep. It shouldn't be too difficult to sneak past them then."

"How did Claudia take the news of your leaving?" Magnes asked.

Jelena winced at the memory of her foster mother's tears. "She's heartbroken. To her, I'm just as much her daughter as I would have been had she borne me herself. She is the only mother I will ever know. It tears me up inside knowing the pain I'm causing her, but she understands why I have to go. If she didn't, she never would have given me my father's ring or told me my parents' story."

"You did tell her about the blue fire?" Magnes asked carefully.

"Yes, and she seemed totally unsurprised, as if she knew about it all along...I wonder," Jelena mused, tugging at a stray coil of hair that had escaped an ivory comb.

"Perhaps she did...Or at least suspected," Magnes replied. "Anyway, you're lucky to have had her to raise you. I just wish I could remember my mother a little more clearly. I have so few real memories of her. They are more like barely recalled dreams."

Jelena had no memory at all of Magnes's dead mother. All she knew of Duchess Julia was what she had been told by Claudia. According to Claudia, the duchess had been everything the duke was not, and her death had been an occasion of great sorrow for the staff. All of the castle's residents were in agreement that Magnes had inherited his looks from his father, but insofar as his soul was concerned, he was definitely his mother's son.

"All the staff loved your mother, Magnes, just as they love you. You will be sorely missed." Jelena paused. "Are you absolutely sure..."

"Yes!" Magnes cried, throwing his hands up in the air in mock exasperation. "I'm beginning to think you don't want me along, and I have to say that my feelings are hurt." He clutched at his heart dramatically and made a tragicomic face. Jelena laughed loudly, but she recognized Magnes's intent. By deflecting her concerns with humor, he hoped to hide from her just how difficult the decision to leave Amsara was for him.

"I'd better get going, then. Cook'll be wanting to start the evening meal soon, and I really don't feel like getting yelled at for being late," Jelena said, a rueful smile playing about her lips.

"Rejoice, Cousin. Your days of servitude are coming to an end," Magnes replied, slipping his arm around Jelena's shoulder as they headed along the wall walk towards the stairwell.

Perhaps so, Jelena thought, *but am I trading an unhappy situation for something better, or worse?*

~~~

This is the last time I'll ever work as a drudge in some lord's kitchen, thought Jelena as she wiped up the last of the staff crockery. No matter what challenges she would face in the coming days, she felt sure of one thing. From now on, she would choose her own path.

The kitchen was quiet now. The rest of the staff had departed, their work finished. Only the kitchen boys remained. There were three of them, orphans all, and they earned their keep by turning the spits, tending the fires, and running errands. They made their beds by the main hearth, huddling together like puppies in winter, sprawling out on the stones in the loose-limbed way of young boys during the hot summer nights.

At present, they were hunkered down beneath the big chopping block in the center of the room, whispering and giggling. They ignored Jelena completely, as they usually did, unless she had a reason to speak to them, which was seldom. Their total absorption with each other would allow Jelena to pilfer the needed supplies much more easily.

She put the last bowl in its place and wiped her hands on her apron. She then made a show of going around and extinguishing the few remaining lamps, leaving the kitchen shrouded in gloom, only the red glow from the banked fire in the great hearth providing any illumination. Keeping a watchful eye on the chopping block, she went over to the door leading out into the yard. With a quick glance over her shoulder, she pushed the door open then shut it, dropping immediately into a squatting position close to the floor.

She held her breath and listened.

The giggling and whispering went on, uninterrupted. Cautiously, Jelena crept toward the pantry, keeping low and holding her skirts up to minimize the risk that she might trip and alert the boys that she remained in the kitchen. She made it to the pantry without being discovered and immediately set about the task at hand. Her apron would serve as a handy carry-bag. She removed it and spread it out on the floor, then proceeded to gather together a supply of small, easily carried food items—cheese, bread, apples, sausages, several slabs of salted and dried fish, a little bag of shelled hazelnuts. Her hand hovered over a pot of preserved sweet cherries—a treat she dearly loved—but she thought better of it and left it on the shelf. *Too big to carry, anyway*, she thought.

Piling the loot into the center of the apron, Jelena folded up the corners and tied them securely in a knot. She then crept to the pantry door to listen. The main room had fallen silent. She could just make out three shadowy mounds by the hearth: the boys, bedded down for the night. Just as she pushed at the door, one of them whimpered and sat up. Jelena froze, then waited anxiously until the boy lay down and flopped onto his stomach. After what seemed like hours to her fretting mind, the sound of snoring signaled that she could now escape.

Moving as quickly and quietly as she could, Jelena made her way to the outer door. Slowly, she pushed it open, wincing at the soft squeal of old hinges, and slipped out into the cool of the night. An owl hooted directly overhead, momentarily startling her and further fraying her already shredded nerves. She lingered a moment more, ears straining to pick up any sounds from within, but the three boys slept on, oblivious.

Clutching the bundled apron to her chest, Jelena hurried off toward the servants' quarters, hugging the shadows cast by walls and buildings. The sounds of late evening drifted on the air—the laughter of off-duty guards playing at dice, the sweet notes of a lute floating from the half-open door of the great hall, the far-off squall of a fussy baby. Her nose caught the scent of night-blooming jasmine mingled with the odor of the stables. Of their own will, her feet slowed their nervous rush to a walk, then rooted themselves to the earth beside the closed keep door. Abruptly, a stark realization struck her like a hard slap across the face.

I'm really leaving.

These were the sights, the sounds, the smells of home. A home in which she was an outcast—despised by many, barely acknowledged by any of her kin, save one—but a home nonetheless. At Amsara, at least she knew where she stood, how she fit in to things. She had learned over the years how to cope with her lowly status, and had made, if not a good life, at least a tolerable one for herself. Now, she stood poised at the edge of abandonment of everything she knew for an uncertain future.

Jelena felt herself wavering and was shocked at the unexpected feelings of loss she had begun to experience. *Why am I feeling this way,* she thought. *Why do I suddenly not want to leave?*

She dashed tears from her eyes in irritation. She didn't want to leave Claudia…that was the problem. She couldn't possibly have any regrets about putting Amsara far behind her. Besides, if she didn't run, in two days time, her freedom would be taken from her, and she would lose the chance to determine her own destiny forever.

There's the magic as well. Don't forget that! She drew in a deep breath to steady herself, gripped the bundle of supplies more securely, and rounded the corner of the keep…

…to collide headlong with a very hard shadow.

"Gods! What the…Who is that! Speak up, right now!"

A wave of dismay, followed closely by fear, hit Jelena at the sound of Thessalina's imperious command. The collision had knocked Jelena back several steps, and the bundled apron now lay in the dirt at her feet. She had to think fast. "It's me, Cousin! Jelena. I…"

Thessalina cut her off before she could speak any further. "What the hell are you doing sneaking around at this hour, girl, and what's that you're carrying?" Thessalina stepped forward menacingly. She stood at least two inches taller than Jelena and possessed a warrior's physique.

Jelena had good reason to fear her cousin. She bent down quickly and scooped the bundle back up into her arms. "It's just dirty laundry. I'm planning to wash it myself tomorrow."

"You're lying, girl. Give me that!"

Before Jelena could react, Thessalina had seized the bundle and pulled it from her arms. She dropped it to the ground, then bent down and with a few jerks, untied the knot to expose the pilfered food. "What are you doing with this stuff? You stole this food, didn't you? Answer me!" Like a lioness stalking its prey, Thessalina unfolded her long limbs into an attack stance, poised to pounce.

The air was heavy with danger, and Jelena knew that she would need to think very fast in order to avoid catastrophe. "I didn't steal anything," she said, sidling slowly backwards. "I'm just taking some provisions for my journey to Veii. I…I was told that it might be a good idea to have some of my own food, that's all. Veii is a long way from Amsara."

"Huh! It's not that far. D'you really think that Duke Sebastianus isn't going to feed you? He paid good money for you, didn't he? Though the gods only know why he'd want a tink like you." Jelena could feel her cheeks burning with anger and humiliation. She was thankful for the cover of darkness, for it hid her eyes from her cousin. If Thessalina could have seen the hate that smoldered there, she would have beaten Jelena for sure. She clenched her hands into fists and prayed that the blue fire would continue to remain dormant. If Thessalina were to discover that she possessed magical abilities...

Thessalina prodded the half-opened bundle with one boot tip. Even in the dim starlight, Jelena could see the ugly expression of contempt twisting the other woman's face. "I still don't believe you, but I'm too tired to deal with it right now," she said. "You'd better get to your room, and stay there until morning. If I catch you sneaking around here again tonight, I'll beat you senseless, and I promise you won't have my silly brother to come to your rescue."

Jelena's body shook with helpless anger as she bent down to gather up the food and re-tie the apron corners securely. Thessalina turned and pushed open the heavy keep door. The flickering firelight from the hearth within briefly limned Thessalina's form with a red glow, turning her shape into something demonic. As the door swung shut on her cousin, Jelena lifted her finger in an obscene gesture, knowing that she crouched just out of range of the slice of light spilling from the doorway, and thus was shielded from any consequences of her small act of defiance.

For as long as Jelena could remember, Thessalina's animosity towards her had been consistent and unrelenting, and because of her lowly status, there had been little she could do to deflect it or protect herself from it. As she started off again towards the servants' quarters, the food bundle hugged tight against her breasts, she swore that tonight would be the last time she would stand and take any kind of abuse from anyone.

If I can't find my father, or if I do and he doesn't want me, I'll go off and find a cave somewhere and live alone. I don't care, just as long as I can choose how to run my own life.

I'm done being a slave!

CHAPTER 8

ESCAPE AND AWAKENING

There was not much to pack. She had very few possessions—the ivory combs that had been her mother's, her father's ring, a small bone-handled knife, a finely made leather pouch that had been a gift from Magnes. Almost all of her meager wardrobe would be left behind, for Jelena fled Amsara this night disguised as a boy. Magnes had provided the tunic, jerkin, leggings, and boots. He'd also found her an old leather cap that she could wear, but only if she sheared off much of her mane beforehand.

Claudia sat on the edge of her bed, watching Jelena and weeping silently as the *snick snick* of the shears filled the little room with the sound of finality, of the inevitability of separation and loss.

Jelena clipped one last lock, then laid aside the shears and brushed the loose hair from her head. Critically, she examined her raggedly cropped coils in the tiny piece of mirror. She swallowed hard as the reflection of a stranger stared back at her, a young woman with almond-shaped eyes, high cheekbones, and bluntly pointed ears. She felt like she was seeing herself—not looking at, but truly *seeing*—for the first time.

Will I look like an elf to my father's people, or a human, she wondered, or will they look at me like almost everyone at Amsara does, with contempt because I am neither?

"All o' yer beautiful hair, all over the floor!" Claudia sobbed, wringing her hands in grief.

Jelena smiled gently. "You have complained my whole life about how difficult my hair is to deal with. Well, now it'll be much easier.

See?" She pulled the cap over her head with a small flourish. "How do I look?"

"Like my baby who's about to leave me forever," Claudia replied tearfully. Jelena sat beside her foster mother and allowed Claudia to enfold her against the ample cushion of her bosom. Neither of them spoke for many moments. There was just too much to say, and yet nothing to be said. Both of them knew that this was the way things had to be.

Finally, Claudia pushed Jelena away and dried her eyes on the sleeve of her chemise. "You'd better get goin'. Yer cousin's waitin' on ye."

Jelena nodded silently, and rose to gather up her things.

"Oh! I'd plumb fergot!" Claudia exclaimed. She reached into a fold of her apron and drew out the strand of blue Kara glass beads that Jelena had worn to the ill-fated Sansa feast. She pressed the necklace into Jelena's hands.

"Heartmother, I couldn't possibly…These were a gift to you from the duchess!" Jelena protested.

She tried to return the necklace, but Claudia's hands fluttered away like fat, featherless birds. "No, no, child. I want you t' have 'em. Besides, what's an old woman like me goin' t'do with such things, eh?"

"I'll treasure them, always," Jelena whispered, her voice hoarse with tears. She tucked the necklace into her bag where it settled down amongst the few other small things that she could call her own.

Claudia went to the door and held it open.

"I love you," Jelena said.

"I love you, too, child. Be happy."

Jelena exited swiftly, not daring to look back, afraid that if she did, she would be unable to leave. The sound of the door shutting behind her seemed to boom and echo within the narrow confines of the stairwell, more like a great stone crashing into place, instead of a humble wood door closing on a small room in which an old woman sat alone, crying for her lost child.

Jelena's heart was breaking as she made for the kitchen garden, half blinded by her own tears. When she reached its fragrant confines, redolent of rosemary, thyme, and jasmine, she dropped the bundled apron and leaned, weak-kneed, against the outer kitchen wall and gave free rein to her grief.

Magnes found her there, sobbing inconsolably beneath the stars that glittered like cold ice embedded in darkest velvet. "I don't know why I feel so…so horrible!" she cried. "I should be delirious with happiness because I'm finally getting out of this awful place, but I'm not!" She buried her face in her cousin's shoulder.

"You have ample reason to grieve, Jelena. You are leaving behind the woman who raised you, who loved you and called you 'daughter,' and you may never lay eyes upon her again. Of course you should be sad. We are about to walk a road that is completely unknown to us, but whatever lies ahead, whether it be good or ill, we'll face it together." Magnes slipped his hand under Jelena's chin and tilted her face upwards. "Courage, Cousin. We'd better get going. The night's a'wasting, and we need to be well away before sun up."

Jelena glanced up at the sky. "There's someone else I need to say goodbye to before I leave, Cousin," she murmured. She turned away from the garden and set out back across the castle grounds toward the keep. Wordlessly, Magnes followed, a comforting presence at her back. She knew that he understood.

The Preseren family crypt—Jelena's destination—lay beneath the high altar of the castle chapel. The two cousins padded silently past the slumbering keep and entered the chapel through a side door set within its southern wall. Quickly, they slipped down the central aisle, past the large wooden altar carved with painted images of gods and saints, to the stairwell at the back that led down into the subterranean vaults. Magnes paused to grab a candle from the altar before leading the way into the crypt.

The air below ground was cool and still. The little flame from the candle cast a feeble glow, but Jelena would have known the way even in total darkness. She had been here often enough before. With unerring steps, she made her way to the very back of the crypt and paused before a plain stone sarcophagus. She knelt and laid her palms flat atop the chilly granite. "Mother," she whispered, "I've come to say goodbye."

Unlike the other caskets, which were fashioned of marble and crowned with detailed effigies of the occupant as he or she had appeared in life, this tomb was stark in its simplicity. No fine effigy adorned its top, only a plain stone lid that bore the inscription:

Here lies Drucilla, daughter of Teomartus and Lucinda of the House of Preseren.

"They put my mother at the very back, away from all of her kin. She was an outcast, even in death, all because she dared to love a man who wasn't human." Jelena began to weep. "Why are people so cruel, Magnes?"

Magnes knelt beside her and slipped his free arm around her shoulder. "Some people are cruel because they are weak and afraid, Cousin." He kissed her lightly on the forehead. "But not all people are cruel. Claudia and I both love you."

"Neither one of us had the chance to know our mothers, Magnes, but at least you have some memories of yours. I have nothing but stories and this cold box." Jelena paused to wipe her eyes, then bent over and pressed her lips to the stone. "I love you, Mother," she murmured. "Even though you're not here, I still feel your love for me. I'm going to find my father...I'm going to find your Zin, and when I do, I'll tell him just what you sacrificed in order to give me life." She looked up at Magnes, and even in the dim light of the single candle, she could see his eyes shining with tears.

"I know that running is my only choice, and I would have gone without you, but I'm very glad you're coming with me, Magnes. I know that sounds selfish, considering what you are giving up, but it's how I feel." She felt her melancholy begin to lift. Magnes's calm, steady strength would be a great comfort to her in the days to come, and for that alone, she was very grateful.

"We'd better go now, Jelena," Magnes urged softly. She nodded, and with a last kiss upon the casket lid, she rose and followed her cousin up and out of the crypt, leaving her mother and all her ancestors behind to sleep the cold slumber of the dead.

~~~

As promised, Magnes had brought the packs and equipment they needed. They took a few moments to divide the food Jelena had filched and to settle the packs and weapons on their bodies. With everything in place, Magnes led the way back to where the castle wall ran behind the kitchen garden. There, they paused to listen. The night hummed with the myriad little noises that fill a green, growing place in spring. Crickets chirped merrily in the trees, and mice rustled in the wild grapevines. High up in the branches of a fruitless plum tree, a nightingale warbled.

Magnes dug around in the pouch at his belt and drew forth a small object. It was too dark for Jelena to see what he now held in his hand, but she guessed it to be the key to the long-unused door. He stepped forward and pulled aside the thick covering of vines to reveal a small, iron-bound portal.

"I oiled the lock a few days ago," Magnes whispered. The key turned with a soft click, and Magnes gave the door a shove. It swung open with a metallic groan that sounded as loud as thunder.

"Damn it," Magnes muttered. "I forgot the hinges!"

They held their breaths and waited. After a few moments, when she heard no cry raised, Jelena dared to breathe again.

Magnes pulled her close and whispered in her ear. "There's a very steep, slippery drop down into a ravine just the other side of this door. Be careful, it's treacherous. I'll go first. Don't start down until I do. I've got to close the door behind us." He turned, ducked through the dark hole, and disappeared. Jelena took a deep breath and followed.

She found herself standing on a narrow ledge at the top of a slope that plunged near vertically into the darkness. She had always known about the natural defenses at the rear of Amsara Castle, but she had never dreamed that, one day, her path to freedom would lead down this perilous route.

Magnes pushed the heavy door shut and stowed the key away in his pouch. "There's no way to lock it behind us, it seems. Good thing Amsara can't be approached from this direction."

"Let's just hope no one comes along and finds the door from the inside," Jelena replied nervously.

"We'll be long gone by then. Ready?"

"As ready as I'll ever be." Jelena hitched her pack up a little higher on her shoulders and adjusted the long knife at her belt. The bow and arrows she had strapped on top of the pack, so they were not readily accessible, but then she planned to use them only for hunting.

They started picking their way carefully down the slope, Magnes in the lead. The surface consisted of a constantly shifting sea of loose soil and small, sharp rocks. Each step sent a new shower of debris rattling down the slope into the pitch black of the ravine. In a matter of moments, Jelena was sweating and breathing hard. It took tremendous effort to stay upright and to keep herself from sliding down to certain injury and the end to any hope of escape. Below, she could hear the sound of water trickling over stones.

After what seemed like hours, they finally reached the bottom of the ravine where they paused briefly to rest.

"Ugh!" Jelena exclaimed. "By the smell down here, I'm guessing this must be the drainage from the castle's sewers."

"All the more reason to get moving," Magnes replied. "C'mon."

They began walking.

Eventually, the ravine spread itself out into the surrounding landscape. Jelena could not tell how far they had come, or in which direction they were heading, but she trusted Magnes's navigational skills. He seemed to know exactly where to go. "Are we headed west, Magnes?" she asked, pushing herself a little to keep up with her cousin's longer, ground-eating stride.

"West and north. I reckon we'll be across the border in three days' time," he replied. He noticed Jelena's struggle to match his gait and slowed down to accommodate her. "We should reach the north-south road soon. I want to follow it until dawn and then look for a place to camp."

Jelena looked back over her shoulder but could see nothing in the darkness, which was just as well. Her life at Amsara Castle truly lay behind her now. She would look forward, only forward, to the new possibilities that awaited her. She would shed her old identity, like a snake sheds its skin, and become a new person. No longer would she be Jelena the bastard. She would be Jelena the free woman, free to make of her life what she willed.

~~~

Far to the north, in a land that for millennia had lain cloaked in perpetual winter, deep beneath a mountain on whose summit crouched the remains of a mighty fortress, some*thing* began to stir.

For over a thousand years, it had remained dormant, its energy dampened by powerful magical wards put in place at the time of its defeat and imprisonment. But time and neglect had steadily weakened the very structure of the arcane energy that had sustained the wards, allowing the thing slumbering in the freezing darkness to slowly awaken.

For a very, very long time, it simply *was*. No coherent thoughts disturbed the dark, still pool of its consciousness. It floated, disembodied, a being of pure energy, existing in a place where no light, no sound, no sensation could penetrate.

Then, with sudden, convulsive force, the very fabric of the universe ripped open, and something pushed through. The being that had been asleep for so long now roused, fully conscious, responding to the familiar energy signature of the magic it had itself created so long ago.

With full awareness came memory and rage, but the spirit was too weak yet to wrestle free of the magical chains that kept it bound in the cold and darkness. It struggled anyway, fueled by its towering fury, but soon gave up in defeat, accepting that, for now, it would remain a prisoner.

The struggle against its bonds had not been a complete failure, however. The spirit did discover the creeping weakness that slowly degraded the integrity of the magic; it was only a matter of time before the wards could be broken and it would be free. In the meantime, it would practice the art of patience, but that did not preclude making use of what tools it could.

Through experimentation, it found that it could extend its consciousness outward, beyond the tons of ice and rock that imprisoned what remained of its physical essence. Even in such an inhospitable wilderness as the high mountains, many creatures, both furred and feathered, managed to eke out a precarious existence. The spirit found the simple minds of these creatures easy to commandeer. They made useful tools, serving as living connections to the outside world. However, the force of its essence drained the creatures of their vital energy, killing them after a time. No matter. There were enough to meet its needs.

It began to search.

Across the frozen desolation of the high mountains and down into the vast forests that lay at their feet, it ranged, merging first with a swift-footed fox, then a snowshoe hare, a sleek black raven and a gray wolf, silent as the shadows. The ravens proved to be the most useful. Their keen eyes saw much; their powers of flight allowed the spirit-being to range over much greater distances—but they tended to die quickly. The wolves, eagles, and big cats lived longer, but they could not get as close to farmsteads and villages without attracting unwanted attention.

The energy signature that the spirit-being searched for was, at first, weak and unfocused, but as time passed, it grew stronger. The spirit now knew that it must concentrate its search in the lands far to the south of its mountain prison, beyond the territory it had once ruled over as a mortal man. There, it felt certain it would eventually locate the vessel that contained the Key.

But finding the Key wasn't enough. The spirit would also need the talisman that it had forged and charged with its mortal hands over a millennium ago. Only by reuniting the Key with the magic of the talisman could it regain its full power and put its plan into motion.

The combination of the two magical energies would unlock the barrier between the living world and the Void—that trackless, howling vortex wherein dwelled unnatural creatures of darkness, fearsome and terrible beyond description. Opening the barrier would release a vast army of these creatures that could be bent to the spirit being's will. With such an army at its back, it...*he* would be invincible, the Destroyer of Nations. No longer The Nameless One, he would reclaim his name and power, and all the peoples of the world would be under his dominion.

This had been his intent a millennium ago, until he had been betrayed by those he most trusted. His magic had been stripped from him. The Key had been stolen and hidden beyond his reach, and his body slain and buried deep beneath the shattered fortress of his enemies. They had sealed him up and warded the chamber, trapping his immortal soul and stifling all self-awareness.

His enemies obviously hadn't anticipated that their magic might fail.

He didn't devote much time to wondering why they hadn't kept a more close watch on the wards; his emotions were distilled down into two only—hatred of all living things, and the desire to conquer and destroy. He would accomplish his plan when he located the Key and the talisman.

He was very close.

PART II

CHAPTER 9

THE GOOD SON

Thunk!

An arrow pierced the center of the target, its fletched end vibrating. Ashinji Sakehera withdrew another arrow from the quiver at his hip, and in rapid sequence, <u>nocked</u>, drew, and fired. The second arrow embedded itself nearly on top of the first. A third arrow followed the first two, then a fourth. Within the space of a few heartbeats, he'd emptied his quiver. Shooting practice always calmed and focused Ashinji's mind, and ever since his return home to Kerala two weeks ago, he'd been doing a lot of shooting.

Captain Sakehera had been given leave to make the journey home from his posting in the capitol at Sendai in order to fulfill a special family obligation. His brother Sadaiyo, eldest of Lord Sen Sakehera's five offspring, and Heir to Kerala, was to be wed. The marriage of the Heir of one of Alasiri's most powerful and important families was a very big event, and as such, no expense would be spared, and all of the obligatory rituals would have to be executed to perfection. As second-born, it was Ashinji's duty to perform the Ritual of Welcoming on the day before the wedding ceremony itself, thereby officially accepting the bride into the House of Sakehera.

Tradition and ceremony were the very foundations of elven society, and Ashinji truly did honor them; yet, lately, those traditions were beginning to feel like heavy chains wrapped around his soul, slowly crushing him with their great weight.

Ashinji walked down the yard to the target and began pulling the arrows one by one from the tightly packed straw. A fly buzzed around his head and tried to land on his nose. He swatted it away as he pulled the last arrow from the target and dropped it into the quiver with its fellows. Wiping his perspiring brow with the back of his hand, he glanced upwards.

The sun, a white-hot eye gazing down from the cerulean sky, made the day unusually warm for early spring. The deep shade cast by the high wall of the yard beckoned invitingly. Ashinji ambled over and sat down in the dirt, back pressed to the smooth-cut stones.

Absent-mindedly, he tugged at the three gold rings that adorned the lobe of his left ear. At the end of each five-year period of service, all soldiers received an earring as a token from the king. In two more years, Ashinji would earn another ring and quite possibly a promotion. Eighteen years was a long time to spend doing something for which he had no real vocation. He would not have chosen the military life for himself had he been allowed to choose.

The second son of Lord Sen Sakehera was a thoughtful young man, and within his highly trained warrior's body resided the soul of a scholar. His temperament had always been more suited to the life of an academic, rather than to that of a captain in the king's army.

Ashinji usually spent much of what leisure time he had studying the texts and treatises of the great mathematicians, both elven and human. His father had always been a little bemused by his offspring's interests but had never actively discouraged them, for Ashinji had always been a dutiful son, ever mindful of the role in life that his family and position dictated for him.

Lately, though, Ashinji had begun to question that role. The second child of every Sakehera generation was bound by tradition to be given to the military. Lord Sakehera himself was a second child, as was his mother before him. It had always been so. The tradition of obedience to one's parents dictated that Ashinji acquiesce to his father's decision that he remain a soldier, rather than pursuing his own dream of a very different life.

Obedience was a virtue he found increasingly hard to live with.

Ashinji laid the bow and quiver aside and stretched his legs out, crossing them at the ankles. He reached around and undid the ties of his light cotton tunic and pulled the garment away from his sweaty torso. Kerala Castle lay quietly drowsing in the heat of mid-day. Ashinji's emerald-green eyes became increasingly unfocused as his thoughts turned more deeply inward. He hadn't been sleeping well since he'd returned home—due in large part to his ever-grow-ing desire to quit the army. The strain put on all of the family by the upcoming nuptials played a part as well.

But mostly, it was the dream.

Since childhood, Ashinji sometimes dreamt visions of such strength and clarity that when he awoke, he could not immediately separate the waking world from the dream state. These special dreams were always prescient, and he had learned that to ignore their mes-sage was to do so at his own peril. All elves possessed some psychic abilities, commonly referred to as Talent. Those with the strongest Talent were usually trained as mages. Lady Sakehera—Ashinji's moth-er—had, as a young woman, trained at a very prestigious school of magic, but had chosen to give up a career as a professional mage for marriage and family. It was she who had first told Ashinji that his dreams were a manifestation of his Talent.

This particular dream always began with him standing alone on the bank of a slow moving river, the sun high and hot overhead. A sound, like the cry of a great beast, caught his attention. He turned his head to seek out the source but he could see nothing save the ranks of silent trees marching down nearly to the water's edge.

Suddenly, he no longer stood alone. A woman appeared before him, dressed in the simple clothes of a servant. She was very young, with a wild mane of dark, tightly coiled hair and eyes that were full of sorrow and loneliness. She appeared to be elven, and yet, there was something different about her that Ashinji could not quite fathom. Within the body of this not-quite elven woman glowed a core of pure, radiant blue energy that pulsed with each beat of her heart. He could sense the immense power of it and its inherent danger, though he also could sense that the woman herself posed no threat; in fact, he felt a powerful affinity toward her, as if she were someone for whom he had been waiting a very long time.

In that peculiar, disjointed way of dreams, he and the woman suddenly stood in a jumbled landscape of fractured, snow-encrusted boulders. The low ceiling of gray clouds overhead spit flurries of stinging ice crystals down upon Ashinji's head. As he watched, the woman's expression slowly changed from sorrow to fear. Darkness bled from the rocks, slowly coalescing into a massive black shadow that loomed over her. A palpable air of menace flowed from the shadow, and the woman shrank from it in terror.

Help me! she cried, reaching for Ashinji with pale, long-fingered hands. As he grasped her hands in his, he saw that, upon one finger, a tiny beast crouched—a miniature griffin. Its feathers were wrought of silver, and its eyes were glowing red pinpricks. The beast hissed and struck. Ashinji cried out in pain as tiny fangs ripped into his flesh. Reflexively, he let go his grip on the strange woman's hands, and she was pulled backwards into the shadow and engulfed.

He always awoke in a sweaty panic, the woman's screams echoing in his head. Unable to return to sleep, he then spent the remainder of the night staring at the ceiling of his bedchamber, trying fruitlessly to wrest some comprehension from his tired mind. Nothing he had ever dreamed before had carried the sense of urgency of this particular dream. He instinctively knew that it presaged an event that would radically alter his life, but whether for good or ill... that wisdom remained hidden from him.

A stray lock of hair, the color of honey, fell across his face, and he pushed it back behind one ear. A hound barked off in the distance. The fly, or possibly its kin, returned to buzz in an annoyingly persistent, erratic flight path around his head.

I really need a bath, he thought.

He rose to his feet, dusted off the seat of his breeches, slung the bow over his shoulder, and headed for the gate.

~~~

"Youngest Son! There you are. I need to go over some things with you."

Ashinji, still damp from the bathhouse, came to sit at the massive oak table that was the central feature of Kerala Castle's main hall. Ashinji had always liked this room for its stark simplicity. The whitewashed walls, unadorned save for the family crest above the flagstone fireplace, sturdy oak furniture, and darkly polished wood floor, gave the hall a feeling of unassuming grandeur.

"Father," Ashinji replied, pulling out a chair and seating himself across from the Lord of Kerala.

Lord Sen Sakehera had been a soldier his entire adult life. Multiple gold service rings adorned both ears, and a very large diamond glittered in the lobe of his right, a symbol of his rank as Commanding General of Alasiri's armies. He had served the royal house of Alasiri for nearly ninety years and was the present king's oldest and closest friend. He ruled over Kerala with a firm, yet compassionate hand, and his people loved him.

Despite his exalted rank, Lord Sen was a humble man —a simple soldier, he'd say, who just happened to have the ear of the king. Today, he was dressed like a gentleman farmer in a plain, unbleached cotton tunic, baggy breeches, and sturdy leather sandals. He wore his tawny hair in a soldier's braid, which reached almost to his waistband.

"Do you wish to discuss the wedding, Father?" Ashinji asked. "I assure you, I'll have the Ritual of Welcoming completely memorized by the time I have to perform it."

"Oh, that. Bloody thing's still eight weeks away, but you'd think it was tomorrow if you listened to your mother. May The One preserve us!" Lord Sen rolled his eyes. "No, no wedding talk. Something much more serious."

"What could possibly be more serious than my brother's wedding?" Ashinji asked, a touch of sarcasm coloring his voice.

"Hmm, yes. What, indeed," Sen replied, a tiny smile drawing up one corner of his expressive mouth. "I'll tell you what, Youngest Son." He held up a sheaf of papers in one hand. "These are reports from the Saihama River district. Several farms have been attacked within the last month by human bandits coming across the river from Soldara. The local sheriff thinks it's the work of a single gang operating from a camp near the fords. She has requested that I send a posse to clean them out."

"You want me to lead it," Ashinji stated, leaning forward with interest.

"Who else but you? Sadaiyo is far too busy being the center of attention as the soon-to-be married Heir, and besides, I can trust you to do the job right."

"Father… Sadaiyo is a perfectly competent fighter and quite capable of performing this task," Ashinji chided gently, "but of course, I will do as you command."

"I just hope that this isn't the beginning of something worse," Sen said, shuffling through the stack of papers in front of him. He pulled out one that bore several official seals. "This report just arrived from Sendai today. It seems that we out here in the east are not the only ones suffering from human incursions. There've been several incidents in the Tono Valley district. Soldaran patrols have been spotted on the Alasiri side of the border, and there have been raids as well. There've been rumors that the Soldaran empress has designs on Tono… that she plans on taking it back."

"Tono rightfully belongs to us," Ashinji said. "Elves have lived and farmed that valley for centuries. It was only because the Soldarans invaded and stole it away from us that it ever became part of the Empire."

"Hmm, yes, and Keizo the Elder won it back for us at the cost of many elven and human lives. The Soldarans have been smarting over that defeat for a long time. Looks like the empress has finally decided it's time for her to avenge her great grandfather."

"How are the Soldarans getting past the Tono garrison, Father?" Ashinji asked. "I thought that Lady Odata kept her troops vigilant."

"She does," Sen replied. "The humans must use trails through the mountains. It's very difficult terrain… treacherous, horse-leg breaking. That's why the raiding parties have been relatively small." He paused for a moment, tugging at his earlobe, then continued. "There's something else that's very disturbing. I've a letter from Prince Raidan. He asks if any of our people have fallen ill with a mysterious sickness. He tells of a plague striking border folk, particularly those living close to human settlements. He says that it appears that a human disease has begun to infect elves. All humans die from it, but our people seem to be able to survive, though it leaves them in a terribly weakened state."

Ashinji frowned with worry. "The nearest human settlement to Kerala is that big castle to the south of us… I forget the name of it, but it's at least three days ride from here."

"Umm, yes. Amsara Castle, seat of the duchy," Sen replied. "It's not the duke's people that I'm worried might bring disease to our folk… it's those bandits."

Lord Sen swept up his papers into a neat pile, pushed back his chair, and rose to his feet. He stood taller than average, a well-built man and still fit, despite being well into his middle years. "I want you to ride out tomorrow morning. Take some of the guard with you. Go to Saihama village first and talk to the sheriff. Find out if she knows of any folk in the village or on the outlying farms that have fallen ill of this mysterious plague. Then, find those bandits and clean them out." His tanned face settled into the hard mask of a man who had come to the conclusion that a terrible calamity loomed on the horizon.

"I fear the future, Youngest Son. I can't shake this feeling that war is coming, and soon. If we have to fight, we cannot afford to have our people weakened by illness. The Soldarans have always had an advantage of numbers over us. Without an army at full strength, we haven't much chance."

"We have to believe that somehow, we'll be all right, Father. What else can we do?" Ashinji rose from his chair. "I'll leave at first light." He turned to go.

"Don't forget to say goodbye to your mother. I know she's all wrapped up in this wedding business, but she would kill me if I didn't insist that you interrupt her for a proper farewell." Sen smiled wryly.

"I will, Father," Ashinji replied. Emerald eyes met gray-green ones in acknowledgment of the unbreakable bonds of love between father and son. "I'll see you when I return."

CHAPTER 10

A CONFLICTED HEART

"Ashiiii!"

The two little girls leapt up from the floor and flung themselves upon their big brother, shrieking with delight. Jena and Mariso were identical twins, the youngest of the Sakehera brood. Twinning was very rare among elves, and the twins themselves were believed to bestow special luck upon their families.

"Whoa! You'll knock me down, you demons," Ashinji cried in mock fear, then burst out laughing as the twins swarmed over him. He scooped up one child under each arm and carried them, giggling and squirming, into the center of the large, open room where two women sat on a low couch, each one bending over something in her hands. The older of the two women looked up, and her handsome face broke into a gentle smile.

"Mother! Mother! Look who's here!" the twins shouted in unison.

"Yes, my pets, I can see perfectly well. You don't have to carry on so. Do let your brother alone so he can come and greet me properly!" Lady Sakehera held out her hand.

"All right, monkeys," Ashinji said, lowering the girls gently to the floor where they collapsed in a giggling heap. He clasped his mother's warm, strong-fingered hand in his and kissed her tattooed palm. He then bent over and kissed his oldest sister Lani's cool cheek, and was rewarded by a demure smile.

Lani was tall, like their father, and just blossoming into young womanhood. She possessed an elegant beauty and a calm maturity far beyond her years. Like Ashinji, she, too, found great pleasure in intellectual pursuits, but she also nurtured a serious artistic talent as well. At present, she and her mother were working in tandem on a large piece of needlework. From the look of the fabric and the complexity of the design, Ashinji surmised that they labored over a wedding robe.

"Come sit by me, Son. Can you stay and talk awhile?" Lady Sakehera asked.

"Of course, Mother," Ashinji replied, settling down on the couch beside her.

The twins immediately began clamoring for his attention. "Ashi! Your hair..." cried Jena. Mariso took up the sentence and finished it. "Can we braid it? Pleeeeese?" Ashinji found the children's exuberance impossible to ignore. Their small bodies hummed with the wild energy of the very young.

"Well, it's still wet, but..."

The girls shrieked with glee.

"Girls, please! Not so loud. Ashinji is not one of your dolls, you know. Maybe he doesn't want his hair braided just yet." Lady Sakehera shook her head in reproach, but Ashinji could see how hard she worked to suppress her laughter.

"All right, monkeys. If you must." He braced himself as the girls climbed over the side of the couch and wedged themselves in behind his back. One of them produced a comb and began attacking his damp locks with enthusiasm.

"Maybe after you two are finished with our brother's hair, you can sit still long enough for me to show you some stitching," Lani's tone crackled with wry amusement. Her clever fingers seemed to move impossibly fast for such intricate work. A single bead of perspiration stood out on the fine skin of her forehead.

A set of ceramic wind chimes hanging in the room's main window tinkled merrily in the warm breeze. Today, the wind came from the southeast, carrying with it the heat it had absorbed during its long journey across the great southern desert.

"I'm going away for awhile, Mother," Ashinji said.

"I know, Son. Your father has told me."

Ashinji studied his mother's profile, trying to glean from it a clue to her innermost thoughts, but Lady Amara Sakehera had been well trained. She was a daughter of the House of Naota, the wife and strong right hand of the Commanding General of the king's army, and a mage of exceptional Talent. If she were fearful over what could happen to her son, she would never show it. Her face remained smooth and calm.

"I hope I'll not be away much longer than ten days or so."

"Perhaps, when you return, you can tell me what has been troubling you these past few days." Amara's eyes, emerald green like her son's, spoke of her desire to offer wisdom and comfort to her child. Ashinji sighed. He had never been able to hide his troubles or fears from her. She was too highly attuned to the psychic energies of all of her family.

The twins put the finishing touches to his hair, securing their handiwork with a leather thong. One of them gave the braid a playful tug as the two of them scrambled off the couch to go attend Lani. The room rang with their bright chatter as the older girl tried to explain what she was doing.

"I've been doing a lot of thinking lately about my life," Ashinji began. He pulled nervously at his service rings, unsure of how to put into words the frustration he felt. He took a deep breath and willed himself to relax. His mother radiated a calm energy, and he allowed his mind to absorb it and use it to ease the flow of his thoughts.

"I am the second-born child of Sen Sakehera, and because of the order of my birth, the direction of my life was chosen for me. Every second child of each generation of our family has always been given to the military. It's tradition. No one's ever questioned it."

"Very few of us have the power to choose the direction of our own lives exactly as we would have it, Son," Amara responded.

"You did," Ashinji countered.

Amara sighed and put down her needle. "Lani, take the girls outside and let them run the dogs for awhile," she said.

Lani's expression indicated that she understood perfectly well the unspoken reason behind her mother's directive. Carefully, she laid aside the sleeve she had been working on and gestured to the twins. "Come along, girls. Let's go and get the dogs. They will be ever so happy to see you," she said brightly. The twins jumped up eagerly and rushed to the door, Lani following in their wake.

"My situation was very different from yours, Son," Amara continued after the girls had departed. "The House of Naota has always been nonconformist. That has been our strength and our weakness. We are a clan of mages, full of eccentricity and madness. My mother never married my father. She chose the practice of magic over the traditional roles of wife and mother. I was raised by my aunts and cousins. When the time came for a choice to be made for my life, neither of my parents had the right anymore to decide what I would become. I was free to make the choice for myself."

"You chose to become a mage, like your mother," Ashinji said.

"In the beginning, yes. I knew my Talent was strong. There were many things that came easily and naturally to me. I believed for a very long time that there could be no other calling for me. Then, I met your father, and suddenly, my perspective on life changed."

A smile, slow and sweet, suffused her face with the gentle glow of a warm memory. "Ai, your father! He came sweeping into my life like a spring storm and turned everything I thought I knew about myself upside down. He convinced me that my life would be much better if I lived it with him in the outside world, rather than in the cloistered halls of a mage school."

"You and my father were lucky enough to be able to choose the lives that suited you best, yet you did not give that same privilege to your children. Why?" Ashinji fought to keep the bitter edge out of his voice, but by his mother's expression, he knew she had heard it anyway.

Amara folded her hands around her son's. She leaned forward slightly and Ashinji caught a whiff of her perfume, a special fragrance imported from the distant and mysterious lands to the east. "Ashinji," she said softly, "I know what is in your heart…there is terrible longing for another kind of life that you cannot have. If I could have given you the freedom to choose, I would have, but it was not possible."

She stood up and moved over to the window. "Our duty binds us too closely now, Son," she continued, gazing out over the gardens below. "We must uphold tradition and consider what is best for the House of Sakehera before all other things, including the personal desires of any of its members. As second born, you were pledged by tradition to military service. Only the king himself can release you from that pledge."

She sighed and turned to face Ashinji. "I beg of you, Son. Try and come to terms with what you must be, and find, if not happiness, at least contentment."

All throughout her speech, Ashinji could do nothing but stare at the jewel-toned flowers embroidered upon the sleeves of his mother's robe. Her words were like stones, piled one by one onto his heart until he felt as if it would be crushed.

Abruptly, he stood. "I must go now, Mother," he stated. Through the open window, he could see Lani and the twins racing across the castle yard towards the gate, three sleek, black hounds bounding along beside them. He had meant to speak to his mother about the dream, but now, all he wanted to do was go somewhere to be alone.

"You will be leaving at first light tomorrow?" Amara asked. She returned to the couch, picked up her needle, and resumed working.

"Yes," Ashinji replied.

"Will we see you at dinner tonight?"

Ashinji considered a moment before answering. "No," he said.

"Then, goodbye, my son. I will see you again when you return."

Ashinji bent down to kiss his mother in farewell. As his lips touched the soft skin of her cheek, he heard her voice in his mind, as clearly as if she had spoken aloud.

I love you, Ashi. I am sorry.

She did not look up at him as he left the room.

~~~

Ashinji finally lay down to sleep, a little past midnight. All of his gear was cleaned, oiled, and ready. An hour before dawn, a servant would come to assist him with armoring. He needed to rest, but his mind kept filling up with a relentless jumble of thoughts.

What am I going to do?

How can I go on like this?

Who is this girl I keep seeing?

Finally, he gave up and climbed out of bed. Pulling on a pair of loose trousers, he tied the drawstrings securely at his waist and went to sit by the open window across the room.

He took a deep breath of the cool night air. The starlight turned the peaks and slopes of the castle's roofs into a mysterious black and silver landscape. Ashinji's quarters were on the uppermost floor at the rear of the east wing; during the day, from his window, he could see out beyond the walls, across rolling green pastures dotted with clumps of trees, to the purple shadows of the vast, forbidding range of the Kesen Numai Mountains, far to the north.

He thought about taking a horse and riding northward, toward the mountains. In three days' time, if he stopped only to sleep for a couple of hours, he would reach the city of Jokyi and its famous university. Once there, he could petition to take the entrance exams; as the son of a lord, he had already received a good primary education. He felt confident he could pass. His dream of a life as a scholar would be within his grasp.

He sighed and shook his head. Could he turn his back on his family, and forsake every value and tradition he had been raised to believe in? It would be a shocking act of disobedience against a father who had always held him in the highest esteem, for had he not always been a dutiful son? He groaned aloud and pulled his hair in frustration. For eighteen years he had lived as a soldier, and, in truth, had found some satisfaction in it. Why, now, had all of that changed?

He stood up to stretch, then went back to his bed and lay down, arms folded behind his head. He was very tired, yet he did not feel at all drowsy. He decided to close his eyes anyway…and was awakened by a soft, insistent knock upon his bedchamber door.

Must be time to get up, he thought. *I slept a little after all…but no dreams.* The wild-haired, sad-faced girl had not come.

He admitted the manservant, who came bustling in bearing a light breakfast—smoked fish, bread, a bowl of honey-sweetened yogurt mixed with berries, and a pot of tea. As he ate, Ashinji recalled his mother's words. Find contentment and acceptance, she had said. The path of his life was set and had been from the very first day he had drawn breath as his father's second born. His mother was the wisest person he knew. Perhaps, in this as in so many other things, he would be wise to heed her advice.

After all, what was his alternative?

"My lord."

"Captain Miri," Ashinji replied, acknowledging the older man's greeting with a short nod. Gendan Miri had been captain of the Kerala Castle guard for as long as Ashinji could remember. He held the stirrup steady as Ashinji mounted his horse, a big, black gelding with a white blaze and large, intelligent eyes. After Ashinji settled himself, Gendan handed up his helmet, which he then hung from the pommel of the saddle. There would be little danger of attack until they reached the area of the last known bandit incursions. He could safely ride bare-headed today.

The first blush of dawn began coloring the sky to the east. The stable yard was dim and cool. The small company to ride out this morning totaled twelve in number: ten castle guards—eight men and two women—with Gendan and Ashinji rounding out the count.

"Have the troops fall in, Captain," Ashinji commanded. Gendan turned and called out the order in a clipped bass-baritone. Jingle of harness and creak of leather, horses stamping and blowing, the muted conversation of troops preparing to ride out—Ashinji let the sounds and sights flow through his mind like water over stones. He did not want to think right now; he just wanted to let the horse carry him along to where he needed to go so that he could do what he had to do and return home.

"The company is ready, my lord," Gendan reported. He maneuvered his ugly dun mount alongside Ashinji's black gelding, who, in a fit of equine ill-humor, flattened his ears and turned to bite. Ashinji checked the animal with a quick jerk of the reins and grudgingly, the gelding turned his head away from the dun.

Ashinji looked over his shoulder toward the main door of the castle, then back to the now quiet company waiting at attention. He sighed.

Time to go.

He flicked the reins and clicked his tongue. The gelding started forward, angling toward the gate, Gendan riding alongside, the company following behind in orderly pairs.

"Ashi, wait!"

Ashinji drew rein and turned in the saddle to see Lord Sen striding toward him. His father's hair hung loose, and he wore only a simple robe and sandals, as if he had just left the warm haven of his bed to come see his son off.

"Whew! Thought I'd missed you," Sen exclaimed as he stepped up and put out a hand to rest on Ashinji's knee. "It's harder to get out of bed the older I get. Just wanted to be here when you left. I know I don't have to tell you to be careful. Don't take any foolish risks. These are only ragtag human bandits, after all, not trained warriors." He looked up at Gendan, and a quick message, conveyed by eyes only, passed between lord and liegeman.

Gendan nodded once, sharply.

Lord Sen turned back to Ashinji.

"I know I can rely on you, Youngest Son." He patted Ashinji's knee and stepped away from the gelding's side.

"I'll return in ten days' time, Father, whether or not I've found the bandits," Ashinji promised. Once more, he urged his mount to walk on toward the gate, which swung slowly open as the riders approached. He led the way onto the sturdy bridge that linked Kerala Castle, which stood on a rocky island in the Saihama River, to the tree-lined shore.

As the company crossed the span, the *clop clop* of the horses' hooves on wood broke the early morning stillness. Birds were just beginning to stir and twitter in the trees as the first rays of the sun shot upwards into the purple sky, kindling the underbellies of the clouds to rose-gold fire. A fine mist writhed among the treetops, but it would soon burn off in the rapidly warming air.

The black gelding blew noisily, then threw his head up and jigged sideways into Gendan's dun, who answered with a swift nip to the neck. The gelding shied away, and Ashinji cursed as he was momentarily thrown off-balance. "I don't think this horse has been ridden enough lately," he commented ruefully as he tried to steady the animal.

Gendan chuckled. "He does seem to be feeling his grain, doesn't he? He'll settle down after a good brisk lope, I should think."

"Huh. Let's hope so!"

Saihama Village lay a day's ride to the east. The company planned to follow a track that paralleled the river for about a league, then cut across open pastureland until they reached the dirt lane that led to the village proper. Once there, Ashinji would meet with the sheriff and form a plan of action. He looked back over his shoulder at Kerala Castle, its whitewashed walls gleaming pink in the early morning light. He imagined that he could just make out the tiny figure of his father standing in the gate, arm raised in farewell.

I wonder how Sadaiyo will feel when he learns that our father sent me to do this job, rather than him, Ashinji thought.

He'll be angry, no doubt, even though he'll know it makes more sense for me to go…but when did my brother ever allow sense to guide him where I'm concerned?

He turned back in the saddle and focused his eyes forward, somewhere beyond the black horse's swiveling ears.

For most of his life, Ashinji had been aware that Lord Sen favored him over his older brother, Sadaiyo. He suspected this was so because he and his father were much more alike in temperament than was Sen and his Heir. Ashinji had never encouraged this. In fact, he had always sought to discourage his father's favoritism, subtle though it was. Try as he might, however, Lord Sen could not conceal the difference in affection he felt for each of his sons. The special bond he shared with Ashinji was just too strong, and because of it, Sadaiyo had nursed a dark, bitter resentment against his brother since childhood.

Ashinji shook his head sadly, knowing that there would be trouble with Sadaiyo when he returned home.

"Begging your pardon, my lord, but you look as if you've got the very weight of the world on your shoulders this morning," Gendan commented, his rugged face a mask of concern. "Something troubling you?"

"Only the usual things, Gendan," Ashinji replied.

Gendan was intuitive enough to know when not to push. "D'you think there's going to be war with the humans, my lord?" he asked instead, changing the subject.

Ashinji shrugged. "I don't know. I pray that there won't be. Alasiri would be hard-pressed to defend itself against an all-out invasion by the Empire."

"Humans!" Gendan spat. "They've overrun practically all the known world, but that's not enough for them. Now, they want to take away the little part of it we elves have managed to hold on to!" Gendan's dun horse snorted and tossed his head, sensing his rider's agitation.

"To be fair, it's not all humans, Gendan, only the Soldaran Empire," Ashinji pointed out. "I daresay a lot of the other human nations conquered by the Soldarans resent them as much as we do."

"That may be so, my lord, but the Soldarans don't want to just conquer us. They want to annihilate us... wipe us from the face of the earth!" Gendan shook his head in bewilderment. "Why do they hate us so?"

"Ignorance and superstition," Ashinji replied. He had studied enough about Soldaran religious beliefs to know that this was the case. As long as most Soldarans were taught that elves were, by their very nature, demonic, there could be no understanding or peace between the two races.

The new sun already burned hot in a perfect, cloudless sky. Ashinji wiped his perspiring brow with the back of his gloved hand. "If war does come, it's going to take everything we've got just to survive," he said. Gendan grunted his assent.

And I'll have to give up on any hope of leaving the army, he thought. *War will require great sacrifices of all of us.*

CHAPTER 11

AMBUSH

Jelena and Magnes walked all night, with only the stars and a tiny sliver of moon to light their way. They passed through rustling fields of growing wheat and orchards awash in blossoms, always heading northwest. Magnes had chosen as their goal the only spot in the Janica River where he knew that the water was shallow enough to cross. To reach the fords, they would have to traverse a small but dense patch of woodland that lay at the northernmost edge of Amsaran territory. Across the river, which marked the boundary of the Empire, lay elven lands.

At dawn, they reached the edge of the forest and decided to stop and rest a few yards into the trees. Magnes went off to forage while Jelena set up their meager camp. It was dark and chilly beneath the thick canopy of oak, beech, and chestnut. The trees themselves were large-boled and hoary, a testament to their great age. This stand was but a remnant of a once vast forest that had covered much of Amsara back in ancient times. With the coming of people, the mighty trees had fallen to the cold iron of the axe blade as the land was cleared for fields and pastures. Somehow, this small patch had survived, most likely due to its closeness to elven territory.

Jelena tried to fight her growing unease by busying herself about the camp. Despite the dim light, she could see well enough to collect a supply of sticks and dry debris, and with flint and steel, soon had a small fire burning. Next, she cleared away the litter of last year's withered leaves and acorns to make a relatively smooth spot on which to spread out the bedrolls. The fire cheered her a little, as did the sunrise, which put to flight some of the darker, more sinister shadows.

Even so, the trees seemed to possess a kind of slow and alien awareness, like strange old men huddled together, whispering secrets over her head. She sat cross-legged on the ground close to the little fire, pulled her blanket over her shoulders, and settled down to await Magnes's return.

The snap of a breaking twig startled Jelena up out of a light doze. She had not realized that she had been asleep until that instant, and a thrill of alarm shot through her. She jumped to her feet and snatched her long knife from the sheath at her waist.

"Easy! It's only me."

At the sound of Magnes's voice, Jelena's fear evaporated, and all of the nervous energy tensing her muscles drained away, leaving relief in its wake. "You scared me half to death!" she exclaimed. "I must have dozed off." She re-sheathed the knife and came forward to see what Magnes had foraged.

"It's these damned trees. They've got me jumpy, too," Magnes said sympathetically. He hunkered down by the fire and laid out his harvest. "It's been a little dry this spring, but there's still quite a lot of stuff growing. I've got some leeks and cleavers, and a few spring beauty roots. We'll have a nice salad." He held up each plant as he named it. "And now, I've saved the best for last!" With a crow of triumph, he dumped a handful of tiny, brilliant red wild strawberries into Jelena's lap. She clapped with delight. With the fruit of Magnes's foraging to supplement the rations they had brought with them out of Amsara, it should be several days before they would be forced to hunt.

"Cook should be noticing I'm missing right about now," Jelena said around a mouthful of bread and cheese. "I think I can hear her yelling."

Magnes laughed.

"When do you think your father will send his guards out to look for us?" she asked, unable to disguise the worry in her voice.

Magnes's face clouded over. "My father won't realize something's wrong until I don't show up with the morning report," he replied. "Once he finds out that I'm not in my chambers and that no one has seen me, then he'll start to worry."

"And Cook'll send someone up to tell him I'm gone, and…oh, no!" Jelena exclaimed suddenly. Sick fear twisted her gut. "Magnes, what have I done… *Claudia!*" Jelena sprang to her feet. She wanted to turn and run and not stop until she had made it all the way back to Amsara.

"What about Claudia?" Magnes scrambled up and grasped his cousin's shoulders. He seemed to sense that she teetered on the edge of panic and wanted to steady her before she fell off.

Jelena looked up into his face, her eyes full of tears and terror. "Your father will want to question Claudia about my disappearance. Magnes, she'll be forced into a position where she'll have to lie to protect me, or else tell him where I've gone, and she won't do that! She'll lie, and she'll be so nervous that your father will know she's lying, and he'll punish her. I can't let that happen. I have to go back."

Magnes shook his head and tightened his grip on her shoulders. "My father may be hard, but he's not a monster, Cousin. He knows how much Claudia loves you, and he understands the need of a parent to protect a child. He'll certainly be angry with her, but he won't hurt Claudia. You don't have to go back."

Slowly, Jelena relaxed. She wiped her eyes and sat back down next to the fire. For a time, she said nothing. Overwhelmed by the enormity of what she had done, she was afraid to think too hard on the consequences. Magnes threw another handful of sticks onto the fire, and Jelena stared into the leaping flames, seeing in her mind's eye her foster mother bowed before Duke Teodorus, trembling in the face of his wrath. The image pierced her heart, but she knew, deep down, that Magnes was right. The duke was a hard man, but he had always treated his servants fairly. Claudia would suffer because of her, but not at the hands of her master.

What's done is done. I can't go back, only forward. I'm sorry, Heart-mother.

Magnes coughed to get her attention. She looked at him, and he held out a strawberry, which she took with a smile and ate. The sun hung well above the horizon now, and the air was growing steadily warmer, heralding another fine spring day. The forest had gradually come to life around them as the sun rose, and the dense canopy above them trilled with birdsong. The ancient trees, which had seemed so mysterious and frightening in the darkness of the predawn, now looked almost friendly. They finished off their small meal and followed it up with sips from their water bottles.

"You'd better try to get some sleep if you can," Magnes said, wiping his mouth on his sleeve. "I'll take the first watch."

"Shouldn't we keep moving?" Jelena asked. Despite the weariness she felt after walking all night, she was willing to go on if it meant staying that much further ahead of any pursuit.

"We have a little time," Magnes replied confidently. "Remember, first they'll search the castle. That'll take awhile. After my father realizes that we're not there, it will take time to organize a search party, and they won't pick up our trail right away. All of this presupposes that my father figures out fairly quickly that your disappearance and mine coincide." Jelena nodded. "So, it'll be hours before any search actually gets underway. Don't worry. I won't let you sleep too long."

Jelena pulled the leather cap from her head and raked her fingers through her cropped curls. She then arranged her pack to serve as a pillow and lay down on the hard ground. The blankets of her bedroll offered scant padding, and despite her best efforts to clear the area beforehand, many acorns and small rocks remained. Fatigue was enough to overcome discomfort, however, and very quickly, Jelena dropped off to sleep.

The sound of her name spoken in her ear woke her. She opened her eyes to see Magnes's face hovering close to hers. His expression was grim.

"Wha...what is it?" she asked blearily. She had been in the midst of a dream—a confused jumble of images and sounds—and wasn't quite sure if she was truly awake yet.

"We've got to go now, Cousin," Magnes whispered urgently. Jelena sat up, fully awake now and jittery with alarm. Magnes pointed back toward the gently rolling terrain they had crossed last night. "I spotted them a few moments ago...a group of horsemen, riding this way. I'm not sure they're from Amsara, but I don't want to wait around to find out."

Jelena imagined the thwarted and angry Duke Sebastianus leading the search for the concubine who had dared to defy him by running away. She shivered as she helped Magnes gather their things and obliterate the evidence of their camp.

"How close are they," Jelena asked tensely. Several crows began screaming raucously overhead, startling her so that she nearly dropped her long knife as she was trying to secure it at her waist.

"We'll have at least a half hour's lead on them...more once they reach the trees. It'll be slow going for them, riding through these woods." Magnes had already smothered the fire with dirt and was busily spreading around the forest litter. "Any decent tracker will be able to tell we've been here if he looks closely enough, but let's hope that they're just searching and not actually following our trail." He wiped his hands on his thighs and hoisted his pack onto his back. "Ready?" Jelena nodded eagerly, anxious to get moving.

As they traveled further into the perpetual twilight of the deep woods, it became difficult to judge the sun's position in the sky, and Jelena soon lost all track of time. They marched along wrapped in a cool, dim bubble, with only the sounds of their footfalls and an occasional birdcall to break the stillness. Once, they startled some small creature that went wildly plunging off into the dense undergrowth.

The trees were getting larger the further into the woods they traveled. The undergrowth steadily diminished, which made for easier going. Jelena was awestruck by the majesty of the deep woods giants. It seemed to her that these trees must have been standing here since the very beginning of the world, when the gods had brought forth order out of the chaos of the Void.

They stopped briefly to rest and drink a little water. Jelena asked Magnes how he knew which direction was the correct one without using the sun. He explained that, as long as they kept the mossy side of the trees behind him, then he knew they were heading north. "Once we reach the river, I'll be able to see the sky again, and when the stars are out, I'll know whether we need to go up or downstream to reach the fords." Jelena fervently hoped that the river was close. She kept imagining that she could hear the sounds of pursuit behind them, drawing ever closer.

They walked in silence for a time. The rhythm of her footsteps lulled Jelena into a trance, so she was unprepared for Magnes's abrupt halt. "Ow!" she cried as she fetched hard up against her cousin's back, knocking her forehead on his pack with a painful thump.

"Shhhh!" he hissed, holding up one hand towards her face. He peered ahead intently, the other hand cupped to his ear. Then, Jelena heard, as well.

Voices.

Magnes signaled that they should change course, away from the still-hidden speakers, and attempt to circle around without being detected. Jelena's heart slammed against her chest wall and her mouth grew dry with fear. She had no desire to find out whether the owners of those voices were friend or enemy.

Slowly, carefully, they moved forward and around, keeping the faint buzz of conversation always to their left side. Jelena had to focus all of her concentration on moving as quietly as she could, and soon, the underarms of her shirt were soggy with sweat. The sound of her breath roared in her ears, and each tiny crackle of leaf or twig under her boots seemed as loud as a thunderclap. Gradually, a growing awareness of a new sound insinuated itself into her consciousness—a smooth murmur, like wind sighing in the treetops. At the same instant, she realized that she could no longer hear the voices.

Magnes stopped and drew her close against him, setting his lips to her ear. "Can you hear it? The river," he breathed. She nodded in assent.

A heartbeat later, the forest erupted around them. Jelena barely had time to register what was happening before she was slammed face down into the ground. A grinning, hairy face pressed itself against hers, and she gagged on the putrid odor of rotten teeth and onions. She heard Magnes shout her name, and desperately she struggled to break free, but the body that pinned her to the earth was too heavy. Her efforts seemed to amuse her assailant, who uttered a low, throaty laugh. She felt a hard tug on her shoulders as her attacker pulled at the backpack. She heard the *snick* of metal cutting through leather straps; then the pressure released as the pack was ripped away from her body and tossed aside. In that instant, Jelena's arms were free, and instinct took over.

In a single motion, she pulled her knife and stabbed upward and back. She heard a bark of pain, followed by a string of profanities, and suddenly, the cruel weight that had been crushing her into the forest floor vanished. She rolled over and scrambled to her feet, crouched, knife blade at the ready. She assessed the scene quickly.

Magnes was standing, but she could see a bright ribbon of blood snaking its way down from above his left eye. "Are you hurt?" he asked in a low voice. She shook her head and moved to press her back to his.

There were six of them, lean and vicious as starving wolves. A seventh lay writhing and moaning at Magnes's feet, clutching at his belly. Blood seeped steadily through his fingers. The youngest, Jelena could see, was a boy of no more than thirteen summers; the oldest, a balding man well into his middle years. They all shared the same cold, hard, desperate look of men with nothing to lose. Each one had a weapon of some sort—knives, a rusty shortsword, a club.

"I guess we weren't quiet enough," Magnes whispered out of the corner of his mouth. He shifted his stance slightly and raised his blood-stained sword a little higher. "We don't have anything of value, except our food," he said in a calm, steady voice, addressing the bandits collectively. "We want no trouble, but as you can see," he gestured to the fallen man, who now lay still and silent, "we are capable of defending ourselves. Please, just take what you want and leave."

Jelena tightened her grip on the hilt of her knife and fiercely willed her hand to remain steady. Her eyes darted from one dirty face to another, seeking in vain for the tiniest flicker of compassion, but there was none, only feral, predatory interest.

The older, balding man spoke. "Give us the girl and we'll let you go," he said, speaking to Magnes but looking directly at Jelena. His eyes glittered like dirty ice chips in his grimy face.

"Impossible. She is my kinswoman and not mine to give. Sorry." Magnes's voice dripped sarcasm. He scowled, then said, "Let me re-phrase. You will leave now, with nothing, or I'll kill the lot of you."

"Magnes!" Jelena gasped. Up until that moment, a blanket of numbness and a sense of unreality had been keeping her fear in check; now, with Magnes's brash words, the numbness abruptly evaporated. The perilousness of their situation became abundantly clear. The balding man threw back his head and guffawed, and the others joined in, laughing and nudging each other as if Magnes had just told them the funniest joke that they had ever heard.

"Get ready to run," Magnes whispered. Suddenly, Jelena felt him lunge forward, and abruptly, the bandits all stopped laughing. She turned in time to see their leader falling backwards in a spray of blood, the hilt of Magnes's boot knife protruding from his throat. For an instant, everyone froze.

"Run, Jelena!" Magnes shouted.

Jelena sprinted towards the sound of flowing water. She could hear Magnes pounding along right behind her, and further off, the sound of pursuit. Panic gave her feet wings as she dodged tree trunks and low branches. She could see the trees thinning out ahead amid a haze of sunlight.

She emerged from the shadows of the forest into the soft light of late afternoon, skidding and almost falling on the loose soil and pebbles of the riverbank. Magnes grabbed her arm to steady her and started running eastward, pulling her along. The bandits burst from the woods a few moments later and, shouting in murderous fury, charged after them.

Never had Jelena had to run for her life before. Now, panting with exertion, she feared she would falter soon if she had to run much farther. Magnes seemed to sense her distress, and she could see the gleam of desperation in his eyes. She risked a glance over her shoulder. The bandits were gaining on them. She and Magnes were going to have to turn and fight.

"Magnes!" she cried, "I can't...we'll have to fight." They slid to a stop, the swiftly flowing river to their right, the forest to their left. The bandits tumbled to a halt a few yards off, panting and blowing like spent horses. Nevertheless, they seemed determined to avenge their slain leader. Slowly, they began to advance. Jelena raised her knife. Bitterly, she wondered why it had to end this way, before she had even gotten started. She prayed for it to be over quickly.

The tingling started like pins and needles in her hands and forearms. Suddenly, blue tongues of flame erupted from her fingers, burning so brightly that Jelena could not look directly at them. So startled was she that she dropped her knife.

"Gods!" Magnes exclaimed in astonishment. Slowly, Jelena raised her hands up and held them before her, a blazing shield of light. She could hear rough cries of amazement and fear, followed by confused chatter as the bandits debated whether the blue fire was real or some kind of trick. All the while, they continued to sidle forward.

Suddenly, the bandits froze in their tracks, staring out beyond their prey further along the riverbank. The ground began to vibrate. Magnes turned and barked a curse.

A group of horsemen were galloping straight toward them, weapons raised.

CHAPTER 12

THE DREAM MADE REAL

The company camped overnight at Saihama Village. The sheriff, an amiable woman named Taura, hosted Ashinji in her own home. She cooked him dinner and offered to give up the bed that she and her husband shared so that Ashinji might have a comfortable place to sleep. Ashinji graciously accepted the meal but declined the bed, explaining that he couldn't sleep indoors while his company slept outside. "It's a pleasant night, the grass is soft on your village green…I'll be fine," he said. "Believe me, I've had to make do with a lot less."

Sheriff Taura laughed heartily. She was a robust, plain-featured woman, well into middle age, with six grown children. Her husband was the village blacksmith. From the look of her ears and eyes, Ashinji suspected that she had some human blood in her ancestry. More frontier people did than liked to admit it. There had been a time, many years ago, when humans and elves had mingled a little more freely, at least out in the border country.

"You're a good man, Lord Ashinji, thinking about your troops first and wanting to share their hardships with them," Taura's husband, Mareo, said.

"It's really no hardship," Ashinji replied.

"I've seen to it that your company all got fed a nice, hot meal with plenty of our good local beer. My husband checked all the horses' shoes as well," Taura said.

"I thank you. Your hospitality has been exceptional."

"You asked me earlier, m'lord," Taura continued, "if anyone in the area had fallen ill with any unknown sickness, and I told you I wasn't sure. Well, I heard later this afternoon that a man out on one of the farms that'd been attacked by the bandits has gotten sick, and it doesn't look like anything anyone has seen before."

Ashinji frowned. "Does the man have strange swellings under his jaw and in his armpits and groin?" he asked.

"Why, yes, I do believe that was what his wife said. So far, he's the only one I know about, but there could be others."

Ashinji finished his dinner and thanked Taura and Mareo for their help.

A sliver of moon winked coyly from behind a cloud, so the stars had the sky nearly to themselves tonight. A short walk brought Ashinji to where his company camped at the center of the village. Gendan and the others greeted him as he arrived. A couple of trestle tables had been set up, and the remains of a substantial meal littered plates and platters. Several oil lamps on poles illuminated the area.

"Looks like you've all had just as good a dinner as I did," Ashinji commented, glancing around at the members of the company sitting or lounging on the grass.

"We've got some beer left, my lord, if you're still thirsty," said Gendan.

"Oh, I think I could manage one more mug," Ashinji responded, laughing. Gendan handed him an earthenware tankard filled to the brim, and Ashinji drained it in several swallows. He wiped his mouth on his sleeve and put the empty tankard down on the table.

"Gendan, Taura tells me that the plague has been reported on one of the farms recently attacked. That could mean that the bandits are infected."

"We've got to find them quickly then, and finish 'em off, my lord," Gendan replied.

"We'll ride directly to the fords tomorrow and cross over onto the Soldaran side," Ashinji continued. "Maybe, if we're lucky, we can find their camp, and if we are luckier still, they'll all be there." Ashinji sat down at the table beside the older man. "I suppose it'd be too much to hope that they can be persuaded to leave without us having to resort to bloodshed. I don't mind telling you, Gendan, that I have no taste for killing wretches, even if they are human."

"I doubt we'll have a choice, my lord," Gendan replied a little sternly, sounding a bit like a schoolmaster chiding a pupil for faulty logic. "The plague's got to be stopped."

"You're probably right, but I pray you're not," Ashinji said thoughtfully.

"Lord Ashinji, Captain Miri!" a voice called out from the darkness. "Kami is going to give us a song." Kami was the youngest of the company, a girl possessed of great skill at arms and an exceptional singing voice.

"We'll worry about the bandits when we catch them, my lord. Right now, I just want to hear Kami sing," Gendan said. Ashinji could see the flash of the captain's even, white teeth in the lamplight.

"A good plan, Captain," Ashinji agreed.

~~~

The Saihama River ran shallow and swift over a bed of gravel studded with larger rocks. These fords were the only place the river could be crossed for many leagues in either direction. The river had always been the undisputed boundary between the elven lands of Kerala on the north side, and the human duchy of Amsara to the south. This was the first time in many years that there had been any trouble. Amsara had never been a threat, despite its relative proximity, and Ashinji preferred to believe that the human lord of the duchy had no knowledge of the cross border attacks.

The horses splashed into the water, ankle deep, and Ashinji called a halt to allow the animals to drink. On the far shore, the forest grew dense and dark. After the horses had drunk their fill, the company continued across and headed west along the gravel-strewn bank, paralleling the trees.

"Stay alert, everyone," Ashinji instructed. He scanned the trees and the ground ahead, looking for any clue that people might be near. Day's end was near, and soon, nightfall would force them to break off their search and make camp.

"What do you say, Gendan? Should we go on or stop for the night?"

"Let's continue on a little further, my lord," Gendan suggested.

"What do you sense, Captain?" Ashinji asked, staring intently into the craggy face of the older man. The shadow of his helmet obscured Gendan's eyes, but Ashinji could see his mouth pursed thoughtfully.

"I had a premonition this morning that we'd find what we were looking for today...no, that *you*, my lord, would find what you've been waiting for." He shook his head. "I don't know what the last bit means, but I have a very strong feeling that whatever it is, it's close by."

Ashinji's heart skipped a beat. "My father has always put his complete trust in your advice, Gendan, and so shall I. We'll continue a little further." He urged his horse onward.

"Lord Ashinji, wait!" Gendan barked. Startled, Ashinji pulled up and turned in his saddle, frowning. Gendan pointed downstream. "Listen."

Ashinji heard it faintly at first, then more loudly. "Someone's shouting... in Soldaran!" Ashinji exclaimed. "They seem to be headed right for us." He checked the chin strap of his helmet and drew his sword. "Let's go!" He spurred his black gelding, and the horse immediately leaped forward into a gallop.

The company raced headlong down the riverbank, Ashinji and Gendan in the lead. Rocks shot out from underneath the horses' flying hooves, ricocheting off the soldiers' leather and metal clad bodies. As they thundered around a bend in the channel, Ashinji spotted a group of humans standing near the river's edge. They all froze for a heartbeat, then turned and began racing away along the bank, all except two, who stood rooted to the spot, either too terrified or astonished to run. Ashinji tightened his grip on his sword hilt and prepared to strike.

Suddenly, like deer startled by hunting hounds, the two humans leapt apart and away, the larger man taking off downstream after the rest of his retreating comrades, the smaller one—a boy from the look of him—running for the trees.

Clever move, thought Ashinji as he twisted in the saddle to mark where the smaller human had gone. For an instant, it had looked as though the boy's hands were glowing with magelight, but that was impossible. Humans had no magic.

"Gendan!" he shouted, pulling up and turning his horse so sharply that it reared back on its haunches. "Go after the main group. You know enough Soldaran to offer them surrender. Kill them only if you have to. I'll go after the boy." Gendan nodded and galloped off, the company riding at his back. Ashinji spurred the gelding into a canter towards the woods.

The trees were large and very close together, and Ashinji quickly decided that it would be pointless to ride in among them. The human boy would be able to evade him with ease. He halted and peered into the gloom, straining to detect any movement. The gelding whickered and looked off to the left, his black ears pointed forward. Turning his head ever so slightly, Ashinji looked out of the corner of his left eye in time to see a slight figure slip from the margin of the woods several yards upstream and start to run in the direction of the fords. He immediately gave chase.

The boy glanced over his shoulder and saw that he had been spotted. He began sprinting hard, his feet a blur on the pebbles, but Ashinji knew the young human could not outrun a galloping horse.

Please don't make me hurt you, Ashinji thought grimly as he bore down on the fleeing boy.

Suddenly, the boy tripped and went down. Ashinji shouted out a curse as he pulled back hard on the running horse, but it was too late to avoid riding over the boy's prone body. He heard a scream of pain as he threw himself from the saddle and ran to crouch beside the fallen human.

The boy lay very still, face down. His left arm was bent at an unnatural angle and blood soaked the torn cloth of his shirt over his ribcage. Ashinji could not see the boy's face, only his shock of tightly coiled, mahogany locks. A shiver of recognition passed through him. Slowly, he reached out, gripped the boy's shoulders, and gently rolled him over.

"Ai, Goddess!" Ashinji exclaimed. The shock of seeing her face drained all of the sensation from his arms and legs, leaving him unable to move. He sat down hard on his backside, staring. It was the girl from his dream!

She moaned, and her eyes fluttered open, alighting on his face. They were bright with pain and fear. She opened her bloodstained mouth and tried to scream but could only manage a croak. She began groping weakly at the empty sheath fastened to her hip as if trying to draw a knife that no longer hung there.

The look in her eyes revitalized Ashinji's enervated limbs. "You must lie still," he said softly in Soldaran. "My horse trampled you, and I do not know the extent of your wounds. I will not hurt you anymore, I swear." He unbuckled the strap of his helmet and pulled it from his head, tossing it to the ground.

If she can see my face, she might not feel so scared.

It seemed to work. The girl stopped moving and began to stare at him, as if transfixed. "I have some poppy juice in my saddlebag," he said. "It will ease your pain. I will go get it now."

Ashinji scrambled to his feet and spotted his horse a few paces away, head down, pulling at a tuft of grass growing among the stones. Quickly, he retrieved the poppy juice and returned to the girl's side. He uncorked the vial and slipped his hand beneath her head. "Drink this," he murmured, lifting her up so that she might sip more easily. Her eyes never left his face as she swallowed the drug. She appeared to be in a trance, with him as the focus. She took a final sip, shuddered, then was seized by a spasm of harsh coughing. A gout of bloody froth bubbled from her lips, and she clutched at her chest, sobbing. Abruptly, her eyes rolled back in her head, and she went limp. Shaking, Ashinji lowered her head gently to the ground, sat back on his heels, and took a deep breath.

Her skin was a shade or two darker than his, and the wild mass of hair, though shorter, was as he remembered it from the dream. She was dressed in plain, well-made clothes—a man's shirt, trousers, leather vest, and boots. Her features bore the unmistakable look of a *hikui,* one of mixed human-elf ancestry.

She was the most beautiful girl he had ever seen.

At that moment, Ashinji felt the world shift beneath him, as if the mighty tidal forces shaping his life had suddenly changed, pulling him in an entirely new direction. He had no idea why, but he knew with the bone-deep certainty of a man of faith that this was meant to be, that he and this girl were meant for each other. He could not—would not—let her die.

He looked up at the sound of approaching hoof beats. Gendan had returned.

"Lord Ashinji! Are you hurt?" the captain shouted in alarm at the sight of his young lord on his knees. He jumped down from his horse and ran over to where Ashinji knelt beside the injured, unconscious girl.

Ashinji waved his hand in reassurance. "No, Captain. I'm unhurt, but this girl here is, and badly. It's my fault. She fell, and I rode over her. Gendan…look at her. She's no bandit."

Gendan squinted down at the girl's drained, slack face and shrugged. "If you say so, my lord…We had to kill a few of the others," he reported laconically.

Ashinji looked at the captain sharply. "Was there no other way, Gendan?" he questioned, dismayed.

"I'm sorry, my lord, but I tried, I really did, but the miserable dogs wouldn't listen!" Gendan replied, clearly exasperated with his young lord. "I told 'em they could lay down their weapons, such as they were, and we'd let 'em go, but their leader just spat at me and then he threw a knife at my face!"

"Goddess' tits," Ashinji muttered.

"Once the three biggest ones were down, the others gave up. We let 'em go, and they all ran like rabbits back into the forest, all 'cept one." Gendan paused and looked thoughtfully at the unconscious girl. "He's not a bandit, either, I reckon. Dressed too well. Says he and his cousin were set upon in the woods by the others. Think this one must be the cousin? He said it was a girl. Hikui, by the look of her. Fancy that!"

"Help me with her, Gendan. Where is the man?"

"We've got him a ways down river. Tied up, just in case he's lying. I figured you'd want to question him yourself. Here, my lord, I'll carry the girl." Gendan stooped down and gathered the girl up into his arms. The jostling of her injured body stirred her partly awake, and she cried out in pain.

Ashinji felt a flare of anger. "Be careful with her, Gendan! She's hurt, and I don't know how badly yet."

"Your pardon, my lord," Gendan apologized, a look of puzzlement on his face. He settled the semi-conscious girl more gently in his arms and began walking. Ashinji gathered up the reins of the two horses and followed. His stomach was a swirling pit of anxiety.

The girl might be so hurt that she would die before he could get her back to Kerala Castle.

When did I make the decision to bring her back to Kerala? he thought. *The moment I saw her face, of course.*

A short walk past the bend in the river brought them within visual range of the rest of the company. Several of the troops stood in a cluster around a kneeling figure. They seemed loose-limbed and relaxed, as if they perceived no threat from their captive. They all snapped to attention when they caught sight of Ashinji and Gendan.

"This is the human, my lord," Gendan indicated the kneeling man with a lift of his chin. Someone had bound his hands securely behind him. An ugly bruise purpled the skin of his forehead just above the left eye, and a deep laceration had made a gory mask of his face.

The human's eyes fastened on Gendan's burden and widened in alarm. "My cousin! What have you done to her? Is she alive?" he cried, struggling against the leather cord that secured his hands. He attempted to regain his feet, but two of the soldiers roughly pushed him back and held him down.

"Enough! Leave him be," Ashinji snapped. The men obeyed immediately with murmured apologies, stepping back from the human, who ceased struggling and fixed his eyes upon Ashinji. Handing off the reins of the horses to a waiting soldier, Ashinji stepped up to the man and drew his knife. The human's eyes narrowed, and his nostrils flared; his entire body went rigid.

"I am not going to kill you. I am going to free your hands," Ashinji explained. He reached behind the man and severed the cord with a single cut.

The human sat for a moment, rubbing his chafed wrists and staring thoughtfully up at Ashinji. "The girl...she's my cousin. Please... tell me. Is she alive?" His eyes, a clear vibrant blue, glimmered with fear, but not for himself.

"She lives, but she is badly hurt, and I am entirely at fault," Ashinji answered.

"My lord, that is not..." Gendan interrupted indignantly, but Ashinji silenced him with a raised hand. The human glanced briefly at Gendan's face, uncomprehendingly, then returned his attention to Ashinji.

"I believed your cousin to be part of the gang of bandits we came here to deal with. She ran; I chased her. She fell in front of my horse, and I could not pull up quickly enough to avoid running over her. I am sorry."

"May I go to her?" the human asked.

"Of course." Ashinji stepped back as the man rose to his feet. He stood a few measures taller than everyone in the company, well built and strong. Gendan was right. This human, unlike the pathetic creatures lying dead and scattered on the riverbank, clearly was no bandit.

"Gendan, give this man his kinswoman," Ashinji ordered in Soldaran, so that the human would understand and know that he was sincere. Gendan complied, transferring the injured girl as gently as he could into the arms of her cousin. The poppy juice was exerting its effect, for the girl hardly stirred. The man whispered in her ear and cradled her close, closing his eyes and resting his bloody cheek against hers.

Ashinji felt torn. There was no question in his mind about the girl. He would take her back to Kerala, but what about the man, her cousin? Ashinji knew that the human would never permit his kinswoman to be carried away while he remained behind. The troops stirred restlessly.

Gendan stepped up and spoke softly. "What are we going to do with these two, my lord?" he asked.

Ashinji fixed Gendan with a determined look. "Have the troops gather some wood so we can burn these bodies," he said, pointing to the three corpses lying on the stones. "We don't know if they carry the plague, but we can't take any chances, so don't anyone touch them with bare hands. Also, make sure that everyone who handles them keeps their noses and mouths covered. After that's done, we'll camp down by the fords. Hurry, it's almost full dark."

"With respect, Lord Ashinji, but you didn't answer my question. What'll we do with these two humans?"

"I've decided that the girl is coming with us. Without a proper doctor, she'll most likely die. The man, well, I'll give him the choice of accompanying her, or returning to his home."

"My lord, you can't be serious! You can't bring humans back to

Kerala Castle!" Gendan's voice crackled with disapproval.

Ashinji rounded on him. "Look at her, Gendan. She is badly hurt, and I caused her to be in this deadly state. I can't abandon her now! Besides that, she is hikui, and that makes her one of our people. She and her cousin are obviously not bandits. Their clothes are clean and well made. I suspect they are from Amsara Castle, most likely retainers of the duke. I will offer them my help. Now, stop arguing with me and do as I say!"

"As you wish, my lord," Gendan bowed stiffly and turned to go. As he stalked off, Ashinji heard the captain muttering in irritation.

Ashinji sighed and turned his attention to the man and girl. The man had settled on a patch of turf with his cousin's head in his lap. Ashinji could just make out his features in the last glow of twilight. Somewhere in the dark woods, an owl screeched. The crickets were beginning to trill brightly in the tall reeds by the water's edge.

Ashinji knelt down in front of the two. "My name is Ashinji Sakehera. My father is Sen Sakehera, Lord of Kerala, the province just across the river from here."

"Magnes Preseren," the man replied. "This is my cousin, Jelena."

"What are you doing out here, Magnes Preseren? You are a long way from the nearest human settlement I know of. Are you servants of the duke?"

The man named Magnes laughed, and Ashinji thought he detected a bitter note. "Yes, we are from Amsara Castle, and yes, you could say we are both servants of the duke."

An unpleasant suspicion began to nag at Ashinji. He stood up. "I want to offer you my help for your cousin, Magnes Preseren, but if you are a wrongdoer fleeing the justice of your master, you must tell me now, or I will take the girl and leave you behind." His voice was hard, the threat behind his words clear.

"I am no wrongdoer, Lord Ashinji, but my cousin and I did flee Amsara Castle because it was impossible for us to stay." Something in the human's voice, a quality of sadness and loss, convinced Ashinji that, in this, he spoke the truth, although Ashinji felt certain that there was much more to the story than the man seemed willing to tell.

"I believe you," Ashinji said, relaxing and hunkering back down so that his face and the human's were on the same level. The girl stirred and whimpered, and Ashinji's heart skipped a beat. Involuntarily, he reached out and touched her shoulder. He could feel the human's eyes boring into his skull like a surgeon's trephine.

Slowly, he withdrew his hand. "I will take your cousin back to my father's house. Kerala Castle is about two days' ride to the northwest, but it may take us longer since we have two extra to carry and no spare horses. We have an excellent doctor there. I suggest you allow me to do this, since she does not have much of a chance otherwise. You, of course, are welcome to accompany her."

A sudden flare of bright orange light splashed outwards, illuminating a broad stretch of the riverbank and woods. The pyre was lit. The hungry, cleansing flames rapidly consumed the bodies of the dead bandits. In the morning, Ashinji would order the ashes and bones to be scattered.

"I won't leave my cousin," the human stated flatly.

Ashinji nodded. "I did not think that you would. When my troops are finished, we will move upstream to the fords and camp for the night." He stood up again and turned to go.

"Lord Ashinji," the human called out. Ashinji turned. "Thank you."

Ashinji nodded wordlessly and went to find Gendan.

CHAPTER 13

THE BEAUTIFUL ONES

Are we your prisoners?" Magnes asked bluntly.

The elf named Ashinji Sakehera smiled slightly and shook his head. "Quite the contrary. You are my guests, and under my protection. When we arrive at Kerala, you will be my father's guests. Perhaps you were expecting us to be... not so hospitable."

"I really don't know what to expect of you, Lord Ashinji. So much of what I have been taught about your people, I'm ashamed to say, is very negative."

"Do you believe what you have been taught...about my people?"

Magnes answered without hesitation. "No," he said.

"How is your head?"

"It aches a bit, but that salve you gave me took away the worst of the pain."

"Good. I have tried to make your cousin as comfortable as is possible under the circumstances."

"I'm grateful," Magnes replied.

After the elven soldiers had finished their gruesome task of burning the corpses of the slain bandits, the entire party moved upstream and made camp by the fords. Lord Ashinji ordered one of his troopers to see to Jelena's injuries. Magnes was impressed by the man's gentle handling of his cousin, and some of his apprehension began to dissipate. Now heavily sedated, her arm splinted and her torso tightly bound in order to stabilize a suspected rib fracture, Jelena lay close by the campfire, cocooned in several blankets with another folded beneath her head as a pillow.

Ashinji Sakehera sat down opposite Magnes and held out a wooden bowl and cup. "Cold rations, I am afraid. No one in my company likes to cook," he explained, smiling ruefully. Magnes took the proffered food with a word of thanks. The bowl contained a round cake of some kind and a hunk of pale yellow cheese. He sipped cautiously at the brimming liquid in the cup and discovered it to be beer, and quite good. He took a bite of the cake and smiled in pleasant surprise. It was delicious, and he eagerly crammed another large bite into his mouth. He looked up to see the young elf lord laughing.

"What is this? It's wonderful," he said, chewing enthusiastically.

"It is journeycake. There are many ways to make it, but this particular batch is made of oats, dried venison, elderberries, and sweetened with a little honey. My mother's recipe. I am glad you like it. We have more, if you want."

Magnes washed down the cake with a swig of the excellent beer. As he ate, he surreptitiously studied the face of his host. These were the first full-blooded elves he had ever seen, and he found himself completely fascinated by them. He had always heard that they were extraordinarily beautiful, and now he saw with his own eyes that that particular rumor, at least, was true. Being no astute judge of male attractiveness, nevertheless, even Magnes could see that the elves' young leader stood out, even among so comely a group.

Magnes estimated Ashinji's age to be somewhere between twenty and twenty-five years although he couldn't be sure; he knew that elves had a much longer life span than did humans. The elf lord moved with the fluid grace of a forest cat and his hair, worn in a long queue down his back, shone like gold in the firelight. Magnes couldn't help but admire the graceful lines of the other man's ears—like Jelena's, except sharper at their tips. A strange, uncomfortable rush of emotion caused Magnes to lower his eyes, worried that the elf would witness his confusion. He took a deep breath to slow his racing heart and drained his cup in one gulp.

Through sheer force of will, he made himself look at Lord Ashinji's face again. The other man seemed unaware of Magnes's inner turmoil. He, too, sipped at a mug of beer and chewed a mouthful journeycake, but his eyes were on Jelena, and Magnes was startled at the intensity of his gaze.

Magnes cleared his throat, and the other man looked up inquiringly. "Your knowledge of Soldaran is excellent, Lord Ashinji," he commented, and silently gave thanks to the gods for keeping his voice steady.

"Does that surprise you?" the elf asked, one eyebrow arching upwards in amusement.

"There will be many things about your people that are going to surprise me, I think," Magnes answered.

"Most people here in the borderlands know a little Soldaran, but I am a bit of an amateur scholar in my free time," Ashinji explained. "I am fluent in your language so that I may study your great mathematicians."

Magnes nodded, impressed.

Just then, the much older man, whom Magnes surmised to be Lord Ashinji's second-in-command, walked up and spoke to his lord. He carried a helmet in his hands.

Ashinji, smiling, reached up and took the helmet from the other man. He spoke a few words and waved his hand in dismissal. "Gendan found my helmet, finally. I was afraid I would have to go searching for it first thing tomorrow morning," he said, switching back into Soldaran. He laid the helmet down beside him and fixed his brilliant green eyes upon Magnes. "Now, Magnes Preseren. Tell me who you really are, and what you and your cousin are doing out here so far from Amsara Castle." The look on his face told Magnes that he would brook no more evasion.

"I didn't lie to you, Lord Ashinji. I just... failed to tell you the entire truth, but I felt justified in holding back until I could figure out what your intentions were. You must admit that our meeting was not exactly under ideal circumstances. Your people attacked my cousin and me. How was I to know that you weren't going to kill us later on?"

"Point taken. Go on."

"My name really is Magnes Preseren, but I'm not one of the duke's retainers. I'm his son... his Heir, in fact. My cousin Jelena is the daughter of my father's dead sister."

Ashinji's eyes widened slightly at this revelation, and he glanced over his shoulder at the sleeping form of Jelena. "Why would two noble-born humans disguise themselves as servants and flee their home? Why did you come here, rather than go somewhere else in the Empire? Did you lose your way and wander this close to the border by accident?" The elf lord seemed genuinely puzzled, yet, there was a probing quality to his questions, as if he were seeking information of the utmost importance.

"It's a long and complex story," Magnes sighed. "It could hardly have escaped your notice that my cousin is a half-elf. Her mother had a liaison with one of your people and suffered mightily for it. The family disowned her, and she died giving birth to Jelena. My father refused to accept his sister's bastard as a member of his house and so allowed my cousin to be raised in the servants' hall. She's lived her whole life as an outsider, despised and abused by most everyone at Amsara."

"Everyone, except you," Ashinji interjected.

"Yes, and Claudia, the woman who raised her. The two of us have always been Jelena's protectors."

"Are all bastard children treated with such contempt among humans?" Ashinji asked.

"No, they are not. Jelena was singled out because of her sire." Magnes paused briefly before continuing. "It shames me to tell you this, but from early childhood, when we Soldarans learn about our religion from the priests and our parents, we are taught that your people—the elves—are the spawn of demons. Elves have no souls and are therefore accursed, doomed never to know the love and light of the gods. Any human who would willingly consort with a demon is despoiled, and the offspring of that union is itself a soulless, accursed creature." He chuckled humorlessly. "This, Lord Ashinji, is the world my beautiful, kind, loving cousin has lived in."

"Please, you may call me Ashinji, for we are both of the same rank, it seems," the elf insisted. "Why is it that you believe differently, Magnes Preseren? You, who are the son and Heir of a duke?"

Magnes shrugged. "I've always been different. I could never accept that the girl I grew up with, played with, loved as a sister, was anything less than a complete being, with a warm, loving soul. It was all just ignorance and superstition, and it always infuriated me."

"We elves are not without prejudice," Ashinji admitted. "Take my captain, Gendan Miri, as an example. He is typical in his attitude toward humans. Oh, he acknowledges that you humans are intelligent and good at many things, but he believes that elves are more evolved… superior, in fact. In Alasiri, we have people of mixed blood—*hikui* we call them—who live among us… not many, but a significant number. I am sorry to say that they suffer legal discrimination, in many aspects of life, but they are not generally despised or abused. If Jelena had been born in my country, she would have had a much better life." He poked at the fire with a long stick, sending a cloud of bright sparks whirling up into the night sky. "Out here on the frontier, things are looser, more tolerant," he continued. "There are a lot of people living out here with a human or two in their family trees."

"How do you feel about humans and…*hikui?*" Magnes asked slowly.

Ashinji regarded him thoughtfully for several moments, as if trying to decide just exactly how to frame his response. Magnes found himself growing uncomfortably warm under that brilliant, green gaze. "I have never spoken to a human before I met you. I, too, grew up with certain ideas about your people that I have never really questioned until now. I am revising my opinion even as we speak. As for how I feel about those of mixed race, I have always felt that they should have the same rights under the law as any *okui*, our word for pureblood."

"So, my cousin is going to be an outsider here as well, made to feel as if she doesn't quite belong…Gods!" Magnes muttered angrily. "She doesn't deserve this. All she wants is to find a real family!"

"Does your cousin know her father's name?" Ashinji asked, leaning forward slightly to look into Jelena's sleeping face.

"He called himself Zin," Magnes replied.

"Hmm. Zin is really just a *bukuza*… a nickname. That is all she knows about him? It would be far more useful if she knew his family name, at least. That way, we would know if he was noble or common."

"Gods! I almost forgot. She carries a ring that belonged to him. It hangs on chain around her neck. I'll get it for you."

"No, no, do not disturb her. Just describe the ring to me."

"It's made of white gold, with a black stone set flush in the band.

There's a griffin, also white, inlaid into the center of the stone." Ashinji reacted as if he'd just heard something completely unexpected and altogether startling. "What? What is it? Do you recognize the signet?" Magnes eagerly asked.

"I...I am not sure," Ashinji replied. He frowned, and pulled on the gold rings in his left ear, staring at Jelena intently all the while. Then he shook his head as if answering a question in his own mind. "I do not recognize it exactly, but it could fit the devices of several noble families, or it could be someone's personal device. My father should be able to figure it out." He rose to his feet and stretched. "I have something in my saddlebag I want you to try," he said, then strode away into the dark.

Magnes leaned over to check on Jelena. She remained deep in a drug-induced slumber. He adjusted the blankets around her then allowed his eyes to slowly scan the campsite.

The man named Gendan Miri sat a few paces away, a very young, strawberry blonde woman at his side. They were deep in conversation, and Magnes focused in on the musical cadences of their speech, allowing the alien words to flow into his ears like warm rain. The elves' language, the sound of their voices, was as beautiful as they were. Most of the others had retired for the night, little more than dark lumps on the riverbank. Two troopers stood guard.

Ashinji returned shortly, carrying something in his hand. It was a small metal flask, which he offered to Magnes. "Have a taste of this," he said, an enigmatic smile on his face. Magnes took the flask and pulled the stopper. He raised it to his lips and took a sip.

Magnes had never been to the southern islands to behold the great volcanoes there. It was said that when they awoke, the mighty mountains belched clouds of burning smoke, and rivers of molten rock poured forth from their steaming maws. The liquid that ran down his throat must surely be a distillation of the essence of those rivers of fire. He gasped and choked, then began coughing helplessly. Tears streamed down his face as he fought to catch his breath. Ashinji deftly snatched the flask from his hands before it could drop to the ground.

When he could finally talk again, he looked up accusingly at the young elf lord. To his chagrin, Ashinji was laughing. "You...you knew that was going to happen, didn't you?" he spluttered.

Ashinji looked a little sheepish, but made no attempt to hide his amusement. "I am sorry, but you should see yourself. I did not know a human could get so red in the face. I hoped that you would be able to take the *muato* a little bit better than you did, but believe me, one does acquire a taste for it. The first time is always the hardest, but you will get used to it," he promised cheerfully.

"I hardly think…hey, that is good." The potent liquor had settled in Magnes's stomach like a red-hot coal, but it was cooling rapidly, and like steam, rose straight to his head. He nodded in pleasure, beginning to feel its full effects. "Tha…tha' has got t'be the strongest stuff ever made, much stronger than anythin' we have back home."

"I knew you would like it. It is a drink shared only between close friends and allies." Ashinji tilted his head back and took a sip. He re-corked the flask and sat down beside Magnes.

"How do you know I'm your friend…or your ally?" Magnes asked, speaking slowly and carefully, so that his words would not slur. His tongue had turned into an unwieldy turnip in his mouth.

Ashinji tapped his forehead with one elegant finger. "I know because I have an instinct about people, and because you have brought something that is meant for me."

Magnes puzzled over Ashinji's words. What, in the names of all of the gods, did the other man mean? Magnes had no more possessions, for everything he had brought out of Amsara had been lost. He could not possibly have anything that was meant for this young elven lord, unless Ashinji had been speaking metaphorically.

Before Magnes could reply, Ashinji slapped his knees and stood up. "Well, it is time that I go to bed. I have left the vial of poppy juice for you, in case your cousin awakes and has need of it. If you need me during the night, I will be close by, just over there." He pointed toward a spot nearer the water's edge. Magnes nodded. "Good night, then."

"G'night." Magnes lay down and snuggled close against Jelena. Exhaustion and the *muato* were pulling him down inexorably toward sleep. He hoped that if Jelena needed him, he would be able to respond. His last thoughts just before sleep claimed him were of Ashinji's odd statement.

Tomorrow, he would ask for an explanation.

CHAPTER 14

JELENA'S ANGEL

Jelena stood alone on a gray, featureless plain. Above her head hung a blank sky and below her feet, gray dust, stretching out until the two met at the horizon. She turned around slowly, looking in all directions, but one direction seemed much like another.

How did I come to be in this place?

She began walking. Her footfalls sent little puffs of dust spurting into the still air. Oddly, she could not tell if she was actually moving forward, even though she watched herself place one foot before the other. She had no way of knowing how long she walked; time did not exist in this strange, gray world.

The sensation started as a dull ache in her chest that rapidly grew into something far more intense. She stopped walking and looked down to see that, beneath her skin, where her living heart should be, a bright light now burned. Its color was bluish white, and so intense that it hurt her to look upon it. Instinctively, she knew that this was the source of the magic that she carried within her—powerful, wonderful, and dangerous. As she stared at the light, it began to pulsate in a steady rhythm, just as her own heart would have, had it still been a part of her.

She covered the light with her hands, but its rays bled through her fingers.

I mustn't let it out… can't let it be seen—but why?

Then, she knew.

Someone, or some *thing*, was searching for the magic—searching for her!

I must not let it find me!

She took a step forward and in the space of an eye blink, found herself standing at the edge of an impossibly high cliff. A wine-dark, restless sea heaved and sighed below. In the strange logic of dreams, only one course of action made sense. She spread out her arms like the wings of a gull and jumped, hurtling down toward the hungry waves. She pierced the surface of the water like an arrow and was immediately seized by a powerful current that tugged her relentlessly downward. Fiercely, she fought against it, stroking hard towards the surface, exploding upward at last with a cry...and awakened to find herself being rocked along on the back of a horse.

"*Shhhh...* I'm here," Magnes whispered into her ear. His arms encircled and held her steady before him. Her arm and chest ached with dull intensity, but she found herself slipping back towards un-consciousness, and she hadn't the strength to fight it. She let go...

...and awakened again, this time on her back, lying in a nest of blankets. She felt uncomfortably warm, and her body hurt with in-credible ferocity. She struggled, but was too weak to free herself. Just as she decided to give up, exhausted, the angel appeared.

It was the same one who had come to her the first time, when she lay dying on the riverbank. She stared up helplessly into the whirling green depths of its eyes, unable to look away. It was breathtakingly beautiful—all gold, emerald, and alabaster. It reached down and laid a hand on her burning forehead, and she sighed at the blessed cool-ness of its touch. She closed her eyes and waited for it to carry her up to the gods on its mighty wings.

~~~

Jelena awoke, clear-headed, to the sound of birdsong. She lay quietly for a few moments and took a mental inventory of her body, relieved to find that all parts were still present and more or less intact.

She opened her eyes and scanned her surroundings. She found herself lying in a very large, comfortable bed in a dimly lit chamber. Sunlight filtered in through the partly opened shutters of a window next to the bed. She sat up and pushed the covers away. A fine, sheer gown of white cotton clothed her body. A tight bandage encircled her torso, just beneath her breasts, and a sling held her splinted left arm tight against her side. She was clean and dry, and a quick check of her hair told her that it had been combed recently. She blushed in embarrassment, contemplating her absolute dependency on her as yet unknown benefactors.

The urgent need to relieve herself drove her to seek a chamber pot. She swung her legs over the side of the bed to the mat-covered floor and attempted to stand, but she was too weak. Her legs buckled, and she fell. Jolts of pain shot through her arm and chest, wringing a scream from her tightly clenched jaws. A warm flood of urine gushed down from between her legs, soaking the gown and the mats upon which she lay sprawled and helpless.

She heard a door fly open and then the sound of footsteps rapidly approaching. A voice—female—gasped, then exclaimed in words Jelena could not understand. She felt hands, strong but gentle, lift her up into a sitting position.

Jelena gaped.

The woman who crouched before her was in late middle age, with a handsome, kind face and soft brown eyes. Her high cheekbones, the upward sweep of her eyebrows, the ears that tapered to delicate points—all were more pronounced versions of the features that Jelena had seen in her own mirror her entire life. "You…you're an elf," she whispered. The fact that an elf woman knelt here meant only one thing.

She and Magnes had reached the Western Lands.

The woman spoke gently, indicating with gestures that Jelena should remain where she sat. Jelena was only too happy to comply. She felt woozy and slightly sick to her stomach. The woman left and returned shortly with a pitcher, basin, a stack of cloths, and a fresh gown, and proceeded to get Jelena cleaned up and back into bed. When she had finished and Jelena was settled, she rolled up the urine-soaked mats and carried them with her out of the room, closing the door softly behind her. Jelena sighed and sank back into the cloud of pillows.

Even if I'm not dead, surely this is what the home of the gods must be like.

She closed her eyes.

She must have dozed off for a while, for suddenly, Magnes was there, sitting by the bed, and she had no memory of him entering the chamber. "Magnes!" she cried, reaching for him with her good arm. They embraced and held each other in silence for a time.

At last, Magnes spoke. "Jelena my dear, dear cousin! I've been frantic with worry. You've been in and out for days. Your fever broke only last night. The doctor wasn't sure you would live."

"Magnes, are we in the Western Lands? I saw an elf woman... here! She helped me...I think she's been taking care of me. Magnes, did we..."

"Whoa! Slow down, Cousin... You've only just awakened. Yes, we made it. We are in Alasiri. How much of what happened do you remember?"

Jelena shook her head. "Not much. Things are pretty confused and jumbled up." She reclined back against the pillows and tried to think. "I remember bandits, and running, and being chased by someone on a horse, then it all becomes a big blur."

"You don't remember telling me about the angel you saw?" Magnes asked with a sly grin.

"I...I do remember something like that... a beautiful face bending over me. I thought it was an angel and I was dying. I saw it twice." Magnes smiled again, enigmatically, and Jelena regarded him with a quizzical expression. "I know now that it wasn't an angel, Magnes. But I saw something, or someone... didn't I?"

Magnes laughed. "Yes, Cousin, you did. Your angel is the son of the lord of this place. His name's Ashinji Sakehera, and his father is Sen Sakehera, Lord of Kerala. We are guests in Kerala Castle. Ashinji brought you here to save your life. It was he who accidentally trampled you with his horse. He was chasing you because he thought you were one of the bandits. You tripped and fell, and he couldn't stop in time." He gently tapped the splint bracing Jelena's broken arm. "The doctor here is amazing. Elven medicine is far more advanced than anything the quacks and leeches can do back home. You had a punctured lung, but he fixed it without killing you. No human doctor would be capable of that."

Suddenly, Jelena remembered her father's ring. She groped for it at her neck but it, and the chain that it hung on, was gone.

"Magnes… my ring! Where is it?" she asked urgently.

Magnes patted her shoulder reassuringly. "Don't worry. It's safe. I have it here." He pulled aside the neck of his tunic to show the ring hanging securely over his heart. "I showed it to Ashinji, and he's promised to take it to his father when you're ready."

"Magnes, there's something else I remember. The blue fire…It came, right when the bandits were about to attack us on the riverbank. Did I…"

A soft knock at the door interrupted Jelena's sentence. Magnes rose from his chair and went to see who had come. "Ashinji, come in. She's awake." Magnes opened the door wide to admit the visitor, who crossed the room in four strides and knelt beside the bed.

Jelena could only stare, speechless.

My angel, she thought.

"Jelena, I am Ashinji," he said. As he held her gaze, Jelena felt a strange pressure in her head, almost as if something struggled to get in past some barrier, something vitally important.

"Ashinji," Magnes scolded playfully, "You've struck my poor cousin dumb."

The emerald eyes turned aside, and the pressure on her mind lifted, leaving her with an inexplicable sense of loss. "She is tired, I think. Perhaps I should go away and come back later, yes?"

Abruptly, Jelena found her voice. "No! Please…stay, Lord Ashinji. There are so many things I wish to know."

"Please, just Ashinji. You, especially, Jelena, need never bow to me." He spoke Soldaran with a lilting accent that sounded almost musical. "I know you have many questions, but there will be time enough for them later. Now, you should eat."

As if on cue, the door opened, and the older woman who had helped Jelena earlier returned, carrying a tray laden with dishes. Ashinji and the woman spoke briefly; then, she handed over the tray to him and withdrew. "Here is some soup, a little cheese, bread, and tea. Please try to eat," he urged. "You have been without nourishment for many days, and you cannot heal properly if you do not restore your energy." He gently settled the tray down on Jelena's blanket-covered lap.

"I'll see to it that she eats every bite," Magnes promised.

"I shall leave you, then, but I promise to return soon," Ashinji said, flashing a quick smile.

Jelena watched him go, and when the door closed on him, it felt like clouds had dowsed the sun. "He…he's…" she stammered.

"Yes," Magnes sighed, "he is."

~~~

Jelena had been in bed for nearly a week. Now, restless and bored, she longed to escape the confines of the comfortable chamber for some fresh air and spring sunshine. Her body was healing with satisfactory speed, and with each passing day, she felt a little stronger.

Magnes was a steady presence at her bedside and served as her informant on the exotic world in which they now found themselves. Each day, he reported on something new he had learned, and it soon became clear to both of them that, despite the many differences that existed between humans and elves, there were similarities as well.

In addition to Magnes's company, Jelena had Ashinji's visits to bolster her spirits. The young elf lord came to see her daily, and Jelena looked forward to his arrival with great anticipation. At first, she had been too tongue-tied to do more than stammer the briefest of answers to his questions, but his patient good humor soon put her at ease.

Ashinji told her much about himself in those first few days. Before long, she knew that he was the second-born in a family of five, that he served as a captain in the army, and that his eldest sibling—a brother—was to be wed in a few short weeks. He did not press her for any personal details, but she found herself telling him the entire bitter story of her life, nonetheless.

At last, the day came when the doctor, a kindly man with twinkling blue eyes, pronounced Jelena fit to leave her sickbed. Her nurse, who she had learned was named Mizu, helped her to dress in the tunic and loose trousers favored by elven women, and brought a semblance of order to her hair with a few cleverly placed pins. She finished by gently rewrapping the sling on Jelena's mending left arm, then slipped a pair of sandals onto her charge's feet.

Jelena studied herself in the full-length mirror that stood in one corner of the chamber. She barely recognized the well-dressed young woman who stared back at her from the slightly irregular surface of the glass. A soft knock at the door heralded Ashinji's arrival. He had promised her a tour of Kerala Castle and an introduction to his parents.

Mizu threw open the door and greeted her young master with warm words. At the sound of his voice, Jelena's heart did its usual flip-flop. She turned away from the mirror to face him.

"You look lovely today," Ashinji said, a smile lighting up his face. "Elven dress suits you." Jelena felt a blush warm her cheeks. No man, besides Magnes, had ever complemented her on her appearance before.

Ashinji wore a sleeveless unbleached cotton tunic, breeches, and sandals. The absence of sleeves on his shirt allowed Jelena to observe, for the first time, the intricate, flowing designs of the tattoos that encircled each of his upper arms. Soldaran men never willingly submitted to tattooing; that was reserved for slaves only. It seemed that elves tattooed themselves of their own free will. The designs were as fascinating as their owner.

"Will Magnes be joining us?" Jelena cursed inwardly at the slight quaver in her voice.

"I assure you, I will behave myself," Ashinji replied.

"Oh, no, that's not what I meant!" Jelena exclaimed. "I would never..." Her voice trailed off as Ashinji laughed heartily. She sighed, realizing that, of course, he understood perfectly well what she had meant.

"Magnes is down in the practice yard with Captain Miri, trying out some of our weapons. Apparently, our swords are not like the Soldaran blades he is used to. He will join us later." He held out his hand. "Come. I will show you around first; then you will meet my parents, and perhaps my sisters as well."

Jelena shyly reached out with her good arm and allowed Ashinji to close his hand around hers. His fingers were graceful and strong, and he held her smaller hand firmly, yet not so tight that she could not easily escape if she so desired. She had no desire to escape...ever.

As Ashinji started towards the door, Jelena held back. He turned to look at her and asked, "Is there something wrong?"

"No," she replied. "There's nothing wrong. It's just...Well, I still can't believe I'm here, is all." She felt giddy with exhilaration and terror all at once. Simply to be alive and standing in this room seemed like no less than a miracle to her.

She took a deep breath and let it out slowly. From somewhere outside, the sound of a bell, deep-voiced and brazen, slowly rang out the hour. Ashinji smiled.

"You are here, and you are safe," he said. "Are you ready to go?"

"Yes. Please...Lead on," Jelena replied.

Chapter 15

Kerala Castle

Ashinji led Jelena along a short corridor to a descending staircase. He slipped his arm around her shoulders, lending her support. She felt grateful for the help—her legs were still a little weak from disuse, and it gave her a chance to be close to him. She wanted so much to rest her head on his collarbone and breathe in his scent—so different from that of a human man—but she dared not. Ashinji had been unfailingly polite and decorous; his behavior was totally in keeping with his high station. It would be shamefully presumptuous to think that he would welcome such attentions, especially from her, a foreigner and a half-breed.

I must keep my feelings under control, keep things in perspective, she thought. *I could get swept away so easily! There could never be anything between Ashinji and me other than friendship.*

Three flights down and through another door, they emerged onto an outside landing above a sunny courtyard. Jelena looked up and saw that she had been lodged on the uppermost floor of a semi-detached wing off the main building. They descended the wooden staircase to the gravel-covered yard below.

"Come. I will lead you around to the front of the main hall," Ashinji said. He released his hold on her shoulders and beckoned with a wave of his hand. Jelena sighed regretfully and started after him, her eyes in constant motion as she took in her surroundings.

Jelena had spent her entire life within the walls and precincts of Amsara Castle, and she knew the details of its architecture intimately, thanks partly to Magnes, but mostly from her own explorations. Kerala

Castle seemed nothing like Amsara at first glance. They crossed the small courtyard and exited through a wooden gate carved with the figures of fantastical beasts. A gravel path led off through a garden of flowering shrubbery. The perfume of the blossoms hung lightly in the warm air, like the sweet promise of spring.

To the right loomed the main bulk of the castle. Built in a series of graduated tiers—Jelena counted four in all—the castle resembled a multi-layered cake crowned by a sloping tiled roof with upturned corners. Rain gutters, shaped like the heads of dragons, adorned each corner. The walls were of white plastered wood, set with many narrow rectangular windows in the bottom three tiers. The fourth and highest tier, Jelena could see, had fewer but much larger windows, a feature she had never seen in any building before. She imagined that they afforded an amazing view of the surrounding countryside. At the moment, most of the castle's upper windows were open to the spring breezes. The entire structure sat atop an imposing base of tightly fitted stone blocks, pierced at regular intervals with what looked like arrow slits.

Off to the left, Jelena could see the castle's inner wall rising like a stone curtain above the garden. The figures of sentries, silhouetted darkly against the bright spring sky, made slow progress along the battlements. The path and the garden ended at a large yard that fronted the castle's main wing. At the top of a short flight of wide, shallow steps, a pair of spear-toting guards flanked the castle's entrance. At present, the heavy rectangular wooden doors stood open. Directly opposite, a gate pierced the curtain wall, topped by a gatehouse built with the same style of sloping tiled roof as the main castle. The massive, iron-bound leaves of the gate proper also stood open, but Jelena could not tell what lay beyond.

Ashinji stopped and opened his arms expansively, as if he wished to embrace the entire castle complex. "This is my home," he said with a touch of pride in his voice. "Through there," he pointed at the gate, "the ground slopes rather steeply down to the base of the hill where the outer wall is built. The main gate leads out onto a bridge that spans the south channel of the river. You cannot really tell from up here, but Kerala Castle is built on a rocky island in the middle of the Saihama River. You Soldarans call the river Janica."

Jelena nodded in understanding. "How far are we from…where you found my cousin and me?" Jelena asked.

"About two days' ride west from the fords. Maybe twelve of your leagues. Come. I will take you down to the lower yard." As they walked toward the open gate, Ashinji continued his commentary. "My ancestor Kaiji Sakehera built Kerala Castle about nine hundred years ago. My family has been here ever since. The original castle was much smaller than it is now. Each lord since Kaiji has added to it so it now takes up the entire island. My father has not done any new construction, but he has done a lot of remodeling, mostly to modernize the place."

As they passed beneath the gatehouse, the two guards snapped to attention. One of them called out what sounded to Jelena like a greeting, which Ashinji answered with a smile and a wave.

"Your language sounds so… I don't know… so *musical*," Jelena observed. "It's beautiful to listen to."

"I would be happy to teach you to speak Siri-dar. It is as much a part of your heritage as is Soldaran. That is, if you choose to stay among us." He stopped walking and turned to face her. Something in his face and eyes, there and gone in an instant, left Jelena feeling a little bewildered. She got the distinct impression of someone filled with intense longing for a thing that they feared they could not have.

Careful, don't get carried away, she cautioned herself.

"I would very much like that," she replied, and was rewarded by his smile, a flash of strong, white teeth. They started walking again down the sloping path that led towards the lower yards. Jelena could see the gate more clearly now, with its double-sided gatehouse and guard towers at each corner. In the yard below lay the stables, the smithy, and what looked like guard barracks. Off to the right lay a large, flat, grassy area, a smaller yard enclosed on three sides by a brick wall topped with a partial roof, and several buildings Jelena couldn't readily identify. The myriad sounds of a working castle, so familiar to a young woman raised in a place much like this one, drifted upward on warm draughts of air.

There were many people about—plainly dressed servants hurrying on various errands, off-duty soldiers lounging in the shade, a small pack of laughing children. Everyone they passed offered a warm smile and a greeting to Ashinji, and he responded in kind. Clearly, Jelena thought, the people of Kerala harbored a great affection for their young lord.

The sound of a bleating goat unexpectedly jabbed a thorn of home-sickness into her heart. She thought of Claudia and had to quickly pretend to wipe grit from her eyes in order to cover her tears. She imagined her foster mother, elbow-deep in suds, calling out orders to the laundry drudges under her command. Later, Claudia would take her midday meal in the kitchen with the other servants, surrounded by people she had known most of her life, yet feeling alone, without the girl she had raised as her daughter. That night, she would re-tire to the room that she and Jelena had shared for so long, and she would truly be alone.

"Ah, here is your cousin," Ashinji announced, breaking Jelena's melancholy reverie. Magnes strode up the path towards them, sip-ping from a waterskin. They walked down to meet him.

"Whew! Your man Gendan gave me quite a workout, Ashinji," Magnes exclaimed. "The swords they make here are excellent, Jelena. And you should see their armor. Truly exceptional. I still can't figure out how it's done, even after examining Ashinji's up close." Magnes's flushed face dripped with sweat, and the linen elven-style tunic he wore was soaked through. He beamed at Jelena. "Cousin, you are looking almost like your old self again. I believe I can see the roses blooming in your cheeks as we speak."

A pair of female servants hurried past them, skirting a wide path around Magnes. They greeted Ashinji deferentially, all the while glancing sidelong at Magnes and Jelena. Jelena wondered at the look in their eyes.

"My friend, if you wish to meet my parents later, then a bath and a change of clothes will be needed," Ashinji said politely. "I mean no offense, you understand."

"None taken," Magnes assured him. "I have gotten used to bath-ing every day, and I quite like it. Jelena, now that you have been freed from your bed, you can discover for yourself the pleasures of the elven bathhouse. It's like nothing we have in Amsara."

"I thought I might take Jelena up to the top of the wall for a view of the countryside…that is, if you feel up to climbing the stairs,"

Ashinji said, smiling at Jelena.

I'd climb a mountain after you, she thought. "I think I can make it," she replied aloud.

"I'm off to get cleaned up, then," Magnes said cheerily. "I'll meet you back at the castle. He turned and headed up the path toward the upper gate. Jelena watched him go, and her heart swelled with love and gratitude. Magnes had sacrificed everything and risked his life in order to help get her here. She had no idea how she would ever repay him.

"Your cousin is a very interesting man," Ashinji remarked as they approached one of several staircases leading up to the battlements. He slipped a hand under Jelena's elbow to support her as they began to climb. "We have had many good talks. It is truly frightening how many misconceptions exist between our peoples. It saddens me deeply."

"Magnes is my best and only friend," Jelena replied. "He has always protected me." Her breath caught in her throat as they reached the top of the stairs and she could at last see out over the wall.

The island upon which Kerala Castle stood reared steeply up from the riverbed and gave the fortress a commanding view of the surrounding countryside. A sturdy wooden bridge connected island to shore. A small guard post stood at the far end of the span. The land spread out in gently undulating folds beyond the flashing, foaming waters. To the east and south lay forest, to the west the deep green of pasture land, crisscrossed with low stone walls. Fat brown and white cattle munched contentedly on the lush spring grass.

Jelena sighed, feeling a measure of peace begin to slide into her soul. She relaxed and let her mind wander for a time, simply enjoying the warmth of the sun on her face and Ashinji's quiet presence at her side.

After a while, Ashinji pointed westward. "That way lies Sendai, where resides our king. It is many days' ride from here. Kerala is at the easternmost border of Alasiri and so faces two human realms—that of the Soldaran Empire to the south and the land of the Urghus to the east. We elves have never had any reason to fear the Urghus. They prefer to remain on their windy steppes, beyond the Kesen Numai Mountains. Occasionally, a trading party will cross the high passes in summer to sell us horses in exchange for luxury goods like silk cloth, jewelry, or steel weapons. The Soldarans, on the other hand…"

"Magnes has shown me books written by Soldaran historians about the wars between the Empire and Alasiri," Jelena interjected, "but it has been many years since there has been any fighting. Surely, you don't think that the peace will be broken?"

Ashinji's brow furrowed and he turned to gaze at her with troubled eyes. "Magnes has said that the Soldarans talk of war, that there are rumors of the empress wishing to reclaim territory that she believes rightly belongs to the Empire, and in truth, we believe that these are more than just rumors. The king has called a meeting of the High Council of Lords to take place at the end of summer to discuss the possibility that by next spring, Alasiri will have to defend against an attack by the Imperial Army."

"Will that mean you would have to fight?" Jelena asked quietly.

"I am an officer. I would lead a company, yes."

Jelena sensed that, behind Ashinji's simple words, lay some very complicated emotions, but she did not feel that she could claim the privilege of being able to share his innermost thoughts and feelings. Instead, she changed the subject. "I want to thank you for everything you've done for me. Magnes told me that the doctor here saved my life, and I am truly grateful. I don't know how I'll repay you, but perhaps I could work here at Kerala for a while, in the kitchen maybe, when I'm stronger. That's where I earned my keep back home."

To her surprise, Ashinji took both of her hands in his. "You do not owe me anything, Jelena. It was I who caused your hurts in the first place. I never would have forgiven myself if…" He stopped speaking and, for an instant, Jelena again felt the strange sensation of pressure inside her skull, as if words that were not her own were struggling to form in her brain. Ashinji's eyes expanded until they filled up her entire field of vision and suddenly, she felt as if she were falling into their green depths.

"Jelena! Jelena, what happened? Are you feeling ill?"

She found herself leaning heavily into Ashinji's chest, with only his arms about her waist to prevent her from collapsing to the stones. "I…I don't know. I felt very dizzy all of a sudden," she murmured. Her face lay against his neck and so, slowly, she breathed in his strange, fascinating scent. An ache flared up below her belly, one that she still believed she had no hope of ever satisfying. With embarrassment heating her cheeks, she quickly pushed away to stand on her own. She lowered her face to hide her discomfiture.

"Perhaps you should return to bed. You can meet my parents tomorrow." Ashinji's demeanor was one of solicitous concern and entirely proper for a good host. Jelena was furious at her body's insistence on flinging up thoughts and feelings that would only get her hurt and cause embarrassment and pity on Ashinji's part.

Damn it! Why am I obsessing over him like this? You have to stop this, you stupid girl! He will never, ever, want you!

"No, no, I'm all right. I want to meet your parents today. I'm very anxious to show your father my ring. The sooner I can discover any information about my father, the sooner I'll be on my way to finding him."

"I do not wish to lessen your hopes, Jelena, but have you given any thought to what you might do if you cannot find your father or any of his kin? Or if..." Ashinji did not need to finish his sentence.

"Or if he, or they, reject me? I haven't given it a lot of thought, no. I guess I should. Ashinji, please tell me the truth. Is there any chance at all that my father might actually accept me?"

Ashinji sighed and turned to stare out over the parapet. When he again looked at her, his face was troubled. "I can only say that we elves hold some of the same prejudices concerning humans as do humans concerning us. I wish it were not so."

Jelena started to speak, but Ashinji held up his hand to stop her.

"That does not mean that all elves feel the same way, nor do we all hold that those of mixed blood are inferior," he continued. "Out here in the borderlands, humans and elves have been quietly intermingling for centuries, so folk are a lot more tolerant. My parents are especially so, and they tried to raise all of their children to be free of prejudice."

Here, Ashinji paused for a moment, and a small frown creased his brow. "I am sorry to say that they were not entirely successful." He did not elaborate, asking instead, "No one here has treated you badly in any way, have they?"

"Oh, no!" Jelena answered quickly. "Though I can tell that not everyone thinks like you do about… what is the elven word for a mixed-blood person?"

"Hikui," Ashinji replied.

"Most everyone I've met has been nice to me, or at the very least, they've not been rude. I've gotten far better treatment here than I ever got back home."

"I am happy to hear that," Ashinji replied, then said, "Your father most likely comes from a border family. He probably would have been raised with more liberal attitudes, which is why he could fall in love with a human woman. So, there is a good chance he will accept you."

Acceptance was all Jelena had ever wanted. Still, she determined that, no matter what, she would make a life for herself somewhere, even if that meant spending it alone.

"I think my parents will be ready to see you now," Ashinji said. "Shall we go?"

Jelena allowed Ashinji to take her good arm again as they descended the stone steps down to base of the wall. She felt surprised and pleased when he did not release his hold, and she permitted herself to lean on him a little as they walked. She imagined she could feel the pressure of many curious eyes bouncing off the back of her neck as she and Ashinji retraced their steps toward the upper gate.

They passed through and crossed the upper yard to the main entrance of the keep. Magnes stood waiting for them, just out of thrusting reach of the door guards' spears. He appeared freshly scrubbed, wet hair plastered to his head. He had changed clothes and now wore a deep green tunic that appeared one size too small for him. Jelena tried to suppress it, but an unintentional giggle escaped her tightly closed mouth.

"I know, I know," Magnes grumbled. He tugged futilely at the hem of the shirt, which hit him just above the crotch.

Ashinji also tried to look sympathetic, but he, too, could barely suppress his laughter. "I am sorry, my friend, but you are so much taller and wider than most of us. It has been difficult finding clothes that will fit you." Magnes nodded his head, hand raised in a gesture that signaled his understanding of the situation. "Follow me, then,"

Ashinji directed. "I will take you in to my parents' private sitting room."

The guards snapped to attention as Ashinji passed between them and stepped over the slightly raised threshold. Jelena followed closely, with Magnes right behind. They were now in a large entryway with corridors running off before and to either side of the door. Jelena, raised in a world of stone and brick, found the smells and sounds of a large wooden building to be new and intriguing. She delighted in the springy give to the floor beneath her feet.

Ashinji led the way down the left-hand corridor. Naturalistic murals decorated the walls, each depicting landscapes populated with animals, birds, and insects. Jelena slowed to admire a scene of a falcon stooping to strike a rabbit partially hidden in a thicket. The detail of the work was both painstaking and breathtaking. She could almost see the delicate twitch of the terrified rabbit's nostrils as it awaited the deadly embrace of its killer.

Duke Teodorus had never had much use for purely decorative objects; artwork at Amsara had been limited to practical things like carpets and tapestries. To hang paintings purely for their aesthetic value would have been a wasted exercise as far as he was concerned. For the first time that she could remember, Jelena pitied her uncle.

They came to a staircase and ascended four flights. Jelena had to pause at the top to rest and catch her breath. Another corridor stretched before them, this one hung with silk banners of brightly woven floral patterns, waving sensuously in the breeze from the large open windows in the opposite wall. At the far end of the corridor, a door stood open. The sound of laughter, high-pitched and full of merriment, drifted through. Jelena's excitement and apprehension surged as each step brought her closer to the one man in Kerala who could possibly help in the search for her father.

Ashinji paused just outside the door. "Wait here a moment," he said, then slipped inside. Jelena groped for Magnes's hand and felt him seize hers in a firm, steadying grasp. They waited in silence, listening to the musical interchange of words between Ashinji and his family.

The squeak of approaching footsteps heralded Ashinji's return. He beckoned them to enter with a sweep of his arm. Jelena held on tightly to Magnes's warm, callused hand, as if, by letting go, she feared she would be cast adrift on a stormy sea, to be swept away and drowned.

The room, like the corridor, was large and airy, but Jelena saw none of the details. Her attention fixed immediately on the little knot of people sitting in the center of the chamber—a man and woman seated in low chairs, a young girl standing behind the man, hands resting on his shoulders, and two children sprawled on the floor at the woman's feet.

"Jelena, Magnes," Ashinji said softly, nodding to the man and woman. "These are my parents, Lord and Lady Sakehera."

CHAPTER 16

A NEW LIFE

Jelena sank to one knee.

"No, Jelena." Ashinji stepped forward to take her elbow and gently pull her back to her feet. "You are a guest in this house. A bow of the head is sufficient to show my parents respect."

"Welcome to Kerala," Lord Sakehera said in heavily accented Soldaran. "Please to sit." He indicated that Jelena and Magnes should seat themselves upon the large cushions resting in front of his chair. Magnes helped Jelena find a comfortable position before he settled down beside her, looking vaguely disconcerted. It dawned on her that her cousin was not used to sitting on the floor at another man's feet.

Ashinji perched on a small padded stool beside his mother. The two children—twin girls—immediately crawled over and attached themselves like climbing vines to his legs. They stared boldly, first at Jelena, then Magnes, their huge gray-blue eyes shining with frank curiosity. The older girl, who looked to be about fifteen years of age, remained standing behind her father, regarding the two visitors with cool interest.

Ashinji spoke up. "These two monkeys are Jena and Mariso," he said, stroking the children's silky blonde heads. "That young beauty over there is Lani." He looked at the older girl, who met his glance with a smile. His voice brimmed with affection.

"We hope all has been good for you since came you here to Kerala," Lord Sakehera said.

"Your hospitality has been exceptional, Lord Sakehera," Magnes replied. "I owe you a tremendous debt of gratitude. If not for your doctor, my cousin would have died. I only wish that there were some way that I could repay you."

Jelena fiddled nervously with the hem of her tunic. She glanced up to find Lady Sakehera staring intently at her, a tiny horizontal line creasing the skin of her otherwise smooth forehead. Jelena began to feel a strange pressure behind her eyes again, not unlike the peculiar sensation she had felt twice before with Ashinji. She rubbed at her temples to relieve the ache. Lady Sakehera's eyes narrowed slightly and the corners of her mouth turned downwards in an almost imperceptible frown. Jelena's heart thumped painfully.

"My son tells me that you come here for to seek your elven kin and that there is ring belonging to your father. Have you now this ring?" Lord Sakehera leaned forward expectantly.

"Yes, my lord, I do." Jelena withdrew her father's ring from its hiding place beneath her tunic. Her awkward attempts to slip the chain over her head one-handed only succeeded in tangling it up in her hair. Magnes came to her rescue, deftly unsnarling the chain and pulling it free. He then stood and dropped it along with the attached ring onto the palm of Lord Sakehera's outstretched hand.

Lord Sakehera brought the ring up to his face and examined it closely. His daughter Lani leaned over his shoulder, craning her neck so that she could get a look at the ring as well. With their faces side by side, Jelena saw clearly how much of the father was in the daughter. Lani's almond-shaped eyes, generous mouth, and well-formed cheekbones were a feminine mirror of her sire's, while Ashinji, by contrast, strongly resembled his mother.

Lord Sakehera thoughtfully scratched his chin. He closed his hand around the ring and nodded his head as if coming to a decision. "My answer to you is, yes, I have seen this, how you say, this symbol meaning certain person or house, this *device* before, but I cannot identify it as yet. However, with permission, I will keep ring and study it, make, ur, *inquiries*."

Jelena could barely keep herself from leaping up and shouting for joy. "Yes, Lord Sakehera! Please keep it for as long as you need to. I am so very grateful! I…I wish to ask permission to stay here at Kerala, if I may. You see, I have no home back in Amsara, nowhere to go really… that is, until I can locate my father or his kin. I will, of course, work for my keep. I was a kitchen servant before I came here."

"Youngest Son, did you not tell me she was niece of duke? How can a man allow family to work as servant? This I do not understand." Lord Sakehera's grey-green eyes glittered with disapproval. He looked to Magnes as if awaiting an explanation.

"My lord, my father is a good man in many ways, but his attitudes concerning your people so blinded him that he turned his back on his own sister and disowned her because she carried a half-elven child. I think that if my aunt had been pregnant with a human child, he never would have cast her out, and Jelena would have grown up as a full member of the family." Magnes paused briefly, as if to collect his thoughts. "Your son has been honest with me about how most elves view humans, and it seems both our peoples have enough misunderstandings and hatred to keep us separated for the rest of time."

"You speak truth, young human," Lord Sakehera answered slowly. Jelena thought that she detected a new note of respect in the Lord of Kerala's voice. "Myself, I hold not these views," he added.

"I came here to protect my cousin and aid her in her search for her elven family," Magnes continued. "I'll stand by her as long as she needs me. If she wishes to stay here at Kerala, I won't try to dissuade her because I think you can help her."

"Jelena," Lord Sakehera rose to his feet. Magnes helped Jelena to stand. "One of my official, um, what is word? Ah, *messengers,* has left service to marry, leaving me with one only person to serve me this way. I give you position. You can ride horse, yes? Good. This way, you stay here, earn keep, search for father. I help also."

"I don't know how to thank you, Lord Sakehera," Jelena answered. "I'm sorry if I sound greedy, but what about my cousin? He needs work as well."

"Lord Sakehera, I must ask you a very serious question," Magnes said quietly. Jelena looked sharply at her cousin, alarmed at the gravity in his voice. "I need to know where I stand here."

Lord Sakehera's eyes narrowed. "Please, what mean you?" he said.

"I mean no disrespect," Magnes replied quickly. "You and your people have treated us well, as I've said, but…" He paused, as if to choose his next words very carefully. "I know you've set guards to keep watch on me, and there are places here in the castle grounds where I've been politely, but firmly turned away by other guards. I understand why you feel you must do this, my lord. We all know of the rumors...Our two countries may very well be at war soon. I could be a spy, for all you know, sent here by the empress through my father."

"You are very...how you say...*clever,* young Preseren," Lord Sen replied slowly. He stroked his chin in silence for a few heartbeats.

Jelena held her breath, waiting.

"Yes, it is true, I have you watched," Lord Sen finally confirmed. "I do this for good reasons...you understand these reasons; you are son of military man. I cannot let you see things or know things that duke can use against me."

"Am I your hostage, my lord?" Magnes asked.

Gods! Ashinji's father thinks Magnes is a spy! Jelena thought, horrified. Her heart slammed against her breastbone, and she felt light-headed with sudden fear. *What if he orders Magnes imprisoned, or worse?*

"Father, I will take responsibility for Magnes," Ashinji interjected. "I brought him here."

"I thank you, Ashinji, but I don't need your protection," Magnes stated firmly. He looked Lord Sen in the eye, and said, "I give you my word... I am no spy, and I swear by all my gods that I will not betray you, Lord Sakehera. I know you have no reason to trust me, and so...if imprisonment is your real plan for me, then all I ask is that you take my cousin under your protection and help her find her elven kin."

A tense, heavy silence settled on the room. Jelena fought hard against the cold, sick panic that threatened to overwhelm her. She opened her mouth to plead with Lord Sakehera for Magnes's life, when, to her surprise, Lady Sakehera spoke.

The Lady of Kerala leaned toward her husband, her voice low and measured. She regarded Magnes coolly all the while, and her words, though incomprehensible, had a curious effect on Jelena. Her fear dissipated, leaving calm in its wake.

Lord Sen listened attentively to his wife, nodding slowly. "My wife says that you speak truth, young Preseren," he said. "She knows how to…look into hearts of men…to see truth there." He took a deep breath, as if coming to an important decision.

"Magnes Preseren, you are duke's son. A man of rank. You shall have position in my guard, if you wish. It will be first time a human works for me. I shall be envy of district!" Lord Sakehera's smile brimmed with sly good humor. "My son will show you where you live. You can eat meals with rest of staff now. I take very good care of my people. You will see."

"Thank you, my lord," Magnes replied, and Jelena heard the relief in her cousin's voice.

"Jelena, Magnes," Ashinji said, "I will take you to the barracks now and show you around." He detached himself from the possessive grasps of his little sisters and transferred them to his mother. Jelena glanced briefly at the Lady. Something about this elegant, handsome woman raised the hairs on the back of her neck. She thought about what Lord Sen had said.

She looks into the hearts of men and sees the truth…and lies as well, no doubt! Jelena could sense the tremendous power hidden behind Lady Sakehera's serene façade.

Clearly, it would be unwise to make an enemy of the Lady of Kerala.

As Ashinji turned to escort Jelena and Magnes from the room, the door swung open and a man entered. Ashinji halted in his tracks. The newcomer strode across the room and stopped in front of Ashinji, blocking his way. He stood with one hand on his hip and arrogance infusing every line of his sleek, well-toned body. The familial resemblance was unmistakable. However, this man's beauty was cold like the icicles that formed on tree branches in the dead of winter. His eyes insolently raked Jelena from head to toe and only settled perfunctorily on Magnes before turning back to Ashinji. He spoke a few words, and Ashinji's lips compressed down to a thin, hard line.

"Jelena, Magnes," Ashinji said tightly. "May I present Lord Sadaiyo Sakehera, Heir to Kerala and my elder brother."

Sadaiyo Sakehera's eyes were grey-green like his father's but held none of their warmth or good humor. He pinned Jelena with a look both contemptuous and suggestive at the same time. She felt a surge of anger and fear, for it was the very same look she had seen in the eyes of some of the less picky Amsara guardsmen, the ones who would try to lift her skirts, then spit on her and call her a dirty tink when she rebuffed them. She felt the comforting presence of Magnes at her back and instinctively leaned into him.

The tension between Ashinji and his brother was palpable. Ashinji spoke, his voice carefully controlled and polite. Sadaiyo responded with a laugh and pushed past him, glaring venomously at Magnes.

"I apologize for my brother's rudeness," Ashinji said quietly. His face had gone very still and pale. "Let us go now." He turned and stalked toward the door, the set of his shoulders betraying his anger. From behind, Jelena could hear Lord Sakehera's voice and that of his eldest son's raised in heated debate.

By the time they had descended back to the ground floor, it seemed that Ashinji's anger had cooled, but Jelena suspected that it never truly dissipated, but always remained simmering just below the surface. In one short exchange, Jelena knew she had witnessed a telling glimpse into a relationship fraught with a lifetime's worth of animosity. She decided, then and there, that Sadaiyo Sakehera was extremely dangerous, and the one person at Kerala she must avoid.

"I take it that your brother doesn't particularly like humans," Magnes commented dryly.

Ashinji sighed. "No, he does not. He has made it quite clear that he thinks my father has made a mistake allowing you to stay here. My advice is to stay out of his way, which should not be a problem. He will be totally occupied with preparing for his wedding, which will be taking place very soon—within the next few weeks. In truth, we will all be occupied with it."

"You don't sound very happy," Jelena observed.

Ashinji shrugged. "He is my elder brother, and the Heir. This is a very important event. I will do my filial duty."

Jelena decided that a change in subject was in order. "Ashinji, I wish to begin my language lessons right away. If I'm to be your father's messenger, I must learn to speak Siri-dar as quickly as possible."

"Cousin, I think you need to fully regain your strength, first," Magnes interjected gently. "Don't forget, you were just released from your sickbed yesterday. I think Lord Sakehera can get along without you for awhile longer."

"I must agree with Magnes. You will not be needed to carry messages just yet, but I can begin your lessons now." Ashinji started pointing to objects as they walked, first calling the thing by its Soldaran name and then following up with the corresponding word in Siri-dar. By the time they reached the barracks, both Magnes and Jelena were sorting out a dozen or so nouns and tripping over the unfamiliar pronunciations. Ashinji patiently corrected their mistakes while trying not to laugh.

The guards' barracks were located above the stables and consisted of a common room, a dormitory for the men, a smaller room for the female soldiers, and several storerooms. At this hour, most of the inhabitants were at their posts, but as the three of them entered the common room, a lone, dark-haired woman stood up from her seat at the long rectangular table in the center of the room. Jelena felt certain that she had seen the woman before, but she could not remember where. The woman came forward and bowed deferentially to Ashinji. He spoke to her at some length, and as her clever brown eyes darted back and forth between Jelena and Magnes, she nodded in understanding.

"I've told Aneko what she needs to know about you, Jelena," Ashinji explained. "She knows that you are to be my father's new messenger when you are healed enough to ride. She also knows that you still require a great deal of rest, so she will look after your needs."

"Jelena, you remember? I care for you by river, me and Kami?" Aneko smiled a little self-consciously, as if embarrassed by her broken Soldaran. She gently took hold of Jelena's elbow. "Come. I show you room where we sleep." Aneko led Jelena into a smaller room, just off the common room, that contained three beds, each with a storage chest underneath. Shelves lined the walls above. The bed closest to the open window appeared unclaimed.

"That one must be mine," Jelena said. She scanned the room then turned back to Aneko. "Surely not all the guards live here. What about the ones with families?"

Aneko's forehead creased in puzzlement for a moment, then she exclaimed and nodded in understanding. "Families have own house. Not live here. Here is for unmarried people only."

"You speak Soldaran very well, Aneko," Jelena commented.

"Who taught you?"

"Grandmother," Aneko replied, and when she did not elaborate, Jelena inquired no further. Instead, she stepped over to the window beside her newly claimed bed. A fine metal mesh, the likes of which she had never seen before, covered the opening. Amazed at the cleverness of the idea, Jelena immediately discerned how the screen allowed air to circulate into the room, yet kept flying insects out. She looked out and scanned the view.

The women's room faced the rear of the building and looked down on the paddocks behind the stables. A few horses stood drowsing in the warm spring sunshine, tails lazily swishing. The earthy smell of horse dung and hay drifted up to permeate the room.

It's not so bad. I can get used to the smell. Besides, I won't be in here that much once I'm better.

She and Aneko returned to the common room. Magnes and Ashinji had seated themselves at the table and were deep in conversation. Jelena went over to join them, slipping in alongside Magnes on the bench opposite Ashinji. Aneko bowed to Ashinji and discreetly exited the room.

"If war comes, I'll be in a very difficult position if I stay here," Magnes was saying. Both he and Ashinji looked glum.

"What are you talking about?" Jelena asked. She felt a twinge of alarm as she looked at the two young men, their faces as serious as if they had just heard some particularly bad news.

"The painful truth," Ashinji answered. "Magnes is the son and Heir of a very important human lord. To stay here in Kerala, in the service of an elven lord, would be seen as treason, I think. And there is the other side of the issue. The son of a powerful human lord is a very valuable hostage. Despite my father's best intentions, he may have no choice in the end. He will have to confine your cousin to Kerala Castle; at worst, he might be compelled to send Magnes to Sendai as a prisoner."

"Jelena, I might need to leave Kerala and go back home," Magnes said quietly.

Jelena leaned her head against Magnes's shoulder. "I don't want you to go. I want us to be together like we always have been, but I realize I must put aside my selfishness if staying here will endanger your life. I love you, Magnes, but I still feel a little guilty that you had to give up everything in order to help me escape."

"Jelena, I've told you that that doesn't matter."

Jelena shook her head. "But, don't you see, Magnes? It does matter, very much. This is your life we're talking about, for the gods' sake!" She looked at Ashinji, who was pulling at the gold rings set in his earlobe. "Ashinji, how certain are the elves that the Empire is planning on going to war with Alasiri?"

"Our intelligence says that it is all but certain, and planned for next summer, just after the worst of the rainy season."

"Yes, that's what I know as well. A little over a year, then." Magnes drummed his fingers restlessly against the scarred wood of the table.

Jelena laid her hand over his, stilling the nervous motion. "Go home, Cousin. Mend things with your father. Tell him about Livie. If he sees how much you love her, perhaps he'll give in and allow the two of you to marry. I'll miss you terribly, but I'll be all right. If I can't find my father, or if…well, at least I have a place here. I can make a good life for myself, I think."

Magnes gathered her up in his arms. "I don't want to abandon you, Jelena," he said, voice hoarse with emotion. "I've always taken care of you. Who's going to protect you if I leave?" Jelena could see that Ashinji had gone very still. His expression was unreadable, but he seemed to be trying very hard to hold back from something, as if there were words within him that he wanted very much to say, but could not.

"I can take care of myself, Cousin. You've helped me get this far; now I can manage on my own."

"I can't deny the logic of your arguments," Magnes sighed. He looked at Ashinji. "I'll need some provisions and a horse, if your father can spare one. I have nothing with which to repay him, as you know, but if there ever is a way, I'll find it."

"Of course, Magnes. There is no need to speak of repayment. My father is a generous man, and there is no hardship in helping you. We will provide you with all that you need, including an escort to the border."

"It's settled, then," Jelena said.

Two days later, Jelena stood at the main gate of Kerala Castle and watched Magnes ride away. The words he had spoken to her the night before kept repeating themselves over and over in her head.

"Jelena, I've seen how Ashinji looks at you. He's drawn to you, and it only seems like it's getting stronger. I know you don't believe any man could love you because of what you are, but that's simply not true. I think Ashinji might. Don't let your fears and doubts prevent you from finding happiness."

Fears and doubts are all I seem to have, Cousin, she thought.

Happiness and the kind of love shared between a man and woman were two things that Jelena had given up on a long time ago. She would count herself lucky if she could somehow manage to find a bit of contentment.

Magnes turned back in the saddle and waved. Jelena raised her hand in response and gave free rein to her tears. From behind, she sensed the presence of another. She turned to see Ashinji standing close by her left shoulder, watching the mounted figures of Magnes and his escort dwindling into the distance. She could feel the heat of his body pushing against her, and the desperate longing to touch him became almost too much to bear.

Could it be true what Magnes said? Could Ashinji really be falling in love with me? How is that possible?

No. Stop fooling yourself. Magnes is wrong. Ashinji is the son of a lord. His parents would never permit him to get involved with someone like me anyway, even if he wanted to, which I'm sure he doesn't.

"I know you are sad, Jelena. Perhaps, one day, if the One permits it, you will see your cousin again." Ashinji rested his hand lightly on Jelena's shoulder, and suddenly, she could take no more.

She sobbed aloud and fled.

CHAPTER 17

A GLIMPSE OF THE FUTURE

During the week that followed Magnes's departure, Ashinji tried to ease Jelena's sorrow and loneliness by spending as much time with her as his other duties allowed.

Jelena's company posed no hardship. In truth, he found himself drawn to her more strongly with each passing day. His first thoughts when he awoke in the morning were of her, as were his last thoughts before he drifted off to sleep at night. She haunted his dreams and preoccupied his waking mind. He found it both exciting and troubling. Ashinji was no callow youth; he'd had his share of affairs, but never before had a woman stirred his soul like Jelena. He felt off balance, like his world had just been upended and shaken out like an old sack.

Early evenings, during the quiet time between the end of the workday and the evening meal, Ashinji liked to ramble about the castle grounds. He invariably ended up on the battlements, where he could soak up the peace of the bucolic landscape in blessed solitude. This particular evening was no different. Slowly, he mounted the stairs toward the top of the wall, his mind already deep in thought.

Ashinji had never given much thought to the idea of romantic love. As the son of a noble house, his duty was to obey his parents, and when the time came for him to marry, he would go before the priests with a bride of his parents' choosing. Love never really entered the picture, at least during the selection process. With luck, the girl would be pretty and of an agreeable nature. With still more luck, they would find that they were compatible, and friendship, then love, would grow between them. Ashinji had known for some time that his parents had been making discreet inquiries amongst several noble families. He had no thought or desire to complain.

Everything had changed the moment he had first seen Jelena's face and had recognized her as the girl from his dream visions. He had known then, with absolute certainty, that they were meant to be together. He must make his feelings known to her, and soon.

His parents did need consideration, though. Lord and Lady Sakehera were far more liberal than most people on the subject of human-elf intermingling, but he wondered if their tolerance would extend to marriage with a hikui. Ashinji loved and respected his parents with all his heart and held his duty to them as one of the central aspects of his life. But in this one thing, he knew he could not obey. If he could not make Jelena his wife, then he would have no wife at all. He must somehow make his parents understand.

The sun had started its slow slide below the horizon. The evening breeze picked up a few stray locks of Ashinji's hair and whipped them across his face, tickling his nose and mouth. He turned his head slightly and spotted movement out of the corner of his eye.

His heart sank.

Approaching him on the wall walk, like an onrushing storm, came Sadaiyo.

"So, Ashi, up hiding on the walls again, eh?" Sadaiyo flashed a grin, all teeth and no warmth.

Ashinji sighed inwardly and steeled himself against the inevitable barbs that Sadaiyo took a perverse delight in throwing at him. "I'm not hiding. I came up here to be alone and think, as you well know."

"Think? About what, Little Brother? Oh, I know. My wedding! That's all anyone can think about these days, isn't it?" Sadaiyo rested his elbows on the parapet, looking smug. "Did you know that my soon-to-be wife single-handedly took out an entire Iinaa raiding party? Single-handedly! And I've also heard that she can love a man to complete and utter exhaustion, then spring from bed to ride to hounds!" He cocked a sardonic eye at Ashinji. "It's a good thing Father and Mother picked her for me rather than you. Such a woman needs a man strong enough to handle her properly. I think she'd end up sucking you dry." He laughed and Ashinji ground his teeth, wincing as hot needles of pain shot up his arms. He looked down to see that he had bloodied his fingers gripping the parapet.

"You've been spending a lot of time with that stray you brought in. I don't blame you. She is very attractive, despite her humanish features… no, because of them, I think. It makes her so…different, so intriguing. Have you had her yet?" Ashinji went cold with fury, but Sadaiyo did not seem to notice. "Wait! This is my prissy little brother I'm talking to. Of course you haven't," he continued, his voice dripping sarcasm. "You know, if you don't want her, maybe I'll take her as my concubine." He paused for dramatic effect. "Maybe I'll take her anyway, even if you do want her." His cruel smile cut like a razor.

"Stay away from Jelena, Sadaiyo," Ashinji replied, his voice low and dangerous.

Sadaiyo raised an eyebrow. "Struck the mark, have I? Is it possible…could it be possible that you actually have *feelings* for this girl, Little Brother? She's a half-breed, you know."

"I am well aware of Jelena's heritage." Blood pounding in his ears, Ashinji fought to keep a grip on his temper, but with each heartbeat, his control slipped a tiny bit more.

"She's a half-breed, and she's kinless. The only thing this girl has to give you that's worth anything is what's between her legs."

Ashinji rounded on Sadaiyo, fist raised.

Sadaiyo stood cool and unflinching, his eyes daring Ashinji to strike. "Careful, Little Brother," he said slowly.

Ashinji lowered his hand and relaxed his fingers. "Ever the charming one, aren't you, Brother?" Ashinji spat, eyes blazing with anger and disgust. "Can't you please just go away and leave me alone?"

Sadaiyo shrugged, a little sneer twisting his handsome mouth. "Don't stay up here too long. You know how much Mother hates it when any of us are late for dinner." He brushed past Ashinji and disappeared down the stairs.

When he felt certain that Sadaiyo had gone, Ashinji leaned back against the rough, unyielding stones of the wall, feeling weak and shattered.

Why do I let him do this to me? he raged silently. He closed his eyes and concentrated on breathing, drawing air in and out of his lungs, until his heart, which had been racing like a runaway horse, slowed and his hands stopped shaking.

Ashinji knew with chilling certainty that if Sadaiyo learned of his depth of feeling for Jelena, he would cast wide his net of hatred to ensnare and destroy her, purely out of spite. Ashinji's pain was like meat and drink to his brother; any chance Sadaiyo had to hurt or humiliate him seemed necessary to his nature. He craved the perverse pleasure of it and reveled in Ashinji's refusal to fight back. Long ago, Ashinji had decided that passive resistance could be the only way to deal with his brother. He would never willingly raise a hand against Sadaiyo, who was, after all, to be Lord of Kerala one day. Blood ties were too strong, too important, and he would owe his allegiance to Sadaiyo because of them.

Ashinji would never openly fight Sadaiyo if given any other choice, but neither would he allow his brother's hatred to poison his own spirit. Much of the time, he remained immune to it, shielded by a mental barrier he had learned to erect in childhood. But, sometimes, a small bit would get past, sliding through a chink in the wall and burning straight into his heart, as it had with Sadaiyo's crude comments about Jelena.

He pushed himself away from the parapet and headed back down the stairs. Crossing the lower yard toward the path leading to the upper gate, he passed several guardsmen and servants. They greeted him respectfully, but he barely heard or saw them, so preoccupied was he with the possible threat his brother posed to Jelena.

Sadaiyo had every right to take a concubine if he so chose, and Jelena would be in a difficult position to refuse. Sadaiyo could not force her, but he could make life nearly impossible for her at Kerala if she turned down his offer. Ashinji knew he must find a way to protect her, but first, he must warn her of the danger she faced.

If you try to hurt Jelena, I will have no choice but to fight you, Brother, with all my strength and to the bitter end, even if it costs me everything.

He would pray to the One that it never came to that.

~~~

In a heavily warded chamber high up in Kerala Castle's east tower, Lady Amara Sakehera put the final touches to her preparations. Carefully, she mixed several incenses together to make the special blend she used for all of her divinations. She checked to see that her scrying bowl contained the proper amount of water and that her altar was tidy. She couldn't abide an untidy work surface.

With all in readiness, Amara sat down on folded knees before the altar and closed her eyes. She began the breathing pattern that would focus her mind and carry it into a light trance. Years of experience allowed her to quickly reach the level where she could easily access her Talent.

Connected now with her inborn magical power, she opened her eyes and carefully lit each of two beeswax candles by simply willing them into flame. Next, she kindled the incense with a thought, and breathed in the pungent smoke to further clarify her mind and sharpen her focus.

Leaning over the shallow copper basin, she gently blew upon the water's surface and breathed out an incantation. She then gazed into the bowl as the water began to roil, slowly at first, then more quickly until a miniature whirlpool had formed at its center. Amara spoke a single Word of power, and abruptly, the water quieted and became as still and reflective as a mirror.

Images began to form, and Amara watched them flicker into focus, then fade in rapid succession. Her pulse began to race as the pictures she saw confirmed both her suspicions and her worst fears.

When, at last, the parade of images had ceased and the waters went dark, Amara sagged backward, shaken and pale. With trembling hands she extinguished the candles and doused the still-smoldering incense with a scoop of sand.

Great Goddess, help us! she cried silently, covering her face with her hands.

Amara allowed herself only the briefest moment of self-pity. She rose to her feet and straightened her clothing. Much remained to be done. First, she needed to contact the others. The time that they all knew would come—had prayed would never come—was finally at hand.

The Key had returned.

CHAPTER 18

THE UNCROSSABLE CHASM

Your progress is excellent, Jelena. I'm amazed at how much you've learned these last few weeks."

Jelena raised her hand and, laughing, she begged, "Please, Ashinji...more speak...I mean, speak more slow!"

"I'm sorry. I'll try to slow down. But, really, you are remarkable."

"You are...very good teacher."

Ashinji had suggested that today they have their language lesson in the gardens below the east wing of the castle. In a shady bower, protected from the midday sun and surrounded by a riotous profusion of flowering shrubbery, he patiently tutored Jelena in Siri-dar by reciting stories from elven mythology, then quizzed her on what she'd heard. She could answer only in Siri-dar; Ashinji supplied any word she could not come up with and corrected her grammatical mistakes as they occurred. Within the deep shade of the bower, the air felt pleasantly cool on the bare skin of Jelena's arms and face. Like Ashinji, she wore a wraparound tunic and trousers of light cotton, hers dyed the color of the summer sky. Ashinji also wore blue, though of a darker hue, closer to peacock.

"Now, tell me what you remember about the story of the twin brothers Aje and Rei," Ashinji gently commanded.

Jelena squirmed a little on the smooth wooden bench. Ashinji had told her that story several days ago, and she didn't know if she could summon up all of the details. Clearing her throat, she began.

"Aje and Rei were brothers of great…rivalry. Whatever one had, so other brother must possess. Aje… had possession of …*owned* magical flying horse, called Ashoya. Rei desired Ashoya and vowed to…remove from, no, *steal* Ashoya from Aje. So, in deep of night, Rei entered place where Ashoya was and jumped on Ashoya and rode him away."

"How did Rei get close enough to Ashoya? This was a magical horse, after all," Ashinji prompted, smiling in encouragement. Jelena's heart skipped a beat.

"Rei…himself dressed in clothes belonging to twin Aje, so Ashoya saw his master's clothes, and thought Rei was Aje." Jelena paused for a moment to think, then continued. "So, Rei rode Ashoya many days north to lands of the trolls…where he hid with the troll king, who was his friend…and…there was cave made of ice…and that is all I remember!" Jelena let out a whoosh of air and playfully crossed her eyes.

Ashinji burst out laughing. "That was very, very good!" he exclaimed. "You made only a few minor grammar mistakes, but all of the words were correct, and your pronunciation is getting much better. I fully expect you'll be speaking fluent Siri-dar by midsummer."

"With heavy Soldaran accent!"

"Well, yes, that will take time to disappear, but…" The sound of the castle's big brass bell, signaling the hour, interrupted. "That's enough for today. It's time I got back." Ashinji sighed, and his face, so cheerful and animated a moment ago, became solemn, and the light in his eyes faded.

Jelena tentatively laid a hand upon his sun-browned forearm, unsure as to how he would react. "What is wrong, Ashinji?" she asked softly. To her surprise and secret delight, he covered her hand with his.

"Jelena, there is something I must tell you," he said, swiveling his upper body so that he faced her. "I think you know that my older brother will be married soon—in three days, to be precise. I won't be able to spend much time with you after today, and I will very much miss your company. My brother Sadaiyo is…he's someone you want to stay as far away from as possible. That shouldn't be too difficult, since you are living in the barracks now. However, when you start your duties as my father's messenger, you will have reason to be at the castle more often."

Jelena shivered in response to the fear for her that she saw in Ashinji's eyes.

"Promise me you'll watch out for yourself where my brother is concerned, Jelena. Whatever you do, don't be alone with him." A lock of Ashinji's honey-gold hair had fallen down across his forehead, and Jelena struggled against the urge to reach up and brush it away from his face.

She swallowed hard. The perfume of the flowers and Ashinji's closeness together conspired to made her dizzy. "I can care for myself, Ashinji, but...I promise I will do as you say." She didn't tell him she had already decided to avoid Sadaiyo. "Your brother, Ashinji...What is it I must fear?" she asked.

Ashinji stood up, pulling Jelena with him. He did not answer her question, but instead, clasped her hand in his and began walking back towards the upper gate. Jelena kept pace beside him, and both remained silent until they reached the barracks.

"Remember the story of Aje and Rei, Jelena," Ashinji said quietly. He squeezed her fingers, then turned away.

Jelena stood at the foot of the barracks stairs and watched as Ashinji walked back toward the castle. He turned around once and waved, just before disappearing through the upper gate. Jelena raised her hand and waved back, wanting very much to run after him.

She thought about Ashinji's last words. The cautionary tale of the dueling twins served as a warning against the dangers of sibling rivalry spun out of control. Jelena knew from other comments Ashinji had made that he and his older brother did not get along. Could Ashinji's reference to the story of Aje and Rei mean that he had feelings for her, his brother knew it, and therefore desired her for himself?

For weeks, Jelena had stubbornly refused to even entertain the idea that she and Ashinji could have any kind of relationship beyond that of friends, and at first, nothing in his behavior indicated that he did not feel the same. But lately, she had detected a subtle shift in his attitude, and she'd begun to wonder if Magnes had been right all along. The way Ashinji looked at her now seemed different. She could feel a definite heightening of tension whenever they were together, and it seemed as though he wished to be as close to her as he could without actually taking her into his arms.

The thought that Ashinji might be in love with her deeply troubled Jelena, for she had some inkling as to what the cost would be to him should he openly declare his love. He could not freely choose his own mate, and even if he could, she knew that his family would deem her completely unsuitable. A marriage between them, even if legal, would be his ruination.

After losing sight of Ashinji, Jelena turned and slowly climbed the squeaky wooden stairs up to the barracks. A raucous chorus of catcalls greeted her as she entered the common room. Aneko, and Kerala Castle's youngest guardswoman Kami, lounged at the long oak table, the remains of a meal before them.

"I see that Lord Ashinji has escorted Jelena home again! Whatever does this mean, eh?" Kami called out in a teasing voice.

"I think it means that our new friend has definitely caught the eye of our handsome young lord," Aneko answered. "Come sit with us Jelena. There is still some chicken left if you are hungry." The older woman waved Jelena over and indicated that she should sit beside her, then added, "I don't think I've ever seen Lord Ashinji so taken with a girl before…Here, have some beer." She filled up a clay mug from the pitcher at her elbow and offered it to Jelena, then topped off her own mug.

"Ai, Goddess, but you're lucky, Jelena," Kami sighed. She rested her chin in her hands, her girlish face wistful. "I wish Lord Ashinji would notice me… Those eyes! I could get lost in them forever."

Aneko snorted derisively. "Whatever happened to 'Oh, I'm sooo in love with Gendan! He's the only man for me!' eh?"

Kami stuck her tongue out at her friend. "Just because I wish Lord Ashinji would notice me doesn't mean I don't love Gendan. I'm not married yet, you know! I'll bet Lord Ashinji is as good in bed as he looks out of it. Jelena, you might be the only one of us lucky enough to find out." Kami winked, her hazel eyes sparkling lasciviously, and Jelena felt her cheeks ignite with embarrassment.

"Lord Ashinji and I are friends only," Jelena protested. "How could we ever be anything else?" She tugged self-consciously at a stray coil of hair.

"Don't say that, Jelena," Kami responded sadly.

"The girl's right, you know." A new voice spoke from the door-way. "She and our lord's son shouldn't even be friends, really. It's not proper, her being a hikui and all."

All three women looked toward the door as the speaker entered the room.

"Why do you have to be that way, Anda?" Kami retorted angrily.

"I don't know what you mean, Kami," Anda replied primly. "I'm just saying that Lord Ashinji should know better than to go all starry-eyed over a hikui."

Anda served as a guardswoman, like Aneko and Kami. The bed that Jelena now slept in had once been hers until she had married a fellow guardsman and had moved out of the barracks. She and her husband had a small cottage of their own now on the castle grounds nearby, but Anda still came around often to visit her comrades.

"Lord Ashinji is wise enough to listen to his own heart," Aneko said quietly, pouring a mug of beer for the newcomer.

Anda lowered herself carefully down on the bench beside Kami and sighed gratefully. "Goddess' tits, but it feels good to sit," she said, rubbing her swollen belly. The young guardswoman, in the final weeks of her first pregnancy, wore a haggard expression, clearly approaching the limits of her endurance. "Ooh, I'll be glad when this baby is out of me! If it wasn't so much fun making them, I'd never have another," she groaned, running a hand through her close-cropped, chestnut hair.

"It shouldn't matter that Jelena is a hikui, Anda," Kami insisted hotly.

"Of course it should! Lord Ashinji is okui. He's high-born and pure and should be with his own kind." Anda reached for a chicken leg. "I'm sorry if I've hurt your feelings, Jelena," she said around a mouthful of meat. "But you, of all people, should know I'm right."

"*Awwwrrr!*" Kami cried in frustration and pounded her fists on the tabletop. She opened her mouth as if to scream again, but Jelena interrupted.

"Please, Kami, no. Anda is right," she said, a catch in her voice. "I know I am not suitable girl for Lord Ashinji. Please do not argue over this."

"I am sorry, Jelena," Anda repeated, then after a short pause, said,

"Several hikui families live in the district, you know. There must be some eligible sons among them. I'm certain if you let it be known that you are looking, Lord Sen could arrange something for you."

Jelena realized that Anda believed her suggestion to be helpful; still, the surge of anger that swept through her caught her by surprise and left a painful knot in her gut in its wake.

"I will not be looking any time soon," she replied.

An uncomfortable silence descended on the room. Anda finished off her chicken leg and started in on a scrap of wing. Aneko sipped at her beer, her expression unreadable. Kami sniffed loudly and traced circles on the tabletop with a forefinger, chin still firmly planted in hand.

Jelena stared at her tightly clenched fists without seeing them, her mind lost in a haze of despondency. A painful cramp in her fingers brought her back to herself, and slowly, she forced her hands to relax.

Kami finally broke the silence with a change of subject. "Lord Sadaiyo's bride is to arrive tomorrow. I've heard that she is a real breaker of both horses and men," she said, smirking.

"Lady Misune is a fine warrior, Kami, and will be mistress of us all one day. You'd do well to remember that," Aneko chided. Oftimes, Jelena noticed, Aneko played the role of disciplinarian, reining in Kami's youthful impudence.

"I'm only saying it because I admire her," Kami sulked. "I wish that I had such things said about me!"

"Your problem, my girl, is that you're always wanting things you can't have," Aneko retorted.

"Ai! You are worse than my grandmother!" Kami shot back.

"Tell me about Lady Misune," Jelena asked, hoping that a bit of gossip would lighten her mood.

"She is the oldest daughter of Lord Dai of Manza," Aneko began. "Manza's the district just to the north of Kerala, beyond the Great Forest. She is supposed to be both beautiful and intelligent, which is why, no doubt, Lord and Lady Sakehera chose her for the Heir. We'll all know soon enough what she's like."

"She'd better be very tolerant," Anda said. "It's no secret that Lord Sadaiyo has a roving eye."

"From what I've heard, I don't think Lord Sadaiyo would dare to stray," Kami chimed in with a mischievous grin.

"Well, I should be getting back," Anda announced. "That husband of mine will be home soon and wondering where I've gotten myself to. He's been as nervous as a broody hen through this entire pregnancy!" She rose ponderously to her feet, belly in the lead.

"Good husbands should be, especially with the first one," Kami commented. "I'll be glad when you're back on duty. I'm tired of working double shifts."

Anda laughed. "I'll remember your words when you're knocked up with Gendan's brat and I'm covering for you! G'bye, all."

After Anda had departed, Kami and Aneko cleared away the remains of the meal, leaving the jug of beer and three mugs behind. When Jelena offered to assist, they politely refused.

"You're still not completely healed, yet. Lord Ashinji ordered us to make sure that you rest," Kami explained.

"I am sick of resting!" Jelena grumbled in annoyance. She felt perfectly fine and ready to start her duties as Lord Sakehera's messenger. To prove it, tomorrow she would go down to the stables and select a mount. When Ashinji saw that she was well enough to ride, he would have to give in and let her work.

The guardswomen rejoined Jelena at the table and Aneko poured more beer. "Don't let Anda get to you, Jelena," she said.

"Anda can be a real bitch, sometimes," Kami added. "It's the way she was raised. You know *we* don't feel that way, don't you, Jelena?"

Jelena forced her mouth into a smile, appreciating her friends' attempts to comfort and reassure her. "What Anda says does not bother me," she lied. "It is something I have heard many times before…in different words, from people I grew up with."

"I've served Lord Sen for many years," Aneko said. "And he's never shown anything but fairness to any person living in Kerala, be they hikui or okui. He's that kind of a man, and he's tried to set a good example for all of us." She took a sip of beer and wiped her lips on the back of her hand.

"I've known Lord Ashinji his whole life," she continued. "When he was very young, back when he lived here at Kerala Castle full time, he had one or two boyish crushes, but they were passing fancies.

Never have I seen him in love…until now, and I can tell you truly, that purity of blood makes no difference to him."

"Please, Aneko! You must not say this thing," Jelena begged. "You know situation of mine. Impossible for me, for us to…Ugh! My Siri-dar is not good enough to make known feelings of mine with proper words!"

Kami nodded sympathetically.

Aneko's kind expression told Jelena that the older woman understood perfectly.

"We commoners are more fortunate than noble folk in some ways," Aneko said. "Most of us get to choose for ourselves whom we would mate with. Lord Ashinji will have to marry according to his parents' wishes, but that doesn't mean that the two of you can't be together. You have won his heart, and that will be yours for the keeping, even after he marries."

Jelena shook her head vigorously. "No! I refuse…not for me the life of a concubine! I left Amsara for this reason. My uncle, he would force me into loveless…how to say what is a binding agreement? I would be concubine only, never wife. I chose to run. I will not…be *slave!*"

She jumped up from the table, upsetting the half-full mug of beer before her, sending the foamy amber liquid gushing over the scarred wood. Sorrow and anger in equal measure threatened to tear her heart to pieces. The air of the common room suddenly lost all ability to nourish her lungs. She had to flee or suffocate.

Heedless of the concerned cries of her companions, Jelena flung herself through the open door and pelted headlong down the stairs into the stableyard. Stumbling to a halt at the bottom, she doubled over in pain and grabbed at her side. She sagged down onto the bottom step and leaned against the sun-warmed wood of the wall. Eyes tightly shut, she willed the pain to pass while acknowledging the not so subtle reminder that her body still had not fully healed.

The vibration of footsteps upon the stairs caused her to open her eyes and look up.

"Jelena," Aneko said softly. She settled down on the step beside Jelena and tenderly caressed her shoulder. "You must love our young lord very much."

Jelena nodded. "With all my heart. From the moment I first saw him."

"Then it's no wonder that you won't settle for anything less than a full partnership with him. I wouldn't either, if I were in your place. I meant no insult to you when I suggested that you consider a…lesser arrangement. I only meant to show you that there was a way to be with him, even if you two can't marry."

Hearing it put so plainly—*you two can't marry*—hurt, with a pain that seared her with its intensity. Jelena wanted to jump up and scream, punch her hand through the wall, tear at her hair, anything to let the pain out lest it consume her flesh and reduce her body to ash.

How can the gods be so cruel? What did I ever do to deserve such punishment? Why did they bring me here so that I could fall in love with Ashinji when they knew that I could never have him? Am I doomed never to be happy?

"Jelena!... Jelena!"

Jelena started, snapping back into the here and now. She turned a wide-eyed stare towards Aneko, who looked down at Jelena's hands, face frozen in astonishment. "What is the matter, Aneko? What are you seeing?" Jelena felt a thrill of alarm.

"Your hands!" Aneko exclaimed. "Jelena, do you know what you just did?"

"Was it…blue fire…from my fingers?" Aneko nodded. "Aneko, know you what is this…this fire?"

"Most people call it magelight or handfire. I've only ever seen trained mages do it." Aneko paused and stared intently into Jelena's face for several heartbeats. "Do you know what this means, Jelena?" she said slowly then answered her own question. "It means that you've got Talent, and a high level of it, at that. Does Lady Amara know about this?"

"N-No," Jelena stammered. "What is this thing, Talent?"

"Magic, Jelena. All elves are born with it. Some have it much more strongly than others." The guardswoman's dark eyes narrowed pensively.

"I…I did not wish to say about it until I knew my place here, but I have had it since…since before I came to Kerala. I knew it was magic, but…"

"This is important, Jelena," Aneko interrupted. "Most hikui don't have much Talent, but you…" She shook her head. "You are obviously different. Lady Amara will want to know. She's a trained sorceress, though I don't think she practices much anymore. She can help you to learn about your Talent."

And so what if I do have Talent? Jelena thought. Did it really matter that she could conjure up magelight—she, a half-human common girl, with no social rank other than that of servant? She would still never be allowed to marry Ashinji.

Aneko must have sensed the change in her attitude. "You can't give in to despair," the older woman said firmly. "You have the makings of a good life here, Jelena. I know that you are searching for your elven kin. If you are able to find them, and they are a noble family and they accept you, then things might change. There might be a chance for you and Lord Ashinji." She paused and laid a hand on Jelena's forearm. "But if it doesn't work out that way," she continued gently, "accept it and move on. You are young and yes, pretty. There are many men who would find you attractive. You might just find one who'll offer you an honorable proposal. Or, with Lady Amara's help, perhaps you could enter a mage school. No hikui's ever done so before, but who knows?"

But I don't want an honorable proposal from any other man, and I'm not sure I want to go to a mage school, even though I do want to learn about my Talent, Jelena thought. She knew Aneko's words sprang from a sincere, heart-felt desire to help Jelena see that she did have options. She appreciated her friend's effort, but she had already made her decision.

If making a life with Ashinji could never happen, then she would make one without him, alone. She would learn all she could about her magic, and if it meant cloistering herself away in some musty school somewhere, so be it. She would love no other man, ever. Her mind could not quite confront the enormity of her decision, not yet. But in time, it would become familiar, comfortable…bearable, even.

"Thank you, Aneko, for advice," Jelena said. "I think I wish time alone, now."

Aneko gave Jelena's shoulder a final squeeze and stood up. "Think about what I've said."

She turned and made her way back up the stairs, leaving Jelena to her melancholy solitude.

CHAPTER 19

THE WEDDING PARTY ARRIVES

Here they come!" Kami cried, jumping up and down with child-like excitement, her hazel eyes sparkling.

All the castle's inhabitants not obliged to be at work were gathered by the main gates, awaiting the arrival of the wedding party. Jelena estimated they numbered at least a hundred people, about a third of the castle's population. The massive, iron-bound wooden gates had been opened a short time earlier, upon the arrival of Lord Dai's herald. Ashinji, astride a big black horse, waited at the center of the entrance, the herald behind and to the side.

Jelena had received a quick lesson in elven wedding etiquette from Aneko last evening. It all seemed quite complicated, but then, so were the nuptial customs of Soldaran nobility. According to tradition, Ashinji's duty as the brother closest in age to the bridegroom began with his greeting of his sibling's bride at the castle's outer gate. He would recite a ritual greeting to the bride's parents, then escort the entire party up to the keep where Lord Sakehera waited with Sadaiyo and the rest of the family.

Once the prescribed greetings and exchanges of token gifts between the parents of the couple had taken place, all would sit down for a midday meal. The bride's face would remain veiled, to keep her hidden from her future husband. Sadaiyo would not be allowed to see or speak to his bride until that evening, after the official Ritual of Welcoming had been performed, the second and most important of Ashinji's duties.

The ritual served as a formal declaration of acceptance by the groom's family; without it, the bride would have no official place in the family, despite a legal marriage. Ashinji had spoken briefly of it, confessing to Jelena that he would be very glad when his part in his brother's marriage would be over.

Jelena had not seen or spoken to Ashinji since their last language lesson three days ago. She threaded her way through the crowd to stand close to the gates, near enough to watch Ashinji and observe the wedding party at the same time.

She fought down the urge to call out to him. Never had she seen him dressed so richly, in brocaded silks of peacock blue and emerald green that matched the color of his eyes. His hair hung unbraided, the sides held up off of his face with a silver clip set with blue and green stones.

Ashinji bowed formally, from the waist, as Lord Dai reined in his horse just inside the gate. The large wedding party numbered at least three score, with many retainers and guards in addition to Lord Dai's family. Several heavily laden wagons brought up the rear. Ashinji urged his mount forward until he and Lord Dai sat shoulder to shoulder. Jelena strained to hear as Ashinji delivered the ritual greeting, but she stood too far away to catch the softly spoken words. Lord Dai nodded once, firmly, and allowed a smile to soften the stern lines of his face. Ashinji then wheeled his horse, and the entire procession clattered noisily through the gates, colorful banners snapping in the air.

Surrounded by guards, a beautiful wooden carriage rolled by Jelena's vantage point, pulled by two sturdy, shaggy-footed draft horses. Carved likenesses of warrior maidens adorned each corner, and the entire brightly painted conveyance flashed with silver and gold leaf accents. As she watched, Jelena thought she saw the merest sliver of a woman's face peak out from between the gauzy curtains covering the window.

Someone jostled her from behind and she turned to find Kami at her shoulder. The elf girl giggled with glee. "Did you see her?" she asked breathlessly. "That was the bride, there in the carriage! Weddings are such fun! Wait 'til you see all of the wonderful food we're going to get. I can hardly wait for Gendan's and my wedding day. Of course, ours won't be nearly so grand." Jelena had to laugh. Kami's high spirits were infectious.

The crowd began to move forward, following in the wake of the horses and wagons toward the upper gate. "C'mon! We don't want to miss a single moment!" Kami grabbed Jelena's hand and pulled her along with the flow of cheerful, chattering people.

The wedding procession passed through the upper gate and pulled up in front of the keep. With Jelena in tow, Kami pushed to the front of the crowd of castle dwellers, who maintained a respectful distance from the proceedings. Kami nudged Jelena excitedly. "Look, there's my Gendan standing there by the door! Doesn't he look incredibly handsome and smart in his parade armor?" Kami's love for Kerala's Captain of the Guards suffused her face with a sweet glow. Despite her ribald talk, no one who knew her had any doubt that Kami's heart belonged to Gendan and no other. Jelena knew what that kind of love felt like; only, for her, there would probably be no happy ending.

Lord and Lady Sakehera stood hand in hand before the open doors of the keep. To Lord Sen's right stood Sadaiyo, coldly resplendent in a beautifully decorated robe of yellow and red silk. Jelena could not help but admire the intricacy of the workmanship, for the entire garment shimmered with an intertwining motif of flowering vines. Every few heartbeats, Sadaiyo would reach up and tug on the high collar as if the stiff fabric irritated his neck.

Arrayed in well-behaved silence behind their elders, the three Sakehera daughters stood with Lani, the oldest, stationed behind her two little sisters, a hand on each small shoulder. Their robes were more simply decorated, but no less finely crafted than their brother's.

Ashinji and Lord Dai dismounted and handed their horses off to waiting grooms, as did Lord Dai's captain, who immediately walked back to the painted carriage. The door swung open, and he offered his hand in assistance to the woman who emerged, blinking, into the sunlight.

By her age and the conservative cut of her dark blue gown, Jelena surmised that this must be Lady Dai. She was a tall woman—stately even—with jet-black tresses confined beneath a headdress of silver wire hung with merrily dancing leaves. After adjusting her headdress to her satisfaction, she allowed the captain to escort her forward and hand her off to her husband. The guard then trotted back to the carriage and held out his hand to the other occupant.

The woman who next emerged wore a resplendent gown of gold and white silk, embroidered all over with tiny pearls. A heavy white veil, secured by a gold headdress wrought to look like a garland of flowers, concealed her face. The captain led her forward where she took her place on her father's arm opposite her mother.

Even though her face remained hidden, there could be no mistaking this woman's identity—Lady Misune Dai, future Lady of Kerala.

Together, with Ashinji in the lead, the noble guests approached their hosts. Ashinji bowed deeply to his father and mother, who acknowledged his obeisance with nods of their heads. He then began to speak in his clear, melodic voice. "My lord and lady, Father and Mother, they who have brought your son and Heir his bride have arrived. Will you welcome Lord and Lady Dai into your home?"

"I welcome you, Lord and Lady Dai, to Kerala," Lord Sen replied.

"I also welcome you and she whom you bring to join with our House," Lady Amara added. Lord and Lady Dai bowed their heads in the proper acknowledgment between social equals; their daughter bowed more deeply, from her waist.

Lord Sen continued the formal introduction. "May I present to you my eldest son and Heir, Sadaiyo." Sadaiyo's bow to his future father-in-law was stiff, as if it pained him to have to show the correct amount of respect. His arrogant visage remained impassive. Jelena's gaze darted back and forth between Sadaiyo's face and his brother's. Ashinji's beauty owed as much to the kindness of his spirit as it did to his physical attraction. Sadaiyo was just as handsome, yet Jelena felt cold fear knot her gut when she looked at him.

Next, the two sets of parents exchanged gifts. Two of Lord Dai's servants came forward at his signal to present a large bolt of fine, sea-green silk to Lady Amara and a bow made of rich, dark wood to Lord Sen.

After a few words of admiration, Lord Sen pulled a small leather pouch from his sleeve.

"I hope these little baubles will bring you some pleasure, my lord and lady," Lord Sen said. He upended the pouch onto his open palm and two black pearls the size of hazelnuts spilled out, their iridescent surfaces gleaming in the sun. A soft murmur of appreciation rippled through the assemblage.

"They are most satisfactory, my lord," Lord Dai replied, inclining his head slightly in acknowledgement of the richness of the gift. Lord Sen carefully dropped the pearls back into the pouch and pressed it into his guest's hand.

"Come. A meal has been prepared," Lady Amara announced. "You must be very tired and thirsty after your long journey." Lord Sen waved his guests forward and everyone visibly relaxed. Jelena guessed that the formal ceremony of greeting had concluded. The two noble families filed up the steps and disappeared into the keep while the servants of Lord Dai began to mill about and the Kerala staff dispersed. A few folk remained behind to mingle. Gendan came forward to speak to Lord Dai's captain. The two men talked animatedly as if they knew each other. Gendan then spoke to the driver of the carriage and pointed toward the east wing of the keep. Jelena watched as the painted coach rolled away, a small knot of servants trotting briskly behind.

"Well, that's it for now," Kami sighed. "Oh, here comes my man!" She scampered over to meet Gendan as he approached and flung herself into his arms. The passion of their kiss made Jelena blush and lower her eyes.

"Jelena! Jelena, c'mere!" Kami called out, waving. Jelena sighed and walked over to where the lovers stood, arm in arm.

"Hello, Captain," Jelena greeted the older man formally.

"Jelena," Gendan replied. Captain Miri had never been very warm toward her, and she knew the reason behind his reticence, but neither had she ever felt any malice from him.

"Gendan has a few hours off, so we thought we'd take a ride out to the old stone circle. Will you tell Aneko where I've gone so she won't come looking for me?"

"Yes, of course." Jelena answered.

"Just wait 'til I get you alone, my girl!" Gendan's voice crackled with mischief. He tickled Kami, and she squealed in response, twisting in his arms to punch him playfully in the chest. Captain Miri had left his youth behind some time ago; Kami had just entered into the fullness of womanhood, but despite the difference in their ages, their temperaments seemed a perfect complement each to the other.

"You two have good time," Jelena said.

"Oh, we always do." Kami sensuously nibbled on Gendan's ear. It seemed to have the desired effect, for he grabbed her by the hand and hauled her off, stumbling and giggling, toward the gate. Kami waved happily, skipping a few steps to regain her balance. Together, the two lovers disappeared through the gate, leaving Jelena standing alone.

Only a few people remained in the upper yard, mostly house servants and the two guardsmen at the doors. Jelena wandered back down to the lower yard, thinking about Kami and Gendan and how lucky they were to be able to love each other openly and proudly. She imagined them making love in the deep grass of the stone circle, and it filled her with a longing so intense, she found it almost too much to bear.

Ashinji had looked so handsome today in his formal clothes, his beautiful hair shining like the fine silk of his garments. In her mind's eye, she replaced Gendan with Ashinji and imagined herself lying in his arms, her naked flesh entwined with his. Gods, how it hurt, knowing that she would never experience the warmth of his love.

The lower yard stood empty, with only the soft cooing of pigeons in the eaves of the barracks to break the stillness. The day's excitement at an end, the castle would quickly settle back into its routine.

Jelena's thoughts turned to Magnes. She wondered if her cousin had returned home, only to find Amsara shut against him. He had committed a serious crime when he had helped her to escape. To make matters even worse, he had turned his back on a marriage contract, an act that most certainly cost Duke Teodorus a dear price, both financially and socially. The duke was a proud man and would not easily forgive such disobedience.

Jelena had known loneliness her entire life, but what she felt now was an entirely new experience. Magnes had been the last link to her old life, the only person in Kerala who knew her entire history firsthand. In a very short time, she had been forced to shed every vestige of Soldaran identity. She now lived, dressed, and spoke as an elf. She had even begun to think and dream in Siri-dar; still, she felt her otherness as acutely as she ever had back in Amsara.

She had found good friends in Aneko and, especially, Kami. Friendship with other women was a pleasure she had heretofore been denied. The easy camaraderie she felt with them amazed her, and yet, she felt the inescapable fact of her *human* blood would forever set her apart from them. The irony of the situation was not lost upon her.

Ashinji had never tried to sweeten the truth for her about elven attitudes towards those of mixed blood. The folk of Kerala were especially tolerant because of their close proximity to human lands and a long history of interaction and commingling, but Ashinji warned that she might encounter prejudice as bitter as that which she had endured in Amsara, if and when she ever traveled beyond the relatively tolerant boundaries of eastern Alasiri.

As a rule, people of mixed race, referred to as *hikui* in Siri-dar, did not have the same legal rights and protections under the law as did full-blooded elves, though within Kerala, Lord Sen had decreed otherwise. Jelena's best hope lay in finding her father or his kin. If she were accepted, then she would be fully protected as a member of his family.

The wedding celebrations would be finished in another three days. At that time, Jelena was to take up her new duties as a messenger, which would give her the opportunity to seek out information on the possible identity of the man who had fathered her. With her ring and Lord Sakehera's help, she felt confident that she would soon know the truth.

Jelena looked up to find that her feet had carried her to the stables without any conscious direction on her part. She thought about going in and choosing a suitable mount, but a voice called out her name from behind. She turned to see Aneko striding briskly towards her.

"Jelena, have you seen Kami? She was supposed to report back here after everything was finished." The older woman looked as if she had just come from the bath house. Her dark hair hung wet and sleek to the middle of her muscular back, shining like an otter's pelt in the sunlight. Her face wore a look of mild annoyance, as if a harmless but none too amusing practical joke had just been played upon her.

"Kami is with Gendan. She told me tell you so you would not look. They went off...uh, to old circle stones."

"Ai, Goddess, that girl! She promised she'd take my shift if I traded with her so she could watch the bridal party," Aneko grumbled. "I can't very well complain to Gendan, now can I? She's going to get herself knocked up long before her wedding day if this keeps on."

"What is 'knocked up'? Oh, yes. Pregnant?"

"You are learning Siri-dar very fast," Aneko said, nodding approvingly. "Soon, you'll be able to curse with the best of us."

"Is pregnant before marriage bad thing here?" Jelena asked.

Aneko shrugged. "Uhhh, it's not what most women would choose, but it happens. There's no shame in it...not much, anyway. If it happens to you, Jelena, no one will think the worse of you."

Jelena looked down at her dusty sandals, hoping that Aneko could not see her chagrin. "I...I was going to choose horse...for me, for riding as messenger."

"C'mon, then. I'll help you." Aneko smiled and started towards the stable doors. Jelena followed, still clenched a little inside.

Like a hidden message woven into the fabric of metaphors that made up a poem, the meaning behind Aneko's words could be gleaned with just a bit of conscious thought.

If it happens to me. If I bear Ashinji a child, there won't be any shame in it. No shame, perhaps, but no celebrations, either.

Best for everyone if that never happens.

PART III

CHAPTER 20

HOMECOMING

The slowly dying sun set the ancient stones of Amsara Castle ablaze with crimson light. Long, dark shadows of towers and walls stretched like questing fingers across the plain below.

Magnes looked skyward to where the fortress squatted atop its rocky perch and felt a sharp twinge of anxiety deep in his gut. The first lamps of evening flared to life on the walls above, shining like stars drawn down from the heavens. Below, at the base of the hill, people made their way home to Amsara village after a long day in the fields. Herdsmen drove cattle into milking sheds and sheep into pens. Their shouts and whistled signals to their dogs pierced the still, sweet air.

Magnes drummed his heels against the flanks of his horse but the animal—weary from the trek south out of Alasiri—stubbornly refused to walk any faster. And so, slowly, but steadily, the elf-bred horse carried Magnes back to his father's house.

He knew the castle guard would have already spotted him some time ago, before the light of day had failed completely, but in the twilight of evening, they would be unable to identify him until he arrived at the gates. He had changed back into the clothes he had worn out of Amsara, so as to give no clue to where he had been these past weeks. Castle folk would be curious enough about his sudden return.

After riding up a series of switchbacks, Magnes reined in the horse at the main gates, which were shut tight for the night. The animal blew noisily and shook its head, then heaved a sigh. Magnes patted its sweat-darkened neck and waited.

A few moments passed before a small square hole opened up in the center of a door set within the gate itself. A pale blur flashed across the opening, and Magnes heard a startled exclamation, followed by loud exhortations to open the door and be quick about it.

The portal swung inward. Magnes dismounted and led the horse through, only to find himself surrounded by excited guardsmen, all talking at once. Someone took the reins from his hand and led the horse away. Another man asked if he wanted a drink. All welcomed him home, and none asked where he had been. They knew better.

"I think I should go to my father now," he said, and the men respectfully fell back.

~~~

At the entrance to the keep, Magnes paused for a moment, then pushed open the door and stepped over the threshold. His eyes immediately swung left to scan the great hearth. The flickering light of the lamps cast dancing shadows across the cold stones of the dead fireplace. The hearth lay bare.

Ghost was not in his usual place.

Magnes swallowed hard and decided that he would deal with that later. For now, he had to stay totally focused on how he planned to handle his father.

It's dinner time, you idiot, Magnes chided himself. *Father won't be here in the keep.*

Duke Teodorus always insisted that the family gather together this one time during the day to eat and discuss family business. Magnes pulled the keep door closed and headed for the great hall.

The sound of multiple voices alerted him to the presence of guests in the great hall this night. Magnes halted just outside the door to gather his wits. He had no wish to face his father in front of an audience, but this particular confrontation could not wait. The door stood slightly ajar. He put an eye to the crack and surveyed the room.

Duke Teodorus occupied his rightful place at the head of the main table. Thessalina sat to his left, dressed in her usual brown and black leathers. To her left sat Father Nath, Amsara's resident priest. To the duke's right, in the chair usually reserved for Magnes, slouched the corpulent Lord Taceo, a minor noble and one of Duke Teodorus's vassals. Taceo's equally rotund wife had wedged herself into the chair on her husband's right.

Father Nath had just made a comment about the divisions in the Soldaran Imperial Council over the empress's plans for war, when Magnes pushed open the door and stepped into the room.

All conversation ceased. Everything, including the very air itself, seemed frozen, as if time had stopped. The sound of his own heartbeat roared thunderously in Magnes's ears.

"Gods…Magnes, you're back!" Thessalina exclaimed, shattering the spell.

"Hello, Father," Magnes said. His feet had mysteriously grown roots that now anchored him to the rush-strewn floor. He could not move.

Duke Teodorus slowly lowered his wine goblet and wiped his mouth on a cloth. His face was still, as inscrutable as that of a stone sphinx guarding a desert temple. His icy blue stare fastened onto his son with chilling intensity.

The tension in the room hung as thick as congealed blood. Nobody dared move or speak, not even Thessalina, whose quick eyes darted from her father's face to her brother's, then back again.

At last, when Magnes thought he could bear it no longer, the duke spoke.

"Tell me, Daughter," he drawled. "What should be done with a son who steals another man's property, runs out on a legal marriage contract, and brings disgrace to himself and his family?"

"Father, I…I," Thessalina stammered, for once at a loss for words.

The roots loosened their hold, and Magnes took a step forward. "Father, please just listen to…"

"*Shut your mouth!*" roared the duke, launching himself from his chair with such violence that it flipped over backward. Lady Taceo screamed in panic and plopped to the floor as her husband, letting out a startled yelp, threw himself sideways to avoid Duke Teodorus's flying wine goblet.

The duke rounded the table and advanced on Magnes like an enraged bear. Magnes stood his ground, and braced himself.

Radiating white-hot fury, the duke halted before Magnes and raised his fist. Unflinchingly, Magnes held his breath and waited for the blow that would surely knock him senseless. He prayed that, when he awoke, his father would be calm enough to listen.

He was vaguely aware of panicky voices raised in alarm, but they did not matter. His entire focus had centered, with the crystal clarity that comes with extreme danger, upon one point. He saw—really *saw*—for the first time, the sheer size of his father's hand—the back of it crisscrossed by an intricate roping of veins, the whitened knuckles dusted with coarse, black hair. The heavy gold signet ring the duke wore on his middle finger would surely leave an interesting mark.

The blow never came.

Slowly, Duke Teodorus lowered his hand. Thessalina stood behind him, gripping his shoulder.

Magnes started breathing again.

A muscle in the duke's jaw twitched, like a little worm jumping under the skin. "We will speak tomorrow. You will tell me *everything*. Now go!" he growled. Magnes looked beyond his father to Thessalina, whose eyes implored him to obey.

He turned and fled through the door out into the night, feeling like a coward. He should have somehow made his father listen. Instead, he had tucked his tail in and had slunk away like a whipped dog.

Slowly, he walked back to the keep. The vacant hearth caused his gut to clench as he crossed the ground floor chamber and made his way upstairs to his apartments. Pain rapidly filled the hollow space that had opened up in his heart.

Snagging a small lamp out of its niche in the wall beside the door to his rooms, he entered and made his way over to the fireplace, where he lit two larger lamps. Slowly, his eyes wandered over the familiar space.

A fine layer of dust coated the mantle. The chamber had a forlorn, abandoned quality to it, as if its occupant had had to vacate in haste, leaving almost everything behind, which, in fact, was what had happened. He sat down at his writing table and trailed a finger through the dust on its surface.

The gurgling pangs in his stomach reminded him that he had eaten nothing since morning. He thought about going down to the kitchen, then decided against it. He could not face anyone else tonight, not even the servants.

Weariness descended on him with the swiftness of a dark winter fog. His arms and legs felt weighted down with rocks as he struggled toward the bedchamber. Somehow, he managed to dredge up enough energy to pull off his boots before he collapsed across the bed, fully clothed. He plunged into sleep before his head hit the coverlet.

~~~

Magnes awoke to the sounds of someone moving about in the outer chamber. He sat up and rubbed his eyes, yawning. He looked down at his rumpled clothing, then cautiously sniffed at his armpits and wrinkled his nose in distaste. He wondered, with wry amusement, what the fastidious and ever impeccably groomed Ashinji would make of him. No doubt his elven friend's perfectly shaped nose would be offended, but he would be too polite to say so directly.

Magnes rolled off the bed and stumped out into the front room, startling the servant who had just finished laying out a meal.

"Ai, gods! Ye nearly scared me out o' me skin, m'lord," the man exclaimed. The delightful aroma of fried bacon and fresh baked bread filled the room. Magnes's stomach rumbled fiercely. "Lady Thessalina told me t' bring ye up sommat to eat," the servant explained. "I hope yer hungry."

"I am ravenous! Thank you, Conrad," Magnes replied. He sat down and began to eat, stopping only briefly to allow the servant to pour him a mug of hot cider.

"Welcome home, sir," Conrad said with affection. "We all missed ye."

"It's good to be back," Magnes answered around a mouthful of bread and apple butter. *I think.*

The servant departed with a promise to send a maid up later to clean and air out Magnes's rooms. Taking a hunk of butter-slathered bread and his mug of cider with him, Magnes moved to sit in one of the sunny, eastward facing window enclosures. He pushed open the pane and drew in a deep breath. The smells of home were wonderfully intoxicating.

From his vantage point, he could look out over a part of the kitchen yard and observe the servants going about their chores. A familiar, stout figure sallied forth from the kitchen, wisps of gray hair straggling down around her ears from underneath her white cap—Claudia, on her way to the laundry. Magnes almost called out to her but then decided against it. He would wait to speak to her in private. She, of all people, deserved to know how Jelena fared.

Magnes licked the last crumbs of bread from his fingers and tossed off the rest of the cider in a single gulp. He ran his hand across the three day old stubble on his chin and grimaced. Now that he was back home, he would be able to shave with a proper razor. Elf males grew no beards, and so, back at Kerala, when he had requested a shaving kit, he had been met with blank stares. Ashinji had finally provided him with a small knife with which to do the job, but it just hadn't been the same.

A knock at the door heralded the arrival of the maid. Magnes opened the door to reveal a young woman in an apron, rags and broom in hand.

"Mornin', sir. Come to clean yer chambers, sir," the maid said with a quick curtsy.

"Um, yes. Well, there's something I need before you can start, and that is a bath," Magnes replied.

The maid looked puzzled. "A bath, sir?" she repeated. Magnes nodded.

"But, it's not ev'n a holiday, sir, leastways, not any I know of. Beggin' yer pardon, sir."

"Yes, right you are, but nevertheless, I want and need a bath. As a matter of fact, from now on, I plan to bathe every day. What d'you think of that?" The maid shook her head, jaw hanging open in complete bewilderment. Magnes burst out laughing at the expression on the young woman's face, convinced that she now believed that he had gone mad while away. "Go and tell Conrad that I need a tub, some hot water, and soap." The maid gulped and nodded, then scurried off.

Some time later, after considerable effort on the part of Conrad and several other servants, Magnes sat in a laundry basin half full of tepid water, scrubbing three days worth of dirt from his body. He sincerely missed the bath house at Kerala, with its deep soaking tub full of hot, herb-scented water. The harsh laundry soap he had to make do with stung and reddened his skin, and even after he had dumped two pitchers of clean water over his head, he still felt a little grimy.

After finishing his less than satisfactory wash, he dressed in clean clothes and left his chambers to the servants. He could delay no longer.

The time had come to face his father.

CHAPTER 21

THE PRICE OF LOVE

Magnes found the duke in the exercise paddock behind the stables, hacking around the circular enclosure on a magnificent gray stallion. He leaned on the wooden railing and watched with silent admiration the skill and artistry of his father's horsemanship.

"Lord Magnes! Yer back!" a familiar, high-pitched voice shouted.

Dari, the young ginger-haired groom skidded to a stop a few paces from Magnes, freckled face alight with excitement. Magnes blinked, doubting the accuracy of his eyes. It seemed to him as if Dari had grown several inches over the last two months.

"How'd you get so big so fast, Dari? I haven't been gone that long, have I?"

"Aye, long enough, sir. Dunno how it happens. I just wake up ev'ry mornin' an' I'm bigger."

Magnes smiled, touched by the boy's simple cheerfulness. "The stallion my father is riding...I've never seen him before."

"Oh, that's his Grace's new warhorse. Arrived just last week, all the way from Kalu...Kalun..."

"Kalundwe?" Magnes prompted.

"Aye, that's it! He's a beauty, he is, sir. I'm not allowed near 'im, though. None of us lads are, only Master Nolus and Lian. They look after 'im."

Magnes turned his attention back to the arena where horse and rider were executing a series of flying lead changes. Dari leaned on the railing beside him, totally spellbound. The stallion moved with effortless grace, powerful muscles sliding beneath shimmering hide like ripples on water. A pair of blackbirds, who just moments before had been squabbling atop a pile of dung, took flight and blew past the stallion's nose, but the horse ignored them, so attuned was he to his rider. As the duke cantered past their position on the fence, the beast snorted, spattering Magnes and Dari with a spray of fine moisture.

Duke Teodorus cantered the stallion in ever tightening circles until he had the horse spinning on his haunches. He then brought the stallion to a complete stop, fully collected and ready to take off in any direction at the touch of a heel. The duke held him thus for several heartbeats, then released him. The horse visibly relaxed and stretched out his neck for a vigorous shake. His ears, which only a moment ago had stood erect with alertness, now flopped lazily.

The duke dismounted and led the horse toward the gate. Magnes slowly walked over to meet him. He lifted the latch and held the gate open as his father and the stallion passed through, then followed behind as Duke Teodorus led his new mount back into the stables.

Lian, the head groom under Master Nolus, waited at the stable entrance to take the stallion from the duke, who handed over the reins with a word of thanks. Dari scurried past with a quick wave to Magnes and disappeared into the dim interior of the barn.

"How was he today, your Grace?" Lian asked as he slipped a halter over the stallion's head. The big horse whickered softly.

"He's settled down nicely," the duke replied. "He's a little stiff on the left hand, but that'll soon sort itself out. The important thing is that he's got a cool head. He listens well, unlike a lot of stallions. That's vital in the heat of battle. He'll not panic and bolt. I think I'll start him on some sparring exercises next week."

"He's magnificent, Father. He must have cost a small fortune," Magnes said, taking care to keep his voice neutral. The duke stared coldly at his son for a heartbeat, then began walking briskly back towards the keep.

Magnes took a deep breath and fell in beside him. "Father, I..." he began, but Teodorus cut him off.

"Be quiet, boy." Magnes gulped and shut his mouth. Father and son walked on in chilly silence. Magnes shot a quick glance at the duke's face but saw only stony impassivity. They crossed the yard quickly and entered the keep. As Magnes followed his father up the stairs to the second floor, he felt like an errant child about to receive a whipping for an especially heinous act of disobedience, which, in a way, was accurate.

After slamming the door to his study behind them, Duke Teodorus crossed the room to sit in a large, padded armchair. He pointed wordlessly to the footstool beside it. Magnes needed no further instructions. He positioned the stool in front of the chair and down he sat, like a penitent before a judge.

"Start talking," the duke ordered. Magnes folded his hands in his lap to keep them from shaking, lest they betray his anxiety.

At first, his mouth could not seem to form the right words. His mind and heart knew what they wished to say, but his tongue turned traitor and refused to cooperate. With an enormous effort of will, he finally broke through the barrier, and the words flowed out in a great rush, like water over a shattered dam.

He told his father all of it. He first spoke of Jelena's despair and desperation. He then confessed his love for Livie and his desire to step aside in favor of Thessalina so that he could marry the woman he loved and live in peace with her, farming the land. He wanted to make his father understand why both he and Jelena had felt compelled to flee Amsara. Neither one of them could face what had been decreed by others for them. He finished by relating, briefly, all that had befallen Jelena and him in Alasiri and his reasons for returning.

Duke Teodorus listened in silence, his face a still-life rendered in cold granite. When Magnes finished, he waited, eyes lowered, for his father to speak.

Several heartbeats slipped by, and still, the duke remained silent. It was torturous, and, Magnes felt certain, quite deliberate.

Just as Magnes decided he could not stand it any longer, his father spoke.

"So. The elf lord let you leave, did he? Stupid of him. If it'd been the other way round, I would've kept his son hostage...in irons."

Magnes looked up sharply. "Father..."

"I am your liege lord and your father," the duke stated slowly, cutting him off. "And as both, I have absolute authority over you in all things. Is this not so?"

Magnes stared at the duke, taken off-guard by the question.

"Is this not so?" the duke raised his voice a notch, and his eyes narrowed dangerously.

"Yes, Father," Magnes conceded.

"Your disobedience cost me a great deal of money, but what is worse, you shamed me and brought disgrace upon our family. You stole another man's property. Do you know what that makes you? Veii and I had already signed a contract. Money had exchanged hands. The girl was bought and paid for."

A flash flood of anger surged through Magnes. The words escaped his mouth before he had time to think of stopping them. "Stop talking about her as if she were a thing! Her name is Jelena! She is your only sister's daughter, for the gods' sake! Why could you never accept her as part of our family?"

"You keep silent while I'm speaking to you!" the duke hissed. Furiously, he sprang from his chair and began to pace. Reflexively, Magnes ducked, expecting a blow. Instead, the duke folded his arms tightly behind his back and continued to rant.

"You are going to pay back Veii out of your own purse, d'you hear? And what's more, there'll be no more talk of you stepping aside. You are the Heir, and that'll never change, so live with it! The marriage contract can be renewed. I happen to know that Orveta has yet to find another prospect for his daughter. This alliance between our two houses is far too profitable to abandon over the foolish whim of a lovesick puppy!"

"Is that what you think I am, a lovesick *puppy*?" Magnes could barely speak through teeth clenched as tight as the jaws of a wolf trap.

"I think that you are the future Duke of Amsara, and it's high time you started acting like it. Now, get out! When I summon you again, you'd better be ready to tell me everything you know about that tink castle and its defenses. *And* I suggest you spend some time meditating on the error of your ways!" The duke turned his back on his son and went to stand by the open window. Magnes opened his mouth to protest, but the futility of it froze his tongue. Instead, he retreated as ordered. He left his father's study and fled to the heights of Amsara's outer wall where he could calm his mind and think.

If only I'd had been able to make Father understand. Gods know I tried, but he wouldn't listen.

Magnes began to regret coming back to Amsara.

Perhaps it would have been better if I'd never returned. I could have gone south to Darguinia or west to the seacoast and gotten passage on a freighter outbound to the Shilluk Islands, he thought. *I still could. After enough time has passed, Father will be forced to declare Thessalina his Heir.*

Magnes truly believed that his sister would make a far better ruler than he ever could be. It was she who had inherited the necessary qualities that made a good leader, not he.

Magnes also believed that, deep down, Duke Teodorus knew the truth of the matter but refused to acknowledge it. The duke was a man who defined his life by tradition, and he would stubbornly cling to it, no matter the consequences, and by tradition, the first-born inherited all titles, lands, responsibilities, and obligations.

All of which Magnes would gladly hand over to Thessalina, without a moment's hesitation.

The sun stood directly overhead now, and the land below lay prostrate under shimmering waves of heat. Magnes wiped his profusely sweating brow on his arm and retreated back down off of the wall and into the relative cool of the partially shaded yard. As he splashed water from a horse trough onto the back of his neck, he spied Claudia crossing the yard, headed towards the kitchen.

"Claudia, wait!" he called out.

The old nurse stopped in her tracks and whirled around at the sound of her name. Magnes watched her mouth form an O of surprise just before her hands flew up to cover it.

As he approached, smiling, she rocked back and forth on her heels. "Ye've come back to us, oh, gods be praised!" she cried, stretching out her hands and laying them on either side of his face when he drew close enough to touch. Of all the servants at Amsara, only she could take such liberties.

He folded her plump fingers into his and squeezed them affectionately. "Claudia, I have news," he said, and her eyes, sparkling with tears, grew wide. "Jelena is safe. She lives now in a place called Kerala, in the service of an elf lord named Sakehera."

"She's found them, then? Her father's kin? Oh, Lord Magnes, this be good news, indeed!" Claudia clasped her hands together and looked heavenward, as if offering a prayer of thanksgiving to the gods.

"No, she hasn't found her father yet, but Lord Sakehera has pledged to help her in her search. In the meantime, he has allowed her to stay and earn her keep as his messenger."

"The elves were acceptin' of her, then? I was so afraid they'd be as cruel to my little lamb as folk was here. It tore my heart thinkin' on it, it did."

"They have accepted her, some more than others, but as a whole, she is treated well. And there's more. When I left, our Jelena and the lord's younger son were becoming close. I know for a fact that she's very much in love with him, and I strongly suspect that he returns her feelings."

"My prayers have been answered! My baby has found a place amongst people who'll love her an' treat her well, even if she be not their kin an' of mixed blood, besides. If the gods're merciful, she'll find her own family afore long."

"There is so much I want to tell you, Claudia, but for now, it must wait. I know you have work to do, and there is someone I must go and see. I just pray that I'm not too late."

"Gods bless ye, Lord Magnes. Ye've brought joy to this old woman. I thank ye!" Claudia took Magnes's hand and fervently pressed her lips to it. She then turned and shuffled off toward the laundry, dabbing at her eyes with the hem of her apron. Magnes stood a moment, watching until the old nurse disappeared from view. A surge of affection for Claudia flooded his chest with warmth. He had very little memory of his own mother, who had died when he was just a baby. Claudia's was the only face he could conjure up when he thought about the idea of a mother's love.

Love of a different sort now occupied his mind as Magnes headed back toward the stables. Dari sat in a patch of shade by the barn door, cleaning tack. The instant he spotted Magnes, the boy put aside the bridle he'd been scrubbing and scrambled to his feet.

"I need a horse, Dari," Magnes called out.

"Aye, sir, right away." Dari turned, cupped his hands to his mouth, and shouted into the shadowy doorway. "Oi! Pip! C'mere, *now!*" He looked over his shoulder at Magnes and grinned. A few heartbeats later, a younger lad of no more than ten summers scrambled out of the barn, bright purple juice smearing his face and hands. Dari cuffed him across his tow head.

"Ow! Wha' was that for!" the child yelled in protest, his face a comic mask of indignation.

Dari looked smug as he shot a knowing glance at Magnes. "That was fer not botherin' t' clean up before you came out here." He slapped the boy again, eliciting another yelp. "And that one's fer sassin' me in front of Lord Magnes. Go and get the chestnut mare out o' the far paddock, and be quick about it." The boy scampered off.

"Since when do you get to boss the other lads around, Dari?" Magnes inquired.

"Since Lian give me permission to, sir. I'm the oldest now. Of the lads, that is. Lian says I'm t' be head groom one day, soon as he's Master. I've got the touch, he says." Dari's voice swelled with pride.

"Yes, you do have a definite way with horses, Dari, but take care that you treat the people under you with kindness. You'll not get the loyalty and respect of the other lads by bullying them. If you show them that you care about them, they will want to give you their best. Believe me, it works."

As Dari listened to Magnes's words of advice, he slowly deflated like a punctured wineskin. Crestfallen, he nodded in understanding. Just then, the boy Pip returned with the mare.

Dari took the halter rope from the child's hand and gave his little shoulder a pat. "Good boy, Pip. Now, go an' get the brushes and picks an' I'll let you help with th' groomin'." The child's face lit up like a candle, and he ran to obey.

Magnes waited in the shade while the two boys groomed and tacked up the mare. After they had finished, he thanked the boys and mounted, turning the horse's head towards the main gate. The boys waved as he left the stable yard, and he raised his hand in acknowledgement.

The guardsmen turned at the sound of approaching hoof beats. Magnes hailed them, and they snapped off a crisp salute as he rode past and out onto the switchbacks leading down off Amsara's rocky eyrie. At the base of the hill, he turned and rode along the outskirts of Amsara village until he came to the road that led south.

Amsara's chief game warden lived with his family on a small homestead about half a mile outside of the village, within spitting distance
of the verge of Duke Teodorus's private woodland hunting grounds.
When they were children, he and Livie would spend hours exploring
every bower and thicket beneath the lush, green canopy. The woods
became their own special, magical playground. Later, when they had
grown from playmates into lovers, the woods served as their trysting
place, enfolding their passion within its protective embrace.

Magnes still felt angry and guilty that he had had to leave so
precipitously, with no time to explain to Livie. *She probably thinks
I abandoned her,* he thought. He prayed that she would be at home
and that she would be willing to listen to him. He recalled how he
had once resolved to set her free so that she would have a chance
for a decent match. He chided himself for his foolishness. As long
as he lived, he could never let go of Livie. His body stirred with the
memory of the last time they'd made love, just before Sansa.

Somehow, they would find a way to join their lives.

He urged the mare into a slow lope. After a while, horse and
rider turned off the main road onto a narrow track that led across
a small, cultivated field. A neat, thatched cottage surrounded by a
wooden fence stood at the far end. A brace of hounds bayed at the
gate as he pulled the horse to a stop and dismounted.

The cottage door flew open and a woman's voice bellowed forth
from the dark interior. "What's all that racket, then!" The owner of
the voice poked her head around the door frame and let out a squeak
of surprise. "Oh, Lord Magnes, as I live and breathe!" The woman
disappeared briefly, then reappeared armed with a broom. She flew
out of the door and descended upon the dogs like a stooping eagle,
swinging the broom in a great arc. The hounds' frantic barks turned
to yelps of pain as they scrambled out of the way.

"Get back, you mangy curs! You know Lord Magnes! What's
the matter with you? Go on, get out of here!" she hollered, and the
dogs, sensing that the time for a strategic retreat had come, backed
off with tails wagging.

"Hello, Mistress Honoria. It's good to see you," Magnes said,
smiling.

Livie's mother had lost none of her formidable energy, even after twenty-five years of marriage and seven children. She ran her
household as tightly as any warship, and she was widely known and
respected as the best potter in the district. Livie, as the eldest child,
was apprenticed to the trade, and already had a reputation as a fine
craftswoman in her own right.

"Hello to you, Lord Magnes. Come in, come in. Don't know what's
gotten into those dogs. Truth be told, they're all bluster and no action." She swung open the gate to allow Magnes to enter the yard.
"I've got some of my homemade elderberry wine if you've a thirst. I
know how much you enjoy it." Her blue eyes twinkled merrily.

"I would love some, Mistress. Thank you." Magnes followed
Honoria into the cool interior of the thick-walled cottage. The two
dogs tailed them to the door then sat on the threshold, whining and
licking their chops.

"Greedy scoundrels," their mistress muttered, though not without some affection. "They know I've been making meat pasties, and
they think they can play me for some more scraps, though the gods
know they've had more than their share already." Magnes laughed at
the tragic looks on the dogs' faces. He sat at the well-worn table that
occupied the center of the large central chamber and waited until
Honoria had poured him a tankard of wine before he spoke.

"Where is Livie, Mistress? It's vitally important that I speak with
her."

Honoria sat opposite Magnes and folded her graceful, long-fingered hands on the table in front of her. She fixed Magnes with a sad,
knowing look that immediately filled him with foreboding. "There's
no easy way of saying this, milord, so I'm just going to say it. Livie's
gone. She's in Greenwood now, where her sister and her family live.
She's got her own shop there, started up just about one month ago.
I've heard tell that folk are already placing so many orders, she'll need
an assistant before too long."

"Then I'll ride to Greenwood tomorrow to see her. She has to
know why I left so suddenly without telling her. She must think I
abandoned her, but that's not true! I would never do that, Mistress.
I know you know how I feel about Livie. I never tried to hide it from
you. I love her, and she loves me. The only thing I've ever wanted is

for us to be together."

Honoria shook her head sadly. For a moment, she seemed too overcome to speak.

Magnes rose from his chair in alarm. "What is it? Please tell me what's wrong!" he cried.

"Oh, Lord Magnes! You can't go to Greenwood to see Livie now."

"Why not?"

"Because she's a married woman!"

Magnes sat down, hard, like a puppet whose strings have just been cut. He stared straight ahead, unblinking, his jaw working as if words were trying to push their way out of his mouth but were unable to breach the barrier of his teeth.

Finally, he managed to speak. "Tell me everything," he whispered.

"She met him when she was visiting her sister, around the time you disappeared. His name is Jonus, and he owns his own land...a fine, large parcel. He's a good, kind man, and he loves her. Oh, Lord Magnes! What was she to do? She had no hope with you, none at all, and we all know that's the truth. You are the future duke! Your father would never consent to a marriage between my daughter and his Heir. When she found out that you'd gone off without a word to her, she cried for days. Her father and I were frantic. We feared she'd kill herself!"

"I couldn't get word to her. There was no time," Magnes murmured.

"Then, one day, Jonus showed up at our door, asking to speak to us about a proposal. He'd come all the way from Greenwood to make his case for our Livie. Well, we told him honestly that we didn't think she was ready to marry, but Livie came out, dry-eyed and steady, and listened while he told her all of the reasons why he would make her a good husband."

Magnes could not bear to look into Honoria's eyes. "And she said yes."

"Lord Magnes, Livie is eighteen years old. She needs to get started on a family of her own. She had a good man willing to make her an offer, a man who was right there and able to marry her. What could you have offered my daughter? Certainly not marriage!"

Magnes laid his head down on his hands. Mistress Honoria's words felt like knives cutting into his flesh, but what made the pain so much worse was the truth of those words. He could see now, with such brutal clarity, the selfishness of his assumption that Livie would always remain willing to accept whatever crumbs of his life he could throw her, never demanding any more of him. How could he have been so cruel, so uncaring, so completely oblivious to the realities of what she needed?

Livie deserved a man who could love her and be a husband to her, a man who could give her legitimate children and help her build a secure life for their family.

The time had come to let Livie go.

He sat up and wiped his streaming eyes.

"The truth is often something that we don't want to hear, yet we need to hear it, nonetheless," he said.

Honoria nodded and patted his hand. "Jonus is a good man. He'll cherish our Livie, I promise you."

"I know he will because you have said it, Mistress Honoria."

Magnes tossed off the tankard in one gulp and rose to leave. Honoria saw him out to the gate and waited while he mounted up. The two hounds sat quietly at her feet, watching mournfully, as if they could sense the great sadness that hung in the air.

"Farewell, Mistress. Give my regards to the warden," Magnes said.

"Gods bless you, milord," Honoria replied.

Magnes turned the mare's head and urged her into a trot towards the road.

He did not look back.

CHAPTER 22

DEVASTATION

When Magnes returned to Amsara late that afternoon, he headed straight up to his rooms and locked himself in. The servant Conrad knocked shortly after nightfall. When Magnes opened the door, he gasped in dismay and said, "Young Master, what're ye doin' standin' here in the dark for?"

Magnes shrugged listlessly in response.

"Well, can I at least come in an' light a lamp or two?"

Magnes shook his head. "Just bring me a couple of flagons of wine…The Rhandon should do. It's good and strong."

Conrad's eyes flashed with worry. "Yes, sir. Straightaway," he said and left to do as he was bid. Magnes waited in the dark, slumped in a chair, eyes tightly shut.

The servant returned quickly with the wine, a tankard, and a small tray of cold meat and bread. Magnes took the wine and told the man to return the food to the kitchen. He closed the door in the bewildered Conrad's face and returned to his chair by the open window.

The moon hung low in the sky, a tiny sliver of silver, barely visible above the castle roofs. Magnes didn't bother to fill the tankard and drank directly from the flagon instead. The wine, dark and strong, soon took hold, and the unbearable pain that gnawed at his insides quieted down to a dull ache. He drank up the first flagon quickly and then started on the second, sipping until he felt completely numb. After a time, he slept.

The discomfort of a full bladder woke him several hours later.

Staggering to the bedchamber, he groped beneath the bed until his fingers snagged the chamberpot. With a sigh, he relieved himself, then wobbled back into the outer chamber to retrieve the wine flagon. With almost no light to see by, virtually blind and still drunk, he blundered into the heavy armchair and crashed to the floor.

Cursing softly, he hoisted himself back up into the chair and sat quietly for a moment until the pain of his cracked shin subsided. When he could breathe again, he groped for the unfinished flagon on the table to his right and managed to grasp it without knocking it over. He shook it gently, and the sloshing sound told him he had enough wine left to sustain his drunken state for the rest of the night. He raised the flagon to his lips and swallowed deeply, then passed out.

He awoke the next morning with a vicious headache and no memory of having fallen asleep again. The empty wine flagon lay on the floor at his feet, a small red blotch staining the carpet beneath its lip.

A soft knock at the door brought Magnes unsteadily to his feet. He swayed a little and sat back down as his stomach threatened to rebel. He breathed deeply for several heartbeats until the wave of nausea passed, then once again tried to stand. This time, he met with success and made it to the door without falling.

"You look like hell!" Thessalina exclaimed. Magnes waved her in and closed the door. "Conrad was worried about you. He asked me to look in on you this morning, and I can see that he was right to worry." She sat down in the window seat with her back to the morning sun. "Magnes, talk to me. All I know is what Father has told me, but I want to hear it from you. Is it true that you took Jelena to the Western Lands so that she could get away from Duke Sebastianus?"

"It's true," Magnes answered. His tongue had grown fur overnight and seemed to be twice as thick as it ought.

Thessalina shook her head incredulously. "But why would you risk so much for her? She was getting a very good deal. She wasn't worth shaming Father and running out on your own obligations, Brother."

"Please, Thess. I...I'm just not up to this conversation right now. Leave me be." He pressed the palm of his hand to his forehead and closed his eyes.

Thessalina clicked her tongue in dismay. "You're hung over. I've *never*...I've never even seen you drunk before! What's going on, Magnes? I know you. This is *not* about Jelena...Tell me what's wrong with you!"

Magnes sighed deeply. Like a terrier with a rat, Thessalina had him cornered, and she was not about to let him go until she had shaken every last detail out of him. "Livie's gone," he said. "She married a farmer from Greenwood. I've lost her for good."

"I'm so sorry, Brother," Thessalina murmured. "I know you loved her."

"It wasn't enough."

"What will you do now?"

"Gods, Thessalina! I don't know. I can't...no, I *won't* marry that stupid creature Father has chosen for me. I'll renounce all claims to the ducal coronet and take priestly vows before I let him force me into such an intolerable match."

"That's foolishness, Magnes. You know you can't just put aside your inheritance."

The alcoholic fog dampening Magnes's brain suddenly burned away in the light of revelation. He abruptly sat up and leaned forward. "I can, and I will. I never wanted the position anyway." He stared into his sister's eyes, trying to gauge her reaction to his words. She seemed genuinely shocked. "Don't pretend that you're surprised, Sister. You and I both know that you should be Father's Heir, not me. The only reason you aren't is because you had the misfortune of being born second in a land where the firstborn inherits everything. Never mind talent or temperament! It's only fitting that I should step aside. If I openly declare my intention to take priestly vows, Father can't stop me. He'll have to make you the Heir."

Thessalina stared, mouth agape in astonishment, unable to speak.

"Where is Ghost?" Magnes abruptly asked. Thessalina blinked rapidly, and he could see her mind start to shift and turn. She now realized the implications of his words, and they pleased her.

"Ghost... Where is he?" Magnes repeated.

Thessalina refocused. "He was an old dog. He died while you were gone. Don't worry. I saw to it that he got a decent burial. I had him put under the old chestnut tree in the back garden—the one we used to climb as children."

Magnes closed his eyes again and leaned back into his chair. He resolved to go say goodbye to Ghost, just as soon as he could stand without retching.

"Would you have someone bring me some willow bark tea, please," he whispered, massaging his temple in a vain attempt to stop the hammer blows inside his skull.

"I'd think long and hard about all of this, Brother," Thessalina suggested, but Magnes thought he detected an undercurrent of eagerness in her voice. He could not fault his sister for her ambition. They both wanted the same thing.

He felt, rather than saw, Thessalina leave the room. A strange lassitude gripped him, and he allowed it to carry him under. He stirred long enough to notice that a steaming mug of willow bark tea had appeared as if by magic on the table by his right hand. He drank it slowly, thankful that someone had thought to sweeten it. When he finished, he heaved himself up out of the chair, made his way to the bedchamber, and collapsed across the quilt, surrendering to sleep.

~~~

Duke Teodorus's ice-chip eyes narrowed when Magnes entered the study. The duke sat at his desk, a small oil lamp illuminating the stack of reports before him. Outside, the castle bell chimed out the hour of Nonis, the last before midnight.

"Details, so many details," the duke muttered. He picked up a large piece of vellum affixed with an ornate seal and waved it at Magnes. "Y'see this? Came today from the capital, signed by Empress Constantia's own hand. It says I'm to prepare and send a report with all speed detailing the strength and readiness of my forces. Bah! We're not anywhere close to being ready for a war, but it seems that the empress is growing impatient. She wants the armies of the Imperium to be ready to march against the elves in fourteen months time—less, if possible! Wishful thinking, I say. Lucky for us, though, you've seen the inside of that elf castle. I've no doubt the empress'll want me to secure it early on, since Amsara lies so close."

"Father, there are things I need to discuss with you," Magnes said quietly.

"And I with you, Son. I have written to Leonus to tell him that our contract can go ahead as planned. With the gods' luck and a little good timing, you should have Leonus's daughter wedded, bedded, and pregnant by fall's end."

"That is what I need to talk about, Father. I don't want to marry that girl."

"What you want doesn't matter," the duke sniffed. "You'll do as you're told. This isn't up for negotiation."

Magnes pulled his hair in frustration. He could feel the pressure building within him, threatening to boil over in an explosion of fury. "Father, listen to me!" he cried. "I *will not* marry Duke Leonus's daughter!"

"I strongly advise you *not* to defy me," the duke growled dangerously.

The dam within him burst and swept Magnes along on the crest of the wave. "I will abdicate my position and take priestly vows if you insist on this marriage! We all know Thessalina should be your Heir, anyway. Give it to her, Father. It's what we both want. Set me free, I beg of you!" he cried.

Without warning, the duke rose from his chair and rushed Magnes, pinning him against the wall by the fireplace. Magnes gasped in surprise, alarmed at how easily his father could hold him. "Please, Father," he croaked.

"*Shut up!* I know what this is all about. Don't think I don't know about you and my game warden's daughter. Who d'you think had the little whore packed off to Greenwood in the first place, eh?"

A red fog shrouded his brain, and Magnes howled.

The next few moments rushed by in a blur of fists, and screams, and the sound of things breaking, and excruciating pain, and still more screaming, and blood.

Blood!

Blood on my hands!

The red fog lifted, and Magnes looked down into the blank eyes of his father.

"Father?" he whispered.

The duke did not answer.

Magnes raised his dripping hands to his face and moaned in horror. He staggered to his feet and stumbled backward, away from the hearth upon which the duke lay, his broken skull resting in a rapidly spreading puddle of gore. A gobbet of hair, skin, and blood dangled from the sharp stone corner of the mantelpiece.

A loud crash exploded behind him. Magnes whirled around to see a chambermaid standing at the partly open door of the study. A heavy tray lay at the girl's feet, shards of crockery and food splattered in a heap upon the carpet. Face white with shock, she pressed her hands to her mouth and stared, first at the duke's lifeless body, then at Magnes.

Magnes nearly choked on the bile rising in his throat. Pointing at the corpse, he croaked, "My father must have fallen and hit his head...We were arguing...Oh, gods!"

The maid's eyes widened with fear. Her mouth worked, but no words came out.

"It was an accident," Magnes whispered plaintively. "I didn't mean..."

Oh, gods, I didn't mean to kill him! Did I?

A wave of weakness threatened to topple him. His muscles began to twitch uncontrollably as his mind succumbed to panic.

I've got to get away, run away, they'll think I murdered him, I'll hang!

It was an accident! Someone please believe me!

The maid opened her mouth and screamed.

Magnes bolted past her and ran, fleeing up towards his apartments, the girl's shrieks feeding his own terror.

Back in his chambers, he stopped just long enough to scoop up his hunting knife and a small pouch of coins he kept beneath his mattress. From his window, he could hear shouts. The maid's screams had been heard.

Got to leave now, or they'll catch me!

Cautiously, he opened the outer door of his chambers and paused to listen. He heard the sound of many feet pounding up the stairs toward his father's study. A heartbeat later, the hoarse shouts of men crying out in dismay, followed by the piteous weeping of the maid sent him stumbling out into the darkened corridor. He turned and rushed away from the main staircase to a smaller, back stairway that led down to a side door in the outer wall of the keep. Under the cover of darkness, he slipped out of the keep and quickly made his way to the stables.

Inside the barn, the soft snores of horses at rest filled the warm air. Silently, Magnes glided down the rows until he reached the stall of his favorite mount. Storm greeted him with a sleepy whicker, and Magnes stroked the horse's velvet nose. Briefly, he pressed his face to the warm skin, then reluctantly moved on to the next stall. He would have to leave Storm behind yet again. He knew that, eventually, he would have to sell whatever horse he rode out on tonight, so Storm must stay at Amsara.

Magnes had never ridden Storm's neighbor, an unassuming piebald gelding. The horse was small, but looked sturdy enough; in any event, he would have to do. Magnes went to the tack room to fetch a saddle and bridle, and soon had the beast ready.

As he led the horse cautiously out of the stall, a childish voice broke the relative quiet. "Oi! Who goes there? What are you doin'?"

Gods, Dari!

"Hush, Dari!" Magnes hissed. "It's me, Lord Magnes!"

Dari appeared at Magnes's side, carrying a stub of candle. He held it up, and in the flickering light, Magnes could see the look of puzzlement on the boy's freckled face. "Lord Magnes, sir. I didn't know t'was you. I was just on me way to the privies. If you don't mind me wonderin', sir, but it seems awfully late t' be goin' out."

"Please, Dari. Listen very carefully. You can't tell anyone you saw me."

"But why?"

"Don't ask me any questions! I need to go now." Magnes immediately regretted the sharpness of his response. "I'm sorry, Dari, but I must go."

The boy let out a startled cry. "M'lord! You...ye've got blood all over yer shirt, sir! Wha' happened? Are ye hurt?"

"Remember what I said to you," Magnes repeated fiercely. The young groom nodded slowly, wide-eyed with bewilderment. Magnes snatched a spare saddle cloth down from the stall railing and draped it over his shoulders; a poor attempt at hiding the incriminating bloodstains, but he could think of nothing else. He clicked his tongue and the horse followed him out into the yard. He checked the saddle girth and mounted, but before he could turn the horse toward the gate, Dari reached up and put his hand on the rein.

"Lord Magnes, will I ever see you again?" The boy gazed up at him, a sad, knowing look in his eyes.

"Dari…" Magnes's voice caught, and he had to pause in order to keep from sobbing. "I don't know. I'll pray to the gods, that I might return home someday. You're a good boy, Dari. I'm sorry you got involved." He looked toward the keep and muttered, "It was an accident."

From the direction of the keep, faint shouts drifted on the night breeze.

"What was, Lord Magnes?" Dari whispered. "What accident?"

Magnes did not answer. He shook the reins and tapped the gelding's flanks with his heels. The muffled clop-clop of the horse's hooves on the hard packed earth beat in counterpoint to his pounding heart. He looked back once to see Dari standing motionless, his face eerily lit from below by the candle stub in his hand.

"Evening, milord," the guardsman said in greeting as Magnes rode up to the outer gate.

"Goin' out so late, sir?" his fellow guardsman inquired.

Magnes had to think fast. He put on a sheepish grin. "Um, well, yes. You see, there's this girl who lives out on the Greenwood Road and, well, her father…"

Both guards guffawed. "Say no more, milord. We get yer meanin'!" the first guard said in a cheerfully conspiratorial tone. His eyes flicked to the saddle cloth over Magnes's shoulders, and his brow furrowed in puzzlement, but he made no comment.

"Aye, that we do," the second added. "We was both young and unmarried once!" The men scrambled to open the gate, just wide enough for Magnes to ride through.

"Will ye be back before or after sunrise, sir?"

"After, most definitely," Magnes replied. He could hear the guards snickering as the gate swung shut.

The night engulfed him, warm and very dark. He had only the light of the stars to see by. Once again, Magnes found himself leaving Amsara in the dead of night with virtually nothing, except that this time, he was the fugitive. The horse proved to be sure-footed and steady as they wound their way down the steep switchbacks and into Amsara village.

Just as he had two days ago, he took the track that skirted the village and ended up on the road that led past the homestead of Livie's parents, the road that would eventually take him all the way to Darguinia, city of the Emperors. A man could lose himself among the multitudes there, shed an old identity, and invent a new one.

All around him, the darkness hummed, alive with the sounds of a late summer country night. A soft breeze tickled the nape of his neck, still wet with the sweat of shock and fear. Loneliness, dense and heavy, settled over him.

He burst into tears and wailed like a child.

Chapter 23

Confessions And Heartache

Is she not the most magnificent woman in all of Alasiri, Little Brother?" Sadaiyo drawled, eyeing his wife-to-be over the rim of his silver wine goblet.

Ashinji had to agree with part of Sadaiyo's assessment—Lady Misune Dai was indeed magnificent, in the manner of a glacier or an ice-rimmed lake in winter. To his eyes though, her cold beauty held no allure.

The Ceremony of Welcoming had taken place earlier that evening. Misune's parents had brought her before the members of the House of Sakehera, assembled in the small chapel reserved for private family worship, clad only in a simple white robe, her hair unbound. There, Ashinji had intoned the ritual chants that bound Misune to her new family; afterward, the bride-to-be retired to the guest quarters so that she might rest for a time before preparing herself for the feast.

"You and she will make a perfect match, Brother," Ashinji commented dryly.

Sadaiyo either didn't notice, or didn't care about the subtle insult. He grinned wickedly. "One more day, and then she'll be mine. I can barely control myself, and she's practically across the room! Come our wedding night, I'll ride her so hard, she'll scream and come like she's never done in her life! Then in the morning, I'll tell you all about it!"

Ashinji sighed and took a pull from his glass. Sadaiyo never tired of this game, and as the evening progressed, he knew that his brother's comments would become increasingly crude. He was thankful that their sister Lani sat well out of earshot, beside their mother.

Sadaiyo turned his attention to the older man seated to his left, a minor lord from Dai's retinue, giving Ashinji a welcome respite. He allowed his eyes to wander over the elegant gathering. The bride now sat revealed—her veil thrown back so that all present might admire her—straight and proud between her father and older brother, Ibeji. Ibeji Dai reminded Ashinji of a young eagle—all sharp angles and glittering, amber eyes.

Brother and sister were deep in conversation. Occasionally, Misune would look up to stare boldly at Sadaiyo, as if taking his measure.

"I see you staring at her, Ashi. What would that delicious little mongrel messenger say if she knew you were lusting after another woman, eh?"

Ashinji glared at his brother, struggling to control his fury, but Sadaiyo's smirk made it all but impossible.

"I understand your envy of me, little Brother. I will soon have a real woman in my bed, while you..." Sadaiyo's lip curled, "you must content yourself with, um, tainted meat."

Ashinji rose abruptly from his chair, tossed off the last of his wine, and excused himself with a muttered apology to his startled parents. Fuming, he stalked from the great hall out into the night, Sadaiyo's mocking laughter ringing in his ears.

Ashinji walked quickly, unmindful of direction, his only thought to escape his brother's toxic presence. He had come perilously close to losing control and had nearly smashed his fist into Sadaiyo's face.

Eventually, his boiling anger cooled, and he found himself among the fragrant blooms of his mother's private garden. He sat down on a wooden bench carved in the shape of two sea creatures entwined, their flukes upraised to form arm rests.

He wondered what Jelena was doing at this very moment. Was she thinking of him, longing for his embrace as much as he longed for hers? He knew that she could feel the tug of the undeniable connection between them. He could see it in her eyes whenever she looked at him. He loved her, and he felt certain that she loved him, but was love enough?

Could his desire to be with Jelena come from selfishness, considering all of the obstacles they would face? She had, by far, the most to lose. She had no family to protect her, and Lord Sen could cast her out with impunity if she became too much of an inconvenience.

No, Ashinji thought. *Father would not do that, even if he thinks Jelena would be trouble for me. He's not that kind of man.*

Lord Sen did know how to take care of a problem, though. He would simply arrange to transfer Jelena's service to another household, as far away from Kerala as possible.

Ashinji stood up from the bench, full of restless energy. He thought of going down to the barracks to see Jelena, but reluctantly dismissed the idea. *No, not yet,* he thought. After the wedding ceremony, he would speak to her, confess his love, and together, they could decide what to do. He spent the remainder of the evening walking the battlements, thinking about his future.

There are seven hundred and seventy seven faces of the Goddess.
All are manifestations of the One.
She has seven hundred and seventy seven names.
All are names of the One.
She who gave birth to the World.
Mother of us all.

The two priests intoned the sacred chant, their voices a steady drone. The bride and groom knelt before the altar, heads bowed, all but immobilized beneath the weight of their heavy, multi-layered wedding robes.

Ashinji knelt behind and to the left of Sadaiyo, clutching in his hand the gold bracelet that his brother would soon place on the wrist of his new wife. Ibeji knelt behind his sister, a similar bracelet in his hand. Ashinji felt hot and miserable in the close, incense-clouded chapel. He wished fervently for the entire affair to be over so that he could throw off his own stiff, heavy garments and go to Jelena. The image of her face—so beautiful and dear—bolstered his strength.

The priests anointed the heads of the bride and groom with sacred oil and intoned the chants of joining. The exchange of bracelets would come next, then the obeisance before the One, and finally, the official pronouncement. Ashinji went through the motions, only because he had to. He felt no happiness, love, or pride. He felt nothing but the desire to escape.

At last, the priests made the final pronouncement. The assembled guests rose and cheered loudly as the Heir and his new wife exited the chapel. The newlyweds headed toward the great hall; there, they would be enthroned in large, ornate chairs like two statues on display, while the guests lined up to present their wedding gifts. Only after all gifts had been received would they be released to return to separate chambers for a few hours of much needed rest before the big feast that evening.

For Ashinji, the painful ordeal had come to an end.

He returned to his chambers and stripped out of his heavy robes, leaving the exquisite garments in a colorful heap on the floor. Redressed in a plain unbleached cotton tunic, breeches and sandals, he hurried down a back staircase and out a side door into the upper yard.

A crowd of people, most richly dressed, some not so, milled about the yard, sweating beneath the late summer sun. The castle swarmed with guests. Every noble family in the district had been invited, and Lord Sen had made it known that any Kerala citizen, be they noble or common, was to be made welcome.

Ashinji avoided the crowd by ducking through the front garden and sticking close to the wall. He made it through the upper gate without being seen and jogged downhill into the lower yard. The barracks area was quiet. Most of the castle staff who weren't directly involved in the logistics of the wedding had been given the day off so they could enjoy the festivities.

Ashinji climbed the stairs up to the second floor barracks where Jelena now lived with the unmarried female castle guards. He stuck his head into the open door and looked around. The common room stood empty.

"Hello? Is anyone here?" he called out.

Silence.

"Hello?" he repeated.

This time, a sleepy voice answered. "Lord Ashinji. I'm sorry. I was asleep and didn't hear you the first time." Aneko appeared in the far doorway and came out into the common room. "I was on guard duty 'til first light," she said, rubbing her eyes.

"I should be sorry, for disturbing your rest, Aneko. I'm looking for Jelena."

"Jelena's not here, my lord. She rode out this morning."

Ashinji bit his lower lip in consternation. "Surely my father didn't send her out with a message," he said.

"No, I don't think so. She said she wanted to go out to the old stone circle for a while. She should be back soon, my lord." Aneko smiled sympathetically.

Ashinji felt himself blushing. *Am I that obvious?* "Aneko, please tell her...tell her that I'll come looking for her during the feast tonight. I have something very important that I must say to her. Promise me you'll tell her."

"You have my promise, Lord Ashinji."

Ashinji left Aneko to her rest and returned to his rooms, successfully avoiding any guests. Fatigued, he sought his bed, where he lay down on the soft feather mattress with a weary sigh. He knew he would not be missed for several hours. Before he dozed off, he vowed that tonight, he and Jelena would be together at last.

~~~

The wedding feast was well underway by the time Ashinji slipped into an empty chair beside Lani.

"Where have you been, Ashi? Mother was just about to send someone out to look for you," Lani said, eyeing her brother curiously.

"I was tired, so I lay down to rest, and I overslept."

"Will you look at them?" Lani indicated the newly married couple who occupied pride of place at the center of the table. "They can't seem to keep their hands off each other. Why don't they just leave right now and go get started?"

Ashinji turned to look at his sister, eyebrows raised in mild shock. "Lani!" he exclaimed.

"Oh, don't look at me like that, big Brother. I'm not a child anymore. I'm practically old enough to be married myself soon. I do know all about sex, you realize." Ashinji just shook his head. It seemed like only yesterday that he cradled baby Lani in his arms and laughed at her comical, infant expressions.

Sadaiyo and Misune did seem quite taken with each other already. They sat with their heads pressed together, whispering earnestly. If Ashinji had not known otherwise, he could believe that they were already lovers.

"Aren't you going to eat anything?" Lani asked. Until that moment, Ashinji had not been hungry, but Lani's question prompted a rumbling response in his stomach.

The castle kitchen had outdone itself. Never had Ashinji seen such a display of the culinary arts presented before in Kerala's great hall. Platters of roasted game, fish, and fowl vied for attention alongside tureens of soups and stews. Mounds of boiled vegetables, breads, cheeses, pies, and fruits rounded out the feast. Ashinji helped himself to a dish of jellied eels. A servant stepped forward to fill his wine goblet.

"Ashi, do you think Mother and Father would consider Lord Dai's son as a prospect for me?" Lani asked thoughtfully.

"Do you like him?" Ashinji responded. "Have you even spoken to him?" He looked over to where Ibeji Dai sat beside his father, his quick, amber eyes darting around the room as if he were trying to memorize every detail.

"He's very handsome. He did look at me and smile, a little."

"You're still too young, little Sister. Enjoy what's left of your girlhood. There'll be plenty of time to think of marriage."

Lani rolled her eyes. "I'm old enough to wonder what it's like," she said.

"What what's like?" Ashinji innocently inquired.

Lani reached over and rapped him on the forehead with her knuckles.

"What it's like to be with a man!" she replied, rolling her eyes with exasperation. Ashinji sighed, suddenly feeling very old. Lani abruptly changed the subject. "Is it true what Sadaiyo says about you and the new messenger girl?"

"I don't know. What is he saying?" Ashinji kept his voice neutral.

"That you're in love with her, but you can't ever have her because she's a half-breed and she's got no family."

"Has he said any of this to Father?" Ashinji asked, trying to remain calm.

Lani shrugged. "I don't know," she replied.

Ashinji pushed aside his plate and rose from his chair. "I have to go. I'll be back in a little while."

Lani looked startled. "You can't leave now! Father is about to make his speech," she exclaimed.

"I promised…I need to go."

He hurried toward the open doors of the great hall, hugging the wall and trying to be as unobtrusive as possible, but he caught the puzzled looks on Lord and Lady Dai's faces and the annoyed expressions on his parents' as he slipped out into the evening air.

The upper yard had been set up as an outdoor overflow area for the feast. Those common people of the district that had come for the celebration, as well as the off-duty castle staff and their families sat at trestle tables under the stars, enjoying the magnificent repast. Ashinji found Jelena sitting at a table on the periphery, surrounded by her guard friends. He stood in the shadows for a while, content just to watch her laugh and talk. She seemed so happy. He thought his heart would burst with love.

He approached and quietly called out her name.

She turned around and their eyes met. Wordlessly, she rose to her feet and walked over to where he waited, her eyes never leaving his face.

"Walk with me," he murmured and held out his hand. A hush fell over the table. Jelena slipped her hand into his and allowed him to lead her away from her friends into the darkness. He could hear their voices start up behind him, like the buzz of excited bees.

They walked side by side, hands clasped tightly, toward Lady Amara's private garden, where Ashinji knew that they would not be disturbed. Having Jelena's body so close was a torment. He wanted to sweep her up into his arms and cover her face and neck with kisses. He could sense the tense expectancy flowing from her, and it only inflamed his desire.

They reached the garden, and he led her over to the sea-creature bench and sat her down beside him. The slivered moon, ensnared in the tree branches overhead, cast very little light; nevertheless, Ashinji could see Jelena's face with perfect clarity.

He still held her hand in his, and he squeezed it even tighter as he started to speak. "I want to tell you something," he began.

"You know that we elves have Talent…what humans call magic. My Talent manifests in dreams that tell me of things that may happen in my future. I've been dreaming of a girl with wild, dark hair and sad eyes…a hikui girl. The dreams started months ago, and I did not understand them until that day by the river."

"The day you found me," Jelena whispered.

"When I saw your face for the first time, I fell down in shock. I knew immediately that you were the girl… Jelena, in the dream, you were calling out to me to help you. You were in some kind of danger. There was a shadow…"

Jelena shivered and drew closer to him. "What think you it means?" she asked, and he could hear the fear in her voice.

"I don't know yet, but I think it has to do with what's inside you."

"Inside me?" she responded.

Ashinji tugged at the service rings in his ear. How to explain without frightening her even more? "It's hard to describe. There's an…*energy,* a force of some kind inside of you, more like a part of you, really. I have no idea what it is, but the shadow seemed to know, and I think it wanted to take it from you."

"Ashinji, you've seen it? It is like blue fire!" she exclaimed. "Do you think energy is part of my elf blood?"

"It didn't feel like any manifestation of Talent, not exactly. It felt more like…like a spell of some kind…Wait, you know about this?"

Jelena nodded. "It came from before I arrived here. Blue fire from my hands. I want to learn about it. Aneko says Lady Amara can help me…I mean, will she help?"

"Yes, yes, I think she will…We can talk about that later. What I have to say now is more important." He paused to breathe deeply before taking the plunge. "I know in my heart that I was meant to find you that day. Whatever this shadow is that threatens you, I will protect you from it. We have a connection, Jelena, one that cannot be denied." Gently, he drew her into his arms and pressed his lips to hers.

For an instant only, she froze then melted sweetly into him. His head swam as if he had just taken a draught of strong wine. Her arms crept up around his waist, and he could feel the curve of her breasts through the thin cotton of his tunic. He embraced her more tightly, and she sighed against him, her lips as soft as rose petals. The heat of passion surged through him, and he knew that if he did not pull away now, he would be unable to stop.

Gasping for breath, he broke their embrace.

"I love you, Jelena," he whispered.

"I love you, too," she breathed.

"Come to my chamber. Stay with me tonight."

Jelena withdrew from him and dropped her head into her hands. "No, Ashinji. I cannot. We…cannot be," she said in her imperfect Siri-dar.

"What do you mean?" Ashinji whispered fiercely. "We love each other, we've just said so! Why can't we be together?"

Her hands fell away from her face, and he could see her cheeks were wet with tears. "Ashinji, my love, you are lord's son. I am nobody, half-breed. I have no family. I live here because Lord Sen take pity on me, give me home and job. I think he likes me, but not enough to let me have you. He will never let us marry." She shook her head emphatically. "I ran away from my home so I could live free, live with… honor. I will not be…less than your wife, even if you do love me."

"I want to make you my wife, Jelena," Ashinji stated firmly. "We'll find a way, somehow."

"No! I will not let you throw away everything for me. I know what family means to you. You go against father's wishes, you lose place, position."

"I don't care about that. All I want is to love and protect you!" Ashinji shivered with growing desperation. He could feel her slipping away from him.

"No. One man already who I love gave up everything for me. I will not let another." The note of finality in her voice stabbed his heart like a knife.

"Jelena, please…don't turn away from me," he begged, grasping her shoulders.

"I must go," she sobbed quietly. "Let me go!"

Slowly, he released her. She jumped up and fled.

He sat very still for several heartbeats, his mind frozen in disbelief. Then, in an agony of perception, he threw his head back, face upturned to the cold, uncaring sky.

"*Jelenaaa!*" he cried to the moon.

CHAPTER 24

THE TEMPLE OF ESKLEIPA

Five days after fleeing Amsara, Magnes came upon a tiny monastery just outside of a hamlet called Gariglen. As he guided his horse through the simple wooden palisade, he made a decision.

He sheltered there a day and a night. When, at last, he emerged, Magnes Preseren, son and Heir of Duke Teodorus of Amsara, was no more. A lay brother named Tilo, dressed in a simple brown robe and armed with nothing more than a knife and a stout walking stick, left Gariglen Monastery that bright Uresday morning. A satchel, bulging with salves and remedies, hung across his right shoulder.

The monks of Gariglen would have their new roof this fall and a stone byre to replace their old wooden one, for Magnes had traded them the horse from his father's stable for the robe, medicines, and the small supply of food that he now carried. The gelding would fetch a handsome price, and a poor herbalist would never have been able to afford a horse in any case. The monks had asked no questions, and they'd accepted the lopsided trade happily.

As Magnes continued to make his way south, guilt haunted his every step. At night, he feared to close his eyes, for the evil dream that plagued him allowed him no rest. His father would appear before him, face like a thundercloud, his life's blood gushing in a scarlet stream from his head. He would raise an accusatory finger, aimed at Magnes's heart.

Why did you murder me, Son? Why?

He would awake, his skin clammy with sweat, fighting for breath.

For a time, he feared he would go insane.

Three weeks of steady travel brought Magnes at last to the city of the Emperors. Darguinia quickly proved itself to be two cities, existing on two very different levels. One was a place of stunning beauty, filled with gardens, fountains, and buildings made of the whitest marble.

The other city was not.

Magnes, as a poor monk with little money, soon found himself in the other Darguinia. He entered a place of narrow, twisting streets and dark alleys, of fetid, open sewers and ramshackle buildings, of crime and disease—a place where hollow-eyed beggars sat in doorways, women and children sold their bodies on the streets to survive, and murder evoked barely an eyeblink.

Magnes had landed squarely in Hell, and he felt that he deserved the place he had made for himself. Even in Hell, though, things cost money, and he was fast running out of what little he had.

First, I need to find shelter, he thought. *Then, I've got to figure out what sort of living I can make.* Hitching his satchel a little higher on his shoulder, he looked around, picked a street at random, and plunged into the crowd.

~~~

The whore lifted her skirts and straddled Magnes where he sat on the shabby room's only chair. Settling her bare rump firmly on his knees, she slid forward and pushed herself onto him. He sighed and shuddered a little. With professional efficiency, she began pumping her hips. Magnes shut his eyes so he wouldn't have to look at her face and gripped the sides of the chair, riding each successive wave of sensation, higher and higher, to a final spasm of release.

It was all quite impersonal and unsurprisingly brief.

"There, told you so, sweet'eart," the woman said. She stood up and carefully pulled herself free, casually wiping between her legs with a corner of her skirt. "Told you I was ten times better 'n that tired old cunt Lorola. Worth th' extra three coppers, right, luv?"

Magnes glanced up, then away. All of the whores in this dangerous neighborhood of tenements and warehouses were well past their primes, but this one, with her cheap red dye-job and heavy make-up, had looked a little fresher than the rest. Still…

"I'm not your love," he said roughly, tucking himself back into his breeches and standing. Almost immediately, he felt a stab of guilt at his harsh tone. He could in no way blame the mess of his life on this woman. "Please," he amended more gently. "Don't call me that." The whore simply shrugged.

His thoughts turned to Livie. The memory of their last time together, of how they had made love and then had clung to each other as if their final night on earth had come, set up such an ache in his heart that he thought he might choke on his despair.

"You have your money," he said quietly. She had insisted on her half-sol fee before coming up to his room. "You need to leave now."

"When you need another ride, you know where t'find me, luv… oops, sorry!" She smirked and left without another word.

Magnes sat down on the edge of the narrow, musty cot and rested his head in his hands. A single tear slid from the corner of his eye, and slowly, he wiped it away with a forefinger. He chided himself, again, for wasting what little money he had left on something so tawdry, but the pain of his loneliness had been so great that the prospect of the touch of another person, *any* person, had proved to be impossible to resist. When this particular whore had propositioned him for the third time, he'd given in.

He then thought of his father.

The image of Duke Teodorus's death-pale face, a constant, lurking presence in his mind's eye, seemed always ready to glide into full view at any unguarded moment. He could still see the crimson of his father's blood, leaking onto the stones from his shattered skull. The memory had lost none of its vivid horror. Magnes moaned aloud and lay down, covering his face with his hands. The little candle on the shelf by the door, the room's only source of light, guttered and went out. He lay, sleepless and unmoving, until sunrise.

Magnes rose at first light and donned his monk's robe. He gathered up his meager possessions—knife, satchel, a waterskin, his walking stick—and left his small room, as he had each morning since arriving in the city four days ago. This morning, though, he had a feeling he would not be returning.

Magnes had found that the brown homespun garment of a holy

brother and healer afforded him a small bit of protection when he walked abroad in the squalid streets of Darguinia's slums. Thieves and cutthroats were less likely to come after him, unless, of course, they needed a remedy; he kept several common ones on him at all times for such eventualities. Not that he really needed protection. He still carried his knife, and his training at arms would serve him well in any fight.

He took one last look around, then headed out into the street, intending to make his way to the temple district. Once there, he would inquire at as many establishments as it took for him to find one that would take him in as a novice.

The morning air already shimmered with heat. The coarse fabric of his robe chafed at neck and chest. Sweat beaded on his forehead and trickled in little rivulets from his underarms and down his back. His stomach rumbled. He thought of the half-sol he had spent on the red-dyed whore last night and winced in regret. A half-sol could have bought him a decent breakfast and a tankard of mead in one of the many alehouses that operated in the neighborhood.

He walked steadily, taking an occasional swig from the tepid contents of his waterskin. After a while, the dirt beneath his sandals became cobbles. The buildings transformed from shabby mud brick to sturdy wood, then stone. Another few blocks and he turned a corner and entered the temple district.

A plan had crystallized in Magnes's mind. He would continue to call himself Tilo and try to get work as an herbalist in one of the temples dedicated to healing, or failing that, he would seek employment as a gardener. It didn't matter, so long as he could work with growing things.

The Green Brothers were not accepting novices at this time, nor was the Temple of Balnath. The elderly priest who came to the door to politely turn him away suggested that he try the Temple of Eskleipa, over at the east end of the district near the Grand Arena. Magnes sat awhile in the shade of the temple porch, mustering his energy for the hot trudge to come. His mouth ached for a drink of something other than warm water; he thought about retreating from the day's heat into a nearby tavern, but then he reminded himself of his dwindling finances.

With a weary sigh, he rose to his feet and set off.

Eskleipa was a foreign god, brought up from the far south of the Empire by a wave of immigration from the conquered lands of the Eenui people. His clergy had proven themselves to be skilled healers; worship of the god had become quite popular, especially among poor immigrants and slaves.

The Temple of Eskleipa looked far less grand than the gleaming marble house of Balnath. Magnes walked up to the plain wooden door of the modest brick building and pulled on a rope dangling from the doorjamb. Somewhere within, he heard the tinkling of a bell.

Time passed, and the door remained firmly shut. Magnes hauled on the bell rope a second time and followed that up with a firm rap with the end of his walking stick. A third and fourth try were equally fruitless, and Magnes had decided to give up when, just as he was turning to leave, the door swung open, and a man poked his head out.

"Yes?"

Magnes blinked in surprise.

He had never before seen a man so old.

"Are you in need of healing, my son? Well, speak up! I'm hard of hearing!" The old man cupped his hand to his ear and peered up at Magnes owlishly.

"No, I don't need healing, Father," Magnes finally managed to answer. "I'm looking for a position as an herbalist. I was told over at the Temple of Balnath that you might accept me as a novice."

"Balnath! Balnath, bah! No Balls-nath, more like. Those quacks wouldn't know their ears from their arseholes. They think tree lizard dung is a cure for warts! Hah!" The old man cackled with derision. "Well, then, young sir, I guess you'd better come in."

His skin was as brown as old wood, and it had been many years since his scalp had last sprouted hair, but the old man's back remained unbent, and the hand that held the door looked untouched by the joint ill. He stood at least a head shorter than Magnes, a twig of a man attired in a gauzy grey garment he had wrapped partly around his waist and draped the rest over his left shoulder. An enormous beak of a nose dominated his oval face.

"I am Brother Wambo," the old cleric said as he led the way into the temple.

"I am Tilo," Magnes replied, following his host through a receiving chamber and out another door into a courtyard.

The courtyard was an inviting oasis of shade trees and flowering shrubs. A tiled fountain stood at its center, the cheerfully splashing water throwing off myriads of bright reflections. The air, so much cooler here than out on the street, hung thick with the perfume of growing things.

Magnes looked about him and sighed. Already, he could feel the peace of the place begin to seep into his body, relaxing it.

"Why d'you want to join with us, eh? Wait! I know! 'Cause the Temple of *Bal*nath turned you away!" The old cleric had abruptly rounded on Magnes and now stood wagging a finger at the tip of the younger man's nose. Magnes stifled a laugh. Brother Wambo looked very much like a cranky old heron.

"We're not nearly so grand as Balnath's temple, no marble pillars and gold leaf here, oh no. You won't see any of the high and mighty here, either, young man, none of *your* sort. Oh don't look so surprised! Did you really think you could hide those fine manners of yours?"

"I...I..." Magnes stammered, then quickly regained his composure. Clearly, his cover story was not going to work, so he decided to take a calculated risk and tell Brother Wambo the truth, or at least part of it.

"Please, Brother, I need a place. I'm a long way from home and just about out of money. I swear to you that I'll work hard, and I'll bring no trouble."

"What about trouble finding you, eh?" Wambo cocked his head to one side and regarded Magnes with hard brown eyes.

"I promise it's all left very far behind me."

"Hmm, well." Wambo's expression softened. "We've never had a Soldaran nobleman petition to join our ranks before, but there's a first time for everything. An herbalist, you say?"

"Yes, I know a lot about plants, both medicinal and food. I can help tend the gardens as well." For the first time in many days, Magnes could feel himself letting go of some of the terrible burden of sadness he had been carrying since leaving Amsara.

"Welcome to our order, Tilo," Wambo said.

"We're a small group here, as you will see. So many needy people!

We are stretched very thin at times," said Wambo as he led Magnes to the refectory.

After his arrival earlier, Wambo had shown Magnes to a small chamber furnished with only a woven rope cot and a single chair. A small window looked out onto the courtyard. Wambo had promised that he would have the room all to himself, a small luxury that had pleased Magnes greatly. He had been allowed to rest until sunset, when the evening meal would be served.

"Sister Melele is our cook. Oh, you'll learn to enjoy what we eat here, but I must warn you. It can be quite a shock to the timid Soldaran palate." Wambo grinned impishly, revealing a mouth full of strong white teeth.

The refectory was a long narrow room dominated by a solid wooden trestle table. Several people were already seated when Wambo and Magnes entered. They all regarded Magnes with varying degrees of curiosity.

"Brothers and sisters, this is Tilo, a young man of conviction who wishes to be one of us," Wambo announced cheerfully.

"Welcome, Tilo. Come and sit by me," a woman said, beckoning Magnes over with a wave of her hand. Magnes obliged, grateful for the overture.

"My name is Ayesha. I serve as the midwife here." Magnes could not help but notice Ayesha's beauty. Fascinated, he caught himself staring at her hair, which had been skillfully arranged into a cascade of impossibly slender braids. Ayesha smiled knowingly, and feeling a little embarrassed by his lapse in manners, Magnes quickly looked away.

"I also look after the women who become ill after childbirth," Ayesha said.

"Then you have a much more harrowing and important job than I do, Ayesha," Magnes replied, daring to look back at her face and finding gentle amusement in her eyes.

"All jobs are of equal importance here, Tilo," she said. "Without a skilled herbalist, I could not offer the poor women who come to us for help many of the most efficacious remedies I know of." Magnes nodded in understanding.

"That is Jouma, our chiurgeon," Wambo said, indicating the

middle-aged man to Magnes's right, "and young Fadili over there, he will be your assistant." Fadili smiled broadly and waved from his seat across the table. "Zemba and Nyal are medics." Wambo pointed to a man and a woman seated opposite Magnes, finishing off the introductions.

"Is everyone in this order from…the south?" Magnes asked, looking around at the people he had chosen to join with. They were all as dark as the wood of the table at which they sat; in contrast, even if Magnes should expose himself to the sun for many hours, he would still be pale when compared to any of them.

"Not everyone," said Ayesha with a smile. "Now, we have a Soldaran brother."

"All of us have lived here in Darguinia for many years," Wambo said, sitting down to Magnes's left. "I last saw our homeland over thirty summers ago. Fadili came into this world right here within these walls."

"It must be hard for you all, being so far away from home," Magnes said.

"Darguinia has become our home. Our work is very important, and the people are grateful. We don't serve the rich here, oh no. Poor working folk, slaves, beggars, and whores—that's who we treat. All of the people who can't afford the fees that Balnath's priests swindle out of their patients. Bah!" Wambo spat in disgust.

"How, then, can the temple afford to buy supplies and support all of us if we charge no fees?" Magnes asked.

"I didn't say that we charged no fees. Of course, our patients must pay something, but only what they can afford, and many times, it's trade. And we have the Arena."

"The arena?" queried Magnes.

Jouma the chiurgeon spoke up for the first time. "The Grand Arena. We hold contracts with several of the yards to provide care and healing for their fighters, both slave and free. It brings in a tidy sum every month, and it's steady."

"It's our Arena contracts that allow us to offer so much for so little to the poor. We'd be out of business without them," Wambo added.

"Tomorrow, we visit the de Guera Yard, our biggest contract,"

Jouma continued. "Yesterday was an off-day, so there won't be any new injuries to treat, just follow-ups and the usual little things—runny noses, headaches, coughs and such. Lady de Guera runs a tight yard. She sees to it that her slaves stay healthy and her prizefighters stay clean, or they don't work. You can come with me if you like."

"Yes, I would love to, thank you," Magnes agreed.

Several more people had since entered the refectory and had taken places at the table. Wambo introduced them as they sat. Last to enter came a young woman upon whose arm leaned a small man. To Magnes's amazement, the man appeared to be even older than Wambo.

"Father Ndoma, the *leke* or head of our order," Wambo whispered into Magnes's ear, indicating the frail elder with a lift of his chin. He waited until the Father's attendant had settled the old man in a high backed chair at the head of the table, then shouted, "*Leke* Ndoma, this is Tilo! He has come this very day to join us as our new herbalist!" Wambo looked at Magnes, tapped his ear and explained, "*Leke* Ndoma is nearly deaf...Has been for at least a year. My lungs have grown very strong from shouting."

"Eh? A new recruit?" the ancient cleric piped in a thin, reedy voice. "Well, where is he? Let him come forward so I can look at him!"

Magnes rose from his seat and approached the *leke's* chair. Unsure of how to demonstrate respect to the elder, he decided to incline his head as he would toward his own father. Just that brief thought of the duke twisted Magnes's gut into a painful knot, but he resolutely pushed his feelings back down into the dark place underneath his heart and sealed them off.

The old man regarded Magnes quizzically. He clicked his tongue and muttered something in a language Magnes did not understand, then asked,

"You are a Soldaran nobleman, yes?" His black eyes glittered shrewdly.

"Yes, Father," Magnes answered. He shifted uncomfortably from foot to foot. The priest's eyes seemed to penetrate through all of the shields Magnes had erected to protect himself, discerning the true man beneath the façade.

"You'll have to speak up, my son. I haven't much hearing left...

Never mind…I know who you are. Welcome." He waved a spidery brown hand, giving Magnes leave to go back to his place at the table.

Magnes returned to his seat, unsettled. What had the *leke* meant by his last remark?

He pondered the question all throughout the meal, which, as Wambo had warned earlier, proved to be highly spiced. His companions, mistaking his distraction for shyness, attempted to draw him out with conversation. He could tell that they were fishing for clues about his background. He fed them only enough details to make up a plausible story. He was the son of a minor noble house, estranged from his family and looking to make his own way in the world. They all seemed to accept him at his word, and he felt a momentary twinge of guilt at the deception, but he told himself that no harm would come of it.

After dinner, Magnes went with Fadili to inspect the pharmacy. He found it to be meticulously organized and well stocked.

"Our old herbalist Tima died last winter of the lung fever," Fadili explained. "She was teaching me." The young man's voice quivered with sadness.

"I'll teach you now, Fadili," Magnes stated. Something about the youth reminded him of Dari. A wave of homesickness weakened his knees and brought tears to his eyes. He wondered if Dari now looked after Storm.

"Are you not well?" Fadili asked. Magnes quickly shook his head.

"I'm fine. It's…it's just that I'm not used to the spiciness of your food, that's all. It has unsettled my stomach a little, but I'll be recovered by morning. Don't worry!" He laughed wanly. "I'll make myself some peppermint tea. That's always good to ease indigestion."

"I'll make it for you and bring it to your room," Fadili offered. Magnes thanked him and made his way back to his little chamber. There, he applied flint and steel to the small clay lamp sitting on a wall shelf by the door and lay down upon his cot.

The straw-stuffed mattress smelled a little musty, but mercifully, seemed flea-free. He would see about getting some fresh straw later. He crossed his arms behind his head and stared up at the wood-beamed ceiling, allowing his mind to drift.

A soft knock at the door heralded the arrival of the tea. Magnes got up to let Fadili in and took the steaming mug from the young novice with a murmured "Thank you" and "Goodnight." He carried the tea over to the cot and sat on the edge, sipping carefully and thinking.

How long ago that fateful Sansa night seemed now, when all of the events that so drastically changed his life had been put into motion. If only his father had not procured that horrible girl, then insisted that he marry her. If only Jelena's choices hadn't been so grim—flight or slavery.

Jelena.

What has become of you, Cousin? Are you happily married to Ashinji Sakehera? Have you found your father yet?

What will happen to you and Ashinji when Soldara brings war to Alasiri? Gods, how I miss you! I just pray that you are safe.

He took a final sip of the tea, got up from the bed and went to extinguish the lamp, then lay down again to sleep.

CHAPTER 25

A NEW THREAT

Ashinji!

Jelena cried his name over and over in her head as she ran, half-blinded by darkness and tears. Somehow, she managed to reach the barracks without falling or running into anyone.

The barracks were deserted. All of the guards either still reveled at the feast or were on duty. She could be alone with her grief. She flung herself down on her bunk and gave in to despair. Her wish had come true, but it was all for naught. Ashinji loved her—*loved her*—but she didn't think that even his love and determination could break the grip that elven societal tradition held on his life. He had said they would find a way, but she couldn't imagine how.

Maybe I should have left Kerala before things got to this point, she thought. *I can still leave...Try to find work somewhere else while I search for my father. But Lord Sen promised to help me, and he can do so much more for me than I could ever accomplish on my own.*

Gods help me, what am I going to do?

What if Ashinji does something foolish, like tell Lord Sen he wishes to marry me? What if his father forbids it and Ashinji dares to defy him?

Disaster!

I can't let that happen!

Tomorrow, she would tell Ashinji that she had been confused, that he had befuddled her with his kisses, that she really didn't love him. He would be hurt and angry, but he would eventually get over her and move on, especially if she left Kerala. The thought of causing him such pain ripped at her heart and brought on a fresh torrent of tears.

I love him so much, but I must let him go. Gods, how am I going to let him go?

Eventually, she slept.

~~~

She awoke with a start and sat up, looking around the dim room apprehensively. The soft drone of Aneko's snores drifted from the far corner, soothing her with its familiarity. The hazy recollection, already fading, of an unpleasant dream made her shiver.

Realizing she had slept all night in her clothes made her desperate for a bath. She rose from her bunk and went to the window to look out. The sun had just begun its climb into the sky. The castle complex lay quiet and still.

Jelena knew that most of Kerala's inhabitants and guests would sleep late this morning. She would probably have the staff bath house to herself. She collected a clean set of garments from her chest and slipped out as quietly as she could.

As she had suspected, the bath house was deserted. This particular facility was one of two set aside for the exclusive use of the castle staff. Because of its proximity to the barracks, the guards and their families made the most use of it.

The rules were simple; the first person to use the bath in the morning built up the fire that the last person to use the bath had banked the night before. Anyone who used the bath during the course of the day would check on the fire and feed it if necessary. The system worked well, for the most part.

The tub itself lay buried in a pit lined with sand and tiles. A wooden deck had been constructed around its perimeter. Benches lined the walls; pegs driven into the plaster at regular intervals served as clothes hangers. An open space against the east wall served as an area for soaping and rinsing prior to the actual bath. The floor had been built with a slope, so that water flowed down and out through a ceramic pipe set in one corner.

The cleverest feature of the bathhouse was its system of taps. Two ceramic pipes protruded from the wall. When unplugged, they delivered streams of running water that served as showers. The water always ran cold early in the morning, but on sunny days, it often got quite warm by noon.

Jelena dropped her clean clothes on a bench and descended the short flight of stairs leading down to the firebox. After stoking the fire with fresh wood, she ascended and stripped out of her rumpled garments.

The shower water felt tolerably cool this morning. Ashinji had once said that elves truly enjoyed washing in cold water before a long hot soak. It made one appreciate the warm water all the more. Jelena wondered how any of them could stand it in winter.

In Amsara, most people bathed their entire bodies infrequently at best, and then usually in connection with a holiday or some other special occasion. Since she had come to Kerala, Jelena had grown to appreciate the benefits and pleasures of daily bathing with clear water and soft, creamy soap scented with herbs. She had come to recognize that part of the reason why she found Ashinji's unique aroma so appealing was that he always smelled clean.

After a thorough scrub and rinse, she slipped into the warm water of the tub with a blissful sigh and closed her eyes. The tub could hold at least six people comfortably, eight if they didn't mind a squeeze. During the early evening when most of the guards preferred to wash, they either squeezed or waited. Jelena liked coming to the bath in the early morning to avoid the rush.

Her mind drifted into fantasy. She imagined Ashinji lying in his bed, asleep. She then pictured herself lying beside him, her naked body melded to his. She lightly brushed his ear with her lips and whispered his name. He awoke and took her into his arms, and as they made love, she entwined her fingers into his beautiful golden hair.

Stop it! Thinking about him—about us—doing those things is no good!

She squeezed her legs tightly together and breathed deeply until the ferocious ache within her subsided.

She soaked until the skin on her fingers and toes began to wrinkle up like dried plums. She pushed herself up out of the tub, skin steaming, and padded over to a large basket containing a neat pile of towels. After drying her body and hair, she dressed quickly, wishing that she had remembered to bring along the small bottle of almond oil she kept for softening her skin. With a grunt of frustration, she engaged her mass of snarled locks in their lifelong battle—she and her comb against the stubbornly resistant tangle of her hair. As usual, they battled to a draw.

I would so love to comb Ashinji's hair, she thought. *It must feel like silk. Stop it!*

The sun had climbed well up above the horizon as she left the dim confines of the bathhouse, blinking rapidly in the rosy light. It dazzled her eyes and prevented her from seeing the figure that approached her along the path.

"Look out!" a man's voice barked as they collided.

She gasped in surprise as strong fingers gripped her shoulders. "Oh! It is you! I mean, begging your pardon, Lord Sadaiyo," she squeaked, her throat gone dry with apprehension. He released his hold on her and stepped back.

"You should be more careful...Watch where you're going, girl," Sadaiyo said mildly.

Slightly taller and heavier than Ashinji, with hair that shaded toward chestnut rather than gold, Sadaiyo looked as if he had just rolled out of bed. He wore only a thin knee-length tunic and sandals, which left little to the imagination. Until this very moment, Jelena felt certain that he had never once spoken to her.

"You're my father's new messenger. Jelena, isn't it?"

Jelena nodded. "Yes, sir. Sorry to have almost ran you...I mean, to knock into you." She ducked her head and moved to step around Sadaiyo, but he shifted his body to block her way. Her cheeks began to warm with embarrassment.

"I'm surprised to see anyone else out and about so early this morning. It was a very, very late night for most of us. I trust you enjoyed yourself at my wedding feast?" His voice sounded blandly pleasant, though something about the way he looked at her sent little sparks of alarm coursing through her limbs.

"Y...Yes, my lord," she stammered. "I...must go now."

"Must you? Why, we've only just met, and I'm quite curious. I would very much like to hear your story sometime. My little brother thinks very highly of you, did you know that?" He moved in closer and Jelena edged away to maintain the distance between them. His eyes locked onto hers and she instantly recognized what simmered within their blue-green depths. She had seen the very same thing in

Duke Sebastianus's eyes when he had looked at her.

"Usually, I don't pay too much attention to the things my brother likes, but this time…this time, it's different."

"Uh, beg pardon, sir, but I do not understand. My Siri-dar not so good," Jelena lied. She understood all too well. Again she tried to get past, and again Sadaiyo blocked her way.

Before she could react, he seized her wrists in an unbreakable grip and held her fast. "Listen to me, girl," he growled. "I've been watching you ever since my snotty little brother dragged you in, and I like what I see. You are far too pretty to languish down here as a mere messenger, and you must know that my brother has nothing to offer you. Your life at Kerala would improve tremendously as my concubine. You'd have your own rooms in the castle, fine clothes, jewels…"

Jelena felt sick. How could a newly married man spend all night making love to his beautiful bride, then the very next day proposition another woman?

She shook her head emphatically. "Please let me go, Lord Sadaiyo," she begged. She tried in vain to break the vise-like hold he had on her wrists.

His eyes flashed grey-green fire. "I'd consider my answer very carefully if I were you," he said in a low, dangerous voice. "Don't be stupid, girl. If I've decided that I want you, then I'll have you, of that you can be certain. It would be a very serious mistake to turn me down, especially in favor of my brother. Think about it." He pulled her roughly toward him and whispered in her ear, "This isn't over." He then dropped her hands and sauntered away, leaving her bruised and shaken.

Jelena's knees turned to water, and she staggered backward, almost falling. Her thoughts fluttered in her head like terrified birds.

What am I going to do? I have no defense against Sadaiyo. He's the Heir. He can do as he likes, and no one can stop him, except…

No. I can't involve Ashinji. Things are already bad between him and his brother. This just might be enough to push him into doing something foolish. No, I must handle this myself, but how?

She ran all the way back to the barracks.

CHAPTER 26

THE HUNT

Seven days had passed since Ashinji had made his declaration and Sadaiyo his proposition, and during that time, Jelena had managed to avoid both brothers.

Ashinji had not sought her out, either; for this, Jelena felt great relief, because her resolve to lie to him about her true feelings had evaporated. She simply could not summon the strength of will to attempt to destroy the bond between them. Better that she avoid him altogether, at least for the time being, until she could figure out a course of action.

As for Sadaiyo, he had been kept very busy entertaining his new in-laws, too busy to spare any more attention for her, thank the gods.

Lord Sen kept her well occupied with carrying messages—orders, mostly, to all of the minor lords of the district. As their liege, part of Lord Sen's job involved directing his vassals in their preparations for the upcoming confrontation with the Soldarans. Much remained to be done. Alasiri had been at peace for over a century, and it was Lord Sen's considered opinion that the elven people had grown soft and complacent.

Today, though, Jelena had no messages to carry. Lord Sen had given most of the staff the day off, and as a bonus, a hunt had been organized for the recreation of Lord Dai and his entourage. The newlyweds were to lead it. Kami had told Jelena that staff members who were not on duty were always welcome to attend organized hunts, provided that they stayed to the rear and did not take any shots without express permission from the lords, a rare and unlikely occurrence.

As a messenger, Jelena was entitled to follow on horseback. Reluctant at first, she eventually allowed Aneko and some of the other guards to persuade her into joining them.

The warmth of the morning offered a preview of the day's heat. The lower yard buzzed with activity. Those staff members entitled to ride busied themselves preparing their own mounts while the grooms readied the mounts of the noble folk. A cluster of castle staff, mainly groundskeepers, laborers and kitchen workers, stood off to one side, well out of the way. They all intended to follow the hunt on foot, keeping up as best they could.

Jelena stood with her guard friends, absently stroking the nose of her favorite horse, Willow. Aneko came stumping up, a little smirk twisting her full mouth. "Kami won't be riding out with us this fine morning, I'm afraid. She's green as an unripe apple and puking her guts out in the privies this very moment."

For the past week, Kami had been ill, especially upon rising in the morning. Jelena's chest tightened with concern. "Maybe she should go see a doctor. Something very wrong could be with her," she said. Aneko roared with laughter, as did several others. Jelena felt terribly confused, wondering if she had made some especially ridiculous mistake with her Siri-dar.

"Oh, she'll be needing the doctor all right, but she's not sick, just pregnant," Aneko explained patiently.

Jelena blushed, embarrassed at her own ignorance. "Does Captain Miri know he is to be a father?" she asked.

"He'll know soon enough," Aneko replied. "I dare say he'll be putting in for that wage increase sooner than he expected. I s'pose their wedding will be moved up as well. Ai, the lords are mounting up. Let's go!"

Jelena climbed onto Willow and settled her bow across the saddle horn and a quiver of arrows at her knee. Aneko had suggested she carry the bow in case an opportunity for the commoners to shoot—unlikely, but still possible—presented itself.

She scanned the group of nobles and caught sight of Ashinji, astride the big black gelding he favored. Her breath caught in her throat. In the midst of talking to Lord Dai's son Ibeji, he abruptly looked up, like a hound scenting a rabbit. Slowly, as if an unseen force pulled at him, he swiveled in his saddle until he sat facing in her direction, catching her in his gaze.

She felt dizzy, and that curious sensation she had experienced before—like thoughts and words not her own were trying to form in her mind—washed over her. A voice called her name; it sounded like Ashinji's but his lips weren't moving.

Lord Sen interposed himself between Ashinji and Ibeji, blocking her view and abruptly the sensation vanished. She exhaled loudly and rubbed her forehead.

"Is your head hurting you?" Aneko asked.

"No…No. I am well," Jelena replied. "All excitement, my first hunt…" She smiled and indicated the hubbub with a wave of her hand.

"Just remember to stay to the rear." Aneko pointed her thumb back over her shoulder.

The cacophony in the yard increased twofold as the hunt mistress brought up the castle's pack of hounds. They were impressive animals, with lean, muscular bodies and whip-slim tails. Their coats gleamed like black satin in the sunlight. Deep, throaty howls filled the air—a raw, primal sound, visceral and wild. Jelena could not help but feel a rush of excitement.

The gates of the castle swung open, and the hunt flowed through. The hunt mistress and her assistants rode at the fore, the pack flowing like black water around their horses' feet. Next came the field of noble folk, followed by the mounted commoners. The group on foot brought up the rear.

Back in Amsara, Jelena had never been allowed to participate in any hunts, and even if she had wanted to, her lowly status as a kitchen drudge would have meant that she'd have had to follow on foot. The idea of slogging through mud and brambles for hours just to witness other people bringing down game had never really appealed to her.

This, however, was entirely different. She had a horse to ride, and social status far beyond anything she had ever imagined for herself. She had friends who respected her. She had, for the first time in her life, a real home.

All of which she now stood to lose if she refused Sadaiyo.

Don't think about any of that now. Just enjoy the day.

The field set out at a brisk jog, heading for a patch of woodland just across the river from the castle. The hounds fanned out and entered the trees, snuffling and growling. The field hung back to allow the dogs to do their work. A well-seasoned pack, they knew their business. Occasionally, the hunt mistress would whistle a series of tones. Jelena wondered what they meant.

After a short time, the hounds emerged, tongues lolling. They had failed to flush any game. The hunt mistress whistled again, and the pack reformed, ready to move on.

The hunt moved as one, a multi-legged beast loping through the golden fields of midsummer. They rode east, toward Saihama village, where, Aneko had informed Jelena, many deer had been spotted recently.

It did not take the dogs long to find game once they had slipped back into the forest. A huge stag careened out of the trees, eyes as big as saucers, the hounds in hot pursuit. The nobles rode hard after it, Sadaiyo and Misune leading the charge. Jelena and the rest of the mounted commoners held back a few moments, then followed at a slightly slower pace. Out of the corner of her eye, Jelena could see the people on foot cutting across at a diagonal to the stag's flight, as if they instinctively knew which way he would run. She bent low over Willow's neck and galloped on, exhilarated.

The stag pounded across an open meadow, trying desperately to loop back toward the shelter of the trees. The dogs leapt and snapped relentlessly at his heels until he abruptly turned and rushed them, head down, in an attempt to sweep them aside with his antlers. The dogs fell back, barking furiously, but they continued to keep the stag encircled, holding him for the hunters.

It ended quickly. Misune had the honor of the killing shot—a single, perfectly placed arrow that pierced the stag's lungs and heart. The beast fell to his knees, gouts of bloody froth dripping from nose and mouth. With a groan, he slumped to his side and lay still. The field let out a great cheer.

Jelena rode up just as Misune took her shot, enabling her to witness the kill at close range. She admired the newest Sakehera's skill with the bow, but at the same time, she felt a twinge of sadness for the death of a noble creature. The stag had run well, and Misune had granted him a speedy, dignified end.

Jelena waited quietly, along with the rest of the common folk, while the nobles discussed where the hunt would ride next. Lord Sen suggested that they continue east to try the woods further on, and the rest agreed. Several servants were assigned to dress the carcass and carry it back to the castle.

The hunt resumed. The hounds soon caught a fresh scent and followed it into the trees. The hunt mistress cautiously went in after them, signaling to her assistants to hang back outside on the forest's edge.

Jelena held her breath, afraid that even the softest of exhalations would break the concentration of dogs and hunters. Willow shifted beneath her with a creak of joint and muscle. The only other sound she could hear was the whisper of the wind in the treetops.

The *blat-blat* of the hunt mistress's horn, along with the explosive barking of the hounds, alerted the waiting field that the game had been flushed.

"Here they come!" someone shouted. Jelena saw a flash of brown and white just within the trees—a doe on the run. Instead of making a break for it out in the open, however, the terrified animal turned at the last moment and headed back into the forest. The hunt mistress's horn sounded again, and her two assistants spurred their horses into the trees.

Jelena could see that the nobles really didn't want to ride among the trees in pursuit. She surmised that they would much rather give chase out in the open where they could have clear lines of sight for shooting.

The barking of the hounds grew fainter as the quarry moved deeper into cover.

Sadaiyo cursed and shouted, "Come on! It's getting away!" He spurred his horse forward and quickly disappeared from view. Like water through a breached dam, the field surged after the Heir, guiding their mounts as quickly as they could between the boles of the trees. Jelena started to follow, then realized that the common people were all hanging back. She turned to Aneko with a questioning look.

"They'll never catch that doe in those trees, not as long as they stay a-horse," Aneko commented. "None of this lot…" she indicated the walkers with a flick of her hand, "…feel like getting trampled while the noble folk blunder about in there. Naw, we'll just wait right here 'til they get tired and come out."

Jelena fidgeted in her saddle, anxious not to miss out on a single moment of this, her first hunt. She made a decision. "I go in after, "she announced. Aneko shrugged and smiled lopsidedly, as if to say that it was no use, but Jelena could do as she liked.

Jelena drummed her heels into Willow's sturdy flanks, and the horse plunged eagerly into the cool shadows beneath the forest canopy. Shouts and whistles echoed among the trees, making it difficult to discern which way the hunt had gone. She decided to let Willow choose the path, for the mare strode along with purpose, as if she knew exactly where to go.

Jelena could hear the dogs now, howling joyfully. *They must be closing in on the doe,* she thought.

Without warning, Willow shied violently. Only sheer luck kept Jelena from being thrown. As she fought to control the mare, she caught a glimpse of a heavy, dark shape in the undergrowth. Bushes shook and leaves flew as an enormous gray-black beast exploded from a thicket beneath Willow's nose and hurtled forward past the plunging horse. An ear-piercing squeal tore at Jelena's ears.

A wild boar!

She and Willow had inadvertently blundered into its hiding place and flushed it out, but the tusker appeared more interested in escape than confrontation. It tore off through the trees and disappeared from sight, leaving both horse and girl shaking with reaction.

Having regained control, Jelena urged Willow forward, now more anxious than ever to catch up to the rest of the hunt. Off to her right, she heard a man call out and decided to head in that general direction. Perhaps she would run into Ashinji. Her heart, having just slowed down, sped up again at the thought of seeing the man she loved.

A man astride a big bay horse came into view—Lord Sen. He sat gazing ahead into the trees, his expression thoughtful, as if trying to decide whether to ride on or stay put. Jelena opened her mouth to call out to him, but he kicked the bay and trotted off. She urged Willow to follow.

Suddenly, the thicket ahead erupted with a furious squeal. Lord Sen's horse screamed in panic and reared, hurling the Lord of Kerala from the saddle. Jelena watched in horror as Lord Sen hit the ground with bone-breaking force and lay unmoving. The horse bolted away into the trees.

The boar stood poised, his small black eyes glittering with porcine fury. His massive head, adorned with a pair of wickedly curved tusks, swung from side to side, snout twitching. Jelena could feel Willow preparing to bolt. Just then, Lord Sen stirred and groaned. With a snort, the boar charged.

Later, Jelena would have no explanation for what happened next; perhaps the One Goddess guided her hands, perhaps the magic within her aided the deed.

She felt her consciousness tear loose from her body and float free to hover above the scene now unfolding in slow motion below her. She watched as, seemingly without enough time to make a shot, she raised her bow, withdrew an arrow from the quiver at her knee, nocked, drew, and fired. The arrow ignited in a flash of blue flame and impaled the boar through its right eye, killing it instantly. The beast crashed to the ground and slid forward in a tangle of limbs to fetch up against the semi-conscious Lord Sen.

Jelena's mind slammed back into her body with such force that she nearly tumbled from her saddle. Shaking her head dizzily, she scrambled off the trembling Willow and ran over to crouch beside Lord Sen.

"My lord! Can you speak? Are you hurt?" she cried, struggling not to gag on the rank aroma of the dead boar. Lord Sen's eyes fluttered open and for one terrible moment, Jelena saw only blankness, then a heartbeat later, a glimmer of recognition.

"My messenger. Where did you come from?" Sen asked. He sounded genuinely puzzled.

Jelena sighed with heartfelt relief. "Do you know what now just happened, my lord?" she asked. He struggled to sit up, and Jelena gladly lent her shoulder for assistance. She peered intently into his face. He looked pale and shaky but seemed more or less intact.

"I startled a boar. My horse threw me. The last thing I remember is thinking that I was going to be very sore tomorrow after taking such a fall." He let out a small chuckle, then gasped and clutched at his side.

"You hurt, where in pain, my lord?" she asked, but he just shook his head, staring first at the slain tusker, then at the bow Jelena still clutched in her hand.

"You saved my life, girl," he said slowly. "Do you realize what that means?" He pointed at the arrow protruding from the boar's eye. Jelena shook her head. "It means that you have earned the right to ask of me whatever you want, and I am obligated to give it to you, no matter the cost to me."

Jelena drew in a sharp breath, not quite believing what she had just heard. Lord Sen regarded her intently, and Jelena saw something in his eyes that she had never before seen in the gaze of a powerful man—respect. She shivered with awe.

"Here, take this," Sen wheezed, his right hand pressed tightly to his injured side. He fumbled with his other hand to release a small ivory horn from his belt. "Blow three short blasts, then three long ones. It will signal the others that there's a rider down." He held the horn out to Jelena, who took it and pressed it hesitantly to her lips.

Her first effort produced a sickly squawk. "Blow harder," Sen instructed. Nodding in understanding, Jelena took a deep breath and blew with all the strength she could muster. Sen bobbed his head in approval.

Almost simultaneously, several horns sounded nearby, answering the distress call. Jelena could feel the vibrations of approaching riders in the litter-covered earth beneath her knees. She glanced worriedly at Lord Sen and silently prayed for them to hurry.

Ashinji reached them first. He tumbled off his horse and threw himself down beside his father. "Father! Are you hurt? What happened?" he cried.

"I'm all right, Son," Sen soothed. "Just a little fall, that's all."

"He is being brave...for you," Jelena stated quietly. "He fell...very hard."

Ashinji looked at Jelena, then his eyes skipped over to the dead boar. "Jelena, you shot this boar, didn't you?" He reached out to touch a fingertip to the bow in her hand. "You saved my father's life." Love and gratitude sparked in his eyes. Jelena wanted to break down and cry; only sheer willpower held back her tears.

Ashinji turned his attention back to Sen. "Father, you must not try to minimize this. Please tell me where you hurt." His tone indicated that he would tolerate no nonsense.

Sen held up his hand as if in surrender. "I think I may have broken a rib here on my right side. That's the worst of it," he said, almost meek in the face of his son's stern concern.

"Great Goddess! Father, you're down!"

Sadaiyo had arrived, along with Misune and Lord Dai. He jumped from his horse and strode over to where Sen lay. "Out of my way, girl," he growled, shoving Jelena roughly aside, sending her sprawling. He squatted beside his father and said, "Are you hurt?"

Jelena scrambled to her feet, still clutching her bow, spitting leaves from her mouth. Her face burned with humiliation. She saw Lord Sen's eyes narrow in anger. "My messenger here shot this beast while I lay helpless. If she had not killed it, you would now be Lord," he said tightly. "I owe her my life."

Sadaiyo raised one eyebrow in surprise and turned to look at Jelena, his expression speculative. She felt a chill race up her spine.

By this time, most of the other nobles had arrived, dismounted and had gathered around the fallen Lord of Kerala. Everyone talked at once, completely ignoring Jelena, although many exclaimed in astonishment over the slain boar. Jelena stood quietly, just outside the noisy circle of people, wishing she could stand beside Ashinji.

As if he had somehow heard her wish, the crowd parted, and Ashinji stepped through and walked up to her. He took her hand and led her into the center of the group where Sen, now up and leaning heavily on Sadaiyo, awaited.

The Lord of Kerala cleared his throat as the crowd fell silent. "This girl here, Jelena is her name, came to Kerala last spring. My son Ashinji found her, wounded and lost, and needing my help. She is in search of her elven kin, and I promised that I would aid in her search. She has been in service to me as my messenger these last few weeks."

Jelena felt like an exotic species of insect pinned under a glass for examination. She kept her eyes firmly affixed to the toes of her boots. Ashinji had released her hand but remained standing beside her, and the steady warmth of his presence gave her comfort.

Lord Sen continued. "When I flushed the boar, my horse reared and threw me. I lay unconscious…helpless. I thank The One that Jelena came when she did. T'was her shot that skewered the great, ugly beast, straight through his eye! I couldn't have done better myself. I owe this girl my life, and she shall have her reward…Whatever she desires." A ripple of shock flowed through the crowd.

"Jelena…Look at me, girl," Sen commanded. Hesitantly, Jelena obeyed. "You shall be the honored guest at my table tonight," he announced, "and I'll make sure that you get the choicest morsels from yonder porker! Now, that's all I have to say. Get me back home, sons." He looked to Ashinji and Sadaiyo, grimacing in pain.

Jelena's head reeled. The reversal of her fortunes had been both swift and shocking. As Sadaiyo and Ashinji assisted their father, Lord Dai assumed command of the hunt. Two riders were dispatched to fetch servants and bring them back to assist with the boar. A frenzy of barking heralded the arrival of the hunt mistress and the pack. Jelena overheard her telling Lord Dai that the carcass of the doe awaited dressing and removal.

Since nothing more seemed required of her, Jelena went in search of Willow. She found the chestnut mare quietly munching shoots a spear's throw away. "There you are, girl," she said, stroking the mare's velvet nose. She hung her bow across the saddle horn, gathered up the reins, and scrambled ungracefully into the saddle.

Then it hit her.

A storm of trembles seized her body. Her thoughts tumbled over each other in a swirl of confusion.

What just happened? Did I really leave my body behind? Is this what it feels like to float on the aether in spirit form?

How did I cause the arrow to burst into flame, and why was it not consumed?

She hugged herself to stop the shaking.

The flame was blue! Blue fire…Magic!

The nobles had all remounted and were moving off. Ashinji and Sadaiyo had assisted Lord Sen back onto his horse and rode along on either side of their father in order to steady him, if needed. Jelena fell in behind, trailing the group at a respectful distance.

When they at last broke the cover of the trees, word had already reached the common folk of the events that had just transpired.

A knot of riders immediately surrounded Jelena.

Aneko spoke first. "Is it true, Jelena? You really killed a tusker about to gore Lord Sen?" Jelena nodded weakly, still too shaken to speak. "D'you know what this means?" the older woman exulted. She didn't bother to wait for an answer. "It means that you'll get what you want, Jelena." She reached over and gripped Jelena's hand and squeezed hard. "It means that there's *hope!*"

Jelena understood Aneko's meaning, but she dared not let herself begin to believe. She knew Lord Sen meant what he had said—she could ask anything of him, and he would grant it—but she didn't think that "anything" included Ashinji…Or did it?

As the hunt made its way back to the castle, despite all her efforts, Jelena felt herself surrendering to hope.

Chapter 27

In Perfect Union

For only the second time in her life, Jelena sat at a high table, surrounded by noble folk, partaking of a rich feast. This time, however, she was among elves, and an honored guest, not an object for sale. None of this made her feel any less nervous.

She wore a gown of russet silk, secured at the sides with tasseled cords, and matching slippers—all borrowed. Only her mother's ivory combs holding her hair at bay and the strand of blue Kara glass beads that had been Claudia's last gift to her could she call her own. She sat directly to the left of Lord Sen, a position normally held by Lady Amara. To honor Jelena, the Lady of Kerala had willingly yielded her place this night to the girl who had saved her husband's life. She sat to Jelena's left, and insisted on serving her guest with her own hands.

At the center of the table, stuffed and roasted to perfection, rested the very reason for Jelena's honored presence tonight—the boar she had so valiantly slain. Even in death, his fierceness had been preserved, for the cooks had left in place his vicious, curving tusks.

Ashinji sat across the table from his mother, where he made little attempt to hide his true feelings. He had exchanged his plain brown hunting leathers for a simple tunic and trousers of dark green cotton, and to Jelena, he looked far more elegant than anyone else in the room, despite the plainness of his clothes. His gaze kept wandering to her face, and she struggled to resist the pull of his desire and not meet his eyes. His behavior was not going unnoticed.

From the corner of her eye, Jelena could see Lady Amara scrutinizing her youngest son closely, and in that instant, she knew the love she and Ashinji shared remained a secret no longer, at least not to his mother. She felt a cold knot of apprehension tighten in her belly.

"Little Brother, I can't help but notice how fascinated you are with our Jelena. Take care, or we'll all think you have designs on her."

Sadaiyo's tone contained equal parts amusement and mockery. He sat in his usual place at Lord Sen's right hand, his wife Misune by his side. Jelena risked a glance in his direction and found him leaning forward, staring at her with frankness bordering on insult. She refused to meet his eyes, looking instead to Ashinji, who nodded his head almost imperceptibly, as if to reassure her.

"Whatever feelings I may have for Jelena are entirely proper and none of your concern, Brother," Ashinji responded. Outwardly, he seemed calm. A tiny muscle along his left jaw began to twitch.

Lord Sen cleared his throat and raised his wine goblet. He looked pointedly at each of his sons, then addressed the gathering. "Raise your cups to this girl in salute, for she saved my life today with her bravery and skill." He turned to Jelena. "Jelena, you shall ever hold a place of honor at my table and in my house." He waited until all the others had raised their goblets, then put his own to his lips and drank.

Jelena felt slightly dizzy, as if caught up in a dream. How was it possible that she, a girl of dubious breeding and no family, now found herself toasted by an entire assemblage of elven nobility?

She remembered the flaming arrow, and the surreal sensation of floating outside of her body. Had that been a dream as well? How could it have been, when the evidence of its reality now lay roasted and sliced on a platter before her?

Sadaiyo's derisive laughter snapped her back to the present. "Look at him! He's hopelessly smitten. Father, I think it's high time you found my little brother a bride. He is obviously suffering from a lack of suitable female companionship. A proper wife is just what he needs to take his mind off, er, other things."

"My wife's cousin has a daughter who is of suitable age, Sakehera. I'd be happy to make inquiries on your behalf," Lord Dai offered.

"She's a charming girl, and quite pretty. I believe you'd find her most pleasing," Lady Dai added cheerfully. She leaned around her husband to eye Ashinji speculatively, who looked as though he'd just been slapped.

Sen nodded. "It's true," he said, seemingly oblivious to his son's reaction. "My youngest son is in need of a wife. His mother and I have several possibilities in mind, but none of them has really impressed us. We'd be very interested in learning more about your cousin's daughter, my lady."

Jelena's heart skipped a beat. A wave of vertigo threatened to topple her from her chair. She felt a hand grip her shoulder and turned to see Lady Amara peering intently into her face.

Abruptly, the room began to fade, and all sound receded to a muted buzz. Jelena's field of vision tunneled down to focus on Lady Amara's face, ageless and beautiful, floating before her like a pale mask. Words skirled softly through her mind.

Do you have any idea what it is that is within you, child?

No, but I am afraid of it.

It is very ancient and powerful. It is of you, and yet it is not.

It made the arrow burn!

Ai, so it did.

I love Ashinji.

I know.

Lady Amara's face receded, and Jelena's senses returned in a rush. She gasped and looked around in confusion. Amara still gripped her shoulder but only to give it a gentle squeeze.

What in the name of all the gods just happened? Jelena wondered. *Did Ashinji's mother just speak to me...in my mind?* Without warning, her stomach lurched. "My lady," she murmured, "Apologies. Just now, I...am not feeling so well." She forced a smile. "Too much...uh, noble food. Not used to...so much."

"Husband, our honored guest is not well," Amara said.

"Oh! Um...I hope it's nothing serious!" Lord Sen seemed genuinely concerned. He rose from his chair, grimacing in pain. A servant leapt forward to lend assistance, but he waved the man off. "I'll have a servant see you back to your quarters," he said.

Jelena shook her head. "No, please. I can walk myself back. Thank you, my lord."

"Let my son walk you back, Jelena," Lady Amara said quietly, then in a clear, strong voice, she announced, "Ashinji will see Jelena safely to the barracks."

Sadaiyo, who had been taking a gulp from his wine glass, sputtered and began to cough violently. Misune exclaimed in dismay and began slapping him between his shoulders. Lord Sen, who also appeared to be taken entirely by surprise, shot his wife a questioning look, but did not object.

"Come, Jelena," Ashinji said. He rose from his chair and beckoned to her.

As she moved to follow, Jelena smiled gratefully at Lady Amara, who nodded in acknowledgment. It seemed that she could now count the Lady of Kerala as her ally. Together, she and Ashinji walked out of the hall into the night.

~~~

At first, Ashinji walked beside her in silence. When they were well away from the open door of the hall, he grabbed Jelena's shoulder and spun her around to face him. He pulled her close and rested his forehead against hers.

"I love you," he whispered fiercely.

She began to shake. So much had changed since she had ridden out to the hunt that morning, but she still dared not let herself hope for a future with this man.

"I love you, too," she replied. "But how can we…?" her voice trailed off, forlorn.

"Come to my chamber. Stay with me tonight. I need you." His voice trembled with desire. "Please!" he begged.

Gods, he felt so good! Not all of the obstacles standing between them and a life together seemed so insurmountable when he whispered to her with such love in his voice. Jelena felt an answering desire flare within her…and she melted. She could resist him no longer. Her lips sought his, and they kissed, slowly and softly at first, then with rising passion.

Ashinji groaned.

"Hurry, my love," he urged, pulling her along toward the outer staircase that led up his rooms.

Ashinji's apartment occupied the entire top floor of a small, newer addition off the east wing of the castle. A servant had already prepared the single, large chamber for the evening. The warm glow of lamplight greeted them as Ashinji ushered Jelena in, carefully closing and securing the door behind them.

Jelena glanced around the large rectangular room and took note of its furnishings. Finely woven mats covered the wooden floors. A low table surrounded by cushions stood near the room's single large window, which hung open to the cool night breeze. A writing desk, chest of drawers, clothes press, and a bed made up the rest of the room's contents.

Ashinji came up behind her and slipped his arms around her waist, then began a series of slow kisses along the slope of her neck. Jelena sighed, feeling herself becoming soft and wobbly. She leaned back against him and allowed his hands to begin the task of undressing her.

She felt the ties of the borrowed gown give way. The silk slithered down her body to land in a liquid heap around her feet. She kicked it aside and turned to face him. Slowly, as if unwrapping the most precious of gifts, Ashinji undid the ties that secured her sheer white undergown and gently pulled it away from her body. With a shrug of her shoulders, Jelena sent it to the mats. Lastly, he removed the combs from her hair.

Jelena now stood clad only in the blue Kara necklace, bathed in the golden glow of the lamps. Ashinji sighed, as if in awe, his face enraptured. "You are…so extraordinarily beautiful," he whispered. He took her hand and led her to the bed.

The bed rested on a low wooden platform. As Jelena sank down atop the silk and fur coverlets, she marveled at the softness of the mattress. She watched with growing excitement as Ashinji quickly shed his clothing until he stood totally revealed to her. As his final preparation before he lay down beside her, he freed his hair from the leather tie that had held it back and shook it out in a glorious fall of gold.

Softly, slowly, he began to caress her body, starting with her face. His hands were warm and gentle, and the natural anxiety Jelena felt began to ease. He reached her breasts and began tracing her nipples with his fingers. She gasped at the exquisite sensation. His hands wandered lower until they rested just above the tuft of wiry hair that guarded the entrance to her most sacred of places.

She turned her face against his neck. The smell of his

body—always intoxicating—now drove her mad with desire. Unsure of what to do, she forced herself to relax and let her knees fall open.

"I have never been…" she started to say, but Ashinji laid a finger on her lips.

"Hush, my love. I know," he replied.

His hand slid down and parted the delicate folds of her flesh, probing ever so gently until he touched a place that sent a bolt of pleasure shooting up through her entire body. She cried out and arched up against him, and he responded by pressing more firmly. Her breath came in short pants now, and she could feel Ashinji breathing harder as well.

He put his lips to one breast and began to suck, causing a whole new wave of marvelous sensations to flood her mind. She could feel his growing urgency, and Jelena knew that they had both reached the point of no return. Every hard curve of muscle spoke eloquently of Ashinji's passion, awakening an answering fire within her.

His breath flowed hot and sweet upon her face as he crushed her body closer to his. She wanted only to melt into him, slip beneath his skin and meld her flesh to his to become one continuous being. As he moved to lie between her legs, she felt the last vestiges of her fear dissolve. She trusted Ashinji completely.

Though she knew it was coming, the pain of the first penetration still shocked her. Convulsively, she dug her fingers into the muscles of Ashinji's back, as if by inflicting this small pain on him, she could lessen her own. She moaned and burst into tears.

Ashinji moved slowly in and out of her, as if he could sense that this part gave her more hurt than pleasure. He covered her wet, salty cheeks with kisses and whispered his love into her burning ears. She felt her mind break loose from its moorings and begin to drift out to where it could more easily process the waves of sensation that crashed over and through her.

Gradually, she became aware that something else lay underneath the pain, a sensation unlike all the others she had newly experienced this night. She felt it pushing her inexorably over a threshold into an unknown world, a world that she desperately wanted to understand. She reached for it—her entire body shuddering with the strain—and then detonated with a soft explosion. Her consciousness slammed back down into her skull, tearing a cry of amazement from her raw throat.

She felt Ashinji's body beginning to shake and, instinctively, she wrapped her legs around him more tightly. He cried out and pushed deep into her, his muscles rigid, then with a final moan he subsided atop her.

Jelena lay very still beneath him, concentrating on the connection between their flesh. She decided that she could stay this way forever, joined with her lover in perfect union.

Ashinji finally stirred and carefully pulled himself free. He rolled over onto his side and gathered her up against him. He buried his face in her hair and murmured, "I love you." After a heartbeat's pause, he added, "And I promise this will only get better and better for you."

Her eyes linked with his. In the lamplight, they gleamed darkly, and the devotion she saw within their depths released a new flood of tears. She caressed his cheek and marveled at its smoothness, so unlike that of a human male.

"I love you, Ashi," she whispered, and kissed him.

Later that night, as Ashinji lay sleeping, Jelena sat up beside him and watched his dreams chase themselves across his beautiful face. She shifted a little and winced at the sting between her legs. She did not mind; the pain served as proof of the reality of her experience.

Fatigue finally overcame her. She lay down beneath the coverlets and snuggled against Ashinji, who stirred but did not wake. She kissed the tip of his ear and laid her hand over his heart so she could feel its slow, steady beat. She closed her eyes and drifted off to sleep.

~~~

The hoarse croak of a raven startled Jelena into wakefulness. She opened bleary eyes to stare at the large, rough-feathered black bird perching boldly on the windowsill. It turned its head sideways to peer at her from an eye that glittered like a jet bead.

Jelena didn't know whether to be afraid or fascinated. She looked over at Ashinji, who sprawled loosely on his back, one arm flung up over his head, sound asleep. The sight of his lean warrior's body, naked in the rosy light of the new day, warmed her with a mix of embarrassment and lust. The memories of the previous night came flooding back, completely dissipating the lingering vestiges of sleep.

The raven croaked again, and Jelena began to feel a little uneasy.

It looks like it's talking to someone, she thought. She decided to wake Ashinji.

She ran her fingers through his silky hair and, kissing him lightly on his forehead and lips, she whispered his name into his ear—softly, lest the raven hear. She felt a little silly, but she didn't want to startle the creature and perhaps cause it to fly into the room. Ashinji muttered something incomprehensible and remained blissfully asleep. She thought briefly of tweaking him *down there*, but decided that she wasn't yet comfortable enough with the idea that she could now touch him like that, and so she shook his shoulder instead.

His eyes fluttered open and focused on her face. Slowly, he grinned, then pulled her down on top of him. She felt his manhood stir against her leg. "This is the single most beautiful sight I could ever hope to see in the morning," he murmured happily. "You...here in my bed...completely naked." He nuzzled her neck.

"We have...visitor," Jelena said in a low voice, and leaned aside so that Ashinji could see the window. The raven had not moved.

"What's this, then! How dare you sit there and spy on us like that! Can't you see we wish to be alone?" Ashinji pulled a pillow from underneath his head and hurled it at the window. The raven let out an indignant squawk. With a downward sweep of its wings, it launched itself off the sill and disappeared.

Jelena shivered and snuggled close against Ashinji. Something about the way the bird had looked at them—*at her*—frightened her.

"What is it, love?" Ashinji asked in a low, concerned voice.

Jelena shook her head, uncertain about why the bird had spooked her so. "That bird...how do you say...Urrr!" In frustration, she lapsed back into Soldaran. "That raven. I don't know how I know this, but there was something...not right, not natural about it. Ravens don't just sit on people's windowsills calmly staring at them."

Ashinji frowned. "There are many ravens here at Kerala," he replied in Siri-dar, "all perfectly harmless, but you're right. It is a little strange. I've never had one actually come and sit on my window-sill before now." He shrugged. "Try not to worry. It's just a raven.

Besides…" His voice became playful. "You have me to protect you from any birds with evil intentions!" He rolled Jelena over onto her back and began to tease her body with his lips and hands, awakening the fire in her still-tender loins.

When he entered her, the pain was brief and swiftly overwhelmed by the ecstasy of union with the man she loved. This time, the soft explosion she had experienced last night became an all-encompassing blast of sensation along every nerve, leaving her wrung out and deliriously happy.

Afterward, she rested in the warm circle of Ashinji's arms, perfectly content, all thoughts of the raven and its strange behavior banished from her mind.

"You seemed to enjoy yourself a bit more this time," Ashinji commented, tenderly stroking her cheek.

Jelena nodded. As before, Ashinji had been gentle and attentive, and her body was learning how to respond properly. "You promised it would get better, and you were right."

Ashinji shifted his body so that they could lie face to face. "Last night changed everything, Jelena," he said softly. "There's no going back to the way it was. In my heart, I am now wed to you, body and soul. All that remains is to make it official. Today, we'll go to my parents and tell them about us."

"Your mother…she knows. I think she is on our side, but your father…" Jelena bit her lip, suddenly afraid of Lord Sen's reaction. Ashinji's father was typically a man of good humor, but he had plans for his youngest son, plans that didn't involve a half-breed kinless girl from Soldara.

"My father will have to understand. After all, he married my mother because he *chose* to. Theirs was a marriage of love, not arrangement. I'm the second child, so dynastic considerations shouldn't play a role in whom I marry since I won't inherit my father's title. He may be angry at first, but eventually, he'll calm down and give us his permission." He kissed her forehead.

Jelena wished she could share Ashinji's confidence. "Ashi, please wait to tell your father a little while more. Give me time to find my father…or my family, so I can say to Lord Sen, this is who I am, these are my kin. Otherwise, I have no…honor." She searched Ashinji's face for understanding, but she could see that he did not agree with her reasons.

"You already have the greatest honor in my father's eyes, beloved. You saved his life. He is obligated to grant you anything that you ask of him," Ashinji pointed out.

"I do not wish to get permission from him because of obligation. I wish him to give it freely because he agrees for us to be together," Jelena responded. "Please, my love. Wait just a little longer."

Ashinji opened his mouth as if to repeat his objection, then gave in with a frustrated sigh. "I'll do as you ask, but only for a short while," he warned. "If my father can't turn up any leads on your elven family by summer's end, we're going to tell him about us. No arguments."

"Agreed," Jelena answered. She stretched and yawned, suddenly reluctant to move, but she knew that she had to report to Lord Sen soon, to find out if he had any messages for her to deliver today. She sat up and swung her legs over the edge of the bed. Something caught her eye, and she looked down to see a small, irregular scarlet blotch upon the cream-colored mattress cover. She drew in a sharp breath then relaxed in realization.

"Don't worry about that," Ashinji said. He sat up beside her and rubbed her back companionably. "I sometimes cut myself during sword practice. The servants won't think anything of it."

The sight of her virgin's blood brought home the reality of her changed circumstances. Back in Amsara, she had given up hope of ever experiencing the soul-satisfying joy of true lovemaking. At best, she had resigned herself to remaining untouched for her entire life. At worst, she had feared eventual rape by one of several castle louts who had grown increasingly more open and persistent in their intentions as she had grown into young womanhood.

She leaned into Ashinji and he slipped an arm around her shoulder. "I...don't feel like I deserve you," she whispered in Soldaran.

"Don't ever say that again," Ashinji chided, placing his hands on either side of her face. "I love you, and that will never change. You are my life. It is I who don't deserve you."

He stood up and helped her to her feet. She wiped away the tears that had sprung to her eyes at Ashinji's heartfelt declaration of love, then bent to gather up her discarded clothing. "Aneko and Kami will know I have been with you," she sighed as she shrugged into the rumpled chemise. "They will…tease and tease."

Ashinji pulled on a pair of breeches and came over to help her with the outer gown, tying up the cords at her waist. He smiled. "Let 'em talk. I don't care if the entire population of Kerala knows about us."

Abruptly, his mood shifted, and he spun her around and looked deep into her eyes with a seriousness that frightened her. "Jelena, you need to beware of my brother," he said in a low voice. "Sadaiyo finds pleasure in anything that hurts me, and I'm afraid that he may try to get to me through you. I don't think he's any physical threat to you, but he uses words like they were the keenest of weapons. Don't believe anything he says. In fact, just avoid him."

Jelena briefly considered telling Ashinji about her encounter with Sadaiyo the day after the wedding ceremony but decided against it. Not much would be accomplished except that it would further upset Ashinji, and besides, nothing had happened. "I will stay away from Lord Sadaiyo. It will be easy. He never comes to the barracks and I almost never see him except sometimes with your father."

"Good. That's good." Ashinji ran his hands through his hair and pulled at the rings in his left ear, a gesture that Jelena had come to recognize meant that he felt upset or preoccupied. He forced his face into a semblance of cheeriness. "Are you hungry?

Jelena thought a moment. "Yes, I think I am," she replied.

"I'll walk with you down to the kitchen, then," Ashinji said. He took her hand. "Let's go."

CHAPTER 28

THE COMING DARKNESS

The raven flew in lazy circles high above the red-tiled rooftops of the castle, its bead-like eyes scanning the landscape below. It had once been a very beautiful bird—sleek and strong—but that was before. Now, it had nearly come to the end of its strength, its life essence depleted in slavery to the alien intelligence that guided its every move.

Hundreds of leagues to the north, deep within his mountain prison, the Nameless One seethed with malevolent triumph. Through the eyes of the raven, he had seen it—the Key, at long last! It burned within its vessel—a cold blue fire—pulsing in rhythm to the beat of the life force that sustained it.

For weeks, he had concentrated his search to the southeast, beyond the Great Forest, but he had been unable to pinpoint its exact position. He had used up many ravens in the search, and his frustration had grown with each passing day. Then, quite unexpectedly, he had felt the unique energy of the Key surge through the aether, alerting him to its location. A nearby raven had been dispatched to a mid-sized castle in the southern borderlands.

Through the eyes of his small tool, he had observed the vessel and had beheld the glorious light of his Key, illuminating its flesh like a beacon. Now that he finally knew the exact nature of the vessel and where it lay, he needed to find a way to get both his ring and the vessel to him. Only then could he resume what had been interrupted by bitterest treachery over five lifetimes ago. It would not be easy. He needed a willing ally in the outside world, preferably one trained in the use of magic. He felt confident he would find such an individual among the ranks of Alasiri's professional mages, one who could be bent to his purpose by the lure of greater power. Were not all magicians driven to a certain degree by the thirst for more power and knowledge?

No, it would not be easy, but it could be done.

A sound like the winter wind sluicing among the high, icy peaks of the Kesen Numai Mountains echoed through the dark chamber deep beneath the ancient fortress—the sound of The Nameless One laughing.

~~~

It is time.

Do you think the girl is ready?

Yes. She has already come to me asking to learn about what she calls her 'blue fire.'

Still...She is very young, and such a burden would be extremely difficult for a trained, experienced mage, let alone a hikui girl!

What other choice do we have?

None...Very well...Begin the girl's training. When she is further along, you will bring her to Sendai. I shall take over then.

There is still the question about our own strength. When the time comes, I fear that, without a full complement, we will be unable to complete the Working.

I am concerned as well, but there is no one suitable that we could invite to join us.

There is my son.

Your son is untrained...because of your family tradition, I might add!

I am beginning to deeply regret that. He is the only one of my children who has inherited the strength of my Talent, it seems.

Does he even know how powerful a mage he could become?

No. I put a block in place when he was a child, after I was certain of the magnitude of his Talent. I have kept it all from him, mainly to spare him the frustration.

Even if you began training him now, yourself, he could never be ready... Not for a Great Working.

He doesn't have to have the skill of a full-fledged mage. He only needs to know how to control and direct the proper energies...and be willing to perform the Sundering, if need be.

Can you be certain he will strike the killing blow if called upon? If what you say is true and he is in love with this girl, he may hesitate at the last moment. I don't have to tell you what that will mean.

He will do what's necessary. My son understands quite well the concept of duty.

The girl's father...You are sure of his identity?

I've seen the ring myself.

It could be some sort of a deception.

Unlikely!

This changes nothing, you know. All must go forward as planned.

I know...This is going to be so hard on my son...I've decided to allow him and the girl to be together so that they might have a little happiness beforehand.

Do you think that's wise? It will only make it more difficult for them in the end. It seems rather cruel to me.

'Cruel' is a harsh word...My son loves this girl. It's not wise, but I've denied my child so much. I've forced him into a life that goes against his basic nature, deceived him about a fundamental part of his being...

You've allowed guilt to cloud your judgment.

Perhaps, but it's a mother's prerogative to indulge her children.

I just hope it doesn't prove to be an obstacle.

When the time comes, they will both do what they must.

Keep me informed.

Of course. I'll contact you again soon.

Amara opened her eyes and took a deep breath. The mental exchange with her colleague in the capital had taken only a short amount of time, but it had required that she expend a great deal of energy to span such a long distance.

She rubbed her eyes and yawned, then stood and stretched in an effort to fight off the weariness that weighted her limbs. Perhaps her colleague was right in pointing out the cruelty of allowing Ashinji and the girl to be together, but when she had first realized the depth of her son's feelings, Amara knew that she couldn't stand in their way. She would be their champion and plead their case to her husband. The fact that he was obligated to grant the girl any request she made of him would make it easier. In the end, he would relent and give Ashinji permission to marry his precious Jelena.

Ashi, my beloved son, how I've wronged you! I should have trained you myself and tradition be damned, but I didn't have the courage to go against my family. Never before have I questioned the rule that only the females of my line could take up magecraft until now...

Amara shook her head. She had no time for regrets. She had too much to do. They all did, they who were the remnants of the once mighty Kirian Society, a sadly diminished order, in both power and prestige. Centuries ago, when the force of Talent had waxed stronger in the elven people, the Kirians held influence second only to the king in affairs of state.

As time passed, the elves saw the strength of their Talent fading; mage schools found it increasingly difficult to find enough candidates with sufficient magical abilities who could be trained as top-level mages, and so the ranks of all the magical orders—the Kirians especially—had become depleted.

Amara had come to accept that the elves must begin to turn away from magic, that science must now become the force to propel their society forward, but many of her fellow mages stubbornly clung to their belief that the elves would always have Talent.

Well, maybe so, but not in the same form as it existed today.

Amara studied her elaborately tattooed palms. The designs were arcane symbols of her magical order. For those who could decipher them, they clearly marked her as a Kirian. She had kept her membership in the Society a secret from everyone in her family except her husband, and even he did not realize the full extent of her involvement. How would he react when she told him what would soon be required of their second-born?

How would Ashinji react?

She knew her son well enough to guess. He would be very angry at first, but not because he had always wanted to be a mage; his passion involved science, not magic. No, he would be furious at the deception itself. His anger would then turn to fear and despair for Jelena, and finally, acceptance.

Amara loved her son and wished that things could be different, but no less than the fate of the material world hung in the balance. The ancient evil in the north had begun to stir. She had seen the consequences of inaction in the waters of her scrying bowl. The thing whose name had been stripped away centuries ago must not be allowed to rise up and escape its rock-bound prison to reclaim its magic.

The task of the Kirians of old had been to put that magic beyond the reach of its creator. The task of Amara and her fellows involved securing that same magic and placing it once again beyond the reach of the one with no name. In order to do this, they would need to perform a Great Working. Currently, there weren't enough of them to provide the necessary amount of energy.

Ashinji's Talent could provide the energy needed...but only just. With no training, placing him in the link during a Great Working could destroy his mind, rendering him permanently insane. Amara must see to it that he learned how to channel the enormous forces that would be directed through him so that he could survive intact.

Jelena was another matter. Amara could see no way that the girl would be able to survive the Sundering. She made a decision.

The entire truth must be kept from both Ashinji and the girl until the last possible moment. The Kirians had no margin for error, and if Ashinji knew beforehand what the Sundering entailed, Amara worried that he might not be capable of going through with it, her assurances to her colleague notwithstanding.

She would pray to the Goddess every day for her son's forgiveness.

Before Amara departed from her work chamber, she extinguished all candles and tidied her altar. Late afternoon sunlight slanted down in golden shafts to the floor through the high windows. The twins would return soon from their riding lesson, and Lani waited for her in the sitting room, eager to begin work on her new tunic.

Amara nearly choked on a sudden wave of anger.

The peace and safety of her children's lives, of all their lives, was soon to be shattered in the terrible chaos of blood and war, and she could see no way to avoid her part in the shattering.

As she made her way down the hall that led to her sitting room, Amara passed by an open window and paused at the sound of her second son's voice. Her breath caught in her chest as the sweet refrain of an old love song floated upwards on the breeze, soft and slightly off-key. Amara leaned over the sill to see her son sitting on a bench in her private garden, Jelena by his side.

They sat, fingers entwined, her head resting on his shoulder. As she listened to Ashinji sing, the melody swept Amara on the tide of memory, back to a time when she had been young and in love with the most beautiful man in all the world. Sen had never been much of a singer either, but whenever he dared, it always sounded sweet to her ears.

Amara turned away and left her son and Jelena to their peaceful tryst. Footsteps weighted down with sorrow, she continued on her way, knowing that it must all end.

I just pray that we all have the strength to survive what's coming.

CHAPTER 29

THE JAWS OF THE BEAST

A h, Jelena, here you are!" Lord Sen called out from across the sitting room as Jelena entered, dressed for riding. As she approached, she walked as steadily as she could in order to hide the lingering soreness in her loins. Lord Sen's natural kindliness would prompt him to ask after what ailed her, and she didn't fancy lying to him.

"My lord," she said in greeting, and bowed deeply.

"I've no messages for you today, so you are free to do as you please. How 'bout that, eh?" Sen said jovially, licking crumbs from the fingers of one hand while clutching a wooden plate littered with the remains of a light breakfast of cheese and bread in the other.

Jelena smiled and nodded.

"Umm, thought you'd like that. There's something else I've got to tell you," Sen continued in a more serious tone. "A royal messenger has just arrived from Sendai. Seems there's to be war with the Soldarans after all. I've been summoned by the king to a war council. Seeing as I'm to supervise things, I need to get my tired old carcass along to the capital as quickly as possible. You, my girl, will ride with me in my entourage." Jelena gasped in surprise.

"I'm going to present you to the king, Jelena," Sen announced. His face took on an uncharacteristic expression of gravity, and his words seemed heavy with hidden meaning. "I've thought long and hard on this, and I've come to the conclusion that he is the one in the best position to help you learn the identity of your father."

"I…I do not know what to say," Jelena stammered. "Thank you,

my lord!" She sank to her knees and lowered her head, overcome
with gratitude.

"Get up, girl," Sen commanded gently, and Jelena rose to her feet.
Smiling, he lifted his eyebrows and indicated with a wave of his hand
that she was dismissed.

Jelena sketched a swift bow and hurried from the room, filled
with excitement. She was to be presented to the king! Surely the king
of Alasiri knew every family important enough to have its own seal.
Lord Sen would show the king her father's ring, and she just *knew*
that he would recognize it!

She made her way down the main staircase and exited through
the front entrance of the keep, heart singing with joy. She thought
of Ashinji, and of how hard it had been to leave his bed that morning. With a little shiver of anticipation, she looked forward to tonight
when she could once again feel the ecstasy of his touch.

Feels like it's going to be another hot day, Jelena thought. She looked
up into the near perfect blue of the sky and decided that a stroll in
the woods directly across the river from the main gate would be a
nice way to spend an hour or two.

The small remnant of venerable oak forest had long been cleared
of any animals larger than a few rabbits, squirrels, and birds. Many
of the castle's inhabitants used its inviting cover of greenery as a
trysting place.

Lord Dai and his entourage had departed Kerala earlier that
morning, and Ashinji had gone along to serve as an escort for part
of the way. He wouldn't be back until evening. Both Aneko and
Kami were on duty, and since there was no one else to accompany
her, Jelena set out alone.

She passed under the sturdy main gates of Kerala Castle and
strolled across the drawbridge, waving to the two guardsmen at their
posts, who responded with languid nods. The waters of the Saihama
River sloshed and gurgled below, blundering wetly around large boulders half-exposed and baking in the heat of the sun. The river ran
low—much lower than usual—even for midsummer. It had been a
very dry year.

Jelena carried only her hunting knife, a water bottle, and a journeycake for her lunch. She had overheard two of the kitchen girls

talking about a patch of ripening blackberries they had discovered a few days ago, only a few steps into the trees, and Jelena hoped to find it. Sweet, juicy berries would make the perfect dessert!

At the far end of the drawbridge, she paused. Something rumpled and black lay on the path just ahead. At first, she thought it might be a piece of cloth, but as she drew near, she saw it was a dead bird.

The raven lay like a broken toy in the dirt, one wing outstretched and stiffened, eyes half-veiled and dull. Jelena prodded the bundle of feathers with the toe of her boot. A trio of iridescent green and black flies buzzed up from the corpse, circled briefly, then settled back down to their feast. Jelena pursed her lips in disgust. She thought about the bird that had been sitting in Ashinji's window earlier. Surely, this couldn't be the same one. Ashinji had said himself that many ravens resided at Kerala; still, the sight of the pitiful, withered corpse filled her with unease.

Stop now, she thought. *Don't ruin this perfect, beautiful day with crazy ideas. A dead raven means nothing except that a raven is dead! A live raven on a windowsill means nothing as well!*

She circled carefully around the dead bird, feeling a little foolish. The cool green shadows of the woods beckoned. She decided to walk straight through and onward to the stone circle beyond. She didn't know why, but for some reason, the ground within the ancient relic felt comfortable and peaceful. Something inside her resonated in harmony with a barely perceived force that existed inside the boundary of the circle.

She left the lifeless raven behind and entered the shade beneath the hoary old oaks. Last year's leaves and acorns crackled underfoot. A large, extremely irritated squirrel scolded her from the safety of a branch overhead. She looked up at the irate creature and burst into laughter. It reminded her of how Claudia used to scold her when she was a child and she would return to their room after a day of adventure with Magnes, clothes dirtied and hair matted with leaves and stickers.

A brief melancholy temporarily darkened her mood. She rubbed at her eyes to ease the sting of tears brought on by the memory of Claudia. She wondered how her foster mother fared without her. Claudia had no one to rub her back at night, no one to soothe the pain she suffered from standing on her feet all day. Jelena had done those things for her once, but could do so no longer. A great gulf of both time and distance separated them now—perhaps forever.

And what of her cousin? Had his father welcomed Magnes home upon his return to Amsara, or had he punished his son because Magnes had refused to bend to the duke's will?

Jelena sighed. She might never learn the answers to her questions. She could only hope that the gods would spare a little mercy for those she had loved and had left behind. She ambled to a stop and eased down onto a fallen log to rest. She still felt some mild discomfort, but she was young and resilient, and nothing would keep her from Ashinji's bed tonight.

As she knew they would, Aneko and Kami had started in on teasing her as soon as she had arrived back at the barracks earlier that morning. Her first flush of embarrassment soon gave way to the realization that her friends' ribbing sprang from genuine affection and caring.

Though still inexperienced in sexual matters, Jelena knew full well what the consequences would be if she and Ashinji continued to be together. Eventually, she would become pregnant. She might, in fact, be pregnant already. She rubbed thoughtfully at her flat, hard belly and tried to imagine it swollen with a child that she and Ashinji had created out of their love. The idea filled her with happiness. She wanted more than anything to be able to hold their child in her arms, but pregnancy any time soon would be too much of a complication. Perhaps the elves had a way—an herb or potion—that a woman could use to block conception, at least for a time, until she was ready to have a baby. She would ask Aneko.

A sharp pop, like the sound of a twig breaking beneath a boot heel, caught her ear, and she looked up and around. Sunlight and shadow dappled the thick trunks of the trees, creating illusions of movement. Jelena stood slowly and peered in all directions but saw nothing. Feeling a little spooked, she decided to press on to the stone circle.

"Beautiful day for a walk in the woods. Mind if I join you?"

Jelena jumped in surprise and spun around to see Sadaiyo standing almost directly behind her. She backed up a few steps, then stood with one hand pressed over her heart, which fluttered like a moth.

How did he sneak up on me like that, she thought.

Sadaiyo cocked his head to one side and arranged his handsome face into a mask of contrition. "I'm so sorry, Jelena. Did I startle you? I can move very quietly when I wish to. Perhaps I should have made more noise." His voice was smooth and sweet, like the butter put into traps to lure mice to their deaths.

"Lord Sadaiyo, I…I am returning now to the castle. Please excuse…" she stammered. He regarded her the way a wolf regards a rabbit it is about to kill. She flashed back to the morning after his wedding, when Sadaiyo had accosted her near the bath house. With chilling clarity, she remembered his words.

If I've decided that I want you, then I will have you.

"Oh, no, no. You're not getting away from me this time. You must know that this is inevitable," Sadaiyo drawled. He began to advance upon her, slowly. "I can make this very pleasant for you…for both of us. I would prefer it that way. But I will be firm if necessary, and that won't be nice for you. Either way, though, it will be *very* nice for me."

Jelena fought down a wave of panic. She had to stay calm and think fast to have any chance of getting out of this. Her choices were extremely limited. She could attempt to fight Sadaiyo off, which would only get her a beating before he raped her, or she could run and hope that she ran faster than he.

She ran.

Sadaiyo ran faster.

He grabbed her from behind by the collar of her tunic and hurled her to the ground, face down. She drew in a huge breath to scream but only choked on a mouthful of debris as Sadaiyo threw his entire weight down on top of her, grinding her face into the forest litter. His breath boomed harshly in her ear. She heaved her body upwards as hard as she could, but he was too heavy. He had her pinned and helpless.

Brutally, he ripped the back of her tunic and pulled it from her upper body, then jerked her trousers down until they were around her ankles. Jelena struggled in vain, her brain reeling in horror and desperation.

Please don't do this, her mind cried, but leaves and dirt filled her mouth, and she could not speak. She felt Sadaiyo force her legs apart with his knee. She needed to stop this *now!*

A small part of her brain realized that her left hand remained free just as her consciousness tore loose from her body. Abruptly, she stood outside herself, watching as Sadaiyo prepared to take her. She saw that her belt remained around her waist, her knife still within its sheath.

She felt the blue fire blaze to life, saw it flare up and out of the fingertips of her left hand and strike the handle of her knife, causing it to glow. Her hand opened, and the knife flew into her palm.

With a jolt, she slammed back into her body. Simultaneously, her hand thrust upwards and back. She felt the blade bite deep. Sadaiyo let out a startled yell of pain and suddenly, his crushing weight lifted off her.

Instinct immediately took control of both mind and body. She rolled over onto her back and kicked out with both feet. Her boots connected to Sadaiyo's chest with a dull thud, sending him sprawling backward onto the ground where he curled up and lay clutching his thigh, groaning.

Jelena knew she had but a few moments left to make her escape. Pulling her trousers back up, she took off running, one hand holding on to the torn remnant of her tunic, the other clutching the waist of her trousers to keep them from falling back down. Terror propelled her headlong through the trees, heedless of direction. Nothing else mattered but getting away.

She risked a quick glance over her shoulder but could see nothing in the gloom. She ran on until exhaustion forced her to slow down to a trot and finally, to a walk. She looked around for a place to hide and spotted a dense thicket surrounding a fallen branch. She forced her way in and crawled to the center where she collapsed, completely drained.

She lay on her side, unable to move. Her limbs seemed to have remade themselves into things of stone. Eventually, her heart ceased its wild gallop and settled down to a steady, slow beat.

Jelena knew she still was in danger, but she simply could do nothing about it. Body paralyzed with shock, she stared blankly ahead.

Only the slight rise and fall of her breasts betrayed her living state.

Her mind drifted, resolutely refusing to focus on anything remotely resembling a thought. She wished only blankness, stillness, peace. She gradually became aware, however, that something pulled at her, insisting that she respond. She resisted at first, still too afraid to move, but the force grew in strength until she at last recognized it. It was...Ashinji's voice, calling her name!

She started up with a jolt, straining to listen. She had heard her name clearly, and *it had been Ashinji* who had called to her. She waited, not daring to breathe, but the only sounds she heard were the normal noises of the woods. She wondered how long she had been lying senseless. The fact that she remained in one piece told her that Sadaiyo had either given up looking for her or hadn't pursued her at all.

Ai, gods! What if I killed him! Her mind shrank away from that horror. It wouldn't matter that Lord Sen owed her a debt for his life. Not even that would shield her from the consequences of the Heir's death by her hand.

Cautiously, she crawled from her hiding place and emerged into the dark of early evening. She stood up, retied the waist of her trousers, and wrapped her torn tunic around her body as best she could. She reached up to gingerly touch her swollen cheek, bruised in the attack. She expected that she would have other bruises on her body as well.

At least he didn't rape me, she thought. *Thank all the gods for that.*

She had to get to Ashinji.

What will I tell him? If Sadaiyo is alive, what will he tell everyone else?

She decided not to think about that now.

She started walking. She soon realized that she had no idea in which direction the castle lay. Well, no matter. The woods were small; soon, she would reach its edge, and when she did, she would just follow it around until she came to the river.

She stumbled, purely by luck, upon the path that led from the castle toward the stone circle. Her legs began to shake so badly that she thought she might stumble and fall, but somehow, she kept going. She had to reach Ashinji. Only then would she feel truly safe.

She spotted the bridge just ahead through the trees. The sun had already retired below the horizon, and Jelena feared that the guards might have already shut the main gates for the night.

The gates stood open. Breathing a sigh of relief, she hurried across the bridge and rushed past the guards. Before they could question her, she ran for the upper gates. She prayed that she would not encounter any of her friends. She knew she would be unable to muster the strength to make up the necessary lie to explain her disheveled state. Yet, she would have to lie, because no one could know the truth except Ashinji.

The two guards at the upper gate were busy eating their dinners and ignored her as she passed. All the guards at Kerala knew her by sight now, and had grown accustomed to her comings and goings from the lower yard to the castle and back.

The castle gleamed softly in the evening light. The flickering yellow of lamplight spilled out from windows on the upper floors. Jelena made her way to the outer staircase that led up to Ashinji's apartment.

"Please be here, my love," she murmured as she climbed the steps. She pushed open the door at the top of the staircase and stepped into the dimly lit hallway beyond. At that same moment, the door to Ashinji's chamber flew open, and he came rushing out. He swept her up into his arms and carried her in across the room, where he deposited her gently onto the bed.

He sat beside her and pulled her close. She clung to him, too exhausted even to cry.

"I knew you were in danger...I could feel it," he whispered, rocking her back and forth. "I rushed back home as fast as I could and tried to find you, but no one seemed to know where you were! And then Sadaiyo showed up bleeding from a deep wound in his thigh. He claimed that he had done it himself by accident, but..." His voice trailed off, and he continued to rock Jelena in silence.

"Tell me what happened, love," Ashinji finally asked.

"Oh, Ashi," she whispered.

Numbly, she told him and then surrendered to the dark.

CHAPTER 30

ASHINJI'S RESOLUTION

In a small, halting voice, Jelena told Ashinji everything that had happened. The trauma of reliving the attack seemed to drain what little energy she had left, for after she finished, she slumped against him and lapsed into semi-consciousness. He held her until he sensed that she had drifted off into natural sleep, then very gently began to undress her. Tears stung his eyes at the sight of the ugly purple bruises on her shoulders, back, arms, and face. After he had removed the torn remnants of her clothes, he tucked her into his bed, then undressed and slipped under the coverlet beside her.

As Jelena lay sleeping, Ashinji stared at the ceiling, his mind seething. The intensity of his anger terrified him, and he felt himself teetering on the edge of a dark chasm. It would be so easy to let go, to fall in and allow the darkness to sweep him away into madness. Only the anchor of Jelena's love could hold him back and keep him from total ruination.

The moon had reached the mid-point of its nightly progress when Ashinji finally gave up all hope of sleep. He kissed Jelena softly, then slipped out of bed and padded across the room to sit on the window-sill. An errant breeze, laden with the scent of night-blooming jasmine, caressed his cheek. He raked his fingers through his hair and glowered into the dark, contemplating murder.

Killing his brother would be personally satisfying, but ultimately disastrous. The penalty for murder was death, so not only would Kerala lose its future Lord, but its only other male scion as well. The House of Sakehera would forever suffer the taint of fratricide.

No, I could never put the family through that horror, he thought.

You'll not die by my hand, Brother. But somehow, some way, I'll make you pay for what you've done to Jelena.

I know I promised Jelena I would say nothing about us to Father and Mother until she found her elven kin, but damn it...that may never happen! The only way I can protect her now is to make her my wife.

He glanced over his shoulder at Jelena's still form.

Not even Sadaiyo would dare cross that line.

He considered Jelena's account of how she had prevented Sadaiyo from raping her. Somehow, she had managed to use her 'blue fire' energy.

Whatever it is, it's growing stronger, Ashinji thought. *She's going to need professional help to learn how to control it...We must tell Mother. She'll know what to do.*

In three weeks' time, Lord Sen would depart Kerala, bound for the capital, to attend the king's council. Both Sadaiyo and Ashinji were to accompany him.

I must convince Jelena to marry me before we go, Ashinji thought.

Jelena stirred and called out his name. He returned to bed and kissed her for reassurance.

"I love you, Ashi," she whispered and drifted off again. He smiled. Only those who loved him called him by his nickname, with the singular exception of Sadaiyo, who never called Ashinji anything without attaching a measure of scorn to it.

Just before sunrise, he closed his eyes and managed to sleep a little.

~~~

Haggard from the long, restless night, Ashinji stalked the castle grounds, searching for Sadaiyo. He had left Jelena curled up in a nest of coverlets, still deeply asleep. After what she'd been through the day before, he doubted she'd wake any time soon. Her traumatized mind and body desperately needed the rest.

Ashinji struggled hard to control his anger; only a cool head would serve him now. He knew Sadaiyo's attack on Jelena had been, in reality, an indirect attack on him. Jelena as an individual was irrelevant; only the fact that Ashinji cared about her really mattered.

It had always been Sadaiyo's favorite method of assault—do harm to his younger brother by harming any person or thing that Ashinji loved. When they were children, it had been Ashinji's pets and toys. Now, it was Jelena.

He found Sadaiyo down in the stableyard, taking inventory of the wagons that would transport baggage to Sendai. He noticed Sadaiyo favoring his left leg and caught himself wishing that Jelena had sliced a little higher and toward the center. Sadaiyo glanced up, spotted Ashinji, and limped over to where his brother stood, arms folded and stony-faced.

"Come to help?" Sadaiyo asked mildly.

"You know why I'm here," Ashinji replied.

"Let me guess. She told you I attacked her. Well, Brother, I'm afraid your little mongrel is a liar. She attacked me." He pointed to his injured leg.

Ashinji stared at his brother with disgust.

"I'm sorry you have to find out about her this way," Sadaiyo continued, "but the truth of it is, she's been pestering me for quite some time now. She came up to me the morning after my wedding and practically threw herself at me, begging me to take her as my concubine. I said no, of course."

"I don't believe you," Ashinji stated flatly.

"Yesterday, I went for a walk in the woods," Sadaiyo said, speaking as if he hadn't heard Ashinji's rejection of his story. "She followed me…practically ambushed me…then demanded that I take her on, and when I once again refused her, she pulled a knife and attacked me! I managed to disarm her but not before she took a few nasty knocks. Then she ran away, obviously back to you, so she could give you her version of what happened." He winced for dramatic effect and rubbed at the wound in his thigh.

"If this is true, then why didn't you tell Father what really happened when you came in last night, instead of claiming that you had wounded yourself by accident?"

Sadaiyo shot Ashinji a pitying look. "If Father knew his favorite messenger had attacked the Heir in a jealous rage, he would have had no choice but to throw her out on her delectable posterior. I felt sorry for her, really. She can't help it if she wants to be with a real man. But don't worry, Little Brother. I've forgiven her. I promise I won't tell Father the true story."

A terrible sadness settled over Ashinji like a clammy gray fog. He stared into his brother's eyes, searching for any evidence of remorse and saw only the usual mixture of amusement and contempt. "I don't think I've ever hated you as much as I do at this moment," he said slowly. Sadaiyo merely shrugged.

"You are, without doubt, lying about all of this, but if Jelena goes to Father, he'll have no choice but to believe you over her." Ashinji paused to draw in a deep, steadying breath, then said, "Mark my words, *Brother...* One day, you'll pay for this." Ashinji turned his back on Sadaiyo and walked away.

"Don't you forget, *Little* Brother," Sadaiyo called after him, "One day, I'll be Lord of Kerala!"

~~~

Jelena had risen and dressed by the time Ashinji returned to his apartment. She sat on the windowsill, chin in hand, looking out over the bright rooftops. At the sound of his entrance, she turned toward him, face alight.

Ashinji shivered as a wave of remorse rolled over him.

It's my fault Jelena got hurt! he berated himself. *I should have done more to protect her!*

"What is wrong, Ashi?" Jelena's voice brimmed with concern as she slipped down from the sill and came over to him.

He took her hand and drew her down beside him onto the cushions surrounding his dining table. "I've been with my brother," he said.

Jelena gasped, and her hand flew to her mouth. "No, Ashi, you did not fight with him!"

Ashinji shook his head, hating to see such fear in her eyes. "No, no, love. I didn't...although I wanted to very badly." He paused, and took a deep breath before continuing. "Nothing but... *shit* and...and *lies* pour from his mouth. I knew he wouldn't tell me the truth, but I had to confront him anyway."

"What...what did he say?" Jelena asked softly.

"It doesn't matter. What *does* matter is protecting you from him. Jelena, we have to go to my parents now and get their permission to marry. It's the only way. Sadaiyo won't dare try anything more if you are my wife. He may be twisted, but he's not stupid."

"Ashinji, your father he is kind, good. But you...you are favorite son. He wants special...pure...*elf* girl for you. I am not special..."

"Don't ever say that!" Ashinji cut Jelena off before she could finish. He took both of her hands in his and brought them up to his lips. Tenderly, he placed a single kiss on each palm. "Jelena, you've given me the greatest gift that I have ever received...the gift of your love. I wish to honor our love every day with my body and my soul. I know you feel you are not worthy...of me, of happiness...It's not true. You deserve to be happy. Allow yourself to be loved by me." He leaned forward and breathed into her ear a single word. "Please!"

Something inside of Jelena seemed to shift, to melt. Ashinji watched her face intently as she wrestled with her emotions. Her hazel eyes went soft and unfocused as she lost herself in her thoughts, then they sharpened up and fastened onto his eyes, filled with a new resolve. "I do love you, Ashi, more than you know. But marry you now...I cannot. Wait! Hear me!" she commanded, raising her hand as Ashinji opened his mouth to object. "I want to marry you...so much, it is painful to me, but I must have a name first. Even if...I find my family and they do not want me, at least I will know who they are... who *I* am. Then, I will feel right to ask your parents to let me join their family."

"Damn it, Jelena...That may not happen!" Ashinji exclaimed, profoundly frustrated with her stubbornness. "I understand your need to know who you really are," he continued more calmly, "but not knowing shouldn't stop us from marrying. Once we are wed, you'll have a name and the protection of our House."

Jelena remained silent, looking tired, hollow-eyed and scared.

"You are afraid of Sadaiyo, of what he is capable of. So am I," Ashinji said quietly. "Have I ever told you why I believe my brother hates me so?" Jelena shook her head. "Sadaiyo had my parents all to himself for many years. I think he believed, naively, that they would have no other children and that he would never have to share their attention or their love with anyone else. My earliest memory of my brother is of him leaning over my cradle and spitting in my face. I was too young to truly understand just what that meant, but in time, I learned the depths of his hostility toward me.

"Sadaiyo has always been very clever and skilled at tormenting me. I eventually learned to cope—to fight back, even—but it made life needlessly difficult for me."

"Why did not your parents stop him?" Jelena asked.

"I said Sadaiyo has always been clever. He never did anything in front of my parents other than taunt me, and all of his most vicious attacks he carefully planned so as to leave no trace of his hands upon them. I could never prove anything, so I usually kept silent and…and…"

Ashinji paused to take a slow, deep breath. Even after so many years, the pain could sometimes flare up so raw and hot, it stopped him in his tracks.

Jelena seemed to sense his hurt, for she moved closer to him and laid her head on his shoulder. "If these memories are too pain-ful for you, Ashi, you do not have to talk about them now," she said quietly.

Ashinji shook his head. "No, I do want to talk…especially to you, now." He kissed her lightly on the lips and continued. "The fact that I am so like our father only makes things worse. It draws us together, my father and me…makes us much more than just father and son; we are friends as well. Sadaiyo has never had that same closeness with Father, and he sees this as a threat. I think he believes Father is looking for any excuse to disinherit him…name me Heir instead, which I know our father would never do."

"You would make a far better Lord than Sadaiyo, Ashi," Jelena interjected. "All here love you. I have heard…seen how much respect in their hearts they have for you. No one loves Sadaiyo. They fear the day he will become Lord."

Ashinji sighed. "The real truth of it, beloved, is that I have never wished to usurp my brother's position. All I've ever wanted is the chance to pursue a life of my own choosing. I was given to the military because that is what tradition dictates for every second born child of our House. I had no say in it, but if I had been given a choice, I would have gone to the university."

"Uni...ver..." Jelena stumbled over the unfamiliar word.

"A place of learning. If I had been born a girl with a high level of Talent, I might have been sent to one of the mage schools... Anyhow, I've never given Sadaiyo any reason to fear me, yet his hostility has only grown worse over the years."

"Your sisters...Does he hate them also?"

"Oddly enough, no. He ignores them, mostly. I think he believes that they are my mother's concern, and are no direct threat to him, although my father dotes shamefully on all three of them."

"As if you do not!" Jelena teased.

Ashinji smiled broadly. "When Lani was a baby, I used to carry her around on my back all over the castle. I taught her how to ride and shoot a bow. She loves mathematics almost as much as I do. And the twins! The twins are...well, they are a force of nature!" Jelena laughed and nodded in agreement.

"My father treats Sadaiyo with the respect due his eldest son and Heir, but I know in my heart he wishes that I had been born first. He can't hide how he feels. Sadaiyo knows, and so any brotherly love he may have had for me has been poisoned beyond hope. The day he assumes the title is the last day I shall ever be welcome in Kerala."

Ashinji had never spoken this bitter truth aloud, though he had carried it for so long within his heart. He felt strangely relieved, now that he had given voice to it—as if by saying the words, he had taken some of the pain out of it and could therefore accept his future exile more easily.

"So you see, dearest love, I am a man with no prospects other than those the army affords me, but I don't care. I'll always have a place, and someday, I still hope to enter the university. The House of Sakehera will be my brother's concern. Do you understand now why the question of your bloodline doesn't matter?"

"But I am half *human*, Ashi. That is still thought of as below elf," Jelena pointed out.

"Yes, you are right. I can't deny the prejudice of many okui—purebloods—against those of mixed race, but things are changing for the better. In Sendai, there is a large community of hikui that has existed for many generations. I'll take you there."

He paused for a heartbeat as his voice caught in his throat. Her beauty took his breath away. "Jelena," he continued, "I want a life with you, whether you know who your father is or not. I want children with you. I never wish us to be separated, ever. Please tell me that you'll marry me."

He searched her eyes for an answer, and she gave it to him in the form of a long, deep kiss.

CHAPTER 31

THE FINAL HURDLE

So. This is the favor you would have from me. My son!"

"Father, don't…" Ashinji pleaded, then fell silent as Lord Sen rose up from his chair, arms crossed, a scowl creasing the corners of his mouth and eyes. Lady Amara remained seated, legs drawn up child-like, on the couch beneath her. Jelena risked a furtive glance at her face, trying in vain to decipher the emotions hidden beneath that smoothly beautiful mask, but she might as well try to read the face of a marble statue.

Sen took a breath as if to speak, but Amara put out her hand to touch his arm, stopping him. "Husband, wait," she murmured. "Listen to what our son has to say first." Sen's scowl deepened, but he deferred to his wife's request, nodding his head in permission for Ashinji to continue.

"Father," Ashinji began again. "Don't be angry with Jelena. This was not her idea. I had to talk her into it. She wanted to wait until she found her elven kin, but I convinced her that she did not need to in order to marry me." He paused to take a deep breath before continuing. "I love Jelena…more than my own life," he declared. "I truly believe the One set her in my path so I would find her and the two of us could join our lives."

As he spoke, Jelena kept her attention fixed on Ashinji's face. His eyes burned with such intensity that she feared he would ignite the very air around him.

Sen's expression softened. "This girl saved my life, 'tis true," he murmured, "and for that I owe her. But…*marriage!* Great Goddess!"

He began to pace back and forth, shaking his head. "I have always been a tolerant man…a fair-minded man. You know this!" he insisted. "I was raised to believe that all of us, okui and hikui alike, are equal in the eyes of the One."

Abruptly, Sen stopped pacing and turned to look at his son. "I…I can hardly bring myself to say it, I'm so ashamed," he said softly. "But I must, nonetheless. Ashi, I know you love this girl, but…"

Jelena's heart sank.

I should have never let Ashi talk me into this! I was such a fool to let myself believe, even for an instant, that we could ever be together!

"She's hikui and therefore unsuitable for the son of Lord Sen Sakehera. Is that what you're trying to say, Father?"

Sen looked away, as if he found the heat of his son's anger and disillusionment too much to bear.

Ashinji threw his head back and a bitter laugh escaped his lips. "So, when it comes right down to it," he said, "everything you've always said you believe about equality is all lies."

Sen flinched as if stung. "This isn't easy for me, Son!" he shot back. "I hate that I feel this way!" His eyes begged for understanding. "I *must* ask you this…Have you considered what marriage to a hikui would mean?"

Ashinji closed his eyes, clearly struggling to rein in his emotions before speaking. "Yes, Father, I have," he replied with the barest tremor in his voice. "I've given it a great deal of thought. I'm just a poor army captain, a second born son, not even worth considering…Why does it matter whom I marry?"

"*How dare you say that!*" Sen hissed furiously. You are a Sakehera! Any child of my House, no matter his birth order, is worthy of consideration!"

Fervently, Jelena prayed for a hole to open in the floor beneath her and swallow her up.

"Husband, please…Calm yourself," Amara soothed. "Ashinji meant no disrespect. He is just trying to point out that he needn't be bound by the same considerations that his brother was."

"Thank you, Mother, but I can speak for myself," Ashinji interjected firmly, though his eyes shone with gratitude for her support. He met his father's anger unflinchingly and said, "My point, Father, is that I am not the Heir...Sadaiyo will inherit your title and all of your lands, not me. It will be his child, his *okui* child, who will carry on your direct line, so you needn't worry. There will be no taint of human blood to sully the future Lords of Kerala." He moved to stand beside Jelena, who had remained sitting on the floor throughout the entire exchange, frozen in place and too mortified to speak.

"Stand beside me, my love," he urged gently, holding his hand out to her. The steadfastness of his gaze infused her nerveless legs with the strength they needed to lift her up. "I've always been a dutiful son to you, Father," Ashinji said quietly, "but in this, I cannot obey. If you won't give us your permission, I'm prepared to give up my place in this family and leave Kerala so that Jelena and I can marry and have a life together."

Ashinji's brave words touched off the spark that lit the fire of Jelena's own dormant courage. Boldly, she met Lord Sen's anguished stare, and said, "My lord, never did I wish for me to come between you and your son, please believe! I am so grateful for all you and my Lady Amara have given to me. I do not want Ashi to give up his family, and I do not wish to leave Kerala myself..." She paused to look into Ashinji's eyes, and added, "He has made up his mind that he loves me enough to do this thing, and I love him too much to give him up now."

Sen exhaled sharply. Something within him seemed to yield then, and the storm brewing in his eyes subsided. He sat down on the couch beside Amara and covered his face with both hands, his shoulders slumping wearily. He remained so for only a moment before looking back up, first at Ashinji, then Jelena. With an air of resignation, he turned to Amara and asked, "Do you agree to this match, Wife?"

"I want our son to be happy," Amara replied, and gently, she laid her hand atop his. "It was not so long ago that you rode through the gates of a certain mage school to claim the woman who had stolen your heart, Husband. We angered a great many people that day, as I recall."

"This is different, as you well know!" Sen growled, but Jelena could see his resistance crumbling.

"It's no different...Not really," Amara insisted.

"I know I am not what you would choose for your son, my lord," Jelena spoke up. "I am kinless and...*hikui*...it is true. I wish I had a father to speak for me, but I don't. There is only me to speak for my-self, and I say to you that my love for your son is pure, even though my blood is not."

Sen rubbed at his chin and frowned slightly, but Jelena had the distinct feeling that his thoughts no longer focused on his objections to Ashinji marrying her. Rather, he seemed concerned about some-thing else entirely, something that he wished to keep hidden.

"Once Jelena is my wife, she will belong to this family," Ashinji said, "and who her father is won't matter."

Jelena felt confused by the sudden, overwhelming certainty that Lord Sen knew exactly who her father was. *If he knows, why is he keeping it from me when he promised that he'd do everything he could to help me?* Jelena wondered. *Is he trying to protect me?*

No, protect my father's reputation, most likely.

Aloud, she said, "My lord, my father and his family will have nothing to fear from me, if I do find them. All I want is just to know who they are."

Jelena fell silent and together, she and Ashinji waited while Sen brooded. The quiet of the sitting room was disturbed only by the little sundry noises that always fill up spaces when there is no conversation to mask them—the sweet tinkle of wind chimes, the distant caw of a raven, the creaks and groans of the castle itself as it settled down more comfortably upon its wooden bones.

At last, Sen pursed his lips and turned to his wife. "Well, I s'pose we can't stand in their way, can we?" he said gruffly.

"We could, but what purpose would it serve, other than to hurt our son and the girl who saved your life?" Amara replied. She laid a tender hand against her husband's cheek. "I think that we must give this gift to our son and to the girl he so obviously loves."

Sen grasped her hand and brought it to his lips. "You, as usual, are right," he replied.

"Thank you both," Ashinji breathed, sinking to his knees before his parents and bowing his head.

"Yes, yes," Jelena added, kneeling beside him, her voice breaking. "I thank you, also!" Unable to stop herself, she began to cry.

"No, no...No tears, girl," Sen grumbled. "I'll start blubbering m'self, and believe me, you don't want to see that!" Jelena couldn't help but smile as she dabbed at her eyes with the cuff of her sleeve. Sen stood up from the couch and added, "Looks like you've got another wedding to plan, Wife. Now, I must be off. I promised Sadaiyo I'd help him inventory supplies for the trip to Sendai."

"Father, Jelena and I must marry before we leave," Ashinji said.

"Hmm, yes, of course. Looks like your mother has her work cut out for her, then. I'm gone!" he called over his shoulder as he stumped out.

Ashinji shook his head. "Father is not happy about this," he stated. He rose to his feet in a single fluid motion and reached out a hand to steady Jelena as she climbed, considerably less gracefully in her opinion, to hers.

"Give him a little time, Son. He'll come around." Amara turned her cool green gaze on Jelena. "Societal tradition is hard to go against, even for a man who believes wholeheartedly that some traditions are wrong. My husband really does hold you in the highest regard, child. You proved to him when you shot that boar and saved his life that your heart is courageous." She paused for a heartbeat, then said, "Jelena, you are going to need all of your courage from this day on."

Jelena nodded, but she felt puzzled; she sensed some hidden meaning behind Amara's words.

"Jelena and I should go, now, Mother," Ashinji said, grabbing Jelena's hand and starting toward the door.

"Ashi, wait," Amara said. "I need to speak with Jelena alone."

Ashinji looked questioningly at his mother but Amara's expression gave nothing away. "Yes, Mother," was all he said. He kissed Jelena lightly on the lips and whispered in her ear that he would see her at dinner, then strode from the room.

Amara waited until the door had shut behind her son before she spoke again. "Come and sit beside me, Jelena." Her voice was gentle, yet still infused with an undertone of quiet authority. Jelena obeyed without question.

"Some weeks ago, you came to me asking for help in understanding the energy you harbor within you," Amara began. "I agreed to teach you all that I could about it. Back then, I wasn't certain what it was that we'd be dealing with, but I've had time to do some research…"

"And you know now what the blue fire is!" Jelena interrupted, excitement riding roughshod over her manners. "Oh! Apologies, my lady," she quickly added, dipping her head in contrition.

"As I've said, I did some research, and, yes, I know what it is now." Amara paused to look intently into Jelena's eyes.

Ashi and his mother have the same eyes, Jelena thought. *So green...like emeralds.*

"I'm going to try something with you, something that my son may have already attempted," Amara continued. "Relax now, and clear your mind of all thought."

"I...I am not certain I can," Jelena said. "Relax, I mean." She still felt a little intimidated by Amara, despite the other's kindness.

"Yes, you can. You have nothing to fear from me...Let your... mind...go...blank..."

Jelena felt herself begin to drift. Her eyelids grew heavy.

Look at me child.

Jelena's eyes widened in astonishment.

Yes, you are hearing me in your mind. This is what we call mindspeech. Every elf is capable of it, but the ability to send and receive mindspeech with any power and clarity is directly proportional to the level of Talent of the individual. The strength of the bond between two people also facilitates its use. I can see by the look on your face that you know about mindspeech already.

"Yes, my lady, I do," Jelena replied aloud. "But I did not think I would be able to hear it...I mean, I know so little about Talent in myself."

There is much about you that awaits discovery, child. I will help you, but you must trust me completely. There is no room for doubt.

"I...I do trust you, my lady," Jelena stammered, unsure of whether she should be excited or afraid.

Try not to use your voice, Jelena. Mindspeech is like thought. Just form the words in your mind and imagine them flowing from your consciousness into mine.

I'll try, my lady...Oh!

Very good! You're learning quickly. Now, continue to do exactly what you just did.

I...I can...feel what you mean now...but my head is beginning to ache!

Jelena rubbed her temples in an attempt to massage away the

pain she could feel building behind her eyes.

Unfortunately, some people do experience pain when they mindspeak, sometimes so much that they are totally unable to communicate mind to mind. My dear husband is such a person. However, I believe that with practice, you will be able to mindspeak with ease.

Tell me about the blue fire, my lady.

Patience, my girl! There are many lessons you must learn first. Now... Your trust will be tested by this first one. I am going to perform a scan of your most recent memories. I must do so in order to show you what a scan feels like so that you can learn to recognize, and most importantly, guard against an unwanted one.

You have nothing to fear, Jelena. I know all about what happened between you and my eldest son.

My lady, I...I am sorry. Ashi and I agreed not to say anything. He...he did not wish to upset you and Lord Sen.

You have nothing to be sorry about, Jelena. I hold Sadaiyo to blame. None of my children can lie to me, and when he told that tale about stabbing himself, I knew immediately that he was withholding the truth. I am truly sorry for what you suffered at my son's hands, child. Sadaiyo has a cruel nature that I have been unable to change, despite all of my best efforts; still, he is my son, and I always try to coax as much good from him as I can. Rest assured that he will make restitution to you in some form.

Thank you, my lady.

Now, relax, just like you did before we began the mindspeech.

Jelena let her mind drift.

The scan, when it first took hold, felt like an itch she couldn't scratch— uncomfortable, but bearable. Gradually, however, the itch grew and changed until, to Jelena's dismay, it morphed into a throbbing pain.

My lady, it hurts! she cried in her mind.

Relax, child. Do not fight me. If you resist, the pain will grow worse.

It feels like the skin is ripping off the top of my head!

Jelena could feel a moan vibrating in her throat, but her ears captured none of the sound.

Just as she thought she could no longer endure the pain, Amara withdrew, ending the scan, and Jelena collapsed. The bitter taste of bile burned her mouth as her stomach churned and her vision swam alarmingly. She felt something cool and hard force itself between her lips—the rim of a goblet, filled with watered wine. She swallowed twice, then pushed the cup away and sagged backward onto the couch, breathing in great gulps.

Somewhere out on the frontier of Jelena's distressed awareness, she felt Amara waiting, strong as a rock, lending her support. Gradually, the nausea subsided, the dizziness abated, and Jelena dared to open her watering eyes.

"Gods," she muttered weakly, in Soldaran.

Amara gave her hand a reassuring squeeze. "Believe it or not, Jelena, you did well. A scan is not an easy thing to endure, even a surface one, especially if it's the first one experienced. Your mind is naturally strong, and you have much more Talent than even I'd guessed. You were actually throwing up a rudimentary shield against me, without knowing what it was you were doing, which is why it hurt so much. I'm quite impressed. As you gain experience, you'll be able to tolerate even a deep scan without too much discomfort. "

"I hope so," Jelena replied. She pressed shaking hands to her head, which felt like an anvil on the business end of a hammer.

"Here, let me ease your head," Amara offered.

"Thank you, my lady." Jelena dropped her hands and let Amara rest her palms on either side of her face. Remarkably, the throbbing in her skull began to subside. By the time Amara released her grip, Jelena's headache was gone.

"A simple pain banishment," Amara explained in response to the questioning look in Jelena's eyes. "One of the easiest spells to learn. Now, I think you've had quite enough for today. Tomorrow, we'll begin in earnest."

Jelena tried to stifle a shiver of apprehension, but couldn't. It seemed that getting to the truth of the blue fire might prove as difficult in its own way as getting to Alasiri had been.

"When shall I return?" Jelena asked.

"Come with my son to breakfast tomorrow. We'll start immediately afterward."

Jelena stood up, a little unsteadily, and turned toward the door.

"And, one more thing." Jelena halted and looked back at Lady

Amara. "From now on, you are considered a member of my family, but until you and my son are officially married, you can't share his bed." Jelena blushed furiously and found an especially interesting spot on the floor to study. Amara laughed, but Jelena heard no mockery in it. "Come now, I know it'll be hard, but it's tradition, and there's nothing that says you and Ashinji can't do other things."

"Yes, my lady," Jelena murmured.

Cheeks still aflame, Jelena beat a hasty retreat, but despite her embarrassment, her heart began singing. She hurried downstairs and out of the castle into the full heat of the summer day. The upper yard lay empty, and the whitewashed walls of the castle shimmered in the glare of a sun that rode high and bright in a cloudless sky.

Ashi and I will be married soon, she thought, and the intensity of her joy swelled so overwhelmingly that she threw her arms out and spun like a top, stopping only when her legs threatened to buckle beneath her.

Abruptly remembering that she stood out in the open, Jelena glanced surreptitiously around her, checking to see if anyone had observed her burst of exuberance. The yard was still deserted, and no curious eyes stared at her from any of the castle windows, at least none that she could see. She headed off in the direction of the barracks.

~~~

Back in the room she shared with Aneko and Kami, Jelena sat on her bed, staring at the ring bequeathed to her by her mother. She held the heavy signet on her palm, trying to imagine the man whose finger it had encircled.

Is he dark like me or fair like Ashinji? she wondered.

Until she had come to Alasiri, Jelena had nothing to base an image of her father on, save her own face, and Claudia had always remarked on how much she resembled her mother Drucilla.

Surely, there must be something of my father in me.

She examined the white gold griffin inlaid in the ring's black stone surface. A signet was a symbol, usually of a person's family or of a society he or she belonged to. Why did she have the distinct feeling that Lord Sen knew her father's identity but chose to withhold the knowledge from her?

Maybe you're just imagining things that aren't there, she thought.

She decided to trust Lord Sen to tell her what she needed to know when the time was right.

After all, I'm to be his daughter-in-law, and a man like Lord Sen would never lie to a member of his family.

Jelena slipped the ring back into the leather pouch that she had taken to keeping it in and put it back in her storage chest. The barracks were quiet; all of the guards were still on duty. Aneko and Kami wouldn't return until sunset, so Jelena had to wait before she could share her good news. She lay back on the bed and folded her arms behind her head.

My life is changing so rapidly, she thought. It seemed like just yesterday that she had been a kitchen drudge, destined only for the life of a concubine, to be used and discarded when her master had tired of her. Now, she would soon become part of a noble elven House, a full member, with all of the concurrent rights and privileges.

Maybe Ashinji is right. Perhaps the One Goddess of the elves did put me on that riverbank so he would find me.

Or, perhaps the Soldaran gods had at last taken pity on her and had released her from their cruel dominion. Whatever the reasons, Jelena would not commit the sin of ingratitude. She vowed to visit the chapel of the One each day to offer up prayers of thanks for her reversal of fortune.

The air felt hot and close in the confines of the bunk room. A horse whinnied in the stableyard below. Jelena could feel sleep stalking her, weighing down her eyelids with pebbles and infusing her muscles with lassitude. She fought for a while—half-heartedly—but soon gave in.

She awoke with a start, the beginnings of a scream tearing at her throat. She sat up and wrapped her arms around her body, shivering despite the lingering warmth in the room. Vague images of something huge and unspeakably evil, trailing tatters of shadow in its wake as it swooped down to envelop her swirled in her mind. Jelena had no idea of the nature of the *thing*, but she had felt its burning hunger, its frantic *need* for...for what? Then it hit her with chilling certainty.

The blue fire!

It wanted the energy that smoldered like banked coals deep within the essence of her being, and she sensed that, though it might not now have strength enough to take what it wanted, its power waxed with each passing day, and soon, it would come for her in earnest.

Jelena scrambled to her feet, swaying a little in reaction to the aftereffects of the nightmare.

I must tell Lady Amara! She'll know what to do!

Jelena ran from the barracks out into the twilight.

CHAPTER 32

THE TRUE MEASURE OF FRIENDSHIP

*D*o not worry, child. The seeds of this nightmare come from your own fears about your Talent, nothing more.

Jelena turned Lady Amara's words over and over in her mind as she slowly walked back to the barracks, but no matter how hard she tried to banish it, the feeling that her future mother-in-law hid something important continued to nag at her.

It's just like with Lord Sen, she thought. *Why do I feel Ashinji's parents know things about me they are trying to keep secret? What could there possibly be to know about me that's worth hiding?*

She shook her head, completely baffled.

As she mounted the stairs up to the common room, she heard Gendan's voice drifting from the doorway. "We've got to send for the doctor!"

Jelena paused, frowning. *What's got Gendan so upset?* she wondered.

"Gendan's right!" Aneko's voice sounded just as distressed. "For once in your life, Kami, please don't argue!"

Jelena hastened to the top of the stairs, heart racing. She rushed through the half-open door and spotted Gendan, kneeling, his back to her. "What has happened?" she cried.

Aneko, who stood beside the captain, looked up and around at Jelena as she approached. The stark look of fear on the older woman's face froze Jelena in her tracks.

"Kami collapsed a few moments ago, Jelena. She's very sick. We need you to go fetch the doctor," Aneko said tensely. Jelena could see now that Kami lay sprawled upon the floor, her head resting in Gendan's lap, still dressed in her dusty armor, as though she'd just come in from guard duty.

"I...don't need a doctor," Kami murmured. Jelena drew in a sharp breath, shocked and terrified at the sight of her friend's bloodless face.

"I told you not to go to work today. I asked you to stay in and rest! Why didn't you listen to me?" Gendan scolded gently, tears streaking his weathered cheeks.

"Jelena, please hurry!" Aneko urged.

Jelena turned and ran for the door. She pounded down the stairs and sprinted across the lower yard. Up the path and through the lower gates she ran, ignoring the shouts of the guards, slowing down only when she had crossed the upper yard and had to think a moment to remember which way to go.

The infirmary lay at the back of the main wing of the castle. By the time Jelena arrived, she was thoroughly winded. Breathlessly, she pounded on the thick, wood door.

The doctor's assistant, a gangly young man, answered the door, listened closely while Jelena gasped out her request for help, snapped, "Wait here!" then slammed the door shut, leaving Jelena alone in the warm darkness.

Anxiously, she waited.

Terrifying thoughts tumbled over themselves in her mind, each new one more horrible than the last.

What if Kami is losing her baby? What if she's dying? What if she dies before I can bring the doctor? Will Gendan blame me?

Just when she thought she would go mad with fear, the door flew open and the doctor stepped through. Jelena immediately recognized her as the woman who had tended the injuries she'd received on the day Ashinji had rescued her from the bandits.

"Lead on, girl!" the doctor commanded, handing her bag off to her assistant. Wordlessly, Jelena turned on her heel and started back the way she'd come, the doctor and her assistant following closely behind.

By the time they arrived at the barracks, Gendan and Aneko had stripped off Kami's armor and clothing, and had put her into bed.

Gendan had pulled up a stool and now sat beside his stricken lover, her small hand clutched tightly in his.

"Doctor Metai, please, you must help my girl!" the captain begged, his voice ragged with fear. The doctor crossed the small room in two strides and bent over Kami, peering into the girl's half-lidded, restless eyes. She pressed her first two fingers to the large vein in Kami's pale throat, then after a few heartbeats, clicked her tongue in dismay. "What exactly happened, Captain?" Doctor Metai asked.

Gendan shook his head. "I don't rightly know," he replied. "I wasn't there, but Aneko, here, was. She came and fetched me just after the bell sounded the hour—said my girl had taken ill."

"We'd just come in from our shift," Aneko explained. "Kami'd been complaining since dawn that she didn't feel well. She insisted it was just the morning sickness and that she'd be all right. She refused to stay in the bunk house to rest, even though Gendan asked her to."

"She's such a hard-headed girl, sometimes!" Gendan added, sniffing hard and wiping his eyes on his sleeve. Kami moaned softly and began to shiver. Gendan stroked her tousled blonde hair. "Can you do anything for her, Doctor?" he asked.

"I'll not lie to you, Captain," Doctor Metai stated. "Kami has fallen ill with a very serious malady. I've seen it most often in young women during the early weeks of a first pregnancy. Sometimes, the girl miscarries. Sometimes, she dies."

"No!" Jelena whispered, her hand flying to her mouth.

"But Kami is strong and healthy," the doctor continued. "With luck and good nursing, she has a decent chance of survival."

"What about our child?" Gendan asked quietly, resting one hand on top of the blanket covering Kami's belly.

The doctor paused a heartbeat before answering. "If the mother survives, usually the child does as well." She motioned for her assistant to bring her bag. "Kami will need constant tending through the crisis," she added, reaching into the bag's depths to withdraw several vials.

"I will watch her," Jelena volunteered. Both Aneko and Gendan looked sharply at her.

"You don't have to do this," Aneko said. "Gendan can find a nurse…"

"No, I will nurse Kami," Jelena insisted. "Captain Miri must work. You must work also, Aneko. I need not work…I mean, there is other messenger…Taba. He can carry all Lord Sen's messages for a short time. I will stay with Kami as long as she needs me." She paused, then added, "Kami is my friend."

Gendan noisily cleared his throat and scrubbed at his eyes with his fists. When he looked again at Jelena, his face shone with relief…and gratitude. "Thank you, Jelena," he murmured.

When the doctor at last departed, she left behind three vials of medicines and instructions on their use. Kami was to be kept warm and the room quiet and dim. Gendan left briefly to shed his armor, and Aneko went to fetch them all some dinner. For a while, Jelena sat alone with Kami, who looked so small and vulnerable beneath the blankets. Kami might be small, but her size misled many. Jelena had seen her friend's skill at arms, had witnessed first-hand the strength of her sword arm.

Kami is a fighter. She'll survive.

"You have to live, Kami!" Jelena whispered fiercely.

I need your friendship!

Kami sighed, and her eyelids fluttered. "Gendan," she murmured. "Sweetheart, where are you?"

"Gendan will return soon, Kami," Jelena replied softly.

"Jelena…You're here." Kami smiled weakly. "I'm so glad." Abruptly, her face crumpled. "I'm scared!" she sobbed. "My baby…"

"Do not worry, Kami. All will be well." Jelena made no effort to hide the tears streaming down her cheeks.

When Gendan returned, he found Jelena huddled beside Kami on the narrow bed, holding her friend in her arms.

~~~

For three exhausting days and nights, Jelena remained by Kami's side, leaving only to tend to the most basic needs of her own body. She slept very little and ate and drank sparingly, ignoring the aches in her own barely healed arm and side.

Kami alternately burned with fever and shivered with chills as the illness raged through her body. Jelena could do little to ease her friend's suffering, other to than bathe the sick girl's forehead with cool water one moment, then pile on more blankets the next. When Kami writhed with nausea and retching, Jelena held a basin to her cracked lips and wiped her mouth afterward.

Gendan came in the evenings after the end of his shift. Lovingly, he massaged Kami's back and limbs with sweet almond oil; his touch seemed to do more to relieve her pain than anything else. Jelena had never witnessed such a tender display of love and devotion between a man and woman before, and she slowly came to realize that, beneath Gendan's gruff exterior dwelt a soul perhaps as kind and good as Ashinji's.

Ashinji came to the barracks each evening to check on Kami and to personally bring Jelena her dinner. He didn't stay long; he seemed to sense that Gendan preferred the nobles not to make a lot of fuss. Lord Sen paid a visit only once, and Gendan seemed greatly relieved when he had gone.

"Don't get me wrong," he'd said. "I 'preciate my lord's concern, but Kami's ours to take care of."

Jelena understood his meaning. Gendan believed that the lives of noble and common folk should intersect only in carefully prescribed ways. He considered caring for his sick sweetheart a private matter, one in which his bosses had no reason to involve themselves.

Four days after she'd first fallen ill, and after having spent the past night in restless semi-consciousness, Kami at last lay sleeping. Groggy from fatigue, Jelena rose from the chair she'd occupied since sundown and stretched her aching limbs. She shuffled over to the open window and peered out, shading her eyes against the sunrise with one hand. Behind her, Gendan's rough snoring rattled the stillness. Drawing in a deep breath of the fresh morning air, Jelena rubbed her eyes and then returned to the bed, where she laid a hand on Kami's forehead. The girl's skin felt cool and dry. Jelena nodded in satisfaction.

It's over, she thought. *Kami and her baby will survive.*

The room had gone quiet. Jelena looked up to see that Gendan had awakened and now silently watched her. The expression in his eyes confused her, and she covered her discomfiture by fussing with Kami's blankets. Gendan rose from Aneko's bed—she had relinquished it to him so that he could stay by Kami's side—and padded over to the window. He, too, took a breath of the cool air, then came over to stand beside Jelena.

"Jelena," he murmured. "I don't know how t' thank you for what you've done."

"Please, Captain, do not thank me. I did this for my friend," Jelena replied softly. She had returned to her chair and now gazed fixedly at Kami's sleeping form.

"I…I've treated you…well, if I've treated you…less than kindly…"

"No, Captain, you have always been polite," Jelena insisted.

"But, I haven't… not really."

"You have, Captain."

"Goddess' tits, girl!" Gendan exclaimed. He laid a hand on her shoulder, and Jelena looked up, surprised. "Will you please let me apologize to you?"

Looking into Gendan's eyes, Jelena could see his contrition and something else as well.

"I was unfair to you, Jelena, because of… well, because of the way I was taught as a boy t' see things…and people, as one way or another. I'm beginning to understand now that sometimes, old ideas need to be let go of, that not everything we're taught as children by our elders is right."

Jelena swallowed hard against the lump in her throat and nodded. She now knew that, from this day forward, she would be able to count Gendan Miri as one of her friends.

Kami moaned softly and stirred beneath her blankets. Gendan immediately moved to kneel beside the bed, where he tenderly stroked her cheek. "Kami, my precious girl, my precious, lovely girl," he whispered into her ear. "I love you…so very much. You and our baby."

Jelena yawned and rubbed at her stinging eyes. *If I don't sleep soon, I'm going to collapse,* she thought. Aloud, she said, "Captain, can you stay with Kami for a time, so I can sleep a little?"

"Ai, Goddess! Of course!" Gendan rose to his feet, shaking his head in chagrin. "You must be exhausted, and I've been completely selfish not t' see. You sleep now, as long as you need to. I'll watch Kami until Aneko comes." He added with a gentle smile, "Call me Gendan, please."

Gratefully, Jelena rose from her chair and went to lie down on her bed beneath the window. She sighed, closed her eyes, and fell asleep.

~~~

Jelena awoke at sundown to find herself alone. She sprang from her bed in alarm and hurried out into the common room to find Aneko sitting at the long table, sipping from an earthenware mug.

"Oh, good. You're awake," Aneko said.

"Where is Kami?" Jelena gasped, her entire body tingling with near-panic.

"It's all right, Jelena," Aneko assured her. "Gendan just took Kami down to the bath house. She woke up feeling much better and begged Gendan to help her...now let's see, how did she say it...'wash the stink off me.' She was very insistent." Aneko smiled at the memory.

"Oh, thank the gods...I mean, the One," Jelena breathed. Her knees wobbled with relief. She plopped down on the bench beside Aneko, who poured her a mug. Jelena accepted it gratefully. She took a long swallow of the spicy beer, and as the drink hit her stomach, it began to growl with hunger. She tried to remember when she'd last eaten and decided that it had been two mornings ago. The stress of dealing with Kami's illness had totally killed her appetite, until now.

"Lord Ashinji was here, asking for you," Aneko said.

Jelena looked up sharply. "When?"

"About an hour ago. I told him you were still sleeping. I asked him if he wanted me to wake you, but he said no, to let you sleep." Aneko paused and patted Jelena's hand. "Tradition be damned, Jelena," she murmured. "You and he belong together. I can see it in his eyes, how much he loves you."

The time had not seemed right before now, because of Kami's illness, to tell her friends of her betrothal to Ashinji, but now that Kami and her child were out of danger, Jelena could no longer hold back the news. She threw her arms around Aneko and cried, "Aneko, the most wonderful thing has happened! Ashinji and I are to be married!"

"Oh, Jelena! Truly?" Aneko exclaimed, then stammered, "But...but, how? How did Lord Ashinji get his parents to agree to such a match?"

She pulled away from Jelena, shaking her head in wonder.

"Lord Sen was not very happy about it," Jelena admitted, thinking back on the tense scene in the family room five days ago. "But Lady Amara and Ashinji, both, convinced him."

"Lord Sen obviously thinks very highly of you, Jelena. You saved his life, after all. If not for your arrow, that boar would have killed him, and we'd all be living under Lord Sadaiyo now. He didn't need too much convincing, of that I'm certain."

"I am not a foolish person, Aneko," Jelena sighed. She took another sip of her beer, a small one this time, for she still felt a little light-headed from the first swallow, and added, sadly, "I know I am not what Lord Sen would have chosen for his son. He wants, how do you say, *okui* grandchildren to raise in his house, not mongrels, like me."

"Don't talk about yourself that way, Jelena," Aneko admonished softly.

Jelena stared intently at the older woman, and a question she'd always been reluctant to ask stood poised on her lips. She let it go. "Why were you and Kami friends to me from the start? You and she...not once have you said anything unkind, never made me to feel...less than...you because of my human blood. Why is that?"

Aneko lowered her eyes and a little smile played about her generous mouth. "Kami and I are both Kerala born and bred, from long lines of border folk on both sides. Out here, most everyone has a little human blood in them, even if some folk refuse to acknowledge it openly. It hasn't always been so unfriendly between our two homelands, you know, and we get regular trade from the human nomads that live out on the steppes beyond the mountains."

Aneko leaned in close and whispered, "My great granddad was a steppe chieftain, so I've been told. My great grandma fell in love and ran off with him...lived with his tribe for over forty years. When he died, she and her four kids came back home to Kerala where she married a rich farmer and lived out the rest of her days." She sat back, grinning. "So you see, my girl, I'm as much hikui as you."

Jelena's eyes widened with shock. "Do others know?" she murmured.

"You mean others like Anda and Gendan?" Aneko shook her head. "No. I pass for okui very well. I've kept it to myself, mainly because no one's ever asked, but if someone should, I'll not lie. Here in Kerala, all folk have equal rights under the law. It's not so in most other places. I'd have to lie if I ever went to live somewhere else, so it's a good thing I never want to leave Kerala!"

"Thank you for trusting me, Aneko. I will never tell anyone, I promise," Jelena swore, grasping the other woman's hands and squeezing.

Aneko's strong hands, callused from years of weapons handling, squeezed back. "I trust you completely, Jelena, but don't fret. I'm not ashamed of my blood, any more than you should be. By the way, Gendan told me what he said to you. He's a good man, our captain. You can count on him, Jelena. He'll be a true friend to you."

"No, no, no, you stubborn girl! I'll not hear any more of this foolishness!"

Both women looked up in surprise as Gendan swept through the common room door, cradling Kami in his arms. He paused to look beseechingly at Aneko, then at Jelena. "Will you please tell this pig-headed girl that she's in no condition to go back to work tomorrow?" he cried in exasperation. Jelena leaped up and ran over to embrace Kami as Gendan gently set her on her feet.

"Thank you, Jelena," Kami murmured, her voice still weak from illness. "Gendan said you stayed with me the whole time. You must be exhausted."

"I am much better now," Jelena replied, wiping away tears of relief and happiness with the back of her hand.

"Gendan won't let me go back to work tomorrow," Kami complained, her pale lips in a pout, but Jelena clearly saw the spark of resurgent mischief in her friend's eyes. Jelena laughed and hugged the other girl again, and her heart swelled so full of joy, she marveled that it did not burst.

"Maybe he'll let you go back the day after tomorrow," Aneko said.

"P'raps," Gendan replied, smiling.

CHAPTER 33

A TRUE FAMILY, A TRUE NAME

*I*t has begun.

Tell me what happened.

The girl came to me last evening. She had a strange dream, a night-mare, really. Some…thing stalked her, something she couldn't name but knew was evil. She is afraid it wanted what she harbors, but, of course, she doesn't understand why.

Nor can she, not yet. What did you tell her?

I explained it away, attributing it to unspoken fears about her Talent. I'm certain that she didn't fully accept it, but she chose not to press me. She is a highly intelligent girl. It will become more difficult to conceal the truth from her as time passes and she grows stronger and more confident.

Did you scan her?

Yes, and I found the energy residue of a magical attack.

Then there can no longer be any doubt. The Nameless One is awake, and he has located the Key. How much time we have before he is strong enough to come after it is anyone's guess, but we must assume that it will be sooner rather than later.

I think it's time for a council. We can no longer sit on our hands, hoping and praying that this will go away.

I agree. You will accompany your husband to Sendai, then?

Yes. Ordinarily, he would expect me to stay behind to run things in his absence, so I must come up with a good excuse; also, there are my three youngest children to consider. It's a very long journey.

The girl needs protection as well, protection only you can provide.

My son would disagree, I think! He and the girl are to be married before we leave.

I still think that's a mistake, especially if we are to use him in the Working.

My son will do what's necessary.

You should tell him the truth now.

No. When we are all gathered in Sendai, I'll tell him. I'll not take away his happiness any sooner than I need to.

There is still the question of the girl's paternity. Has your husband decided what he is going to do?

He is torn. We all know what a scandal this will cause, but my husband won't lie to his oldest friend. Also, he swore to help the girl find her kin, and he won't go back on his promise.

Try to get him to reconsider. This could complicate matters immensely.

He won't.

Then I suppose we'll just have to find a way to deal with the consequences.

Ai, Goddess! How did we let this happen? Why were we not more vigilant? We knew that the Key was due to reappear during our tenure! Why did we not search for it so that it could be secured? And why...why did we allow the wards to fall into disrepair?

We've been shamefully complacent. I'll be the first to admit that, and as head of the Society, I must take responsibility. But now is not the time to indulge in guilt. Protect the Key, continue training the girl, and we'll all meet in Sendai.

Until then.

~~~

Jelena and Ashinji were joined in a small ceremony held in the family chapel, attended by the Sakehera clan and a select few among Jelena's friends on the staff. The simple nuptials stood in sharp contrast to the lavish affair that had been held for Sadaiyo and Misune, but this was perfectly proper. Ashinji was, after all, the second born child, and Jelena had no family at all. Still, the simplicity of the proceedings suited Jelena just fine. She needed no spectacle to confirm her love for Ashinji.

That morning, Jelena rose early to prepare herself to become Ashinji's wife. She began with a leisurely soak in the staff bath house,

followed by a light breakfast in the barracks common room, surrounded by the people who had come to mean so much to her since
her arrival at Kerala.

When the time came for her to dress, Aneko assisted her with a
little help from Kami, who, though recovering rapidly from her illness,
still tired easily. The wedding robes Lady Amara had provided were
not nearly as sumptuous as the many-layered extravaganza an elven
lady of high station would wear, but Jelena thought them beautiful
just the same. A sheer undertunic of fine white cotton rested against
her skin. Over that went a robe of lightweight, cream-colored silk,
embroidered with a simple design of flowering vines along the borders. The main garment—a robe constructed of heavy silk and dyed
a glorious yellow—cinched at her waist with a green sash. The image
of a crane—symbol of good luck—embellished the back from nape
to hem. The sleeves, with their long tippets, were slashed to reveal
the delicate pattern decorating the robe beneath. To finish, yellow
silk slippers graced her feet.

Jelena declined the headdress of gilt-silver made to look like a
cluster of flowering vines, choosing instead to secure her mane with
her birth mother's ivory combs. About her neck, she hung the string
of blue Kara glass beads—her dearest bequest from her heartmother,
Claudia. Beneath the layers of rustling silk—resting against her heart
and secure on its silver chain—hung the ring of her unknown sire.
It seemed right that this small thing that had once belonged to the
man who had helped create her should accompany her on this, the
most important day of her life.

After the last tie had been secured and all the layers arranged
to perfection, Aneko applied a rose-colored stain to Jelena's lips and
a light dusting of powdered eggshell to her face. Jelena refused to
allow anything more elaborate in the way of makeup, believing she
would only look foolish if done up in formal style. She wanted to
stand at Ashinji's side as herself, not some poor imitation of a high-
born elven lady.

After one final check of herself in a mirror borrowed from Aneko,
she emerged from the barracks to applause and exclamations of admiration.

"Jelena, I would be honored if you'd allow me to escort you to your wedding." Jelena, fighting back the tears that threatened to spoil her simple makeup, nodded in assent as she linked her arm with Gendan's. The gruff Captain of the Kerala Guard stood as living proof that an essentially good heart could be liberated from seemingly insurmountable walls of bigotry, even if those walls had existed since childhood.

With Aneko and Kami trailing behind, Gendan walked with Jelena from the barracks to the castle proper. It was midway through the month of Nobe by the elven calendar, Actea by Soldaran reckoning. Though fall approached, the days remained hot and would be so for many weeks yet. By the time the wedding procession reached the chapel doorway, Jelena felt miserably and thoroughly wilted.

Aneko must have seen her distress. "You look beautiful!" she whispered, and Kami nodded in agreement. Jelena flashed a nervous smile and gripped Gendan's arm more tightly.

"Are you ready to become our Lord Ashinji's wife?" Gendan asked.

"I've been ready since the day I came here," Jelena answered aloud, but a tiny, nagging worm of doubt plagued her.

I'm sure Ashi loves me and gods know I love him, but is this the right thing to do? Can I, a mere hikui with no name of my own, ever really be worthy of a man like him?

Gendan raised his hand and pounded on the polished wooden chapel door three times, then pushed it open and escorted Jelena out of the sun into the cooler, incense infused interior.

As soon as she stepped across the threshold, she felt the unmistakable pull of Ashinji's presence and her gaze immediately alighted on his face. His luminous eyes—so full of joy and passion—ignited her body and soul in response.

He held out his hand, and she heard his voice in her mind, clear as a solstice bell on midwinter's eve.

Come to me, my love.

All doubts and fears were swept away.

~~~

The ceremony proved to be an exercise in endurance for Jelena, despite its supposed simplicity. After well over an hour of kneeling, her muscles began to ache so much she feared she would be unable to move once released from the posture of supplication before the altar of the Goddess.

The priestess, an elderly woman dressed entirely in white, intoned the prayers in a throaty, singsong contralto. A bluish-gray cloud of incense hovered overhead, and the pungent aroma in the close room, combined with the discomfort of her body, made Jelena light-headed. She could feel herself swaying on her knees and prayed that she would not topple over.

She knew she was supposed to keep her eyes down during this part of the ceremony, but she couldn't resist a quick glance at Ashinji. Dressed in emerald green and gold—his favored colors for formal attire—he appeared perfectly composed, eyes cast reverently downwards, hands folded in his lap. A detailed representation of a willow tree adorned the back of his robe. The same emerald-studded clip Jelena had first seen him wear on the day of Misune's arrival at Kerala bound his hair. The only other jewelry he wore were the gold military service rings in his left ear.

Jelena looked down at her own hands clasped demurely before her and tried to concentrate on the deeper meaning of the prayers, but she found it difficult to understand the words—intoned in classical High Siri-dar—of a language no longer spoken in everyday conversation.

It'll be over soon, my love.

Jelena inhaled sharply. *Ashi, can you hear me?*

Yes, and quite clearly!

The priestess came forward, a small gold vial in her hand. She raised the vial and decanted three drops of oil onto her index finger and traced a sigil on Ashinji's brow. She then repeated the same upon Jelena's forehead. Next, she went back to the altar and returned with twin bracelets of twisted gold, one in each hand. She touched each bracelet to her lips, then indicated that the bride and groom should hold out their right wrists. She slipped a bracelet first on Jelena, then Ashinji.

This is the last bit, love.

The priestess laid her hands on the tops of their heads and intoned the final prayers. She then stepped back and smiled, gesturing for the two of them to stand.

Ashinji rose first and bent to assist Jelena, who had to stifle a groan as her abused muscles protested. Stiffly, she turned with Ashinji to face her new family.

Lord and Lady Sakehera stepped forward to embrace her. "You are our daughter now," Sen murmured as he kissed her cheek. Next came Lani, cool and beautiful in blue, the twins flanking her. Lani embraced her and whispered, "Welcome Sister," and the twins shyly presented her with a bunch of yellow irises.

Is this really happening? Jelena thought.

A strange sensation of unreality gripped her, as if everything that had just come to pass had happened to another girl whom she now watched from the windows of her eyes. Only when Sadaiyo and Misune came forward did she finally come back into herself.

"Welcome to the family… Sister," Sadaiyo said. He leaned forward as if to kiss her on the lips and instinctively, Jelena recoiled. At the same time, Ashinji stepped between her and his brother. Sadaiyo simply shrugged and offered an insolent bow instead.

"Well, I don't know about everyone else, but I'm starving. Let's go eat," Lord Sen directed, and if he noticed the tense moment between his two sons, he pretended not to. He took the arm of his wife, and led the way back to the family's living quarters.

The family, along with the priestess who had performed the ceremony, celebrated the marriage quietly in the large sitting room where they always gathered for communal meals. Jelena had been obliged to thank and bid farewell to Gendan, Kami, and Aneko at the chapel door. Before she had departed, Kami had whispered a quick invitation to Jelena and Ashinji for her own nuptials to Gendan, to be held a week hence. Jelena had joyfully accepted.

Jelena and Ashinji ate their first meal as husband and wife from the same plate, symbolizing the new unity of their lives. Jelena drank freely of the sweet, light wine decanted especially for the occasion, but left the strong, dark beer strictly to Ashinji and his father and brother. The only other time she could remember being so happy was on the morning she had awakened in Ashinji's bed for the first time. Not even Sadaiyo's subtly mocking presence could spoil her mood. She was beyond his reach now, and forever.

When, at last, the meal ended and Lord and Lady Sakehera gave them their final blessing, it seemed as if their feet couldn't move fast enough. They had been apart for almost two weeks, and their need for each other had become nearly unbearable.

With much giggling and unsteadiness—they were both a little tipsy from too much drink—the newlyweds made their way back to what would now be their shared private quarters. As soon as Ashinji shut and barred the door behind them, Jelena began pulling at the laces of her wedding robes, desperate to be free of the confining garments.

"No, wait," Ashinji whispered. Gently, he caught up her hands in his and pressed them to her sides. "I wish to be the one to unwrap my bride...slowly," he bent to kiss her neck, "...one layer at a time." Jelena shivered at the soft touch of his lips on the delicate skin of her throat. She sighed and let her head fall back, her entire body swaying now to the slow beat of rising passion.

Ashinji first removed the ivory combs from her hair, laying them down on the room's only table, mindful even now of how precious they were to his new wife. The blue Kara necklace followed, along with the griffin signet ring. Next, he unwound the sash from around her waist and tossed it aside. Both outer robes then slipped to the floor, leaving Jelena clad only in her sheer undertunic. Here Ashinji paused to remove his own wedding robes. As they slid off his shoulders to the floor, he shoved them back with his foot and stepped forward to enfold Jelena in his arms.

They stood thus for several heartbeats, each drinking in the other's unique scent, reveling in the sensation of a shared embrace. Then Ashinji swept Jelena up and carried her across the room to the bed.

The sun had not yet set, so the windows had been shuttered and the room lit with the soft yellow glow of brass lanterns. Ashinji sat Jelena down on the edge of the bed and knelt before her.

"I know you've never allowed yourself to believe that this day would ever come, but see..." he covered her hands with his, "Here it is. You are my wife, I am your husband...and nothing can ever change that. I will love you forever." He touched a finger tip first to the bracelet on her wrist, then to the one on his, the symbols of their union.

Jelena nodded mutely, too overcome to speak. A single tear spilled over the rim of her lashes, quivered there but an instant, then fell to splash the back of Ashinji's sun-browned hand.

"You think you're not worthy of me, but it is I who am the unworthy one. Every day I give thanks to the One for granting me the gift of your love…Every day, Jelena!" Tenderly, he removed her slippers, bent his head to kiss the top of each foot in turn, then stood and removed the last of his clothing.

Jelena inhaled sharply at the sight of Ashinji's naked body. Though she had seen him in arousal before, now her eyes took him in with a newer, deeper perspective. Her own sacred center answered the call of his desire with a rush of fire through her loins. Eagerly, she wriggled free of her undertunic, and with a sigh, she lay back onto the bed—soft as a cloud—and welcomed her husband into her embrace.

Their lovemaking was fierce, joyous, tender, magical. At the moment of climax, something happened, something near mystical in intensity; later on, when Jelena tried to put it into words, she could find none that were adequate. It felt as if her consciousness and Ashinji's had merged, and for a time, they shared a co-mingled essence, each aware of the other's deepest emotions. There were no words, only feelings, illuminated by the brilliant blue fire that burned at the core of Jelena's being.

When at last the roaring flames of their passion had burned down to warmly glowing embers, they clung to each other, their faces wet with tears and sweat. They didn't speak—they had no need for words. Their minds were now joined as securely as their bodies had been.

Eventually, they slept.

~~~

Kami and Gendan were married a week later in a solemn ceremony attended by most of the Kerala guard and quite a few of the castle's general staff. Jelena and Ashinji held pride of place as the guests of honor, and even Lord and Lady Sakehera stopped by during the raucous celebration that followed to offer their congratulations.

Kami, who had nearly regained all of her strength, glowed with happiness. The normally gruff, taciturn Gendan brimmed with good humor, offering one toast after another to his new bride, to his comrades and friends, and to the Sakehera family.

Though outwardly all seemed joyful and festive, Jelena couldn't help but sense the anxiety that ran beneath the surface of the celebration like a hidden current in the ocean's depths. Five days hence, Lord Sen and most of the castle guard would leave Kerala to journey to the capital so that the King's Council could convene. All present knew what would be discussed behind the closed doors of the council chamber.

War loomed like a storm on the horizon, and the elven nation must somehow prepare to battle for its very existence against an enemy with at least three times its strength. Much blood would be spilled in the most desperate fight the elves would face in over a thousand years.

As Captain, Gendan would ride out at the head of the Guard, but Kami would not be accompanying him to Sendai. Her recent illness and advancing pregnancy precluded her taking the long, exhausting journey. She would not even have the comfort of Aneko's company, for as First Sergeant, Aneko was needed on the march. Jelena felt sorrow for her friend; Kami should not have to go through so much of her pregnancy separated from her husband.

With any luck, however, they would all be back home by winter's end, and Kami could give birth with Gendan by her side, unless…

Unless the Soldarans decide to press their attack early, before the spring rains end, Jelena thought. So much uncertainty! No wonder melancholy haunted the smiling faces all around her.

With the celebration still going strong, Ashinji and Jelena at last took their leave later that evening and retired to their tower apartment for some much needed sleep. Over the last few days, Lord Sen had kept Ashinji busy assisting with the logistics of moving the entire household. Jelena spent most of her time studying with Lady Amara, though she did deliver the occasional message.

Lord Sen had informed Jelena that she need not continue to carry messages for him.

"I have never not worked, and I am not stopping now, just because I married your son, Father!" she announced to a bemused Lord Sen, who wryly gave in and didn't press the issue.

The days passed quickly, and on the eve of departure, after the family had finished dinner, Sen took Jelena aside. "I've got something very important to tell you, my girl, something I should have told you a long time ago," he said.

Sen wore a troubled look, and Jelena's heart jumped nervously in her chest. "What is it, Father?" she whispered. "You look so serious. Should I be worried?"

Sen patted her hand reassuringly. "It's about your father. I think I know who he is."

Jelena gasped, then frowned. "You think? Then that means you are not sure," she responded. Eagerly, she searched his face, looking for some clue that her father-in-law did, indeed, have the information she so desperately wanted.

Sen sighed and shook his head. "No...no, I'll not dance around it. I'm sure, though I wish I'd found a different answer," he replied. Jelena sat very still, her eyes locked onto his. "You see, my dear," he continued, "your sire is...well, let's just say that things will become very complicated for him when your existence is revealed."

"My father is of a noble family, then, but one which won't accept a hikui as one of their own. Am I right?"

"Partly so, yes. But there is much more to it than that." Sen leaned in close and the intensity of his expression stopped Jelena's breath. "Jelena, when my son announced his intentions to marry you, well...you know I was not thrilled, and I feel shame even now when I think back on the things I said. I'm just an old soldier and a farmer, a simple man who's struggled to rid himself of old notions. But even old dogs can change. I've come to love you as if you were my own blood. I want you to always consider me your father, no matter what happens with your own sire."

"Now, I am worried, Father," Jelena murmured.

"When you showed me your ring, I recognized it immediately, but I couldn't tell you the truth about it then. I knew nothing about you. You might have been out to deliberately deceive, or you, yourself may have been deceived. I couldn't take the risk until I had observed you and could find out for myself just what you were about.

"Then, you proved yourself to me beyond all doubt by bravely risking your life to save mine. Still, I'm ashamed to admit, I held back...not because of you, but because of the difficulties I knew would occur once your father and his family found out about you."

Jelena bowed her head and clasped her hands tightly together to keep them from shaking.

Why am I so upset? I knew this could happen.

She made a decision. "If knowing of my existence will cause so much trouble, then perhaps it's best that my real father never find out about me," she said, raising her head and meeting Sen's gaze firmly. "I have found everything I have ever wanted right here in Kerala. You are all my family now. I do not need any other."

"Jelena, my dear, that might be easiest for everyone, but I've given it a great deal of thought. Your sire has a right to know that he has a daughter. He's unmarried, you see, with no other children."

"I know that I cannot inherit any of my father's titles or lands because I am hikui," Jelena stated. "I am no threat to the rest of his family, or to any future heirs he might have."

"That's true, under ordinary circumstances, but your father is no ordinary man. He could change the law if it suited him to make you his Heir," Sen responded.

Jelena's eyes widened in bewilderment. "Who is this man?" she asked. "Tell me his name!"

Sen paused, as if, even now he were plagued with doubts. Finally, he spoke. "Your father is Keizo Onjara, King of Alasiri."

About the Author

Leslie Ann Moore has been a storyteller since childhood. A native of Los Angeles, she received a doctorate in Veterinary Medicine from the University of California. She lives and works in Los Angeles, and in her spare time, she practices the art of belly dancing. *Griffin's Daughter* is her first novel.